IT FEELS LIKE THUNDER

by

L. Jean Voss

This is a work of fiction. Any resemblance of any of the characters to persons living or dead is strictly coincidental.

FIRST EDITION

Copyright 1993, by L. Jean Voss
Library of Congress Catalog Card No: 92-62002
ISBN: 1-56002-242-6

UNIVERSITY EDITIONS, Inc.
59 Oak Lane, Spring Valley
Huntington, West Virginia 25704

Cover by Jason M. Piel

Dedication

For My Parents

with special thanks to Rena Bezilla, Donna Brown, Nancy Cooke, Cindy Emmel, and Anne Kaufman—my true friends who helped me find my way.

Chapter 1

Small decisions have a way of building on one another. They mesh and twine together until, with the force of an avalanche, they lead to events that crash down and sweep up everything before them. While some might call it fate, gamblers attribute such forces to chance, even though a gambler lives, as do we all, unaware of the little choices, the whims and impulses that change the course of one's life.

Certainly no epic thoughts of fate or chance or the will of the gods troubled Graham Andrew McNair as he idled in the shade of a train depot in Millersville, New York. Recently arrived from Albany, and before Albany from Rutland, Vermont, Graham had left the train that was to take him back west solely because an annoying brush salesman from Philadelphia had attached himself to him. Graham had less interest in brushes than he did in cholera jokes, and these seemed to be the salesman's only items of conversation.

But that was the east for you, he thought, watching the noon train steam into the depot and longing to be back west of the Mississippi where brush salesmen rarely dared to go. Soured on train travel, he resolved to outfit himself with a horse and saddle and provisions that afternoon. He had no need to buy guns, as he wore a forty-four forty Colt's revolver at his hip and carried a Winchester rifle snug in a saddle boot. Not even being east of the Ohio River could lull him into traveling unarmed.

It was a hot day for all that it was only May, and Graham pushed his black hat back off his forehead. In his opinion, that year, 1873, was bound to be a troublesome one. A bar room shootout on New Year's Eve had set the tone for the following months; if he hadn't killed that drunk cattleman, Graham never would have had to come so far east in the first place.

Of course, it was hard to say which was more irksome—being east or being bored. In his mind, the two went hand in hand, and so, he pricked up his ears at the sound of angry voices coming from the stock cars off to his right. An argument was as good entertainment as he could hope to find in such a place; therefore, Graham strolled along the depot wall until he was close enough to see what was going on.

From a distance, it looked as though some businessman was arguing with a wrangler—they were really going at it, too. The businessman was wearing a brown pinstriped suit and a derby hat. He had a prissy look about him, and his face was red. His high starched collar was beginning to wilt from the heat and his sweat. The businessman wasn't tall, but the wrangler was even less so; Graham could not get a clear look at him because the businessman stood between them.

When he was close enough to see them both clearly, Graham stopped in surprise. The wrangler, who he had thought was a teenaged boy, was a young woman, not much more than a girl, really. She wore jeans and boots and chaps; her hair was pinned up under a gray cowboy hat, and the sleeves of her white broadcloth shirt were pushed up over her elbows. She wore gloves—leather cavalry-style gauntlets that flared up over her wrists.

Graham moved closer until he could overhear their argument. He didn't need to get too close, for neither of them troubled to lower their voice.

"Miss Chapman," said the businessman, pulling nervously at his moustache. "If you'll just have your father come and sign for the horse, we can get this matter taken care of . . ."

But the girl interrupted him impatiently.

"My father is in New York City," she said. "Besides, there is no reason for him to sign anything. I run our family's horse farm and have full power of attorney."

"Do you have documents proving that?" The agent asked.

"Not with me."

"You are under-aged and female," the agent said. "You cannot be held legally accountable. Perhaps if your foreman would sign this . . ."

"My foreman doesn't know how to write."

"If he could make his mark . . ."

That was the wrong thing to say, Graham thought, smiling to himself as the girl's eyes flashed so angrily that the agent involuntarily stepped backward.

"I selected this horse," she snapped, advancing on him. "And I arranged the terms of sale with Mr. Larrites. I signed the sales agreement, and I paid the $200 downpayment. Now you either let me sign the receipt, or you can keep the horse, and I'll sue you both for breach of contract."

The agent flushed, and Graham noticed that sweat was trickling down the back of his neck.

"This is very irregular," he stammered.

"No, you're very irregular, and you can be sure I'll tell Mr. Larrites that. He's done business with me for four years and with my grandfather for twenty years before that," the girl advanced on the hapless agent. "You won't have a job after he gets the letter I plan to write about this incident. You'll never get a job worth having in New York, Pennsylvania, or Vermont, either."

While the agent wavered, indecision showing plainly on his face, the girl took the clipboard from him and, plucking a pen from his pocket, signed the receipt. Then she handed him $200, took her copy of the release, stuck the pen back in his pocket, and walked away from him without another word.

The agent silently mouthed some words which plainly expressed his opinion of the entire transaction. Graham was glad that the agent had not said them aloud for, as a gentleman, he could hardly have allowed such insults to a lady's character to pass unavenged.

The girl stalked down to a wagon stationed by one of the freight cars. Unobtrusively, Graham followed her, staying close to the side of the depot. He stopped a few yards from the wagon, and looking around, he noticed that several townsmen had also gathered nearby, apparently expecting some excitement.

Four wranglers lounged near the wagon, which was loaded with supplies. She seemed to become less pleased when she saw the wranglers doing nothing, and Graham noticed that they shuffled uncomfortably as she neared them.

"Well, what's going on?" She demanded. "Where's the horse?"

"He's right riled up, Miss Kelly," said the largest of the three, a regular bear of a man. "We're having a right hard time with him."

"What do you mean? Who's having a hard time with him? You're all standing around like school boys!"

Some faces reddened a bit at that. The bearish man, however, was unaffected by her irritation.

"Ray went up to git 'em," he said. "Thet horse's already chased Sam outta there, and he just about bit a hole in his groom. Doc's tending to 'im."

"Thet horse is mean, Miss Kelly," said another of the wranglers.

"He's not mean," Kelly said, annoyed. Jason thought any horse with a little spunk was mean. "He's just upset from the train ride."

Just then an enraged squeal and the sound of hooves thudding against wood came from inside the car. Another thud and Ray came tumbling down the loading ramp, landing in a heap at the bottom. There was some laughter from the spectators.

"Jason, Vic, go help him," she said. As they hurried over to him, Kelly turned a baleful eye on her head wrangler. It was too hot out to stand such trials to her patience.

"Ray's got no business being in there, Zion. I thought I told you to do it."

Zion was unperturbed.

"I had no say. By the time I got back from the feed store, they'd dared Ray to do it, an' he was in there."

"Well, he just lost a job," Kelly said. "And if he's bothered that horse he'll lose a sight more."

"Seems he's learned a lesson," Zion remarked.

Kelly did not answer. Vic and Jason were helping Ray hobble toward the wagon. He had been kicked in the thigh, and his leg wouldn't take any weight.

Kelly took a lead rope from the wagon. None of this would have happened if she'd not been tied up arguing with that stupid man. Now she had a lamed-up wrangler and a thoroughly upset four-hundred-dollar horse.

"I've had enough of this," she snapped. "Get Ray in the wagon and tie his horse to the backboard. I'll go get the stallion."

Zion opened his mouth as if to speak, but Kelly silenced him with a look. Graham moved closer. It would be interesting to see how this female cowboy fared with the wild animal who was trying to kick the box car apart. The other spectators also stood silently, too interested in the proceedings to think of talking or getting on with their business.

Oblivious to her audience, Kelly strode over to the car and trotted up the ramp. Ray spat.

"Good riddance."

Zion fixed him with a warning look.

"A man would say that to her face," he said.

Graham, the wranglers, and a crowd of about twenty passersby watched, waiting to see what would happen. Ten minutes passed, and there was no sound or movement from within the stock car. The crowd watched with growing interest, and Zion began to worry, but Kelly did not come tumbling down the ramp as Ray had.

Then she appeared at the top of the ramp, a powerful dark bay horse standing beside her, nervously sniffing the air and flaring his nostrils. The horse pricked up his ears and snorted, eyeing the train yard warily. Kelly let him look until he relaxed. With her right hand, she held the lead rope six inches under his chin, and with her left, she held the other end of the rope. She started down the ramp slowly, so that the incline would not hurry him. It had taken some patience to get him calm enough to lead, and she knew any sudden noise or motion would startle him up again. If she could just get him down the ramp and ponied between two good cutting horses, everything would be fine.

Then, halfway down the ramp, the train whistle shrieked.

The stallion reared. Kelly felt the lead tear from her right hand, but she kept hold of it with her left. The ramp was narrow, and in his panic, the horse lost his footing. He leapt off the side of the ramp, and Kelly leapt with him.

Kelly landed on her feet, caught her balance, and then threw all her weight backward, jerking the stallion's head around and breaking his flight. He danced back away from her, but she did not try to stop him. Instead, she moved forward with him, letting him have his head.

After a few moments, he stopped. Kelly took a better grip on the lead rope, which had nearly been torn from her hands. She began to talk to him in a soothing voice but did not try to approach him. If she scared him or if the train whistle blew again, he'd tear the lead rope from her hands and take off. None of them were mounted, and he would be in Canada before they caught him.

Gradually, he began to relax. His head lowered a little, and the whites of his eyes disappeared. Slowly, Kelly moved toward him, until she was close enough to pat his neck, which she did until he was calm enough to be lead.

The loungers had watched the entire scene breathlessly, and when she took hold of the lead rope, they breathed a collective sigh of relief and began to talk. The sudden noise made the horse paw the ground and shuffle his feet, but Kelly firmly lead him back to the wagon.

She nodded to Zion, who crept toward them and attached another lead rope to the horse's halter. Then Zion mounted up, tying his end of the lead rope to his saddle horn. Kelly took the far end of her lead rope and moved toward her own horse, letting the stallion stand where he was. Then she mounted her horse and wrapped the lead rope around her saddle horn.

She let herself relax a little. The stallion was now tied between two good horses, a fifteen-foot lead rope on either side of him. She rubbed her right arm, which ached from having been jerked so hard.

"Vic, get that wagon going," she said quietly. "We'll follow you."

Vic obeyed, and the creaking of the wagon made the stallion snort and dance between the two leads, but the two horses held him steady.

Kelly let the wagon go for about fifty yards. She checked to make sure the lead was secure around her saddle horn, then she lifted her right hand to signal Zion that it was time to go.

As they started out, Kelly looked briefly along the wall of spectators who lounged in the shade. They all looked away when her eyes fell on them. It irked her that, no matter what she did in Millersville, it seemed to attract such attention. Her lip curled a little in contempt.

Her eyes stopped abruptly as they met Graham's. She knew somehow that he had been watching her for awhile. The thought flustered her, especially as she knew immediately that he was not from the town or anywhere nearby, either. The gunbelt he wore, the lines of his face, and the alertness of his stance all spoke of wildness that you just didn't see in Millersville; a wildness that belied his immaculate black suit and freshly starched white linen.

He grinned suddenly and tipped his hat to her. Kelly flushed and looked away quickly. Then she looked back and saw he was still grinning at her. Annoyed at his boldness, she tipped her own hat to him, raising one eyebrow inquisitively. Then the stallion began to rear, and she had no more time to consider strangers.

But Graham watched after her until she was out of sight, then he remained there in the shade for some time, eavesdropping on a conversation several of the townspeople were having.

"Ain't it a shame the way she bullies them wranglers?" One of them said, shaking his head. "Be damned if I'd stand for it."

"Twenty-five dollars a month might change your mind," said another. "Best wages in the state. She raises the best horses, too."

The first man spat. "Mr. Jinson's down south are as good."

"Then why does she always take blue ribbons at the state fair?"

"It don't matter," said a third man. "Place'll close down when she gets married next month."

"Not if she bullies her husband like she bullies them wranglers."

The townsmen laughed, and slowly dispersed to go about their business. Graham looked after Kelly and Zion as they lead the stallion home, not looking away until even their dust had vanished from the horizon.

At last he left the depot, pleased with his morning's entertainment. Maybe there was some hope for the east yet.

Chapter 2

The day was nearly over by the time Kelly had an opportunity to reflect on that morning's events. Getting the stallion settled had been difficult. No sooner was it finished then an unexpected horse dealer had shown up. Kelly had spent the rest of the day with him. He was, in her opinion, inordinately fussy considering he hardly knew what he was talking about. Still, he had purchased a fine pair of four-year-old carriage horses for five hundred dollars. Kelly was pleased with the sale, but it had been tiring.

Now she watched the sun set over the west pasture. The new stallion was racing around the near paddock, getting the kinks out of his legs after the long train ride. But Kelly wasn't thinking about the horse, or the foals he could help produce. Her minding was considering her rapidly approaching marriage. She knew that, once she was married, she would be expected to stay in the city and give up this farm and her work. She had been lucky to escape her fate for even this long.

Kelly didn't particularly like her fiancee, Robert Lawton, but her father had proposed the match, and Kelly had never learned to say no to her father. The cold, scornful disdain he had toward her always left her inarticulate and scared. Now that her grandfather was dead, she had no one to take her side, and she had no stomach for the way fighting with her father made her feel.

The sun was almost flush with the horizon now, and Kelly squatted, pulling a grass shoot from the ground and chewing it slowly. She couldn't imagine life anywhere else; she couldn't conceive of spending her days some way other than this. But if she defied her father, she knew he would take the farm away from her somehow—he woud sell it or send her away. Whether she married Robert or not, she knew she would lose this life she loved. So what difference did it make?

She spat out the chewed-up bit of grass and sighed. Time was running out. The clouds were gathering, and there seemed to be nothing she could do except endure the storm. She was trapped, and she had no idea what to do about it.

Her mind turned to more practical matters. It was time to check the barns one last time before she went up to the house for supper. She also had to tell Zion to be ready to make a trip into town tomorrow. The money from the past two weeks' sales had to be taken to the bank, and it wasn't safe for her to go alone.

She went to one of the four large barns. It was shadowy inside, and the warm smell of horse filled the air. Everything was neatly swept and clean. It always made Kelly feel good to walk through the barns in the evening, smelling the clean smells of straw and hay, knowing all these fine animals were snug and well cared for.

Kelly walked to the last stall on the right side of the barn, where a fine dark bay gelding stood pulling hay down from his rack. As Kelly approached, he stopped eating and poked his head over the stall door, whinnying softly.

Kelly stroked his nose and pulled a carrot from her back pocket. She spoke to him; this was her pet horse.

"Sorry we didn't get out for a ride today," she said. "I brought you a carrot though."

She fed him the carrot and continued to pet him. This horse had been her grandfather's birthday gift to her when she was ten years old, and the horse had been a long-legged new born foal. She had named him Phoenix, and now, remembering the knobby-kneed scraggly-haired foal he had been and seeing the strong, fast, proud horse he had become, she thought the name was apt.

Zion came up behind her, shuffling his feet so as not to startle her.

Kelly turned and looked at him; Phoenix nuzzled her shoulder.

"Good evening, Zion," she said. "Everything closed up tight?"

"Yes'm," he said.

"Good. We need to go to the bank tomorrow. Can you be ready to go around eight?"

"Course. Thet's a fine horse you bought today."

"Thanks. He'll be a handful though. I don't want anyone messing with him." Saying this made her remember the morning's trouble. "How is Ray?" She asked.

"His leg's not broke, but it ain't well, either," Zion

answered. "I reckon it'll be a week afore he can ride out of here."

Kelly considered the matter. She had been annoyed with Ray for disregarding her orders earlier, but as Zion said, he had probably learned a lesson, and he was a good horseman.

"Well," she said. "There's no hurry. He can stay if he likes. Tell him he can work on cleaning all the saddles and harnesses while he's off his feet."

Zion nodded. It was no work for a horseman and plenty enough punishment.

"Go on to the bunkhouse and get some dinner," she said to him. "It's been a long day."

"Sure," he replied. "Good night."

"Good night."

He left the barn. When she heard the door shut, Kelly unbolted Phoenix's stall door and went inside. She was halfway minded to saddle him up and go for a ride, but it was getting dark quickly, and it would be dangerous to gallop across the fields as they usually did.

She sat down in the clean straw. Phoenix dropped his head so she could stroke his nose, then after a moment, he went back to pulling hay down from his rack. Kelly rested her head back against the wall, thinking about that morning at the stockyard. Getting that horse off the train had been a close thing. She should have had at least one of the wranglers mount up before she had tried it. Next time she would be more careful, she thought, rubbing her sore arm. Heat and aggravation were no excuses for carelessness.

Thinking over her trials in the train yard, she remembered the stranger who had grinned at her. Frowning, she tried to figure out how come he had seemed so alien and yet so familiar. She decided that something about him put her in mind of her Grandfather Chapman, though her grandfather had been taller and lankier and had worn a beard.

"He was probably catching a train out of here," Kelly said to Phoenix. "Though I don't know why he would need all those guns to ride a train."

Kelly sat there for another hour. Although she was hungry, she was in no hurry to go up to the house and eat supper. If she waited until seven o'clock, dinner would be over, and she could eat in the kitchen by herself instead of the dining room with her widowed Aunt Sally. It ruined Kelly's digestion to eat with her aunt, who only took interest in two subjects: religion and Kelly's lack of refinement. Neither subject particularly interested Kelly, who would much rather speak to Phoenix than her aunt.

Aunt Sally had moved in to chaperone her after her grandfather had died, which Kelly had thought was ridiculous. What did she need a chaperone for? And now that she had one, what good did it do? She never even saw her aunt unless she was too hungry to wait for her dinner. Kelly was up and out of the house before dawn to get the day's work started, and Nell, the cook, always sent a lunch basket down to the barns for her at noontime.

"It gives her something to do, I guess," Kelly said aloud. "Plus she gets to give herself airs over the townspeople."

It was full dark, and Kelly stood up, brushed her jeans off, and went up to the house, yawning. She went in the back door, pausing on the porch to remove her boots.

"Evenin' Miss Kelly," Nell said to her. "I kept a plate warm for you."

"Thank you, Nell. I appreciate it." Kelly sat at the table, and Nell put the plate in front of her; it was loaded with a chicken breast, mashed potatos and corn. Kelly began to eat. She had missed lunch that day because of the buyer.

"There's beans," Nell said. "But you never did like beans much. There's also more chicken in the pantry, if you want it."

"Thank you," Kelly said, swallowing. "These potatos are especially good."

"Nice of you to say so. Leave them dishes in the wash pan," Nell said. "I'll get 'em in the morning. Good night."

"Good night, Nell."

Nell hung her apron behind the door and left the room. Kelly cleaned her plate, then went into the pantry and got another piece of chicken. She was just sitting down at the table when her aunt stepped into the room.

Kelly's aunt was in her late forties. She was well-educated and well-mannered. She never raised her voice and spent most of her time doing delicate needle work that would have driven Kelly insane in moments. Sometimes, just watching her aunt work so patiently and endlessly on such fine embroidery gave Kelly fits.

"Good evening, Aunt," Kelly said, unconsciously straightening her back and smoothing out her voice.

"Good evening dear," her aunt responded, looking her niece over with a critical eye. Aside from the girl's shocking choice in clothing, she could find nothing that needed correction. Her posture and table manners were excellent, and her voice was quiet and ladylike.

"You missed dinner again," her aunt said. "I believe you delay in coming up for meals so you can eat by yourself."

Kelly lowered her eyes and didn't answer. She didn't really like eating alone, but the pressure of spending an hour or so in her aunt's company spoiled her appetite.

"It's father's fault," her aunt went on. "He let you run wild. He spoiled you so. I had hoped that my presence here would have a civilizing influence on you."

Kelly knew that her aunt had just summed up her family's opinion of her character, though of course, none had dared to voice it while Grandpa had been alive. Kelly often wondered why they considered being spoiled worse than being ignored completely. Arguing was useless, however, and Kelly had learned that, the less she said to her aunt, the sooner her aunt would tire of annoying her.

But that evening, Aunt Sally had something on her mind besides her niece's faults.

"I came to tell you that I had a letter from your father today," she said.

Kelly flinched. Her father never wrote directly to her; he always wrote to his sister, who passed his orders or scoldings along to Kelly for him. This particular letter no doubt dealt with her coming marriage. Kelly gripped her fork tighter and listened carefully.

"On Friday," her aunt said. "You are to take the noon train into the city. He will have a carriage waiting for you when you arrive."

Kelly dropped her fork.

"Friday! I can't be ready Friday!"

"Modulate your voice dear."

"There's no one to run the farm!"

"It's been sold already," her aunt went on calmly, apparently unaware that she was speaking about the end of the world. "The sale takes effect June first. I suppose those . . . men . . . can tend to things until then."

Kelly pushed her plate away; her appetite had vanished, and she felt ill.

"I won't go," she said dully. "I want to stay here."

Her aunt frowned.

"I'll wire your father to that effect," she said. "I'm certain he will come out here to persuade you, though I doubt the trip will do his temper much good."

There was no threat in her aunt's voice, only a calm statement of fact. Kelly felt sicker. She stood up, wanting to leave the room so her aunt would not see how upset she was.

"I'll be ready," Kelly said, her voice steady and calm.

"Good."

"I think I'll go to bed now," Kelly said. "Good night, Aunt."

"Good night dear."

Kelly hurried out of the kitchen and upstairs to her room. Once safely inside, she flopped down on the bed and tried to think. Coherent thought eluded her. She had run out of time.

Chapter 3

As the sun began to streak the sky pink, Kelly washed herself and dressed for the day ahead. No matter what was going to happen on Friday, there was work that need to be done today. She would also have to tell the men about the sale. It was just like her father to pass down some high-handed order with no concern over how it affected anyone else. The wranglers would be worried about their jobs, of course, and there was no reassurance that she could give them.

She went down to the barns without pausing to eat breakfast. Her stomach was all in knots, and eating was impossible. The men were feeding the horses. Kelly greeted them and went to Phoenix's stall. She fed him herself, brushed him down, and saddled him. Zion appeared as she was leading him from the stall.

"Morning, Miss Kelly," he said, tipping his hat.

"Good morning, Zion," she said. "Are you well this morning?"

"Well enough."

"Good. Would you please gather the men in the barnyard?" she asked.

Zion nodded and stumped off to do as she said, thinking that Kelly looked poorly that morning, as though she hadn't slept.

When the wranglers were assembled, Kelly led Phoenix from the barn and tied him to a fence. Then she went to talk to her men.

"I hate to give you such news on a beautiful day," she said. "I heard last night that the farm has been sold."

She paused as the men murmured for a moment. When they were quiet again, she went on.

"The sale goes into effect June first, two weeks from now," she said. "I don't know what plans the new owners have, and I'm sorry I can't promise you that they'll want to keep you all on. But I'm going to give you all your wages for June today. If they pay you again, well, consider it my thanks for the good work you all have done here."

She counted out each wrangler's money and handed it to them herself.

"If you want to move on, I understand," she said when she finished. "Though I hope you'll all stay on for a bit. I've never had such a good crew, and that's the truth. I hate to see this happen."

Feeling dangerously close to tears, Kelly signaled to Zion that it was time for them to go. After they had mounted up, Kelly looked at the men as they slowly went about their work, knowing she would miss them. Despite occasional spots of trouble like the previous day, she felt a camaraderie with those men. She had cleaned stalls and carried hay bales and water buckets and had taken plenty of lumps at breaking time, and they had favored her with some warmth for it. After all, someone had to be the boss and say what needed to be said, even if it was hard to hear.

Zion saw her look and knew what she was thinking. No one would work as hard as Kelly did unless they loved their work. It seemed a shame to him that she felt more at home among horses than she did among her own people, or any people, for that matter.

"They'll be fine," he said. "But how are you?"

Kelly turned away from her musing.

"You're a good man, Zion," she said, offering him her hand, which he shook.

They rode west over the hills. It was ten miles to town, a good outing for Phoenix, she thought as they cantered along. She liked to start the day off with a wild ride across the pastures before dawn, but this morning, she'd been too worried and too tired from her sleepless night. Riding to town was better than nothing, but distracted as she was, she could not enjoy it properly. She did not even race along as she usually liked to; instead, she rode sedately beside Zion, who noticed the change but did not comment on it.

When they reached town, they rode to the bank, a two-story building that had an impressive set of stone steps. But it didn't have any hitching posts in front of it, so they tied their horses in front of the general store. Zion cut himself a plug of tobacco and sat on the steps. He often said that he hated banks, so Kelly always went in by herself.

She was halfway up the stairs when the doors burst open,

and a man backed through them. He fired two shots into the air.

Instinctively, Zion flattened himself on the ground. Kelly was too stunned to move. She watched the man turn and hurry down the steps. He was carrying a canvas sack, and Kelly recognized him as the man who had grinned at her the day before.

Graham paused when he saw her and held his gun on her for a second. Their eyes locked, and Kelly shook her head at him. The faintest trace of yesterday's grin crossed his face, then he continued down the steps.

When he reached the bottom, Frank Gaynor, the bank guard, appeared in the still-open doors, a bloody weal on his forehead. Graham had his back to him and did not seem to hear him; he was busy keeping an eye on Zion, who lay between him and his horse.

Frank stopped on the same step that Kelly stood on and raised his revolver. Kelly saw that he planned to shoot the stranger in the back. Before she knew what she was doing, she shoved Frank so hard he nearly fell over. He got off a shot just as she pushed him, but it sliced harmlessly through the air.

Graham whirled and fired so quickly Kelly did not even see him raise his gun. But she did see Frank thrown backward off his feet, crumple into heap, and then roll down the steps until he came to rest just in front of her, blood flooding from a hole in his chest and puddling around her feet.

When she looked up, Graham had untied his horse and swung into the saddle. He had fired again, scaring the other horses tied nearby. Several horses had torn free and were milling about in a confused way; Zion's gray mare and Phoenix were among them. Kelly ran down off the steps as Graham wheeled his own horse around and made to gallop out of town. The loose horses began to follow him.

Unwilling to see her pet horse run off, Kelly ran after the horses. The horses were stampeding, raising a storm of dust in their fear, but Kelly never hesitated. She ran in among them and over to Phoenix. Unable to stop him, she ran alongside him for two strides, then grabbed a handful of his mane and sprang onto his back, landing in the saddle with a thump.

Kelly heard two more gunshots, although she had no idea who was firing. Phoenix began to run flat out. She did not lose her seat, but neither could she stop him. The reins were dangling, and he was terrified. Kelly had ridden enough runaway horses to know that he was going to run until he was exhausted or no longer scared, whichever came first.

They cleared the town in a matter of seconds. Kelly's horse was running alongside Graham's, as were one or two of the other horses that had pulled free. Even if Kelly could have stopped him, she probably wouldn't have. To her mind, there was nothing like the feeling of having a horse run wild beneath her, especially if it carried her away from a perilous danger.

She heard more shots being fired. The wind whipped her face, and Phoenix ran more strongly. It was exhilarating. Kelly leaned forward against his neck and wished he'd never stop.

Several miles out of town, Graham reined his horse in. Phoenix had been slowing down for some time, and now, he began to trot. Kelly spoke to him soothingly for few moments, and he began to walk. Graham watched all this quietly, then nudged his horse up alongside her.

"You ought to turn back now," he said. His voice was faintly amused. He looked at Kelly, but his face did not reveal any of the curiosity that he felt. As he waited for her to reply, he noticed how easily she sat in the saddle, even though her feet dangled free of the stirrups and she had not recovered her reins. He also remembered how she had swung onto the galloping horse as gracefully as an Indian.

Kelly did not answer. She couldn't think of anything to say that didn't sound silly. Graham watched her, clearly expecting an answer.

"I'm not going back," Kelly said finally. He did not respond, and this made her nervous, but she forced herself to say nothing more.

"You should go back," he said at last. "They'll make you a hero for trying to save that bank guard."

"I didn't try to save him," Kelly said without thinking.

"Why'd you push him then?"

"I pushed him so he wouldn't shoot you in the back," Kelly replied.

At this, Graham stared at her so hard that she felt herself flush. To escape his stare, she slid off her horse and collected the reins, then she remounted. Graham stopped his horse and waited for her.

It was in his mind to ask her why she had done such a thing, but he didn't. That was her own business and none of his.

"Aren't you supposed to get married next month?" He asked instead.

Kelly flinched, startled. "How did you know that?" She demanded.

He didn't answer, and Kelly supposed she was the only one who treated her engagement like a secret. Probably everyone in Millersville had been discussing it for months.

"I am," Kelly said, "But I sure don't want to."

She said no more about it, and he asked no more questions. They walked on in silence for a few moments, letting the horses catch their wind.

"Well," Kelly said. "I'd best get on my way. Can you point me to the nearest town?" She was unfamiliar with the state beyond Millersville.

"Where are you going after that?" He asked.

19

"To San Francisco," she said impulsively. It was the furthest point west that she could think of.

"I don't know where the nearest town is," Graham said. "It's been over ten years since I've been this far northeast. You'd best ride with me a few days."

Kelly's mouth fell open.

"You can't be serious."

"It's not safe for you to travel alone," he said. "It's the least I can do, after you saved me from being shot in the back." His voice was serious to the point of mockery, but Kelly was too flustered to notice.

"I hardly think it's safe for me to travel with you," she said, indignant that he should think her so naive.

"Why?" He asked in a bland way that made Kelly wonder if he remembered that not more than fifteen minutes ago she had watched him shoot Frank Gaynor in the chest.

"You just robbed a bank and killed a man," she replied cooly.

He raised an eyebrow—at her words and at her tone of voice.

"You ought to be wary of speaking so boldly to someone you don't even know."

"I say what I think," Kelly replied. "If you don't care for that, we ought to part company right now."

Not a flicker crossed his face at her words, not anger or amusement or any other emotion.

"Then what do you think of yourself?" He asked. "You helped me with both endeavors."

"I did not!"

He looked sideways at her, and Kelly had to admit that he had a point, but at the time, it hadn't seemed that way. Everything had happened so quickly.

"All right, so what if I did?" She asked.

"Then we ought to get along well together," he said.

They were now riding through a heavily wooded area. Kelly considered her position. She had no intention of riding back to Millersville or of going home, for she knew what awaited her if she did. Traveling with this bank robber might be dangerous and it might not, but to her, a possible danger seemed less threatening than a certain one.

After all, she thought, Frank had been shooting at him, and you couldn't expect him to just stand there and get shot. Of course, this didn't excuse the bank robbing, but such matters did not disturb her. As far as she was concerned, he could rob all the banks he liked as long as she missed the noon train on Friday.

"Maybe for a few days," she said, looking at him carefully. Up close, she thought, he seemed less like a stranger.

Though surprised by her answer, Graham did not look it. He didn't particularly want a traveling companion, but if he was to have one, he could think of worse—a brush salesman for example.

"Good," he offered her his hand, which she shook firmly. "I'm Graham McNair. I don't believe I caught your name."

"Kelly Knowlton," she said giving him her mother's maiden name instead of her own last name. Graham, who knew her real last name was Chapman, let the alias pass without comment.

And they rode west together.

Chapter 4

Kelly had lost all track of time and was nodding sleepily when Graham announced, "We'll camp here."

He dismounted and unsaddled his horse, then began to clear a place for a fire. Kelly too dismounted. Yawning, she stretched to get the kinks out of her legs and then unsaddled Phoenix. The trees loomed eerily around her, and the sound of rushing water came from close by. Kelly began to feel uneasy.

Graham was busy with the fire, and Kelly, because she felt awkward standing there doing nothing, took both horses by their bridles.

"I'll water the horses," she said. Graham looked at her briefly.

"Don't wander too far," he said.

Kelly nodded and led both horses into the woods toward the sound of the stream. Although she was used to riding, her legs felt numb and shaky, and she stumbled from weariness now and then. She found the stream with no difficulty and let both horses drink. They had been riding slowly for the past hour or so, so she let them drink all they wanted, leading them into the water so their legs could have a soak.

When she returned to the camp, Kelly tethered both horses to a bush. Graham had a small fire going. It was a cool night, and the thin broadcloth shirt she was wearing was not warm enough. She was grateful for the fire, but wondered if it were a good idea to have one.

"Is it wise to have a fire?" She asked.

Graham was unrolling his blankets. He looked at her when

she spoke but did not answer.

"You could answer me," Kelly said, nettled by his silence. "Even if it was a foolish question."

"We're in Canada by now," he said. "It's safe enough."

Kelly was stunned. That meant they had ridden a good eighty miles—at the very least. No wonder her legs were so tired.

"Here." Graham tossed her a blanket.

Kelly caught it and put it around her shoulders. "Thank you," she said.

"We'll get you outfitted at the next town we run across," he said, squatting near the fire. "I'm going to boil up some coffee. Do you want some?"

"No thank you," she replied. "I never learned to drink coffee."

Kelly realized she was hungry but hesitated to say anything about it. Instead, she sat near the fire and, with some difficulty, pulled her boots off. Her feet were swollen from the long ride, and she rubbed them, thinking that, if she weren't so tired, she'd go stand in the creek for a while.

Graham finished with the coffee and pulled two apples and a few corn pones from his saddle pouches. He tossed Kelly one of the apples. She caught it, and then he tossed her a corn pone.

"There's more corn bread if you want it," he said.

"Thank you," she said. After eating the apple down to the core and polishing off the corn pone, she thought about the horses.

"Do you have anything to rub the horses down?" She asked.

He handed her the rag he kept for that purpose. Kelly brushed both horses as well as she could and gave them each half of her apple core. She spent as long as she could with the horses, then went back to her blanket and wrapped herself up in it. Graham silently offered her another corn pone, which she accepted.

She was warm now and began to feel sleepy. The day's events seemed remote, almost as if they had happened in a dream. She leaned back against her saddle and drifted off to sleep untroubled by either regret over the past or fear of the future.

Graham watched her sleep for awhile, fascinated by the peace of mind that her face reflected. His decision to take her along had been a quick one, and despite what he had told her, it had nothing to do with the shoot out at the bank. It had more to do with what he'd seen yesterday at the trainyard. Watching her arguing with the shipping agent and wrangling that stallion had given him the first twinge of loneliness he'd felt since he'd left home in 1858. He wasn't sure why, though, unless it was because she had grit, and he respected that.

He wrapped up in his blanket and pulled his hat down over his eyes. Inspired, perhaps, by Kelly's example, he slept more soundly than he had in months and did not wake up at all during the night.

Kelly woke with a start just after dawn. She was disoriented, and for a moment, her eyes tried to make the clearing look like her bedroom at home. Then the mirage vanished, and yesterday came rushing back at her.

Everything was still. The horses were standing quietly, but Graham's blankets were empty, and he was nowhere to be seen. Kelly sat up and tried to pull her boots on, but her feet were still swollen, and they didn't fit.

Graham stepped out of the woods, his rifle over one shoulder. He carried a rabbit by its hind legs.

"Good morning," she said, wondering if he had bothered to sleep at all. It must have been midnight before they had made camp, and it couldn't be five o'clock yet.

"Good morning," he replied, his voice slightly mocking.

"Is there something foolish about saying good morning?" She asked irritably.

"Not a thing," he said. "You want to water the horses?"

"Sure."

Still barefoot, Kelly went and untethered the horses.

"Put your boots on," Graham said to her as he started skin the rabbit.

"I can't," Kelly said, but she saw his point. She was liable to cut herself or get snakebit walking barefoot to the stream. So she stood beside her horse and jumped onto his back. She could ride to the stream and then get off and soak her feet. Maybe after that, her boots would fit.

Graham watched her ride into the woods. He knew plenty of men who couldn't get on a horse without a saddle to pull themselves up with.

When she reached the stream, Kelly let both horses drink. She slid off Phoenix's back stood in the cool water, savoring how it felt running over her tired feet. She washed her face and hands and rinsed her mouth, then got back on her horse and rode back to camp.

After roasting and eating the rabbit, they broke camp. Kelly had managed to get her boots on, but she rode with her feet out of the stirrups for the rest of the day. Riding along with her feet dangling, she thought that she felt better than she had in months. Why hadn't she thought of just riding away from the whole mess weeks ago, she wondered. Now that it was done, it seemed so easy.

The country was rough, and they rode single file, Graham leading. He rode easily, but with an erectness that made her think he'd been in the army for a good while. She herself had never been able to get so straight in the back when she rode, despite her grandfather's nagging. There must be something about wearing a uniform and being yelled at a lot that put starch into your spine.

Despite Graham's statement that they were in Canada and were safe from pursuit, it seemed to Kelly that he was hurrying. He kept up as fast a pace as the country would permit and only allowed a half-hour stop for lunch. Kelly did not appreciate it on top of the previous day's excitement and the night before's sleeplessness, but she was determined not to complain. The faster and futher she got from Millersville, the more relieved she felt. A sore behind and sleepy eyes seemed small prices to pay.

They rode hard for an hour after lunch, then dismounted and walked a while to rest the horses. The country had flattened out a little, and they walked side by side. They had not spoken since breaking camp that morning, and Kelly was bored with the silence.

"Do you mind my asking how long you were in the army?" She asked.

Graham looked over at her, surprised by the question, although no one looking at him would have thought him even interested, much less surprised.

"Who says I was in the army?" He asked.

"The way you sit your horse does," Kelly said.

They walked on a few more paces, and Kelly wondered if he was going to answer her.

"I went in in '62 and came out in '70," he said. "You have sharp eyes."

To Kelly, there wasn't anything sharp about it; it was as easy to see as the nose on his face. She was pleased by the compliment though, and it made her feel bold enough to continue the conversation.

"My grandfather fought in the Mexican war," she said. "Did you fight down south in the late conflict?"

"No, I was out west," he replied. "You should be careful how you speak of such things. Tempers tend to flare over them. A southern man might take offense at such a question."

"But you're not," Kelly said. "I knew you weren't. Not with that Yankee accent."

"Yankee accent?"

"From Vermont, I think. I do—used to do—a bit of horse trading up there."

"I see."

His tone indicated that he had had enough of her questions. Kelly pulled her gloves off and let her hands cool. She could think of nothing else to say, so she let the conversation lapse and went back to thinking about her escape.

Her good spirits started to fade as darkness fell, and Graham showed no intention of stopping. Again, they did not stop until well after dark, and Kelly was dismayed to feel her knees wobble when they finally did dismount.

They made camp. Kelly tended to the horses. Graham was

even less communicative than he had been during the day before, but it didn't bother her as much. She was tired and irritable and didn't want to talk to him anyway. She had a feeling he was trying to see how long it would take for her to complain about being tired. That thought rankled her, since it hadn't been her idea to go along with him anyway.

Sleep did little to refresh her. She woke up feeling as irritable as she had been before going to bed. She did not wish him a good morning, and they did not speak at all. Kelly tended the horses silently except for talking quietly to Phoenix as she saddled him. She glanced up to see Graham looking at her. On seeing his questioning look, she favored him with an icy stare. She didn't expect someone who didn't like talking to people to understand why she spoke to her horse.

They came through the woods to the northern shore of Lake Erie. They followed the shore line, and Kelly enjoyed seeing the vast blue expanse of the lake. It was hard to imagine that there was another shore on the other side.

Although he did not share Kelly's fascination with the lake, Graham knew there was a better chance of finding a town near it. He needed to get her outfitted as soon as he could. He had only brought provisions for one, and they were quickly running out. Also, she would probably be less irritable once she had her own gear. He knew it was irksome to depend on another person.

Early in the afternoon, they sighted a good-sized settlement. Kelly was relieved. They had not seen another person since having left Millersville two days before. It also meant she could get her own food and bedroll and a warmer shirt. And a hairbrush, she reminded, herself, grimacing as she thought of how knotted her hair must be by now.

Graham surveyed the settlement with a careful eye.

"You had better wait here," Graham said to her. "I'll get what you need."

Kelly did not like that idea. She wanted to see the town for herself and do her own shopping.

"I don't want to wait here," Kelly replied. "I can do it myself."

"There's probably a notice out on you," Graham said. "You ought to stay here."

"It's more likely there's a notice on you," Kelly returned. "With a bigger reward, too."

Graham did not seem perturbed by this statement. He reached into one of his saddle wallets and removed a bundle of banknotes.

"Here," he said and, seeing her surprise, explained. "It's your cut of the bank money."

It was on the tip of her tongue to refuse it, but then she thought the better of it and accepted the money. If she refused it, he would want to know how she planned to buy what she needed, and she didn't want him to know that she had over a thousand dollars.

Kelly never did learn the name of that town—it was more of a village, really. A few businesses lined the wide central street which was surrounded by a scattering of houses. Some of the houses were made of hewn logs, some of planed lumber. Kelly and Graham's first stop, the general store, was made of lumber.

Graham excused himself, saying he would go get grain for the horses, and Kelly went in alone. The clerk stared at her, but Kelly hardly noticed. She was used to being stared at. There was no one else in the store.

"Good afternoon," she said, taking a quick moment to look over the store's stock.

The clerk nodded in reply.

"Let's see," Kelly said. "I'll need two of those striped wool blankets. Do you have a slicker that would fit me?"

The clerk set the blankets on the counter, and pulled a slicker from the shelf behind him. Kelly unfolded it and tried it on. It was a size or two too big, but she could roll the sleeves up.

"Do you have any ready made shirts?"

The clerk jabbed his thumb at a table in the front of the store.

"Over there," he said.

Kelly examined the shirts. They were cheaply made and tended to be gaudy. She rooted through the pile until she found a solid blue one that looked as though it would fit. She added it to her pile on the counter, then wandered around the store, picking up a canteen, a small knife, and a hairbrush. As an afterthought, she picked up a package of needles and some cotton thread. Kelly was no great hand at sewing, but if clothes were going to be so hard to come by, she'd have to practice up.

"Is that all?" The clerk asked her.

"Let me think a minute," Kelly said, looking around. She could use a spair pair of jeans, but didn't see any. She had no idea whether or not they would stop again soon, but decided to wait. If she bought regular men's pants, they would never stay up without suspenders, which she had no intention of wearing.

"Hairpins," she said, suddenly. "Do you have hairpins?"

The clerk walked to the end of the counter and returned with a small box.

Kelly could see nothing else that she needed.

"Add a bag of that horehound candy, and that'll be all, thank you," she said.

The clerk added her purchases up on a piece of paper while Kelly checked the prices on everything. Having plenty of money was no reason to get cheated for want of normal caution.

"It all comes to twenty-one dollars and fifty-eight cents."

Kelly frowned. That sounded wrong.

"Let me see that, please," she said, motioning for the paper.

The clerk handed it to her. Kelly checked over his arithmetic.

"You added the hairpins in twice," she said. "It should be twenty-one thirty-two."

The clerk went back over the paper so slowly Kelly thought she might as well pay the twenty-six cents; it beat growing old and dying in a general store.

At last he nodded.

"Twenty-one dollars and thirty-two cents is right. Sorry about that."

"It's all right," she said handing him twenty-two dollars and reminding herself to count the change.

After receiving and counting the change, she tied the blankets and the slicker into a bed roll and carried the other things wrapped up in the new shirt. She nodded to the clerk and left, not bothering to notice if he nodded back.

Graham had not returned from wherever he had disappeared to, so Kelly tied the bed roll behind her saddle, and stowed everything else in her saddle bags. Then she sat down on the store steps and waited for him.

He came walking down the street a few minutes later, carrying a large sack, which Kelly guessed held the grain. She was not prepared to discover that it also contained a rifle, saddle boot and revolver.

"What's all that for?" She asked. "Don't you have enough guns already?"

Graham ignored her second question.

"I took the liberty of buying these for you," he replied. "You'll need them sooner or later."

Kelly frowned. Maybe she would need a gun, but she doubted it. And anyway, it wasn't any of his business.

"I appreciate it, Mr. McNair," she said, not sounding very appreciative.

"The name is Graham."

"But don't you think you should have asked me?"

"No."

"Why not?"

"There's no point in asking someone about something they don't know anything about." Graham handed her the weapons. Kelly accepted them reluctantly.

"I can shoot a little," she said, trying not to sound defensive.

"Glad to hear it," he said, stowing a sack of grain in her left saddle bags.

Kelly set the guns down. Before he could tie the saddle bag closed, she was at his elbow. She took the flap from his hands and checked inside the bag to make sure the grain wasn't on top of her candy bag, which she wanted in easy reach so she could get to it while riding. Graham stepped back out of the way and put the rest of the grain in his own saddle bags.

"See to those guns," he told her. "We ought to get out of here."

He noticed that several of the townspeople were standing in the street, watching them. He wasn't going to be able to slip in and out of towns unnoticed while traveling with a pants-wearing female.

"You have a hard way of speaking to people," Kelly said, although she did as he had said.

"You go on the scrap too easy," he replied, mounting his horse.

Kelly had some trouble getting the rifle boot tied to her saddle in a way that pleased her, but at last she accomplished it and mounted up, puzzled as to what she should do with the revolver. She guessed that he hadn't been able to locate a holster for it because she was small waisted for a gunslinger. The thought made her smile, and she pushed the revolver in the middle of her bed roll.

Graham hurried them out of town; Kelly would have liked to ridden slower and seen more. She deliberately slowed Phoenix down and trailed behind Graham, who was annoyed. Didn't she realize everyone was staring at her? The townspeople would talk about nothing else for weeks—months maybe. While Graham wasn't concerned about being followed for the bank robbery, he thought it unlikely that Kelly's family, whoever they were, would let her just ride off without a word. Sooner or later, someone would pick up their trail.

When they had cleared the town, she rode up beside him.

"If you aren't worried about being pursued for the robbery," she asked. "Why do you ride so fast all the time?"

"Don't you think your people will send someone after you?"

Kelly frowned. She had not thought of that. They would probably be just as glad to be rid of her.

"Maybe," she said. "But probably not."

Her answer surprised Graham into asking one question more than he had planned.

"Not even your folks?" He asked. "Won't they worry over you?"

"No," Kelly said firmly and with no trace of emotion in her voice.

He did not question her further, and she volunteered no more information. But the thought he had planted in her mind would not go away. Kelly's father would not worry over her, but he would be furious when he heard what had happened at the bank. He would not come after her to save her, but he might to punish her.

Kelly put the thought away. It was probably next to impossible to find someone in this wilderness, anyway.

Kelly was enjoying the slower pace they had been keeping for the past hour and was sucking happily on a piece of candy when Graham reined in. They were in a clearing about fifty yards long and twenty wide.

"What do you think about having a shooting lesson?" He asked.

"I don't think it's necessary," Kelly said. "But of course, I bow to your expert opinion."

Graham didn't react to her sarcasm, and Kelly wondered if he had even noticed it. Instead, he dismounted and tied his horse to a tree. He felt there was only one thing more important than getting west as quickly as possible, and that was teaching Kelly to shoot, and to shoot well. She had the nerve to defend herself, but it was wasted without the means.

"Get the revolver I gave you," he said.

Kelly dismounted, tied her horse beside his, and pulled her revolver from within her bed roll.

"It's more likely you'll need to use this before the rifle," he explained. "Do you know how to sight?"

"You line these two little knobs up, right?" Kelly asked, pointing to the sights at each end of the barrel.

"Right. But if you need to use a revolver, you don't have time to think about it."

"That doesn't make sense," Kelly said, frowning. "How can you aim without thinking?"

Graham thought for a way to explain it.

"Remember how you got up on your horse when he was running?" he asked.

"Sure."

"Well, how did you do that?"

Now Kelly was silent as she thought.

"I've done it for so long I can't think exactly how I do it," she paused. "I just see myself doing it—in my head, if you know what I mean—and then it happens."

Graham nodded.

"It's the same thing with using a revolver. You practice until it comes natural."

"Maybe," Kelly said doubtfully. "But I don't think I need to get that good at it. I don't intend to get into any shoot outs."

"No one ever does," Graham answered. "But they have way of happening anyway."

"You sound as if you know from experience," Kelly said, remembering how easily, almost carelessly, he had sent a bullet through Frank Gaynor's chest.

He ignored her comment.

"Sight on that tree," he said, pointing to a small oak tree about twenty yards away.

"Have you robbed other banks?" Kelly asked, not wanting to be diverted from her line of thinking.

"Have you?" He asked, his eyes glinting a little. Kelly refused to be put out by his question.

"No, that was my first," she said. "I didn't mean to be insulting." Graham relented a little. He couldn't really blame her for wondering about such things, even if he was annoyed by her boldness in asking about them.

"I took a little spare traveling money from a bank in Iowa right after I left the army," he said.

"I didn't think they had banks in Iowa," Kelly replied.

"Well they do. Now sight on the tree," Graham said.

Kelly sighted on the tree and fired three times, taking a moment between each shot to adjust her aim. Only the last shot hit the tree. Her ears rang from the noise.

"Looks like we have some work to do," Graham said, secretly impressed that she had hit the tree even once.

Kelly removed the spent shells from their chambers. Graham handed her three new shells.

"Let's move closer," he suggested. "If you hit more, we can figure out what direction your aim is off in."

They moved a few yards closer. Graham explained to her that she was firing low and to the left. Kelly listened carefully. When she had taken over the farm at age fourteen, one of the first things Kelly had learned was that no one person was good at everything. Smart people accepted this and took every opportunity to learn from those who knew things they didn't.

She knew very little about Graham, but when it came to life outside of Millersville, New York, she had no doubts that he knew a whole lot more than she did. Therefore, if he said that she needed to learn how to shoot well, she would take him at his word and apply herself to the task.

Kelly practiced the rest of the day. By the time it was too dark to shoot anymore, she had a headache from the noise and her nose was sour with the acrid smell of gunsmoke, but she felt pleased with her progress.

When they finally sat down to eat supper, Kelly found that her right hand was sore from the unfamiliar demands on it. After she had eaten a few bites of supper, her headache eased somewhat.

"So let me see if I've got all this straight," she said, setting her plate on her knee. "My revolver and my rifle take the same kind of bullets, except my rifle isn't a rifle, it's a carbine. It's a carbine because the barrel is four inches shorter, which means that it's less accurate over distances but not so heavy and awkward for someone with short arms like myself."

Graham looked up briefly but didn't correct her on any point. Kelly, taking this to mean that her recitation had been accurate, went on.

"Both the carbine and the revolver are .44 caliber, and if I use the wrong caliber bullets, the guns could blow up in my hands. When I get more comfortable with them, you'll file down the hammer notch, which will make the trigger more sensitive so

I will have to be more careful. I should never put a bullet under the hammer unless I know I'll need it and never draw on anyone unless I plan to shoot. If either gun gets wet . . ."

"Why don't you eat some supper?" Graham interrupted.

"I want to make sure I have all this straight in my mind," Kelly said.

"You do. And if you don't, it'll keep until morning."

An edge had crept into his voice, so Kelly went back to eating her supper, silently reviewing the rest of the day's lesson in her head. When her plate was empty, she looked curiously over the fire at Graham, who was taking a swig from his canteen.

"What do you do," she asked when he set the canteen down, "if you don't rob banks?"

"I play cards and scout for the army now and then," he said, the edge in voice more apparent. He felt that he had answered enough questions for one day. "Is there anything else you want to know?"

"What kind of cards?" Kelly asked him, deciding to ignore his sharpness. Aside from Aunt Sally, everyone in her family was sharp practically all the time, and if you wanted someone to shut up, you said so in plain English so you wouldn't be misunderstood. "I used to play poker with my wranglers when they needed to round out a game."

"Win much?"

"Hardly ever," Kelly said, pleased because he had answered her.

"I never met a cowboy yet who was any good at cards," Graham commented.

"I'm not a cowboy," Kelly said.

"What are you then?"

"I'm an equestrian," she said, after a moment's thought. "We never kept a cow."

Graham's face twitched. Kelly couldn't decide if he was trying not to smile or if he was trying not to frown.

"Is that why your horse has got such a high-flown name?"

"He's a fine horse," Kelly said, a little miffed.

"I never said he wasn't."

"I suppose you never named your horse," she said.

"You're right. I never saw a horse yet that would answer to his name."

Kelly shook her head. She never could understand why most people had so little imagination.

"Sometimes horses are better to talk to than people, and how can you address one properly if you don't know its name?"

Graham could not tell whether or not she was joking. Her face was perfectly serious, and he'd seen plenty of cowboys who acted right dotty about their favorite horses. Well, to each his—her—own.

"You sure whoorahed that horse dealer like a cowboy would have," Graham said, although he knew a cowboy would have used fewer words and more violence.

"That was his own fault," Kelly said. "There wasn't any reason for him to be so difficult about the receipt."

"Nor was there for you to be."

"Wasn't there?" She asked heatedly. Thinking back on that incident made her almost as angry as she had been when it had been happening.

"All you had to do was let your foreman sign it."

"That's the most ridiculous thing I ever heard," Kelly snapped. "Zion can't write and doesn't even understand what a downpayment is."

"Well, legally . . ."

"Who are you?" Kelly interrupted sarcastically. "Daniel Webster?"

"No, and I'm not some horse dealer either," he replied, meeting her sarcasm with coldness. "So watch the tone you take with me."

"Then don't lecture me," Kelly said. His conversation seemed so annoying that she had a suspicion that he might be doing it deliberately.

Graham said nothing more. He had not expected her to get so riled just from talking, but since she had, it was better to let it drop. They finished their meal in silence. Graham washed the plates with water from his canteen. When he was done, he took a deck of cards from his jacket pocket and began to shuffle them aimlessly. Kelly was watching the horses. They had had a short day of riding, and she wasn't sleepy yet.

But she was bored. She wished she had a book to read or that Graham was less tricky to talk to.

"Let's play some cards," he said suddenly, startling her. "If you want to, that is."

"Sure," Kelly said, glad to have a diversion.

They played five-card draw for matches. Graham had never cared much for two handed poker, but Kelly turned out to be a fairly good player, and the game was interesting. It was midnight before Kelly said she was tired and wanted to go to sleep. Her pile of matches was smaller than his, but not by enough for him to feel smug about it. As she wrapped up in her blankets and lay back against her saddle to go to sleep, Graham wondered if her earler deprecation of her abilities at poker had been a bluff. A good gambler never bragged about card playing.

As he fell asleep, he made a mental note to be more careful about underestimating her.

The night passed quietly. A little after three in the morning, a raccoon scampered down from a tree, startling both horses, who snorted and pawed at the ground as the furry intruder waddled away.

At the horses' noise, sleep fell off of Graham, and he was completely awake in an instant, his revolver drawn. He listened carefully but heard nothing except the usual night sounds. The horses were grazing quietly again.

He sat up and looked around. The fire had died into embers and gave off little light, but his vision was excellent, and he could discern no movement.

After listening a while longer, he relaxed, but he did not go back to sleep. He had learned that sometimes it was a big mistake to assume there was no danger just because your senses told you so.

A few feet away, Kelly slept peacefully, oblivious to whatever had disturbed him. He thought the girl could sleep through an avalanche, and for someone supposedly used to getting up early, she sure tended to be grouchy in the mornings. The previous two evenings, he had noticed that, when they dismounted to make camp, her knees had been wobbly with fatigue. She had never said anything about it, but he guessed that she was pretty exhausted from all the hard riding they were doing.

His need to hurry puzzled him, because there didn't seem to be any particular reason for it. No one had pursued them after the bank robbery. If Kelly's family did send someone after them, it would be a special detective or a hired-out marshal, either of which would probably get lost ten miles out from town.

They had encountered no problems so far, and the weather was fine. Still, he felt a need to get the east behind him for good. It was so peaceful and quiet that he felt edgy. In truth, he hadn't really needed a road stake all that badly; he'd only robbed that bank out of boredom and irritation.

Kelly mumbled something in her sleep and rolled over once. Graham envied her ability to sleep so well. To him sleep was a dangerous, helpless time. During the Indian campaigns, he'd seen sound sleepers wake up with their throats cut, dying before they could even realize what had happened to them.

He remembered a scouting patrol he'd been in the year he finally left the army.

They'd been caught in the open but had managed to reach cover in a river bottom and had only lost four men on the way. The remaining men had hunkered down when darkness came, only to hear the agonized screams of one of their fallen comrades from across the stream. Lord only knew what those Indians were doing to him, but he'd screamed all night. They lost two more men that night, and just before dawn, two other men turned their revolvers on themselves.

The remaining four, Graham among them, had met the Indians' early morning attack halfway. Only Graham and a bucktoothed private from Indiana ever made it back to the fort. Graham often wondered about that private. He had been white faced and shaking with fear through the entire fight, but he hadn't lost his nerve during the night when two seasoned campaigners had. Graham decided that maybe it didn't have as much to do with courage as it did with a man's determination to live.

But white men were just as murderous. He'd come east after shooting a cattle dealer in Nebraska. The man had come at him drunk and firing wild, but to the law, that counted for nothing against the fact that the man was a regular church goer with a large family. There was nothing more dangerous, in Graham's opinion, than a drunk with a gun in his hand.

True, whiskey destroyed a man's aim, but it also eliminated his regard for his own life. A man worried about dying can be shown the error of his ways. A man thinking only of killing someone else, no matter what the cost, was very likely to succeed. Graham still wasn't sure why the man had come at him, although he had gathered that the man's friends had put him up to it on a dare. What a stupid reason to die, he thought.

Sunrise was about two hours off, he judged, holstering his revolver and laying back down. They were about back in the States by now, and once they got through Illinois, they could slow down. Once he could smell the Mississippi river, he'd feel better. He fell asleep quickly, and in the morning, he hardly remembered that his sleep had been disturbed.

Kelly woke before him that morning. She sat up and yawned, looking around at how peaceful everything seemed in the thin morning light. After pulling her boots on, she stood and started walking to the woods because she had to go to the bathroom. Her feet crunched some sticks laying near the fire, and Graham sat up abruptly, his revolver drawn and pointed at her.

Kelly froze. Graham blinked; he had been dreaming of Indian raids, and it took him moment to recognize her.

"I give up," Kelly said, holding her hands above her head. "Don't shoot."

Graham holstered his gun, a sour look on his face. Kelly laughed and walked off, wondering what could possibly make a man so jumpy.

The next week passed swiftly. Graham resumed their hurried pace, but stopped earlier to continue with Kelly's shooting lessons. She had good eyes and reflexes; he was pleased with how quickly she developed a steady hand and good aim. It was not necessary that she become a sharpshooter, though it was essential that she understand that being willing to shoot made up for pin point precision.

But that was one lesson he couldn't really teach her. It generally came as a shock to people when they realized that other people were willing to kill them and that the only way to prevent it was to shoot first. It would especially shock someone raised in as civilized a way as Kelly had been. He could warn her of it, but in the end, he knew, it was either in her, or it wasn't. Only an actual scrap would reveal the intensity of her instinct and will for survival.

Chapter 5

The land flattened out, and occasionally, they rode by farms. Graham was certain they were in Illinois; however, they seemed to be a bit far north of where Graham had intended, and so, he chose an angling course southwest. At midmorning one day, they found their road blocked by a river.

The river was lined with trees, and they halted in the shade. Kelly removed her hat and wiped the sweat from her forehead. The river was wide, and the current looked strong. She hoped they would not have to cross it but waited silently while Graham considered it for a moment.

"Let's scout downstream and see if there's a better crossing," he said, much to Kelly's relief.

They rode downstream for a half an hour, until they came upon an area where the river was flanked by low banks, and the current seemed to have lost some of its strength. The river was wider there, but Graham doubted they would find a better place. He saw some old wagon tracks in the mud, which indicated that someone else had used that crossing, although he couldn't say what success they'd had.

"Wrap everything up tight in your slicker," he told Kelly.

"What about my rifle?" She asked.

"Don't worry about it, you can clean it when we get across."

Kelly followed his directions and tried not to look nervous. She had never swum a horse before, and while she was generally fearless when it came to anything having to do with horses, something about that river unnerved her. She strove to maintain her calm, however, knowing that if she were scared, Phoenix would be too.

As it turned out, neither horse would willingly enter the water. After some cajoling and a lot of firmness, Kelly managed to get Phoenix in, and then, Graham's horse followed with little difficulty. As the horses waded into the water, Graham could tell that the current was stronger than he'd thought. He hoped the horses would not have to swim, but as they walked further and further into the river, the water rose higher and higher.

They were a quarter of the way across when Kelly felt Phoenix's feet leave the river bed. He began to swim with a jerky, panicky motion. Kelly tried to calm him, but water was rushing over her, pulling at her so strongly she had to use both hands just to hold on to the saddle horn. Graham's horse, which was a more experienced swimmer, had now outdistanced them and was nearly ashore.

Then she felt Phoenix start to roll over. Before she could get free of the saddle, he had rolled on top of her, and she found herself completely under water. She kicked free of the saddle and pushed herself away from the horse with all of her strength. She was afraid he would kick her as he thrashed around.

Now she was completely disoriented. The water was rushing around her, pulling her downstream, but she had no idea where the surface was until she suddenly bobbed upward and broke through it, gasping for air.

She had begun to swim but was unable to make much headway against the current, when suddenly she ran up against a small mud bar. She scrambled onto it gratefully and lay there panting for air.

When she sat up, she realized that she had been pulled quite a ways downstream. She could not see Graham or either of the horses. She wondered if Phoenix had drowned and what she should do next. Because she was tired and too scared to try and swim any more, she decided to wait and see if Graham would find her.

Graham had reached the bank and had turned to see Kelly's riderless horse thrashing around in the water. He scanned the river for signs of Kelly, but saw nothing but the swirling, muddy water. Her horse finally made it ashore, and Graham led it as he rode downstream.

Downstream, the river grew wider and the current swifter. He felt sure in his heart that she must have drowned and was cursing himself for having misjudged the river, when he spotted something on a mud bar about fifty yards further down river. The river bank was wooded, and he could not tell what it was he saw, so he hurried both horses until he had a clear view. Then he breathed a sigh of relief. It was Kelly.

She waved to him, and he waved back.

"Don't swim," he shouted. "I'll throw you a rope!" He tied Kelly's horse to a tree. He planned to walk his horse into the river, hoping to get close enough to her so that his rope would reach her.

Sitting on the mud bar, Kelly was so relieved to see him that she felt tears rise in her eyes. She heard him shout, "Swim" and something else she couldn't hear. She was afraid to swim, but she couldn't think how else she could get to shore, so she dove back into the river and began to swim toward him.

Graham heard the splash and looked up in amazement. What the hell was she doing? Was she crazy?

Kelly swam strongly, but the current was fierce, and it dragged her further downstream. She could not judge how much headway she was making; the bank seemed miles away. She closed her eyes and swam until her fingers struck the steep muddy bank of the opposite shore.

The bank was slippery and wet, and there were few good hand holds, but Kelly clutched it frantically and began to pull herself up. When Kelly reached the top, she was soaking wet and covered with mud. She flopped down on a patch of grass and waited for Graham to find her. She would have gone looking for him, but she was exhausted, and besides, she had caught a glimpse of him following her downstream as she swam.

Hearing some noises in the brush, Kelly sat up and tried to wipe her muddy hands clean on the grass. It didn't help much.

Graham appeared a second or two later, leading both horses. Kelly looked up to smile at him but couldn't when she saw that his face was clouded with something like anger. He stared at her until she flushed and dropped her eyes.

"Are you crazy?" He demanded.

"No," Kelly said, taken aback by his tone.

"You must be stupid then," he said, throwing her horse's reins at her. "I never saw anyone act such a fool."

"Don't yell at me," Kelly said, her voice quivering with insult and rising in anger. "I hate being yelled at."

He swore. Both horses moved uneasily, upset by his sudden anger.

"When I tell you things, it's for your own good," he said, his voice angry but low. "I ought to stripe your leg."

Kelly scrambled to her feet. Her chest heaved with anger, and her hands shook with fatigue, but there was no way this bank robbing army scout was going to lay a hand on her.

"I'd like to see you try!" She shouted.

Graham stepped toward her, and Kelly snatched up a club-sized stick.

Graham did not come any closer. There was something faintly ridiculous about the situation, and it could only get more so, especially if she hit him.

So he stepped back, turned, and walked a few steps away from her. Kelly held on to the stick; she had an idea that he was trying to get her to drop her guard. She could not figure out why he was so upset; it wasn't like she had fallen off the horse on purpose.

When he faced her again, he was so calm that it seemed impossible that he had ever been angry in his life.

"You could have drowned," he said as though it wouldn't have mattered if she had. "I was going to throw you a rope, that's why I told you not to try and swim."

Kelly dropped her stick. She felt sick all of a sudden.

"No, you told me to swim," she said defensively, but she knew that she had misunderstood him because of the roaring of the river and the water in her ears.

Graham decided the least said about it, the better.

"You'd better change your clothes," he said. "The things rolled up in your slicker ought to be dry."

Kelly took the bundle from behind her saddle and went into a thicket of trees. She stripped off her wet clothes and dried herself with her blanket. She dressed swiftly, but because her boots were soaked through, she did not put them back on. She could ride barefoot until they dried.

She rolled her wet things back into the slicker and went back to the river bank. Graham was seated on a rotting log waiting for her. He watched as she tied the bundle back behind her saddle.

"Where's your hat?" He asked.

Until then, Kelly had not missed it.

"I don't know," she said. "It must have come off in the water."

Graham looked at the sun. It was now late afternoon.

"Well, we'll go for another hour or so and stop early. I expect you're worn out."

Kelly mounted her horse and did not answer. She was still offended because he had yelled at her. But Graham did not seem to care whether she answered him or not. He mounted up and headed his horse upstream. Kelly followed him, feeling angry and sick and wishing very much that she had the gumption to go her own way.

When they camped that evening, Graham did not suggest that they play cards, even though poker games had become a matter of habit in the evenings. Plainly, Kelly was still angry, and he knew that she would refuse to play. Neither of them spoke—Graham because there was nothing to say, and Kelly because she was still mad.

The next morning, trouble started as they were breaking camp. Kelly had saddled her horse and was ready to go when Graham offered her his hat.

"Here," he said. "You'd better wear this; the sun'll be fierce today."

"No, thank you," Kelly replied icily.

"Take it," he said again. "Or you'll be sunburnt."

"If I take it," Kelly replied. "You will be sunburnt."

"Not as badly as you'd be," he said. "I'm more used to the sun and was never so fair skinned anyway."

Kelly's mouth set in a stubborn line. Graham saw it and knew that further argument was useless. He scooped some dirt into the tin can he used for making coffee and added some water from his canteen. He stirred the mess with a stick until it was thick, black mud.

Kelly watched this with growing apprehension. She had a terrible suspicion about what the mud was for. That suspicion was confirmed when he approached her with the can.

"If you won't wear the hat," he said. "You'll wear this."

Kelly shook her head and backed away from him.

"I won't either. You are not putting mud all over my face."

"Then you do it," he said, offering her the can.

"I said no," Kelly replied, glaring at him.

He grabbed her so swiftly that she couldn't twist away in time. She tried to wrench her arm free, but he tripped her, and she fell to her knees. Before he could improve his grip on her arm, she had torn free and was scrambling away. Graham dove after her and caught her legs. Kelly kicked violently, but he would not let go.

They wrestled on the ground for a few more minutes, and then Graham managed to pin Kelly face down on the ground by holding her hands behind her back and putting his knee in the small of her back. Still, she struggled so violently he couldn't let go with one of his hands to get the can. He looked around and saw it didn't matter anyway; the can had fallen upside down during their struggle, and it was now empty.

He held her down for another moment, then let her go. She scrambled to her feet immediately. He swore and kicked the can, wondering how anyone could be so full of pure cussedness. He was only trying to help her.

He turned to tell her so, and she punched him in the face so hard that he nearly fell over.

Though caught off guard, Graham kept his balance, and when she stepped in to hit him again, he was able to block her fist and grab her arm. After grappling with her for a few moments, he managed to pin her arms to her sides in a bear hug. Kelly continued to struggle. She was so enraged at having been pinned down again that she resolved to shoot him the moment he let go of her.

But Graham was not in the habit of making the same mistake twice. He did not let her go; he waited until her struggling tapered off.

"Are you finished?" He asked.

"Yes," Kelly said, but she wasn't. She still planned to shoot him as soon as he let go.

"I'm not a fool," he said, as though having read her thoughts. "I'm not letting you go until we settle this."

"I won't be bullied," Kelly snapped, "Not by you or anyone else. And I won't be yelled at or manhandled either."

Graham let go of her then, but as he did so, he pulled her revolver from its holster and pushed her away from him. He wasn't taking any chances.

Kelly stumbled, then caught her balance. Her face was red, and her hands shook with anger. Graham now looked entirely calm, but she was pleased to see a thin trickle of blood coming from one corner of his mouth.

"That's fair enough," he said. "Now let's go."

"I'm not going anywhere with you," she said, her voice trembling.

"Don't be stiff-necked," he said. She apparently did not appreciate how forgiving he was being. His mouth hurt like hell, and he felt bruised all over; she'd gotten some good ones in during their fight.

But she also seemed to have no intention of mounting her horse or doing as he said. He couldn't very well pack her over her horse. Despite his anger, he didn't think of leaving her there or letting her ride off alone. Especially now that he thought he understood how she felt; she was used to being in charge and taking orders rankled her.

"What are you going to do?" He asked. "Sit here in the middle of nowhere?"

Even angry as she was, Kelly knew she had few choices, but she couldn't believe that he was going to act as though none of this had happened. It was humiliating.

"I want my gun back," she said.

"You can have it this evening," he said, unloading it and sticking it in his belt. As an afterthought, he went over to her horse and removed her rifle from its saddle boot.

That settled it for Kelly. She felt grimly vindicated because he was now sufficiently impressed with her to take her guns away. She began to calm down and consider things more rationally. Unless she was ready to go out on her own, she had to make the best of the situation.

Her face was sweaty from her exertions, and she looked up at the sun. He was right about getting sunburned; a fact she had never contested, not even in her own mind. For her, it was more a matter of not having wanted to accept his high handed offer of assistance, and that was now settled.

So she retrieved the can he had kicked and made some more mud, which she carefully daubed on her face, leaving only her eyes and lips uncovered. Graham watched her without comment. He didn't think anything she did would ever surprise him again.

When she was done, Kelly mounted her horse. She felt ridiculous but acted as though having her face covered with mud was nothing unusual. She was relieved when it became apparent that Graham was not going to poke fun at her. He sat on his horse, gingerly feeling his jaw.

"Who taught you to punch like that?" He asked.

"No one," Kelly replied. "I never hit anyone before in my life."

Graham spat to clear the blood from his mouth.

"You have a talent for it," he said.

"Thank you," Kelly replied. "I was inspired."

They headed due west, and for the next three days, they did not stop early for shooting lessons, even though Graham gave Kelly her guns back at sundown as he had promised.

Chapter 6

The mud did the trick though. In fact, Kelly thought as she examined her skin four days later in a hotel room mirror, it did a better job than a hat. Still, she had stopped to wash it off before they had ridden into town, even though it had been after dark. Graham hadn't said anything about the delay, though she knew the situation amused him considerably. He could laugh all he wanted as far as Kelly was concerned; she wasn't one to cut off her nose to spite her face.

A few blocks away, Graham was thinking much the same thing as he walked down the street from a local saloon to the hotel where they were staying. He had been in an all-night poker game that had just broken up. The cards had played in his favor, and the bright heat of the morning sun reminded him of the fight he and Kelly had had near the river.

Instead of heading straight back to the hotel as he had originally intended, Graham wandered around the town for a while. They were now less than a day's ride from the Mississippi river, and the town was sizable. After some looking, he came upon a haberdashery store.

The store had barely opened, but the clerk greeted him cheerfully.

"Good morning sir," he said. "It's a fine morning to be out early."

Graham nodded. Store clerks annoyed him almost as badly as brush salesmen. He went to the back of the store and examined the hats offered for sale. The clerk watched him look for ten minutes, then stepped forward.

"We have the finest selection of hats in town," he said. "Is there something in particular you were looking for?"

"This one," Graham said, holding up a black hat very much like his own. "Do you have it in a smaller size?"

"Yes sir. That's an excellent choice. One hundred percent wool felt. Sheds water like it was oil skin and warm as fur in the winter. It's silk-lined for comfort in the summer. What size did you need?"

Graham thought a second. It was hard to guess Kelly's size because she always wore her hair up, but if he bought it a little big, she could always put newspaper around the inside band to tighten it up, or in the winter, she could wear a muffler under it to keep her ears warm.

"This will do." He said, picking up a smaller version of the same hat. "How much?"

"Five dollars."

Illinois prices, Graham thought, handing over the five dollars, but at least you got quality for them.

"Can I wrap this for you, sir?" The clerk asked, ringing up the sale on an ornate cash register.

"Yes."

The clerk wrapped the hat in brown paper, securing it with string. It made for a lumpy package.

"Will that be all sir?" The clerk asked when he was done wrapping the hat. "Perhaps I could interest you in a fine linen shirt?"

"No," said Graham, taking the package and going to the door, which the clerk held open for him.

"A good day to you, sir," he said as Graham walked out.

Graham nodded in reply and started back to the hotel. He'd probably missed breakfast by now, and while that didn't matter to him, he wanted to catch Kelly before she went out.

But he need not have hurried. Kelly had slept late, enjoying her first night in a bed since having left home, and she too had missed breakfast. Now she sat on the bed dressed only in her clean shirt and camisole, relaxing and thinking about going out to find some food.

She knew they wouldn't be leaving for another day or so. The night before, Graham had said that he wanted to play a few nights of poker before they headed across the Mississippi and into the more sparsely populated plains. Kelly had no objection; she looked forward to getting rested and taking a real bath.

There was a knock at the door. Kelly snatched her jeans from the bed and hastily pulled them on, not bothering to tuck her shirt in.

"Who is it?" She asked.

"It's Graham."

Kelly opened the door a crack and peeked out. It really was him so she opened the door and let him in. He carried a lumpy package wrapped in brown paper.

"Good morning," she said. "You're up early."

Graham did not mention that he had never been to bed yet, since the thought had not occurred to her.

"I had some things to do," he replied. "This is for you." He offered her the lumpy package.

Kelly took it, too surprised to say anything but thank you. She stood there awkwardly for a moment.

"Aren't you going to open it?" He asked.

"Of course," she said, sitting down on the bed.

The package was very light. She untied the string and carefully unwrapped the paper. She was impressed when she saw the hat; it put her in mind of the ones her grandfather used to wear, and he never wore anything but the best.

"It's really lovely," she said softly, lifting it from the paper and looking it over. She stood and went to the mirror and tried it on. It was a little large, but when she put her hair up properly, it would fit fine.

Graham was pleased, thinking the hat much more becoming to her than the beat-up gray hat she'd lost in the river. The gray hat had made her eyes gray, and now he could see that they were really a changeable shade of blue.

"It looks a lot better on me than mud, don't you think?" She asked, wrinkling her nose as she remembered how badly the mud had smelled.

Graham laughed, and Kelly was so startled she nearly dropped the hat. She had never heard him laugh before.

"I must have looked pretty bad," she said. "I didn't think you even knew how to laugh."

"You would've looked worse burnt red."

Neither of them spoke for a moment. Kelly realized that he was still looking at her reflection in the mirror. She stepped away from it, folding her arms across her stomach.

"Well, thank you for the hat," she said. "I apologize for hitting you."

She did feel bad about having done such a thing. It hadn't really been called for, except that she had been pushed passed the limits of reason. After all, he had taken the time to help her and not many people in her life had ever done such a thing.

But their fight near the river had been far from his mind, and now that she had recalled it to his attention, he brushed it off.

"No need, I should have seen it coming," he said. "But you should watch that temper of yours. Someone else might have hit you back."

"You mean someone else might've tried to hit me back," Kelly said.

It was hopeless. Graham doffed his hat to her.

"Pardon me, my mistake."

Kelly sensed he was highly amused, but she didn't care. He just didn't give her credit for having any sense, though maybe now he would at least give her credit for having some gumption.

"How big a hurry are you in to get to San Francisco?" He asked, changing the subject abruptly.

"Where?" Kelly asked, startled by the question.

"Your folks. San Francisco? Remember?"

"Oh. No hurry," Kelly said hastily. "It's not like they know I'm coming."

"Do you want to telegraph them?"

"No, no," Kelly thought fast. "They might tell my father where I am."

Graham nodded, but Kelly doubted that he believed her. Well, who cared? He could think what he liked as long as he didn't call her on it.

"I'd like to stay here for another day or so," Graham said. "Since you're in no hurry."

"I said last night that we can stay as long as you like."

"And if you're interested," he went on. "There's a way you could help me out playing poker tonight."

Kelly pricked up her ears, interested to think that she played cards well enough to help him out with it.

The plan Graham had outlined to her was simple enough. They would play it straight, except on his deal he would stack the deck to her advantage. Kelly was not comfortable with the thought of cheating, but since they would enter and leave the game separately, there was little chance of them getting caught.

They worked the games for two days. Kelly found the play exciting. She went to the saloons unarmed, but before they rode out of town, she purchased a gunbelt. Wearing it made her feel a little silly, but as they rode a ferry across the Mississippi, Kelly began to feel that she was on an adventure as exciting as those her grandfather used to tell her about.

Chapter 7

When they left town, Kelly noticed that they slowed down considerably. They also resumed her shooting lessons and their nightly poker games, though now Graham concentrated on teaching her to cheat. He privately doubted that she had any family to go to in San Francisco, and by now, it was plain that she had no intentions of going home. She would have to learn a trade, and poker seemed the best available option.

The country was now a little hillier, crossed here and there with tree-lined rivers. They often paused in these creek bottoms, savoring the shade and letting the horses drink. Late one afternoon, they stood in such a stand of trees. The day was furiously hot. Graham had removed his suit jacket earlier on in the day, and now Kelly took a drink from her canteen.

"Let's walk for a bit while there's shade," she said.

But before Graham could answer, two rifle shots sounded abruptly and so near to them that Kelly thought she heard them whizz through the air. Both shots struck a small cottonwood tree beside Graham, spraying him with a hail of splinters. The horses shied and tried to wheel about. Kelly flattened herself on her horse's neck and tried to calm him. She could not see who was firing, but Graham had drawn his revolver and spurred his horse forward, his eyes fixed on a rise ahead of them to their right.

As he rode out of the trees, he could see someone hastily mount a horse and gallop away. He gave chase for a moment, coming close enough to see that the figure riding away was only a boy, probably not more than fourteen. Graham gave up the chase and turned back toward the stand of trees.

Meanwhile, Kelly examined the tree the bullets had hit. Not more than six inches in diameter, the bullets had scored it across one side, leaving a deep, ragged gouge.

"It was a boy," Graham said, riding up. "Dressed like a farmer. Probably thought we were a couple of deer."

Kelly's eyes left the tree. If those bullets had been one more foot to the left, she thought, Graham would be dead. She looked at him, meaning to say something to that effect. Instead, she noticed that he hadn't escaped unharmed after all.

"Your arm is bleeding," she said.

Graham looked at it, surprised. He hadn't even felt it until she had spoken.

Splinters from the tree had torn into his upper arm, some of them quite deeply. Although blood ran freely down his shirt sleeve, it wasn't a dangerous wound. Of all the stupid luck, he thought disgustedly, examining it, knowing that, if he hadn't taken his jacket off, it wouldn't have been such a mess.

Kelly dismounted and rooted through her saddle bags until she found her needles.

"What are you doing?" Graham asked her.

"This ought to do for the smaller ones," she said, holding up a needle. "Do you have any whiskey?"

Graham shook his head.

"Mount back up. We can tend to this when we get to town."

"You said that would be two or three days," Kelly replied. "Your arm could get infected."

"It won't," he said. "Mount up."

Kelly's face set stubbornly.

"Who doesn't want mud on their face now?" She asked him.

Who indeed, Graham thought as he dismounted. He took his whiskey bottle from his saddle bags and handed it to her. She poured a little over the needle as he stripped his shirt off and sat down on a rock.

Kelly washed the blood from his arm with water from her canteen. He flinched when she touched his arm.

"Sorry," she said immediately. "I'll try not to make this hurt anymore than it has to."

Graham did not answer. He motioned for the whiskey bottle, which she gave to him, thinking he must really be hurting if he couldn't talk from it. She was unaware that Graham had not flinched in pain; he had flinched because her touch sent a shiver down his spine.

Kelly examined his arm carefully. There were five or six sizable chunks of wood embedded in his arm, some of them pretty deeply. The smaller splinters worried her more. They could work in deeper and were much harder to see.

"This may take a while," she said at last. "I apologize in advance if this hurts."

He flinched again when she spoke. Kelly frowned, puzzled.

She had not even been touching him. But the puzzlement fled her mind as she considered what needed to be done. She would have to pick the larger ones out with her fingers, and the thought made her a little squeamish.

"Fire away," Graham said, taking another healthy swig from the whiskey bottle.

Kelly worked over his arm for nearly an hour before she was satisfied that all the splinters were gone. They had not spoken while she had worked. Graham had taken regular pulls at the whiskey bottle; Kelly had frowned with concentration, biting her lip and wincing now and then, even though he didn't seem to be in any pain.

Her hands were slimed with blood when she finished, and she washed them with water from her canteen as he poured whiskey over his arm to disinfect it.

Kelly ripped her extra shirt into strips and bound his arm tightly. Graham stood and surveyed her handiwork.

"Feels better already," he said. "Next town we come to, I'll get you a new shirt."

"We can call it even," she replied. "A shirt for a hat, fair enough?"

"Fair enough." He stood and put his own shirt on. Kelly wiped her hands dry on her jeans. He was looking at her oddly, and it made her uncomfortable. At first, she thought he might be insulted because the hat had been meant as a gift, but she dismissed that thought. He wasn't a petty sort of person. Perhaps the whiskey had affected the focus of his eyes or something.

She was only partly right. Graham wasn't thinking about hats, and the whiskey hadn't bothered his eyes, though it was responsible for him having allowed his face to reflect his feelings. He turned abruptly away when he saw the uneasiness in her face, regretting that he had drunk so much. The wound hadn't been all that painful, but the whiskey had been necessary to keep his skin from jumping when she touched him and had stood so close that her breath occasionally tickled his ear.

They remounted, and the horses, fresh from their rest, went on gladly. As they left the creek bottom, Kelly asked if they would stop early that night. Graham didn't answer, and they didn't speak again until the next morning.

"Are you angry about something?" Kelly asked as they ate their breakfast. Eighteen hours of silence were enough for her, especially when they had been getting along so well.

"No," Graham replied.

Kelly sighed. This was going to be like pulling teeth, she could tell.

"Does your arm hurt?"

"Not much."

"Well, why are you so quiet?" she asked, irritation plain in her voice.

"Because there's nothing to say," Graham said, giving her a look that indicated the conversation was foolish.

"There's always something to say," Kelly said. She was impervious to his looks. If he wanted her to shut up, he'd have to say it straight out.

Graham stood and kicked the fire out. After looking up at the sky for a moment, he said, "Nice weather," and went to saddle his horse.

Kelly gave up. She saddled Phoenix and gathered her things, prepared for another day of quiet riding. It was better, at least, than having to listen to a lot of foolishness. Anyway, Phoenix was in fine fettle, she thought, patting his neck affectionately. Their long journey had made him leaner, but healthily so, and his spirit was as high as ever.

They had not gone far when, suddenly, Phoenix snorted in fear. Before Kelly could see what he was afraid of, he reared and, coming back down, leapt forward at a mad gallop.

With some difficulty, Kelly brought him back under control. He was no longer running wildly, but she could not get him down to a walk again either. He was cantering, but Kelly had him so collected that he was practically running in place.

"Come on," she said to him, "There's nothing to be so upset about, calm . . ."

Her words ended abruptly as she was thrown violently over his neck. She heard a sharp crack and hit the ground hard. She scrambled to her feet; despite the breaking sound that she'd heard, nothing felt broken. Then she looked back to see if Phoenix had run off and saw that he lay motionless on his side. Kelly's stomach turned over as she ran to him. Even from a distance, she knew it was bad.

His right foreleg had been caught in a hole, and it was badly broken. Kelly could see a jagged edge of bone piercing the skin.

All at once, the sun seemed blazing hot, and sweat trickled down Kelly's neck, soaking the collar of her shirt. In that moment, she knew that Phoenix would never stand again, never walk again, never be her companion again. He raised his head and looked at her; she could see her image reflected in the brown of his eyes.

Graham rode up and surveyed the scene silently. Kelly did not seem to be hurt, so he rode on a few paces and waited.

Kelly unbuckled her saddle, and after some tugging, she pulled it from under him. Then she knelt by his head and undid the bridle. She patted his neck and spoke to him until he whinnied, a sad, hurt sound that made her sob. There was only one last thing she could do for him, and she would do it, no matter how much it hurt her. She stroked his nose once more, then stood up and stepped away from him.

Kelly drew her revolver and pointed it at his head, steadying it with both hands. She squeezed the trigger, and the gun roared, shattering the stillness that seemed to have descended everywhere. Phoenix jerked once, then his head fell to the ground, and he lay still. Kelly saw that her bullet had gone right between his eyes.

It seemed wrong to leave him there on the plains for the crows and wolves, and Kelly lingered for a moment. She looked around, and the vastness of the plains seemed to swell up around her. The sky seemed endless, and she wondered where the next town was and if it was possible to walk that far.

Then she draped her saddle bags and bridle over her shoulder and hefted her saddle. She walked to where Graham was waiting, still seated on his horse.

"His leg was broken," she said.

Graham dismounted. Without a word, he took Kelly's saddle and placed it on top of his own on his horse's back. He did the same with her saddle bags and bridle.

They began to walk. Graham estimated it would take them three or four days to reach some kind of civilization—depending on how Kelly held up. Most cowboys didn't take to walking very well.

Walking beside him, Kelly was too upset to even care how far they had to walk. For years, Phoenix had been her best friend and only companion. It seemed impossible that one minute he had been alive and full of spirit, and the next, he had been laying on the prairie mortally wounded. It didn't seem possible that he was dead. Thinking of it made her feel empty and sick, so did remembering that she had shot him.

Kelly sniffled; she was on the edge of crying, and she was not particularly concerned with trying to hide the fact. She was too upset to be embarrassed.

Graham snuck a look at her out of the corner of his eye and saw that she was crying some. He could not imagine why anyone would cry about a horse, especially someone as sensible as Kelly, but there she was, crying.

Silently, he took a handkerchief from his pocket and offered it to her. Kelly accepted it and wiped at her eyes but knew that she wasn't done crying yet and wouldn't be for a while.

Kelly was thinking about how, back at the farm, Phoenix used to jump out of his paddock and follow her around like a pet dog. They'd ridden like banshees over the hills of New York and had watched silent sunrises on frosty mornings. At the end of long, hard days when she'd been so tired that her legs and arms had ached, Phoenix had greeted her with a pleased whinny and had nosed her pockets for carrots. Many nights while waiting for a foaling to begin, she had curled up in his stall and napped.

"I guess I talked to that horse more than I did to anyone else except my grandfather," she said tearfully. The thought was so strong in her mind she couldn't help but say it.

She was too busy grieving to notice, but Graham was looking

at her with something like understanding in his eyes. Though he had not considered the matter before, he suddenly realized that, even when surrounded by people, it was possible to be alone—as alone as someone who roamed the wild places and went months without seeing another human face.

The thought hit him hard, and without thinking what he was doing, he put his arm around her shoulders. Kelly, though greatly surprised, did not shrug his arm away. It was comforting, somehow, and she knew how hard comfort was to come by in the world.

Chapter 8

Three and a half days of walking put them in a little cattle town northeast of Topeka. After putting Graham's horse up at a ramshackle livery stable and getting rooms at the better of the town's two hotels, Kelly wanted to buy another horse. They had done plenty enough walking as far as she was concerned.

There were no horses for sale at the stable where they had boarded Graham's horse, but an elderly stable hand suggested she go over three blocks and try her luck at the local stock trader. Kelly decided to go immediately, and Graham offered to go with her.

"You don't have to" she said. "I've bought plenty of horses in my time."

"Oh, it'll be interesting to see how an equestrian goes about horse trading," Graham replied. "Maybe I can pick up some pointers."

Kelly couldn't tell from his face whether or not he was joking but knew it wasn't likely that he was serious. She knew it amused him to devil her over such things, though for the life of her she couldn't imagine why.

"You have a perverse sense of humor, Mr. McNair," she said, smiling a little.

The stock yard was hot and dusty, and it smelled like manure. Kelly wrinkled her nose in disgust. There wasn't any reason for such a smell, not even in high summer. All you had to do was have your manure hauled away every day or so.

Some men were carrying water buckets from a well outside the barn to the stalls inside. Kelly saw no one who looked like they were in charge, so she and Graham circled the barn until they came upon a small office with "B.T. Boone & Sons Stock Dealers & Livery," written on it. Graham opened the door for her, and Kelly stepped inside.

A man wearing sleeve garters was sitting at a desk, reading some papers. He looked up when the door opened, stared at Kelly, then rose to his feet to greet them.

"Good afternoon . . . folks," he said. "I'm B.T. Boone, what can I do for you today?"

This last was directed at Graham. Kelly broke in before he could answer.

"I need a riding horse," she said.

Boone looked at her briefly, then looked back at Graham.

"What did you have in mind, sir?" He asked.

"I'm doing the buying here," Kelly said. "You can either speak to me, or we can go elsewhere."

Boone hesitated, then looked her in the eye for the first time. Kelly smiled politely and met his gaze squarely. His face reddened a little, and he dropped his eyes, but when he spoke, his voice was polite.

"Of course, my apologies, Miss. What did you have in mind?"

"A gelding with good wind and sound limbs."

"Might I suggest that a mare would be more suitable?"

"Rubbish," Kelly said. "Mares are temperamental. I want a gelding."

"Very well then," Boone said, slipping his suit jacket on. "I'll show you what we have at the moment."

He led them to a round paddock with ten horses of varying sizes and colors milling about in it. Boone was extolling the virtues of each animal and of his establishment in general, but although Kelly nodded politely at times, she was not listening to him. Graham trailed along behind them, watching carefully but staying out of the way.

"Now that gray over there is a good animal," Boone was saying. "I've ridden him myself, and you couldn't ask for a sweeter-tempered animal."

Kelly turned a critical eye on the gray. His tail was too high set, and she'd never yet seen a horse with a high-set tail that could jump worth a damn. Of course, she wouldn't be doing much jumping, but it never hurt to have the option. His knees also looked lumpy, as though they'd been injured and were still puffy from it.

"How about that chestnut over there?" She asked.

"Good animal," Boone said, secretly annoyed that she had honed in on the best horse in the pen. He had hoped to sell her a lesser animal for a higher price. "But a trifle spirited, perhaps."

"Does he bite or kick?"

"Not as a vice," he said. "But that one with the four white

legs now, that's a fancier looking horse but just as sweet as the gray."

"I'd like to see that chestnut up close," Kelly said.

"Of course," he said. He turned toward the barn and yelled, "Jack! Come and catch this horse!"

"Don't bother him," Kelly said, climbing the fence with her bridle over her shoulder. "I can do it."

Before he could protest, Kelly had jumped down off the fence and into the corral.

"Want your saddle?" Graham asked her.

"No, thank you," she said.

The other horses moved out of her way as she walked toward the chestnut, and as she got closer, the chestnut started to walk away too. Kelly followed him patiently, walking slowly, until he stopped, and she was able to touch him. After stroking his neck for a few moments, Kelly put the reins over his neck and slipped the bridle on him. He accepted the bit with a minimum of fuss. She patted him again and tied him to the fence.

From looking at his teeth, she guessed he was about six years old. She felt his legs over, and then picked up each foot in turn, examining his hooves for signs of disease or cracking. All four were sound. His coat, although dusty, was healthy, and he had no saddle galls. He seemed a little thin, but well muscled. The right feeding should set him straight.

Now that she was finished looking him over, Kelly untied him and, taking hold of his mane, swung on to his back. He tensed and stood stock still, but he did not buck or shy. Kelly guessed he hadn't been ridden in a while, though he seemed to have been well broken.

After a second's urging, she got him to walking. There was a larger, empty paddock a little off to the right.

"Mr. Boone," she called. "I'd like to ride him around that paddock over there. Can you open the gate for me?"

He opened the gate to the paddock in which she was riding. She walked the horse out of the holding paddock and over to the empty one. Once there, instead of waiting for Boone to catch up with her, she leaned over and down, holding a handful of mane with one hand and opening the gate with the other.

Boone watched her. The gate latch was quite a reach for her, but she hung off the horse's side, one hand holding his neck and one leg stretched over his back, until she could undo it. Then she pulled herself effortlessly back up onto the horse's withers. She might look and talk like green meat from back east, and maybe she was, but she sure could ride. He looked sideways at Graham, who had not yet said a word to him.

"If you don't mind my saying so, sir," Boone said to him. "A lick or two would cure her willful ways."

He blanched as Graham turned a cold eye on him.

"If anyone's going to get beat, it's you."

Offended, Mr. Boone sat down on a hay bale and watched his customer ride.

Now that she had more room, Kelly put the horse through his paces. He was not very responsive to the reins but was very sensitive to the shifting of her weight. She found she could direct him better by letting go of the reins altogether and shifting her weight in the direction she wanted him to go. His paces were smooth, and he was sound. He also liked to go; Kelly had a feeling he was speedy when inspired.

After a half-hour ride, she decided to buy him. Mr. Boone was sitting on hay bale looking bored and disgruntled. Graham was leaning up against the barn wall, smiling and watching her ride. Kelly rode up to the fence, leaned over and undid the gate, then rode over to them.

"Well, he needs a bit of work," she said. "But I might risk it. How much are you asking?"

"That's one of our finest horses, Miss. One hundred and twenty-five dollars."

Kelly laughed. Graham looked up, startled. It was a soft, playful little laugh like he'd never heard her make before.

"You are joking, of course," she said. "I think seventy-five dollars would be a little more appropriate."

"Miss, I can assure you I paid one hundred dollars for that horse not a week ago, and since that time, he has received the best of care. I must make some money on the transaction."

"I think eighty-five dollars would probably allow you a reasonable profit," Kelly replied, sliding down off the gelding's back.

"If eighty-five is your price, Miss," Boone said, "Perhaps I could interest you in the gray we spoke of earlier."

"I would not pay eighty-five dollars for a horse with broken-down knees," Kelly said, "Ninety for the chestnut."

"Ninety would get you the chestnut with white stockings," Boone replied, "I can have the animal saddled for you, if you like."

"That chestnut is a mare," Kelly said, "I distinctly said that I want a gelding."

Boone scratched his ear, annoyed. This girl had no business even knowing what a gelding was, much less how to tell one from a mare.

"If it's this horse you're set on," he said, indicating the chestnut Kelly had just ridden, "I can assure you I paid top dollar for him and . . ." his voice trailed off. Kelly was looking at him with a knowing expression on her face. He flushed, suddenly certain that she knew he was lying and, in another minute, wouldn't hesitate to tell him so.

"Perhaps I could go as low as one hundred dollars," he said.

"Ninety-five and I'll board him inside for three days," Kelly said, "In your finest box stall at full price."

Boone considered it. He'd bought the horse for seventy dollars. Any price over seventy-five dollars was pure profit; he'd not fed the horse anything but hay, and hay was cheap. He could jack up the price of the board to soothe his ego.

"Done," he said, taking off his hat with a flourish. "And may I compliment you on your fine selection."

"Thank you, Mr. Boone," Kelly said, her face expressionless although she was thinking that Boone would probably stiff her on the cost of the board. Oh well she thought, let him have his little victory. "Have one of your men set him up in a single stall, and we can go arrange the bill of sale."

Twenty minutes later, Kelly and Graham left the stable. Kelly was happy with her horse and not even bothered by the fuss Boone had created over letting her sign the papers. She'd dealt with much worse in her time.

Graham had not said a word during the entire transaction, but now, he walked along beside her looking very amused.

"Well, did you enjoy your afternoon's entertainment?" She asked him as they started back to the hotel.

"Indeed. I can't abide a man who wears sleeve garters."

"Neither can I. Especially one who tries to take advantage of a woman. I wouldn't pay one hundred and twenty-five dollars for any horse I've seen since leaving home. "

"I thought ninety-five was a little low, myself," Graham said,

"It was. I would have gone as high as a hundred and ten," Kelly said. "But I'll bet Mr. Boone didn't pay more than seventy-five dollars for him."

"How so?"

"There's no sense in it. You can't count on finding someone willing to pay so much for a horse, especially not in a little place like this."

No, there wasn't much difference in how an equestrian and a cowboy went about horse trading, Graham thought, though maybe equestrians used better grammar.

From looking at the sun, Graham guessed that it was about four o'clock. He was minded to play some cards that night; his rode stake was not holding out as well as it usually did.

"I might as well move my horse over to Boone's," he said, thinking it would make things less awkward when the time came to leave.

"Oh, I'll do it for you," Kelly offered. "I imagine you're in a hurry to get to work."

"Not really, but I would appreciate it," Graham said. He didn't particularly want to mess around with his horse after having had his suit brushed.

"It's no trouble. I want to go back anyway and get some of the dirt off that animal."

Graham considered asking her to wait until morning, but it

might start an argument, and what was he worried about anyway?

"Don't be too late," he cautioned her. "This isn't a wholesome place after dark."

Kelly decided he meant nothing but to help her, so she accepted this advice with a smile and wished him good luck at his game. She went down Harley Street, and he continued down Main.

Unbeknownst to them, two men stood across the street, watching them attentively. As Kelly went to the barn and Graham to the saloon, the taller of the two, a sometime thief and part-time cowboy named Bob Puller, spat reflectively.

"Sumbitch shot my brother in Platte River," he said.

His partner, a one-eyed man named Abe Nibos, nodded.

"Don't I know it. Lost my eye in thet fight."

"I reckon we can settle his account tonight," Bob said.

Abe remembered the scrap in Platte River well, though it seemed Bob had forgotten the details or else he wouldn't speak so confidently. An argument over a poker game had exploded when Bob's brother had drawn on Graham. Graham had put a bullet in his forehead and turned on Abe, who had drawn an instant after Bob. Abe had lost his eye, but at the time it had seemed like he'd gotten off easy, since even with one eye, it was easy to see his friend's brains splashed on the wall.

"I reckon there's a better way than pulling down on him in a saloon," Abe said.

"'Course there is," Bob replied. "We'll ambush 'im on the way out of town."

Abe considered it, but knew that he wanted a little better revenge than sending Graham McNair down to hell in an instant. Abe felt he deserved a more lingering kind of end.

"Listen," he said to Bob. "You saw that girl what was with him?"

"Yeah, so?"

"I'll shoot her, then we'll tell him about it," Abe paused. "That'll make him so mad he won't be able to shoot straight."

Bob thought that over.

"Well, he mightn't care. She's likely just some whore he picked up with."

"It'll still touch his pride," Abe argued.

"That's so."

"'Sides, it'd be like an eye for an eye," Abe said.

"I didn't know such things were mentioned in the Bible," Bob replied.

"They ain't, exactly."

"Well, I oughter do it then, since it was my brother that got kilt," Bob said.

"I don't like that," Abe said. "Twas my idea."

"You'll know how ter rub his nose in it better," returned

Bob.

"I reckon." Abe considered it. It would be more to his credit if he killed Graham; probably no one had ever even heard of the girl before.

"All right," Abe said. "Now listen . . ."

Unaware of their plotting, Graham played cards but bowed out early because his luck had run cold. The saloon had a no-guns policy, and Graham had been obliged to check his gun belt at the door before entering. Graham disapproved of such policies and was dismayed to see that they were becoming so popular.

Night had fallen, and he was sitting at the bar when Abe walked in, stopping on the threshold to eyeball the room. He soon spotted Graham.

Graham set his whiskey glass down, and his hand fell instinctively to his hip when Abe walked straight over to him. His hand came up empty though, and he picked his whiskey glass back up.

"'Evenin' Mister," Abe said, standing beside him.

Graham nodded but did not reply.

"How's the whiskey here?" Abe asked, looking sideways at him.

"Good enough."

"Let me buy you another," Abe said, signaling to the bartender.

The bartender poured two shots of whiskey for them, then walked away. Abe picked his up and sipped it. Graham watched him. Abe appeared to be unarmed, and Graham wondered what he was up to.

"You ought to drink up," Abe said. "It's the last drink you'll ever have. Sides you might need a bracer."

"Hardly. Get crosswind of me again and that one eye of yours'll be staring at hell."

"Not likely," Abe said, finishing his drink. "Course, if so I'll have some company. Some yellow-haired company, too, I reckon."

Abe saw Graham's face shift as understanding came to him. The look that replaced Graham's poker face gave Abe a flash of the jimmjamms, but it was gone so quickly that Abe soon forgot it.

For Graham understood the situation better even than Abe. He knew it was likely that Abe was still traveling with that no-account hard case Bob Puller. He knew that Kelly was alone at the livery stable, and that night watchmen could be bribed. He knew that, while he stood there chinning with Abe, anything could be happening.

But he also knew the next few minutes were crucial.

As Abe tried to think of something else biting to say, Graham simply turned and walked to the saloon door. Startled, Abe froze in confusion; Graham was supposed to ask him what he meant and try to fight him. Abe didn't have a gun, but he carried a nine-inch bowie knife under his jacket.

Abe reached for his knife and started after Graham, who turned abruptly and, snatching up a chair, smashed him over the head with it so hard he fell to the ground. Graham started forward to hit him again but stopped short. Abe was out for the count, and it would be a waste of time to try and make the damage permanent. He collected his gun belt and left the saloon.

Chapter 9

Meanwhile, Kelly had finished her work. She left the stall, bolting the door, then picked up the brushes. The silence in the stable struck her as somewhat odd. She could not imagine why there was no night watchman. Maybe he had snuck out for a drink or something.

Kelly put the brushes back in the saddle room. She paused for a moment, listening to the horses much their hay. There was a creaking noise from the front of the stable. It had a stealthy sound to it that she didn't like. The lamp flickered unpredictably, and she couldn't see anything in the shadows beyond its uncertain light.

Then she heard it again. Her hand fell to the butt of her revolver. She told herself that she was being silly, that it was probably the watchman, and that she should call out and ask who it was. But something stronger than reason held her back. She stepped away from the lamp until she, too, was in the shadows, and then, she drew her revolver.

One of the horses nickered and moved suddenly in its stall. All of a sudden the silence seemed to crawl down her back, making her shiver. The horses had stopped eating. Her skin broke out in gooseflesh. There was someone out there, and whoever it was, was between her and the door.

She heard the click of a gun hammer being drawn back, and the sound seemed to paralyze her—until she saw the gleam of metal from the darkness to her right.

She threw herself behind a stack of hay bales near the tack room just as the roar of a gunshot filled the room. She landed hard and scrambled to her hands and knees. Another shot sounded; it struck the hay bales above her head. She ducked instinctively as bits of hay rained down on her.

She looked down and saw that she still held her revolver. She tried to listen for clues as to where her assailant stood, but she could hear nothing except the pounding of her heart and the racing of her blood.

Finally, she heard footsteps. From their hesitant sound, Kelly guessed that whoever it was didn't know whether or not she'd been hit. The footsteps stopped, and Kelly heard the click of a revolver being cocked. She shifted around so that her head and feet positions were reversed. Then she moaned softly as though she were in pain.

Another creaking step sounded. Kelly tensed herself. She thought he must be about eight paces away, just in front of the aisle of stalls. Everything seemed magnified, the dust on the floor in front of her nose, the roughness of the hay against her side, the frightened noises the horses were making. Kelly heard the floor boards creak as he shifted his weight, ready to take another step.

Kelly threw herself up from the safety of the bales and fired three times. She had a clear glimpse of the man's startled face as he swung around and brought his gun up. Then she was thrown back against the barn wall so hard she saw stars. There was a curious numbness in her right shoulder, and she slumped against the wall, gasping. There was a roaring in her ears, and she could not hear anything, not even the sound of the frightened horses rearing and snorting in their stalls.

Her head cleared a little, and she pulled herself to her feet. Her only thought was to make sure that whoever had been shooting at her was dead. She could see blood on her shirt and knew she had been shot, but she felt no pain, only numbness. She had to make sure she was no longer in danger before the numbness gave way to pain.

Graham was hurrying to the livery stable when he heard the first shot. His heart skipped a beat, and he ran faster, but not more than twenty seconds later, he heard three more shots, the last of which was so loud that he knew it must have been two shots fired at almost the same time.

He drew his revolver and entered the stable cautiously. The horses were riled, but he could hear no human sound. He saw the lamp flickering in the carriage bay and crept silently toward it.

Gun smoke hung in the air, and the first thing he saw was the body of a man lying face down in a large pool of blood, a revolver clutched in his hand. He seemed to have been shot several times in the chest. Then, from the shadows on his right, a voice asked:

"Is he dead?"

Graham spun around and saw Kelly half-standing, half-leaning against a stack of hay bales. Her right side was drenched in blood, and her face was white as a sheet, but she still held her revolver.

Holstering his gun, Graham rushed over to her. He put an arm around her waist and eased her to the floor. When he tried to take the gun from her hand, she would not let go of it.

"Let me have the gun, Kelly," he said.

"Is he dead?" She asked again.

"I've never seen anyone deader," he replied. "Let go of the gun."

She did. After unloading it and sticking it in his belt, Graham tore her shirt open and saw that the bullet had gone just below her collar bone and was still in the wound. Although she was bleeding badly and quickly losing consciousness, he was relieved to see that there was no blood coming from her nose or mouth.

Kelly was unconscious now, but when he picked her up, she moaned in pain. People were gathering at the stable entrance, but no one saw him as he carried her out through the office and disappeared down an alley. There was a doctor about three blocks away; a doctor who could be trusted to keep his mouth shut.

Chapter 10

Back at the saloon, Abe had picked himself up off the floor, gingerly feeling his jaw to see if it were broken. He heard the gunshots coming from down the street, but he had no great hope that Bob had succeeded in killing Graham and the girl both. It was best to clear out of town in a hurry, before Graham came looking for him.

Five blocks away, Dr. Arnold Cooke was reading in his front room when he heard someone banging on his back door. Having heard several gunshots a few minutes ago, he had expected someone to come knocking sooner or later. The fact that it was sooner must mean that someone was alive but hurt pretty bad.

He opened the door, and Graham rushed in without waiting for an invitation. Dr. Cooke asked no questions but lead him to the side room he used for his office.

While he hastily lit a lamp, Graham laid Kelly on the examination table. She was very pale and bleeding badly. Dr. Cooke brought the lamp over beside the table and examined her shoulder. Though surprised to find that his patient was a young woman and not a boy as he had first thought, there was no time to ask questions about how such a thing had come to be.

"We need to get the bullet out and get her stitched up. Should I wake my wife, or can you help me?" He asked Graham.

"I'll help. What do you need?"

"Hold her up so I can try to get some laudanum down her."

Graham propped her back up and tilted her head back. The doctor put a bottle in her mouth and let some of the drug flow into her mouth. Kelly choked, coughed, then swallowed. Graham laid her back down and wiped her mouth and neck with his sleeve.

"Hold her down while I probe for the bullet," Dr. Cooke said, washing his hands. "I can't give her enough laudanum because she's out, and it is going to hurt."

Graham nodded. Dr. Cooke selected a probe, disinfected it, and bent over Kelly's shoulder. Graham took hold of her upper arms.

Kelly had been still since he'd first picked her up to carry her out of the barn, but as the doctor's probe disappeared into her arm, her back arched and her arms twisted so violently that he almost lost his grip on them. Though still unconscious, she tried to escape the probe and the hands that kept her from doing so. Sweat stood out on her forehead, and her eyes, though unseeing, opened and tears ran from them. She screamed.

The doctor worked on, oblivious to his patient's contortions, but Graham felt his nerve quake. He had seen far worse. He had seen men have their legs amputated with no morphine, wide awake and aware of what was happening to them. He had seen men die screaming of gangrene. Now he took hold of himself angrily. This needed to be done, and his sudden, foolish squeamishness could kill her.

"It's way in there," the doctor said, straightening up. "I'm going to have to open the wound some to get to it."

Kelly had relaxed when the doctor had pulled the probe from her shoulder, but she writhed again as he used a scalpel to lengthen the wound. Graham took a fresh grip on her shoulders. She was strong, and the pain made her efforts to free herself unpredictable.

Dr. Cooke set the scalpel down and picked up some forceps. He probed the wound again. Kelly jerked so violently that she managed to free one hand and strike him in the chest.

With some difficulty, Graham recaptured her wrist and pinned it back down.

"Sorry about that," he said, not looking up from his task. "Hold her tight now, I'm going in after that bullet."

Graham held her wrists so tightly he feared they might snap under the pressure. But he knew that the less she moved, the less it would hurt.

After a tense moment, the doctor held the bullet aloft. Graham loosened his grip on her wrists a fraction. The worst was over.

"Got to clean the wound out and stitch her up now," the doctor said, dropping the bullet on the floor.

Graham continued to hold her down, although her struggles had decreased. At long last, the wound was closed and the bleeding stopped. The doctor set about washing things up. Graham looked at the clock and realized they had been at it over three hours.

"Will she be all right?" He asked, letting go of Kelly and stretching his fingers out. They were cramped up from having held her so tightly.

"Ought to be, if she doesn't get blood poisoning or an infection. She needs to stay and bed and eat up. She lost a lot of blood." He looked at Graham, remembering his earlier curiosity. There must be one hell of a story behind this. How did this girl come to be shot, and why was this hard case so worried over it? Well, no matter, if he asked, like as not he'd be told some lie, so it was better to just let it alone.

"How much do I owe you, Doctor?" Graham asked taking his wallet from his coat.

"Oh, ten dollars should cover it."

Graham gave him twenty, and the doctor handed him the laudanum bottle.

"Take this," he said. "Give her a spoonful when the pain is bad, but only for the first week. Where are you all staying? I'll stop by and see how she's doing in the morning."

"At the Grand Republic," Graham answered, pocketing the bottle and picking Kelly up. "I'd appreciate it if you'd keep this as quiet as possible."

"Certainly."

"Thank you."

Dr. Cooke opened the back door for him, and Graham carried Kelly outside. She was limp in his arms, and that was somehow worse than having her screaming.

Chapter 11

An unknown time later, Kelly felt herself lying in bed. The closer she came to wakefulness, the worse she felt. Her shoulder ached and throbbed as though it were filled with hot needles, and her throat and mouth were parched. She opened her eyes blearily and recognized her hotel room, but she had no idea how she had come to be there. The last thing she remembered was brushing her horse down. She tried to think, but she felt dizzy and sick, and her mind was numb; it was like straining to see through a dense fog.

"How do you feel?" Asked a voice that Kelly vaguely recognized as Graham's.

He was sitting in a chair by her bed. He needed a shave and his eyes were tired. She tried to speak, but her mouth and throat were too dry, and she began to cough instead.

Graham poured her a drink of water from a pitcher on the bed table. He helped her to sit up and steadied the glass while she drank. Kelly slurped gratefully, not minding the water that spilled on the bed clothes. Her shoulder hurt worse when she lay back down, but she didn't care; it had been worth it.

"How bad's the shoulder?" He asked.

"Bad," Kelly croaked. "What happened?"

"You were shot. Don't you remember?"

Kelly shook her head. She looked at Graham again and realized that the front of his shirt was stained with blood; she wondered sickly if it were hers.

"You're going to be all right, though," he went on. "The doctor got the bullet out and stitched you up."

Kelly was more awake now. She realized that her back also hurt, but for the life of her she couldn't think why. The light in the room also seemed funny; it looked liked the sun was setting, but it had been seven o'clock at night the last she could remember. She wanted to ask how long she had been out, but she couldn't think of the words.

"You bled a lot," Graham was saying. "That's why you feel weak, but don't get alarmed over it. A week or two in bed and you'll be good as new."

"What time is it?" Kelly asked froggily.

"'Bout six o'clock," he said. "You were out cold all last night and all today. The doctor had to dope you up pretty good. You fought like a bear when he tried to get the bullet out. I had a time holding you down."

It was too much for Kelly to understand. Her mind was tired, and she could not understand why he was talking so much. She fell back asleep and did not wake up again until the next morning.

Graham stayed in the room for another two hours. By then it was plain she was going to be out for a while, and he was beat. He felt her forehead and was relieved to find it cool. It meant she wasn't going to get blood poisoning and had escaped an infection. Without those complications, she should recover.

He went to his own room and stripped off his clothes. He knew that Abe must have skipped town shortly after the shooting. Graham regretted not having been able to kill him immediately, but he also knew it was only a matter of time before he ran across Abe again, and when he did . . .

For Abe had guessed correctly; attacking Kelly Knowlton was the best way to get at Graham McNair. Unfortunately for him, however, Graham was still alive and in perfect health; therefore, for all intents and purposes, Abe Nibos was a dead man.

Chapter 12

To Kelly, the following days seemed a blur—hazy with pain and laudanum. She had trouble remembering where she was or what had happened, and at times, she found herself asking for her grandfather, who was dead, or for her mother, whom she had never known. Graham stayed with her almost constantly, but at times, she had trouble remembering who he was.

As the days slipped by, the pain lessened until she was able to go long enough with laudanum to recover her mind. Her shoulder began to itch unbearably, and that was almost as bad as the pain had been.

Dr. Cooke stopped by several times, and each time, he told her and Graham how well she was healing. Kelly supposed that she should be grateful for the reassurance, but privately thought that, considering how miserable she felt, in order to have such an opinion, Dr. Cooke must have gotten his medical training by mail order catalog.

Nonetheless, barely two weeks after having been shot, Kelly was able to sit up in bed, feed herself, and read. Graham now let her be for long periods of time and tended to vanish when the doctor came.

He was gone now, and Dr. Cooke was examining her shoulder. Kelly had liked Dr. Cooke immediately because he never tried to evade her questions and never mislead her about her prognosis.

"Can you lift your arm straight up?" He asked her.

Kelly tried. She made it half way before the pain stopped her.

Dr. Cooke nodded.
"Wiggle your fingers."
Kelly did.
"Does that hurt?"
Kelly shook her head.
"I can turn pages in a book, too," she volunteered.
"Good. You can put your shirt back on."
　Kelly had become adept at dressing herself with one hand, and she managed the shirt without any help.
　Dr. Cooke watched her, not wanting to give her instructions until he had her full attention. He still could not quite figure out how this girl had come to be shot. Although he had no proof of anything, he also felt that her injury was, no doubt, tied to the dead man who had been found in the livery stable the same night she'd been shot. There were a good few questions he would have liked to ask her and Graham, but he kept silent. It was plain that Graham would not look kindly upon his inquisitiveness.
　Kelly finished buttoning her shirt.
"Well?" She asked. "How am I doing?"
"Better than I would have expected," replied Dr. Cooke. "Stay in bed for another week to ten days, then we'll see. If you must get up, keep that sling on. It's very important that you not reinjure that shoulder and start the bleeding up again."
　Kelly nodded, trying to hide her disappointment at having to spend so long in bed.
"Thank you, doctor," she said.
"It's no trouble," he replied. "I'll be back in a week but do not hesitate to call if you have some difficulty."
"Thank you, I won't."
"Good bye, then," he said.
"Good bye."
　He left the room, and Kelly slumped back against the pillows. After a short while, she picked up the local newspaper from the foot of her bed and started to read it.
　Kelly read only a few paragraphs before throwing the paper down impatiently. She'd read the entire paper before Dr. Cooke had shown up, and it hadn't been all that interesting then. Now, there was nothing else to do but sit around and think—think about how much her shoulder hurt and wonder what was going to become of her. Neither subject was pleasant to contemplate.
　She had enough money to pay the doctor and the hotel, but she doubted that Graham would want to hang around this dirty little town for another ten days. Even after that, she would have to take it easy; she would be a lot of trouble. Surely he would consider his debt to her paid and head off on his own.
　He had never indicated by word or deed that he was intending to leave, on the contrary, he had been very kind, almost worried. But Kelly couldn't think of a single reason why he shouldn't leave now that she was almost better.

And even if he didn't, she was frightened now and wanted very much to go home. Running away didn't seem exciting anymore; it seemed dangerous and stupid. Whatever had she been thinking of?

"I wasn't thinking at all," she said aloud to the empty room. "That's the whole trouble."

Of course, going home wasn't a whole lot to look forward to either. The farm had been sold. She had missed her train by over a month, but she doubted that would make anything more pleasant; it would make things worse. Her thoughts were interrupted by a knock at the door. The woman who owned the hotel usually brought her lunch at about this time, and Kelly answered the knock irritably.

"Come in."

Unexpectedly, Graham walked in with the tray. Kelly was surprised to see him; she had not expected him to turn up until the next morning.

"How are you today?" He asked, setting the tray beside her on the bed.

"Better. And yourself?"

He nodded. "What did the doctor have to say?"

Kelly surveyed the tray without much appetite.

"I'm to stay in bed another week, then we'll see," she said as unconcernedly as possible.

"That's not too bad," he said, sitting in the chair beside her bed. "You'll be interested to know that no one cares about Mr. Puller's death. There won't be any trouble over it."

"Who?" Kelly asked, startled.

"The man you shot," Graham explained.

"Oh," Kelly picked at a piece of corn bread. She didn't want to think about the shooting. She could remember everything now, except for what had happened after she'd been shot. Graham had filled her in on that, even though she'd made it a point not to ask about it.

"I expect you'll want to move on soon," she said to him, thinking that it was better to ask him and get it out into the open rather than wait until he disappeared without a word.

"As soon as you're ready."

"I meant on your own," Kelly said.

Graham looked at her curiously, wondering what craziness she was thinking about now. You had to watch her every minute, it seemed.

"San Francisco's still a ways off yet."

"You can go on if you want," Kelly said. "I'll understand."

"I don't want. I said I'd see you to California, and I will."

Obviously, this news didn't relieve her mind. Graham saw her frown deepen.

"What's wrong?" He asked. "Aside from your shoulder hurting."

"I'm not going to California," she said tiredly.

"What about your relations there?"

"I haven't got any relations there," she said. "I don't know why I ever said such a thing."

She was too worried to even care much about having been caught in such a lie. Especially since he'd probably known she was lying the moment the words had left her mouth. She fully expected him to be angry, or scornful, but instead, he smiled at her.

"I thought so," he said. "You'll never make a good liar. It doesn't come naturally to you."

"I ought to go home," Kelly said.

Graham was silent for a moment. Part of him thought it was the right thing to do. It certainly would be safer. But safety wasn't the only thing to consider. It was first in her mind because she was flat on her back with a bullet wound. And though she didn't know it, that was more his fault than hers.

"I didn't think you cared much for your home," he said. "Won't they take this out on you?"

Kelly could imagine the scandal her running away had caused; her father must have been furious. He would punish her. Kelly remembered the last evening she had spent at home, when she had watched the new stallion race around the paddock. That was the home she wanted to go back to, but she had to admit that wasn't an option any more.

While Kelly thought about home, Graham knew it was time to tell her about Abe. He could not have foreseen what had happened, and only by incredible luck could he have prevented it, but the fact remained that she had been shot because of him. It would not be honest to keep it from her.

"I ought to tell you something about the man who shot you," he said.

"What?" Kelly was hardly interested. She had more important things on her mind.

"He was a hard case from Kansas," Graham said. "I had some trouble with him and his brother and a friend of theirs two years ago. It came down to me killing his brother in a brawl."

Kelly was listening now. Graham was looking off out the window as he spoke, and his eyes were troubled.

"I understand," she said, interrupting him. "You don't need to tell me anything else."

"Don't I?"

"No. You don't," Kelly said firmly. "He's dead, and I'm alive, and I'll never again wait that long to shoot first."

That was the bones of it, Graham thought as Kelly started eating. She looked like she'd gotten her appetite back.

"Do you want some of this?" She asked him.

Graham shook his head. Something he had said had changed her mind completely, but he didn't know what it was.

If he had asked her about it, Kelly would have told him that his news about Bob Puller had changed her mind. She had not done anything wrong to invite his attack, and she had taken hold well when faced with it. She was alive, and Bob was dead and maybe that made her what Graham liked to call a "hard case."

Certainly being such gave her an edge over those who weren't, and those who weren't made up most of the world. At least, she amended, it was so in Graham's opinion, and it was his opinion that she relied on in dealing with this untamed world that she found herself in.

When she finished eating, he left the room. After dropping the tray off in the kitchen, Graham headed for the saloon. He needed a drink.

On the way, he tried to understand why he hadn't immediately offered to buy her a train ticket to home. It was the sensible thing to do, but it had never occurred to him. He told himself that it was her choice and that he had little say in what she did, but he knew that wasn't entirely true.

Standing at the bar a few minutes later, Graham stared at his whiskey and realized that his thoughts were tinged with guilt because he knew he couldn't stand the thought of not seeing her ever again.

Chapter 13

From that point on, Kelly recovered quickly. So quickly, in fact, that it surprised both Graham and Dr. Cooke, who pronounced her fit to ride at the beginning of August with a caution about sparing her arm as much as possible.

"It's healing well," he had said, "But be careful about lifting heavy objects. If you ride and the arm gets tired of dangling or holding the reins up, wear a sling. And don't let your horse jerk it around."

Kelly accepted his warning graciously and thanked him for all his help. When Dr. Cooke left the room, she and Graham made plans to leave the next day. Because she had been confined to bed for so long, Kelly wanted to buy a few things on the way out of town, and so they agreed to leave around midmorning.

Now Graham was down the street at the gunsmith's and Kelly was just leaving the dry goods store, pausing briefly on the threshold to let her eyes adjust to the bright outside light. It was nearly eleven o'clock, but the streets were strangely empty. There had been a saloon brawl the previous evening, and Kelly guessed that people were still unsettled from the ruckus.

That seemed likely, after all, she felt a little unsettled herself at the moment, she realized as she stowed her things in her saddle bags, taking special care with the two books she had purchased. Books were bound to become scarce commodities the further west they rode.

Out of the corner of her eye, she could see two men coming down the sidewalk. They were not looking at her, and they were talking about the weather as though they were farmers.

But they weren't farmers. They both wore gun belts—fancy ones too. Also, they walked with an alertness that reminded her more of Graham than it did of any farmer she'd ever seen.

She stepped back away from her horse. As she did so, her attention snapped up the street, where she could hear some kind of commotion going on. A large, blowsy-looking woman leaned from a second-story window, shrieking at a man who bolted from the building's front door and ran down the street. Kelly relaxed, and at that moment, she was knocked to the ground by one of the two men who had been walking by her. He had taken advantage of the diversion to leap at her, and Kelly found herself flat on her back with her arms pinned to the ground.

Surprised though she was, Kelly reacted swiftly. She brought her knee up between his parted legs as hard as she could. He howled and released her arms. She shoved him off of her and rolled away from him, only to look up and find herself staring down the muzzle of the Colt .45 the other man held two feet from her face.

"Get up," he said.

Kelly obeyed.

"I'm John Caldwell. I'm with Pinkerton's detective agency. Your father hired us to bring you home."

"I don't want to go home," Kelly said.

"That don't count for much," he replied, stepping forward and relieving her of her revolver. "You all right Ben?" He asked his companion, who was now sitting up.

"Almost," Ben replied. Kelly's knee had been partly blocked by one of his thighs, otherwise he would still be rolling on the ground.

"Now, if you'll come quietly, I won't have to tie your hands," Detective Caldwell said to her.

Kelly considered her options. Knowing they were Pinkertons changed the situation considerably. There was no chance they would shoot her, although they probably wouldn't mind roughing her up a little if she resisted them. She also thought briefly that it was the perfect opportunity to give up and go home; no one could blame her for being dragged off by two armed men.

Then she thought of having to face her father after having been brought home like a wayward child.

"Can I get my saddle bags?" She asked meekly. "All my things are in them."

John motioned to Ben, who was now standing again. Ben rifled through both bags, looking for weapons. He found nothing except some ammunition, which he pocketed, and some clothes and food, which seemed harmless enough. He nodded at John, who looked narrowly at Kelly.

"All right, but I'll truss you up like a Christmas turkey if you do anything foolish."

Kelly stepped over to her horse and untied her saddle bags.

She slid them from behind the saddle. Ben pulled her left arm roughly, ready to lead her away. Kelly swung around and hit him in the face with the saddle bags. As soon as she felt his hand leave her arm, she sprinted down the street.

John had been expecting her to try something of the sort, though he had not been prepared for the strength and determination with which she had attacked his partner, who had fallen to his knees, momentarily blinded. Unmindful of his injured partner, John ran after Kelly.

Kelly felt him following her and knew she couldn't outrun him. Just as the thought crossed her mind, he grabbed her right arm and yanked her backward with all his strength.

Pain tore through her recently healed shoulder. Kelly screamed and nearly blacked out. Tears rose in her eyes. He was now twisting her right arm up behind her back and pulling her backward. All thoughts of resistance had left Kelly's mind. The only things that mattered were the pain in her shoulder and her need to end it. She screamed again. Her assailant was unmoved by her screams. He intended to hurt her, and because he was ignorant of her recent wound, he thought she was exaggerating the pain so he would loosen his grip.

Then his world exploded as he felt a pistol butt smash the back of his head. He stumbled and released Kelly, vaguely realizing that he was being attacked. He reached for his revolver.

Graham had heard the commotion from inside the gunsmith's. He left the shop just in time to hear Kelly scream as her arm was being twisted. The sound triggered a cold blooded anger in him that he hadn't felt since leaving the Indian fighting business. It was a hard, thinking kind of anger.

He strode up behind the Pinkerton and smashed the back of his head with the butt of his revolver. After the Pinkerton let go of Kelly, Graham holstered his gun and grabbed the man under the arm pits, steadying him with one hand and punching him in the solar plexus with the other. The Pinkerton man heaved and slipped helplessly to the ground. Graham kicked in the ribs so hard he flipped over, rolling several feet backward. His revolver had fallen from his grip, and now, he reached frantically for it. Just as his fingers brushed it, Graham stomped down on his hand. There were sickening snapping sounds, and the Pinkerton man screamed. Graham kicked the gun away and pulled him to his feet.

Kelly had been on the verge of blacking out when suddenly, miraculously, her arm was released. She fell to her knees, panting. Pain still surged though her arm, and she felt sick. She wiped the tears from her eyes and saw Graham stomp on John's hand. She watched numbly as he methodically set about beating the Pinkerton man senseless. There was a cold deliberateness about him that made her skin break out into gooseflesh. She looked away and saw the Pinkerton man's gun lying within her reach. She picked it up.

Meanwhile, Ben had recovered a little, although his eyes were still watering badly. Blearily, he saw his partner being tossed around like a rag doll, and he drew his revolver as Graham threw the now-unconscious and badly bleeding John into a dry watering trough.

Graham spun around as he heard the click of a revolver hammer; Kelly heard it too. She raised her revolver, meaning to shoot Ben, when Graham dove for her, knocking the gun from her hand and grabbing her arms, rolling them both out of Ben's sights.

Ben fired twice, both shots striking the wall of the building in front of which Graham had been standing. Still belly-down in the dirt, Graham drew his own revolver and fired once. Ben yelled and dropped his revolver; he had been shot through the wrist.

Graham leapt to his feet and ran over to Ben, who was clutching his bleeding wrist. Graham picked up the discarded revolver and threw it far down the street, then he hurried back to Kelly, who was kneeling in the street, looking sick and disoriented. He squatted beside her.

"Can you ride?" He asked. Her face was dusty and tear-streaked, but she did not seem to be bleeding anywhere.

"Do I have to?" She replied.

"Yes."

She nodded and tried to stand, Graham helped her. Her shoulder still throbbed, but she no longer felt faint. She mounted her horse without assistance, but her right arm hung useless by her side, and she held the reins with her left hand.

"Get out of town as fast as you can and ride like hell straight south," Graham whispered to her as she mounted. "I'll catch up with you."

Kelly nodded and spurred her horse into a run, she cut through the west side of town, then rode south. She had no idea what Graham had been thinking about when he had told her what to do and less idea how he would catch up to her. It didn't matter. She almost hoped he didn't. She kept hearing that Pinkerton man's fingers snap, and the sound made her almost as sick as the pain in her arm.

Kelly rode south the rest of the day. At first she rode at a pretty good pace, but then, realizing that no one was following her and worried because Graham had not yet reappeared, she slowed down. The day wore on, and the sun sank lower and lower in the sky. Finally she stopped and made camp in a sheltered spot near the base of a butte.

Unsaddling her horse was awkward because her right arm was still so painful she was afraid to use it much. She tended to her horse as best she could and tethered him close to camp. After some thought, she decided to risk a small fire.

It was full dark before she sat down on her blanket and ate a cold supper. After, she undid her shirt halfway and examined her shoulder. The wound had not reopened, but the skin was badly bruised. Kelly thought she might be bleeding some inside, but since she didn't feel dizzy or weak, it couldn't be too serious.

She stayed awake for some time, expecting Graham to reappear at any moment. But as the night wore on and he did not turn up, she began to doze. She woke every now and then, startled by some noise. Toward dawn, she slept a little more soundly, and she woke just as the sun was beginning to rise.

Chapter 14

As Kelly dozed near her campfire, Graham rode into a small town east of where Kelly had been shot. Through having kept his ears open while Kelly had been confined to bed, he felt certain that Abe was either in this town or recently departed from it. Abe had taught him a valuable lesson about being too merciful, and Graham was minded to thank him for it before riding south to find Kelly.

He left his horse tied near a noisy saloon and began his search. There were four places Abe was likely to be: Johnson's Prairie Oasis, a saloon at the north end of town; The Barking Dog Saloon or the Grace Dancehall, which were across the street from each other; or Nell Dove's House of Heavenly Delight, a brothel down the street from the dance hall.

Graham decided to check the saloons and dance hall first. Any brothel with such a high-flown name was likely to be too expensive for Abe, unless he'd had a streak of luck at the poker table, which was unlikely. Besides, it was bad manners to shoot up a brothel. Graham intended to finish his quarrel with Abe before rejoining Kelly. He didn't plan for either of them to get ambushed again.

Abe was playing cards in the Barking Dog Saloon and did not see Graham walk in. Graham took a place at the bar and ordered himself a whiskey. He watched the game for a few moments, confident that Abe would not see him amid the noisy crowd. Abe was packing a Colt, but that made little difference in Graham's mind, because he knew Abe to be a slow draw and a terrible shot.

Graham called the bartender over and told him to send a whiskey over to Abe. One of the waiters delivered it. Abe looked up, startled. He asked the waiter who had sent him the drink, and the waiter pointed to Graham, who, when he saw Abe's eye lock onto him, raised his glass in a toast and took a sip from it.

Abe went pale. Graham pulled his jacket back away from his revolver; he hoped that Abe would be scared enough to throw down on him right there, and for a moment it seemed that Abe would cooperate with that plan. Then he seemed to get a hold of himself somewhat, and he went back to his game.

Abe continued to play poker. Graham stared at him the entire time, and it made Abe even more nervous. His nerve broke after the second hand, and he left the saloon hurriedly, and Graham did not follow him right away. Abe was too stupid to give him the slip now that he was so close. He finished his whiskey and paid the barkeep, then he left the saloon through the back door, in case Abe might be planning on ambushing him. He strolled down the street just as Abe vanished into Johnson's Prairie Oasis.

Because there were no windows or doors in the back of the building, Graham positioned himself in the alley to the left of the building, figuring that when Abe came out, he would go to get his horse, and in order to do so, he would have to walk past the alley.

Then he settled down to wait.

Less than an hour later, the door banged open. Graham crept along the side of the building until he was in the shadows where the alley met the street. Abe hurried by carrying his traps.

"Hello, Abe," he said.

Abe stopped short and peered into the shadows, trying to make out who was addressing him. Graham let him peer for a moment, then stepped into the light. Abe dropped the bundle and tried to draw his revolver.

But Graham's right hand moved like lightning, and the movement ended in the roar of a gunshot. Abe was thrown backward, and his half-drawn revolver flew from his hand; his body came to rest against the sidewalk. Graham's bullet had taken him in the left side of his chest.

In the gloom, it was hard for Graham to see where his bullet had gone or if the man was still alive. Abe's gun was out of reach, but Graham approached the body carefully anyway. Abe did not move, and now that he was closer, Graham thought the man's eyes seemed lifeless. But since it never hurt to be sure, Graham held his own gun ready and ground the heel of his boot into the bullet hole. Abe did not respond, and Graham was now sure he was dead. He holstered his revolver and walked away.

No one had, as yet, shown any interest in the shot he had fired, and Graham doubted anyone ever would, although sooner or later everyone would assume he had done it, even if there was no proof. Graham was unconcerned. A mean, small-time drifter like Abe Nibos wasn't worth avenging as far as the law was concerned. And if by chance the law did take an interest, well good luck to them. They would need it.

Chapter 15

Kelly broke camp slowly, wondering what she should do. Graham had said ride south, but she didn't want to go south; she wanted to go west. True, he may have planned to meet her along the way, but she had no way of knowing if he had even made it out of town. Anything could have happened. It worried her that he had not found her yet.

At length Kelly decided to go west. If he had planned on giving her such a head start, then he must have planned to track her, so it didn't matter where she went, so long as he had a starting point when leaving town.

Her decision made, Kelly mounted up and, suddenly, was distracted from her worry by her first real view of the plains and the endless sky floating over head. She had never imagined being able to see so much of the world all at once, and the sight was overwhelming.

All that day and the next, Kelly rode west. There was no sign of Graham, and near dusk on the second day, she decided that he wasn't going to turn up. The plains rolled on endlessly; it seemed she was the only person in the world. She felt very small when she looked up at the empty sky.

With such open country, she felt that she would be able to see any town or person or approaching danger within about a hundred miles, which was plenty enough time to get ready for anything.

On the third morning, Kelly rose before sunrise but did not break camp until midday. She wondered if she shouldn't ride back and see what had become of Graham. If he had met with some trouble back in town, perhaps she could help him in some way. She dawdled around her campsite worrying about it, then decided she had to know what had happened. She kicked out her fire and mounted her horse turning him eastward and riding hard.

Toward dusk she scanned the horizon and saw another rider riding toward her from the northeast. She reined in and waited. It had to be him, she thought, straining to see for sure, but she kept her rifle ready in case it wasn't.

Her caution proved unnecessary. In another twenty minutes, the rider was close enough for her to see it was Graham. She booted her rifle and waved to him. He waved back.

"Hey there," he said reining in. "You're headed in the wrong direction."

"I was going back to see what had become of you," Kelly said.

Even in the fading light, he could see her face all upset. He had expected her to be worried a bit over traveling alone, but not to be worried over him.

"I just took the long way around town," he said. "How's your arm?"

"It's still sore," Kelly replied. "But the bruise has gone down some. That first day it was every color of the rainbow."

"I'll bet."

They rode until full dark, then made camp on the prairie. Kelly fussed with the horses a little longer than usual. Her saddle didn't fit her new horse very well, and he was beginning to develop saddle galls. Since she had no other saddle, Kelly decided to try padding it with her extra jeans. She would have preferred to ride without the saddle, but without it she had no way to carry her gear.

Sitting in front of the cheery fire, listening to the horses munch grass and watching Graham fiddle with his deck of cards felt so familiar that Kelly spoke without realizing that Graham had been gone for three days and would not know what she was talking about.

"Arnie's getting saddle sores," she said. "My saddle's pinching him."

"Arnie?" Graham asked.

"My horse."

"However did you land on that name?"

"I named him for Dr. Cooke," Kelly explained. "Because they are both smart and even-tempered."

Graham supposed it was Kelly's way of honoring the doctor who had saved her life, and if so, it confirmed his opinion that cowboys acted oddly about their horses and brought to mind something else they needed to speak about.

"Well, if you're not going to San Francisco, where do you want to go?" He asked.

"I don't know." Kelly thought for a moment. "How do you decide where to go?"

"That depends on a lot of things," he said. "I like where I am and what I want. I'll take you anywhere you want to go."

Kelly thought some more.

"I want to see the mountains," she said finally. "Can we go there?"

"Sounds like you want to see the Colorado territory," Graham said thoughtfully. "It's still plenty wild out there."

"You said anywhere I wanted," Kelly said stubbornly.

"So I did. That's where we'll go then. I haven't been that way in a year or two myself."

Kelly nodded, pleased. Her bold way of talking suddenly put Graham in mind of Alice Wesley, an old acquaintance of his from Kansas. Alice had moved to Denver some years ago and ran a saloon there. Of course, Alice didn't like being so far west and, even two years ago, had been telling anyone who would listen that she was saving up to move east, but if she were still in Denver, maybe she could help him with Kelly.

As he saw it, Alice and Kelly ought to take a shine to each other. If they did, it would make him feel better about turning her loose in the midst of the rawest wilderness he had yet seen.

"Whatever took you so long to catch up to me?" She asked, breaking into his thoughts. "I'd about given up on you."

"I had some business to attend to," he said.

Kelly decided not to ask what that business was. She had a sudden vision of him thrashing that Pinkerton man, and it made her shiver. Graham noticed.

"Cold?" He asked.

"No."

"I can build up the fire if you want."

"No, thank you," Kelly said. Thinking back on that day troubled her. "Can I ask you something?"

"Ask and I'll tell you."

"Why did you stop me from shooting that Pinkerton?"

"Because you might've killed him, and you can't kill Pinkerton men and go unnoticed."

"But you nearly beat that other one to death."

"Nearly doesn't count."

"I see." The distinction was not lost on her, though she thought it a pretty fine one. Remembering the fight they'd had near the river, Kelly marveled that she had punched him in the face and cut his lip and had gotten away with it, but he had about killed that Pinkerton man just for twisting her arm a little. It also made her wonder why she had never been afraid to be alone with him, not after watching him shoot Frank Gaynor, not after their fight, and not now.

She couldn't decide if she was just too foolish to know what a chance she was taking, or if that grin he'd given her in the train yard was the only true measure of his character she'd yet seen. Looking at him now across the campfire, he just looked like anyone, handsomer maybe, and more alert, but not like a real-life desperado like the newspapers told about.

Kelly laid back against her saddle and looked up at the sky, as always, taken with the stars and the sky and how they seemed so endless. She half wished that she never had to see another dusty little town spoil the horizon.

She fell asleep without realizing it; the past two restless nights having taken their toll. Her dreams were confused and unformed, and she woke with a lingering sense of excitement that did not fade, not even after a short day's ride southwest that brought them into another town.

"There's only just one room," Graham told her as they stood in the front room of the Willkenson Rooming House, Graham just having spoken to the proprietor. "You take it at night, and I'll take it during the day. How's that?"

"All right, I guess," Kelly said. It seemed like one of them could go somewhere else, but since he didn't suggest it, she decided not to either. "I'll go down to the barns and see about those saddle galls on Arnie's back."

Graham took both their traps upstairs. Kelly left the hotel and went down to the stable. After some searching, she found a good curry comb. She went to work cleaning the dirt from the base of his coat; Arnie seemed to delight in rolling on his back in the night, and he was now just as dirty as he had been on the day that she had bought him. It was hard, dusty work, and it tired her arm.

But, after a couple of hours, Arnie looked clean enough to suit her. She patted his neck affectionately and dabbed some goose grease on the galls. It was hateful to see so good a horse suffer from such an unnecessary ailment, but with care, they ought to clear up in a week or two.

It was only midafternoon. Kelly was at a loss as to what she should do. She couldn't go back to the hotel unless she wanted to sit in the parlor and be bored. Walking around the town didn't interest her. Eventually, she decided to take Arnie out for a ride.

Not wanting to saddle him and risk irritating his galls, Kelly just put a bridle on him. She led him from his stall and jumped onto his back.

She rode out of town and into the countryside for about three miles, then she circled the town and came back in from the south. Two miles out of town, she caught up with a group of five cowboys, who were coming into town from their cow camp. They hailed Kelly as a fellow drover, then when she got close enough to tell she was female, they greeted her courteously and began to rib her for riding bareback.

Kelly ignored their ribbing, until one of them, a squat little man in bad need of a shave, went a little too far.

"She don't need a saddle, 'cause that horse can't more than walk," he said. Kelly bristled.

"Maybe so, but even walking, he makes that crow bait of yours look lame."

The cowboys guffawed.

"You tell'em missy," one of the cowboys shouted, pleased at the prospect of an argument. "Tate ain't never learned how to speak to a female yet."

But the other cowboy rode up beside her.

"Bet you ten dollars he can't out run this horse of mine," he said.

"I'll meet your ten and raise you five that he can," Kelly said.

Some of the cowboys hooted at her bravado. Tate hesitated, a little cowed by her confidence. It would be terrible if he lost. His friends noticed his sudden lack of enthusiasm.

"What's s'matter Tate?" One asked, clapping him roughly on the back. "Y'ain't scared, are ya?"

There were more hoots. Tate's face reddened.

"Alright," he said. "Down main street to the church and back to this corral."

"Fifteen dollars?" Kelly asked.

"That's the ticket."

They shook hands.

The whole group of them rode to the south end of the main street. The street itself was a good thirty yards wide, flanked by a raised board sidewalk that fronted the stores and houses that ran along the street.

Kelly took a short grip on her reins and scooted as high on her horse's withers as she could. He danced nervously, knowing something was afoot. She did not look over at Tate, whose horse pranced nervously beside her own.

"Steady now," said one of the cowboys, who had appointed himself in charge of the event. He raised his revolver into the air and fired.

Both horses leapt forward in a cloud of dust. Kelly had a confused impression of flying dust and screaming people. But she had gotten a better start and was a length ahead, and soon she was in the clear. Tate spurred his gelding on and closed the gap. For a moment, they ran neck and neck straight down the street, then he edged his horse to the left, nudging Kelly toward the sidewalk.

Because she had no saddle, Kelly feared he would try to get close to her and pull her off her horse. Instead of waiting for him to try it, she deliberately guided her horse closer to the sidewalk, and when she was close enough, she jumped him up onto it.

Kelly yelled wildly and beat Arnie's flank with her hat. He never missed a stride. They galloped down the sidewalk for ten yards and outdistanced Tate by a length. Then she jumped Arnie back down off the sidewalk.

The end of the street was rapidly approaching. Kelly reined in some and wheeled her horse around, then yelled and brought her hat down on his flank again. He leapt forward with such strength that she slid back off his withers until she was nearly on his rump. She had kept hold of his mane, however, and was able to pull herself forward again.

Tate had made better time turning around and was now two yards ahead of her. Tate let fly with the rebel yell, and Kelly aped it as best she could, using her hat on her Arnie's flank. They surged forward and caught up with him, Kelly breaking off in mid-yell, coughing from the dust. Then they were past him, and the corral loomed in front of them.

She streaked past the group of cheering cowboys, and unable to stop, Kelly popped her gelding with her hat again. He jumped the corral fence, landed running, and jumped out the other side.

Jarred from the second landing, it took Kelly a moment to rein him in and turn around. Then she loped back to where the cowboys sat on their horses, whooping and laughing. They rode up around her, clapping her on the back and offering to buy her drinks. The only person who didn't look happy was Tate.

"C'mon now Tate," said the cowboy who'd fired the starting shot. "Be a sport. She won it fair."

He handed Tate a whiskey bottle. Tate took a healthy swig to clear the dust from his throat, then handed Kelly her money.

"Alright now, what the hell is going on here?" Boomed an angry voice.

The cowboys quieted suddenly. A tall man wearing a sheriff's badge and a disgusted face stood a few feet away. He was flanked by two deputies. All three men wore sidearms and carried shotguns.

"Why, Sheriff Alan," said the head cowboy, "We just had ourselves a little race to settle a question of horsemanship."

"That's a sorry damn excuse for tearing the town up, scaring innocent women and children. You damn cowboys got to learn some manners."

He stepped forward, his eye falling on Kelly. Because she was the only one bareback, he knew her as the rider who had been up on the sidewalk.

"You there," he said to her. "What kind of damn fool are you? Don't you know better to ride on the sidewalks? Ain't you got any sense?"

"That ain't no way to speak to a lady, sheriff," the head cowboy said reproachfully.

The sheriff suddenly stood stock still. He was close enough now to see that Kelly was a girl. He gaped at her a second.

"Of course I know better sheriff," Kelly said. Her cheeks were flushed, and she was still keyed up from the race. "And any damn fool ought to know I do."

The sheriff's mouth set in a grim line.

"Boys," he said, addressing his deputies. "Take that other fool down to the jail." He reached up to pull Kelly from her horse, but she backed Arnie away.

"You will come with me," he said to her. "Or I'll shoot you off that horse."

No one moved. None of the cowboys were armed, and Tate had already dismounted and was being led down the street. Kelly shrugged and slid off her horse.

"No need to get in a dither," she said.

The sheriff pulled Kelly by the arm, leading her toward the jail.

"What about my horse?" Kelly protested.

Sheriff Alan ignored her question and continued pulling her down the street.

"Don't fret, missy," called one of the cowboys. "We'll take keer of him."

"Take him to the stable on Third Street," Kelly yelled, waving back at them with her free hand. The sheriff let go of her arm, and she walked quietly beside him. Her mind was on the race she'd just run. Aside from her fear that the cowboys would run off with her horse, it did not occur to her to be concerned about being taken to jail.

The jail was a long rectangular building two blocks over. The sheriff opened the door and pushed her inside. Kelly looked around curiously. She stood in an office with two desks and a large gun cabinet. There was a door in the back wall between the two desks. Kelly guessed it lead to the cells.

One of the deputies replaced the shotguns in the cabinet. The sheriff sat at one of the two desks and opened a large, leather-bound book.

"What's your name?" He asked Kelly.

"Mary McNair," she said without hesitation. The sheriff looked up at her, his pen poised to write, but instead of writing, he beckoned to his deputy. They conferred quietly for a moment.

Kelly continued to look around the office; there was a board with wanted posters tacked on it. She scanned them, wondering if, somewhere, there was such a poster with her face on it. If so, she hoped that no copy of it had ever made it so far west.

"You in town by yourself?" The sheriff asked at last.

"No," Kelly replied. "I'm here with my brother. Can I send word to him about where I am?"

"What's your brother's name?"

"Graham. Graham McNair," Kelly answered.

The sheriff set his pen down. This had to be handled carefully. If the girl was telling the truth, then he was in grave peril.

"I've known your brother for a while," he said. "He never

mentioned no sister to me."

"We're even then," Kelly replied tartly. "I've know him all my life, and he never mentioned no sheriff to me."

He set his pen down and rubbed his chin thoughtfully.

"You all don't look much alike," he observed.

"Well, thank goodness," Kelly said good naturedly. "The last thing I need is a moustache."

The sheriff narrowed his eyes at her. Yes, the situation called for caution. Graham was not likely to be happy over having his sister called a damn fool and hauled off to jail. He'd be less happy if she were charged with something. Sheriff Tom Alan liked lawing and took pride in his fearlessness, but there was also something to be said for being smart. Upholding the law was only enjoyable as long as you were alive.

In the end, he sent a deputy to find Graham. The other deputy escorted Kelly back to the cell block and locked her in an empty cell. Kelly looked around the cell and wrinkled her nose. There was dirty straw on the floor and a bucket half-filled with what looked like urine. She poked at the bunk with a finger and jumped back as several fleas leapt from the blanket covering it.

There were two cells across from her and one beside her, and judging from how the place smelled, they were all in the same condition. There were three men in the cells across from her, two of whom appeared to be asleep. The other was Tate, who looked aggravated at her.

"It's not my fault," she said to him. "How'd I know the sheriff would take such an objection to a race?"

"You shouldn'ta gotten up on the sidewalk," he said.

"You shouldn't have tried to ride me into it," she replied.

They said nothing further. Not wanting to sit on the filthy cot, Kelly squatted in the middle of the cell. She sincerely hoped they wouldn't hold her long.

When the cell block door opened again, it was dusk, and Kelly, who was still squatting in the middle of the cell, stood up quickly. She had begun to worry that she might be stuck in jail overnight. The sheriff stepped in, and to Kelly's relief, Graham was with him.

"I appreciate you not holding her on charges, Tom," Graham was saying. "It would break her mother's heart."

Kelly squashed an impulse to laugh at the solemn note in Graham's voice. She had known he'd back her up but hadn't thought him capable of such dramatics.

"I always try and do the right thing," Sheriff Alan said. "Jail time wouldn't do her no good."

Graham had his own opinion about that but kept silent as he unlocked the door to Kelly's cell. Kelly didn't look any worse for wear, although her face was dusty, and her hair straggled from under her hat.

"Thank you sheriff," she said graciously, stepping from the

cell. "What about Tate?"

"Tate? Tate who?" The sheriff asked, straining to be polite.

"The other damn fool you arrested with me," Kelly explained. "He's right there. Shouldn't you release him too?"

"I didn't arrest you, miss," Sheriff Alan said hastily. "I just took you into custody so's that riffraff in the street wouldn't do you no harm."

"And I appreciate it," Kelly said. "But it seems awful hard that a hard-working cowboy should have to stay in jail 'cause of a little race I dared him to."

"Well, I'll look into it," Sheriff Alan said. "If he ain't drunk, I'll release him."

"Thank you so much, sheriff," Kelly said.

Graham took her firmly by the elbow and started for the door.

"Thanks again, Tom," he said. "I sure won't forget this."

He said nothing else until they were far from the jail. Kelly walked down the dusty street beside him, pleased that she had won the race and the fifteen dollars.

"I'm not even going to ask how you decided to take a gallop down the main street sidewalk," Graham said, interrupting her thoughts. "I trust you had a sound reason."

Kelly shrugged.

"He was going to try and pull me off my horse, that or run me into the sidewalk. So I just jumped onto it," Kelly paused, Graham looked like he'd just bit a lemon. "I'd bet him fifteen dollars that Arnie n'me could out run that nag of his."

"I thought you were just going to see about those galls."

"I had to pass the time somehow," she said. "So I went for a little ride, bareback, and these cowboys took it on themselves to annoy me."

Graham didn't answer, but she was used to that.

"I'm going to the stable," she announced. "Those cowboys said they'd see about my horse. I want to make sure they did."

She ran off without another word. Graham sighed and pushed his hat back off his forehead. Maybe going to Denver was the best idea after all. If Alice were there and Kelly took a liking to her, it could solve all his problems.

He settled the matter in his own mind that night at the saloon. The only talk at the bar and the tables was of the wild race down main street that day and the blonde haired girl who could jump fences bareback. If they went west at first light tomorrow, Graham thought, they might be able to outrun the talk.

He broached the subject with her in the morning as he took the room.

"What do you think of heading for Denver?" Graham asked.

"I don't know," Kelly said. "Why Denver particularly?"

"It's getting on toward winter and bad traveling weather. It's about as far west as we'll safely get. It's a big enough place to provide a good living, and I may still have some friends there, though I may not. I've not been out that way for a good two years or more."

"What kind of friends?"

"Friends that could help you get settled."

"Is it far from the mountains?"

"Less than a day's ride."

"All right then," Kelly said. "When do we leave?"

"First light tomorrow?" He asked.

"Good enough," she said. "Won't you need some sleep?"

"No."

Kelly shrugged.

"It's up to you."

"First light tomorrow then," he said.

"Good night then," Kelly said, "Or, I guess I should say good morning."

"Good morning," he replied, stepping into the room.

Kelly turned and went down the stairs to get breakfast. Graham watched her go, hoping she had the sense to stay out of trouble today. Then he closed the door and bolted it.

"She has the sense, I expect," he said. "Just not the will."

He sat on the chair and pulled his boots off. Why she had bothered to make the bed, he did not know, but people from back east did strange things sometimes. He took off his gun belt, then rebuckled it and hung it from the bed post, glad that the room was on the second floor so he didn't have to worry about the window.

He stripped down to his long johns and got into bed, turning onto his left side. His last thought before drifting into sleep was that the pillow smelled like Kelly.

Chapter 16

Even though the trip was uneventful, it took them over ten days to reach Denver. Early on, Kelly noticed that they were getting started later, riding slower and halting sooner, but she never questioned Graham as to why he no longer seemed to be in a hurry. The slower pace was enjoyable, and her shoulder was almost better. She felt less exhausted and more alive, especially now that she no longer had to pretend about going to San Francisco. It was also a relief to know that she would never have to go home.

The plains had taken on a more rolling look, and they were interrupted here and there with buttes. Clouds passed so low overhead that they cast incredibly black shadows, making the ground look as though it had been burned over. Every now and then, a traveler would pass, usually too far off to see clearly, but twice they passed families riding in large covered wagons. Kelly would have liked to ridden with them for a while and ask where they were going, but Graham always spurred ahead before she could suggest it.

"What's the hurry?" She had asked him the second time this happened. "I was curious to know where they were from and where they were going."

"There's no point in it," he had replied. "They'll take you for a bandit and run you off."

"How do you know?"

He had not answered, and Kelly had let the subject drop, though she brought it back up that evening as they ate.

"You don't care much for settlers do you?" She asked. "You

always speak so badly of them."

"No, I don't," his tone told her that he didn't want to discuss it. Kelly decided not to question him further. She finished her supper and took one of the books she had bought out of her saddle bags. She leaned back against her saddle and began to read.

Graham finished eating, then rinsed both their plates with water from his canteen. He sat back down by the fire and fiddled with his deck of cards for a moment.

"What's that you're reading?" He asked.

"It's some stories by Nathaniel Hawthorn," Kelly said without looking up.

The name meant nothing to Graham, who could read very well but had never regarded it as a form of entertainment.

"Read one aloud if you like," Graham said. "I wouldn't mind some literary diversion."

Surprised, Kelly nodded and flipped back to the beginning of the story she had been reading. She sat up closer to the fire and began to read aloud.

Graham leaned back against his saddle. The story didn't interest him much, but Kelly had a good reading voice. He listened attentively for an hour, at which point the story was over, and Kelly closed the book, saying she was going to sleep.

As was his habit, Graham stayed awake another hour or two. The next two or three days should see them to Denver. They could slow down a little more, he thought, after all, there was even less reason to hurry now than there had been before.

Denver appeared on the horizon on their tenth day out. Kelly was not precisely sure what day of the week it was or of the date, although she knew it was near the beginning of September.

They rode into town toward sun down that day. Denver was larger than she had expected, larger and more civilized. But not all that civilized, she thought, as she watched two men come to blows over an argument about whose mule was stronger.

Graham seemed to know where he was going, so Kelly let him lead on while she looked around at the town. He halted in front of a livery stable and dismounted. Kelly followed suit.

"If you'll see to the horses, I've got some tracking to do," he said. "Meet you back here in an hour."

Kelly nodded, and he walked off.

"Hey there," she called to a man who was lounging near the barn door. "Do you work here?"

The man nodded.

"Do you have room for two more horses?"

The man nodded and motioned for her to lead the horses into the barn. She did so, wondering why men hated to talk.

Meanwhile, Graham walked two blocks west and four south, looking for Alice's saloon. It was right where he remembered it, and when he walked by the open door, he caught a glimpse of Alice, who was standing behind the bar talking to some bearded man who looked like a miner.

Pleased that his plans were working so far, he went down to the Royal Monarch Hotel, only to find there were no rooms available. The two other hotels were also full. The only other available lodging possibility was one of the town's sporting houses, but he could hardly put Kelly up in such a place, and he never could stand to spend more than a night in one himself. Well, they'd check again after seeing Alice. Maybe something would open up.

Kelly had fed, watered, and brushed both horses down by the time he returned to the stable. She was leaning over Arnie's stall door feeding him a piece of candy when he walked in.

"Do you feel up to some cards tonight?" Graham asked her.

"I suppose."

"We can get a game going for a while, then come back here for our traps. All the hotels are full up."

"Sure," Kelly said. "Did you find your friend?"

"Right where I expected. Alice never did like to move around."

"Alice?" Kelly pricked up her ears, pleased at the prospect of meeting another woman. "Does she play poker?"

"Sometimes. She owns a saloon—the one we're going to."

"Let's go then."

They walked out of the barn and down the street. Graham was pleased at Kelly's enthusiasm and at the prospect of scamming some miners. It seemed that coming to Denver had been the right thing to do after all.

Chapter 17

Alice Wesley had seen a lot of commotion in her thirty-two years, and while she didn't mind particularly, she did dream of the day when she could close up her saloon and move back east. Though not an impossible dream, it was one that required a good sized bank role, for it took a bit of money to maintain a respectable life back east if you weren't married.

She could wait if she had to. Alice had patience, and she wasn't afraid to work hard either.

Keeping up the second largest saloon in Denver wasn't any easy job, especially with all the shiftless help she'd had lately. Lars, the bartender, had been with her over a year, though her pharo dealers had come and gone like a bad smell in a shifting wind, and she couldn't keep a porter to save her life. Her troubles were compounded by the fact that her last pharo dealer had stabbed her last porter during an argument. The porter had died, and the pharo dealer had been lynched.

Well, no matter, winter was setting in soon, and winter always calmed things down a bit, even when you took the effects of cabin fever into consideration.

Alice shook her head, considering it. People were so shiftless out west. A customer stopped at the bar, asking for a drink. Alice poured him one, then went back to her thinking. She always worked behind the bar with her bartender, and because this particular night was slow, she set about polishing shot glasses as she surveyed her establishment.

Opposite the bar was an open space with ten round tables. Card games occupied four of those tables; the others were surrounded by men drinking and talking. Toward the front of the room, in an alcove to the left of the door, the pharo table stood unmanned, and Alice hated to think of the money slipping by until she found another dealer. To her, every dollar earned meant one less day until she could move east again.

Alice held the glass she was rubbing up to the light. It was spotless. She set it back under the bar and picked up another. The saloon door opened, letting in a quick breath of fresh air, and she looked up to see the newcomers.

Well, for heaven's sake, she thought, look what the night air blew in. If it wasn't an ex-army captain and sometime hell raiser by the name of Graham McNair. Alice hadn't seen him for over two years, and last she'd heard, he'd gotten into a bad scrape up in the Nebraska territory and had headed east to let things cool a bit.

She wasn't too surprised to see him again, what with all the Indian trouble the law had other things to worry about besides a gunman who had killed an onery cattle dealer. But you could have knocked her over with a feather when he walked in beside a blonde haired slip of a girl who was packing a gun and a lively pair of blue eyes.

Alice had known Graham for ten years, but she had never even heard of him traveling with anyone since he'd left the army, much less take a woman along for company. It sparked her curiosity. In her opinion, he was the coolest blooded man she'd ever met. It was uncanny at times, and now here he was . . .

It staggered her imagination.

They took interest in a three-man game going on at the tables. After a few minutes, they joined it. Alice watched their play for some time. To her practiced eye, it was plain that they had some kind of scam going, but she couldn't figure it. Graham always had been clever about such things.

It was near closing when the game broke up, and Alice was relieved to see that it broke up peacefully. Graham came over and sat at the bar; Kelly lingered near the pharo table, examining the set up.

Alice poured Graham a whiskey.

"Hidy," she said, smiling.

"Hidy yourself," he replied, returning her smile. "Fine establishment you have here, ma'am."

"Alice Wesley is the name," she said. "What's yours, pilgrim?"

"Graham McNair," he said, appreciating her caution. It was always prudent to find out if someone was using an alias before throwing their name around a saloon.

"Seem's I've heard that name," she said, "in connection with some unpleasant business up in the Nebraska territory."

"You may have," Graham said. "I've got a cousin by the same name as myself, and he is a reckless character."

"It must be your cousin I heard of," Alice said, a wicked gleam in her eye. "The Graham McNair I heard of always traveled light. You seem to have have some blonde-haired baggage with you, pilgrim."

Graham sipped his whiskey and ignored her reference to Kelly. Alice was always terribly interested in other people's business, but she was kind-hearted, so it was best to ignore her nosiness.

"Yes, this is a fine establishment," Graham went on. "How is the town?"

"It's a little wild," Alice said. Her bartender was herding the stragglers out of the place; Kelly evaded him and sat next to Graham. "For a peace loving man like yourself. Your cousin now, he would like it here."

Kelly didn't understand what she was talking about, but Graham smiled in a way that made her faintly jealous. Then he turned to her.

"Kelly Knowlton, this is Alice Wesley, proprietress of this establishment."

"I'm pleased to meet you," Kelly said, offering Alice her hand. Alice shook it firmly.

"Any friend of Graham's is welcome here," she said, looking Kelly over.

This was no common whore he'd picked up to pass the time with; she wasn't some poor-white sod buster's daughter either, Alice thought. For one thing, the girl spoke like she was educated, and for another, she had an unsettling amount of direct self-assurance. Alice remembered the rumors she'd heard about a runaway girl having shot a Pinkerton man in Kansas. At the time, she'd put it all down to drunken exaggeration, but this girl looked perfectly capable of such an act, and it was no secret that Graham McNair attracted trouble like a buff hunter drew flies.

"You want a drink?" Alice asked her.

"No, thank you," Kelly replied. She was looking Alice over just as Alice had looked her over. Alice's eyes were alert and shrewd, but warm. Kelly felt the woman was appraising her, but her smile was friendly and real, and Kelly was grateful for that after having spent so long among strangers who were often hostile and dangerous. Her hair was an alarming shade of red, and Kelly wondered if it were dyed. She had never seen dyed hair before.

"Where do you come from, child?" Alice asked her. Kelly was irked at being called a child, but sensed it was meant kindly—or perhaps to rankle Graham who had snorted at the word.

"East," she said.

"Been traveling long?"

"More than a month," Kelly replied.

Alice's opinion of Kelly rose. It never paid to tell a stranger too much about yourself.

"Been traveling with this pilgrim long?" She asked, jabbing a thumb toward McNair.

"Seems like a while," Kelly said. She could tell the conversation was amusing Graham, but she had no idea why.

"Well, I got a place over on the next street," Alice said. "You two can stay with me while you're in town. I've got plenty of room."

Kelly was about to accept and thank her for her kind offer when Graham, who was apparently alarmed by the idea, spoke hastily.

"No thanks, we can get rooms at the Monarch," he said.

Alice pricked up her ears. Rooms? Why on earth would they need more than one? Was he putting up a blind, and if so, why bother? She stole a glance at Kelly, whose cheeks had reddened slightly; she had also picked up on his reason for refusing Alice's offer. Alice chortled to herself. It looked like it might be an interesting winter after all.

"Oh, I've got plenty of rooms," Alice said airily, emphasizing the plural. "I take in boarders sometimes, but the last lot I had were so rowdy I threw 'em all out."

"That seems fair enough," Kelly said. The idea of staying with Alice appealed to her. "But we'd pay you for your trouble."

"It's no trouble," Alice said.

She noticed that Graham seemed annoyed at Kelly's acceptance of her offer, but she put it down to him being irked at not having the final say. In reality, he was considering letting Kelly go with Alice while he got a room at the Monarch. Of course, all things considered, it would be for the best. But Alice was wild; he ought to make sure that she didn't get Kelly into trouble before she got good settled. He'd better stay with her a while yet.

"All right then," he agreed.

"Good," Kelly said happily. "Can I help you clean up, Mrs. Wesley?"

Alice, who had been taking a sip of whiskey, choked when Kelly said this. Graham shifted uncomfortably on his seat, then stood up.

"I'll go get our traps from the stable," he said, tipping his hat to them both and leaving.

Kelly felt embarrassed, knowing that she had said something wrong but not knowing what.

"Did I say something wrong?" She asked.

"No, no," Alice said, after coughing to clear her throat. Her eyes twinkled with amusement. "Just call me Alice."

It seemed disrespectful, but Kelly hardly felt she could refuse.

"If you wish," she said. "What can I do to help?"

"Come on in the back and help me wash these glasses,"

Alice said.

Kelly followed her, rolling up her sleeves as she went.

"I expect you've been traveling for a bit," Alice said as she poured hot water from the stove into the dish pan.

"Ten or twelve days since the last town," Kelly said. "I lost track of time somewhere along the way."

"Well, you can get a bath at my place," Alice said. "And get out of those pants and into a nice clean dress, if you've got one along."

Kelly smiled and picked up a dish towel.

"I don't. I always dress like this."

"Always? Why?"

"Back home I ran a horse farm and had to do a lot of riding. I always wore pants."

Alice started washing the glasses, frowning because Kelly's story just didn't sound right to her. Why would an educated female from the east wear pants and work horses? Maybe the family was short on men folk, she thought, deciding not to ask about it right now. Besides, Graham had probably told her to keep still about such things.

"You can have a bath, anyway."

"Thank you. I would dearly like one."

"That was some good poker you all were playing."

"Thanks."

"I've made some good money playin' cards," Alice said. "But it don't pan out regular enough for me, that's why I bought this saloon."

"Have you owned it long?" Kelly was fascinated to think that Alice owned and operated the place all by herself. It was one thing to manage your own family's property, but it was quite another to start your own business.

"Going on six years," Alice said. "When I got here, this was about the only drinking place, and I made some good money. There's more watering holes now though, and it's a mite harder to break even. Especially with my pharo man gone."

She looked over at Kelly, who was studiously drying glasses. Under that cowboy hat and smudged face was a pretty girl. Alice knew from her own experience that a female pharo dealer was worth her weight in gold, especially one smart and good with cards like Kelly seemed to be.

"What happened to him?" Kelly asked.

"Who? Oh, Bernie. Well, he had to leave town sudden," Alice said. It was better not to advertise the dangers of the profession. She would wait a day or two and see how things stood, then ask if Kelly would fill the pharo cage for her.

When the cleaning up was done, they said good night to Lars and walked to Alice's.

"Shouldn't we wait for Graham?" Kelly asked.

"He knows the way, I reckon." Alice said. "I'd lay odds he's already holed up asleep."

Alice lived in a one-story, five-room house three blocks from the saloon. The entire front of the house was a sitting room; the back was half a kitchen and half a bedroom, and the middle was two more bedrooms. A shotgun hall ran from the front to the back. Kelly thought it was the most curious looking house she'd ever seen.

As Alice had guessed, Graham had disappeared into one of the middle bedrooms. Kelly found her things in the other. Alice occupied the room off the kitchen, which made sense to Kelly, because it was sure to be the warmest room in the winter time.

Tired and glad to be in a house again, Kelly took her clothes off and folded them neatly. The room was small and sparsely furnished with only a bed and a wash stand, but the quilt on the bed was cheerful, and everything was clean. She let her hair down and brushed it out, then crawled into bed. She fell asleep almost immediately.

The next day, Kelly slept late. She woke to find the house empty. Alice had left a plate of food in the stove for her breakfast, which Kelly ate hungrily.

After washing her breakfast dishes, Kelly decided to take the bath she'd been promised. She found the washtub in a lean-to behind the house and put it in her room, then half-filled it with water from the pump. There was a large iron stew pot on the stove, which she also filled with water and set on to boil.

Alice came in the back door just as the water had begun to steam.

"Good morning," Kelly said. "I'm setting up to take a bath. I hope you don't mind."

"Not at all. Make yourself at home. Did you find the tub?"

"Yes, in the lean-to."

"And your breakfast?"

"Yes. Thank you. It was very good."

"There's some softsoap in the pantry if you want it."

"I do. Thanks."

Kelly got the soap and put it near the tub in her room. When she got back to the kitchen, her water had begun to boil. Alice helped her carry the heavy pot into her room.

"Don't pour it all in," Alice said. "Leave some out to rinse your hair with."

Kelly poured in enough to take the sting out of the cool well water. Alice started making her bed. Kelly hesitated. She did not want to bathe in front of a stranger, but the water was getting cold, and Alice showed no sign of being in a hurry to leave. Perhaps she was being prudish.

Kelly took her clothes off and stepped into the tub.

"Where do you come from, anyway?" Alice asked her, fluffing the bed pillow. "You talk like you're from the east."

"I am," Kelly said. "From New York State. My people

owned a bit of land up there."

"Farmers?"

"Well, we had a horse farm near Rochester, but my father had some business in the city."

"New York City?"

"That's the one."

Alice looked at her curiously.

"He must've had some money then," she said. "Why ever did you run away?"

Kelly wasn't sure how to answer that. She took some soap from the gourd and rubbed it into her wash cloth. "I never did get along with him," she said at last. "And he wanted me to marry this man."

"There's worse things than marrying a man," Alice said. "Although I don't know if I can think of one just now. Was he old or ugly or something?"

Kelly had hardly known her fiancee, and she had never thought about whether or not he was attractive.

"No, he wasn't yet thirty, I don't think. I suppose he was handsome enough."

"Did he drink?"

"I don't know. I barely knew him."

"Well, were you sweet on someone else?"

"No. I never had time to think about things like that," Kelly said. Alice's questions were beginning to upset her a little.

"So you just up and ran off with Graham McNair?"

"I didn't mean to," Kelly said, nettled by the sly note in Alice's voice and what it seemed to imply. "It just kind of happened."

She told Alice how she had found herself in the middle of a bank robbery and what had happened after that, but she neglected to tell her about having seen Graham the day before in the train yard.

"Passing strange," Alice said. "But I've heard stranger. I once knew a woman in Dodge City who married the man who shot her first husband. She said she liked a man who could accomplish something. But she always was flighty, Nola was. She's been married twice since then even."

Kelly didn't see what that had to do with anything, but didn't say so. Instead, she scrubbed her feet.

"Well then," Alice said. "How old are you? Twenty?"

"Seventeen," Kelly said.

It was possible, Alice thought. She looked young but acted old.

"That's a good age. I reckon I was about twenty when I first came to Kansas. Dodge City, it was, and what a wild time. Cowboys shootin' the town up, Indians shootin' the country up, and the army raisin' hell both places."

"Is that where you met Graham?" Kelly asked.

"Yes ma'am," Alice said. "I was livin' with an gambler by the name of Phineas Faulk, though I would bet he changed his name oftener than he changed his linen—and he was a dandy, too. I reckon Graham was a scout then. He sure spent a lot of time in saloons, more than most pony soldiers, so he must've been scouting."

"Whatever happened to Mr. Faulk?" Kelly asked. The bath water was beginning to cool, so she wet her hair and rubbed soap in it.

"Don't waste a mister on him," Alice said. "Well, he took a bullet in a brawl over a high stakes card game. It left me in a bad way, but Graham saw I got the money that was owed to me from that pot. Never stake a man at poker, honey. If they don't lose it or get shot for it, you'll still have a time getting your cut of the winnings."

"Did he die?"

"Not straight away. He was down with blood poisoning for a week before he went."

"What did you do then?" Kelly was nearly done scrubbing her hair.

"Well, if you're worried I took up with Graham McNair, you're worrying over nothing, although he did cut quite a figure in his uniform, let me tell you. I bought into a saloon on First Street and ran the pharo table. We did right well. After a while, I sold out and bought this place here. I reckon I can sell this place in another few years and move back east."

"Can you help me rinse my hair?" Kelly asked.

"Sure. Stand on up."

Kelly obeyed, shivering a little from the coolness of the room. Alice poured the remaining water over her head. Kelly stepped from the tub and wrapped herself in a towel. The bath water had turned a muddy brown.

"Looks like you brought a good part of Kansas with you," Alice said.

Kelly dried herself and sat on the bed.

"How ever did you get that scar?" Alice asked her, pointing to her shoulder.

"I was shot," Kelly said, hastily covering it with a towel. She had not thought much about the scar until now; it had always seemed a trifle next to nearly dying. But, now that Alice mentioned it, it sure was ugly.

"Mr. McNair let such a thing happen?"

Alice's tone seemed to imply that it was Graham's fault. Kelly bristled a little but changed the subject without arguing the matter.

"So what will you do when you go back east?" She asked.

Alice noted Kelly's umbrage at her comment about Graham and her haste in changing the topic.

"I'll tell you," Alice said. "I'm going to buy a big old house, and I'm going to paint it blue. Then I'll take in boarders and laundry so everyone will know it's a respectable place, and I'll go to church every Sunday wearing a brand new hat."

"That sounds like a good plan," Kelly said, thinking that Alice might be a little crazy from having been west too long.

"It keeps me straight," Alice said. "Else I'd wander around lost and get into trouble. You got a plan?"

"No," Kelly said. "Though I'd like to raise horses someday."

"You'll need some money to do that," Alice said. "Holler when you're dressed, and I'll help you tote that bath water out."

"All right."

Alice left the room, banging the door shut behind her. Kelly dressed in her clean clothes, thinking over what Alice had said. Why couldn't she have her own horse farm? She knew how to run it, and as Alice had said, all it took was some money.

She and Alice toted the washtub out back and emptied it. Kelly sat at the kitchen table and dried her hair while Alice rummaged around in the pantry.

"You want to go to the store with me?" Alice asked from within the pantry.

"Sure," Kelly answered. "As soon as my hair is dry."

Graham had still not returned an hour later, but Kelly's hair was dry, so she and Alice headed to the store. On the way, their conversation consisted mostly of Alice telling stories about her past adventures. Kelly listened with amazement and, occasionally, with disbelief.

They walked through a section of town that Kelly had not seen the previous day. Alice was talking about an Indian raid on a settlement in Kansas, and Kelly, who was hardly listening, looked around the street. Her eyes fastened on a large two-story building that looked like a hotel. Two women who were wearing nothing but their camisoles and bloomers were hanging out an upstairs window, calling to the men who passed below.

Kelly stopped walking and stared. Alice walked on a few paces, then realized she had lost her audience. She walked back to where Kelly was standing, mystified by Kelly's interest in the sporting house across the street.

"What is that place?" Kelly whispered before Alice could say anything.

Alice tilted her head to one side questioningly.

"That's Maybelle's House," Alice replied, amused. "Do you mean to tell me that you rode all the way through Kansas and never saw a sporting house?"

Kelly shook her head. She had heard the term before but had not been sure what it meant. Now she had a much better idea.

"You mean those are bad women?" Kelly asked, using the only euphemism she could think of.

Alice put her hands on her hips.

"I mean those are sporting women," she said. "I have yet to

see a bad woman though I've seen a good plenty of bad men."

Kelly flushed and looked away from the house. Apparently, Alice had much different ideas about such things than did people back in New York.

"I wasn't trying to insult anyone," Kelly said.

Alice relaxed a little.

"No, I guess you weren't," Alice said. "But I think we'd best have a little talk when we get back to my place."

"What about?" Kelly asked.

"Things you need to know," Alice replied. "Come on, it's gettin' late."

Chapter 18

For a few days after her "talk" with Alice, Kelly found it was hard to concentrate. Her ears were still ringing from some of the things that Alice had told her. Not all of it was a surprise to her, of course, especially as she had supervised the horse breeding at her farm for the past four years. But the specifics were interesting, and Alice had been pleasantly blunt about the whole thing. Kelly had always had a hard time understanding innuendo.

Alice was blunt about almost everything, and as time went by, Kelly found herself liking Alice more and more. Alice never got angry about anything and spoke her mind without encouragement. Sometimes she spoke about things that no one really wanted to hear about, but in those instances, you could tell her so, and she would not take offense.

Life slipped in to a routine. Alice and Graham went to the saloon nearly every night, Alice to keep charge of the place and Graham to play cards. Although they both frequently asked her to go with them, Kelly generally declined. She spent her days riding out around town on the pretext of exercising their horses. Alice had nearly had a fit the first time she found out that Kelly was riding alone outside of town.

"You're just asking for trouble. Anything could happen to you," Alice had fumed at her as they sat eating dinner. "Tell her she ought to stop, Graham."

Graham had looked up from his plate, and his eyes had met Kelly's. Kelly had been furious over Alice's interference, and it had shown clearly in her face. Graham had smiled and gone back to his eating.

"I don't believe I'll take a hand in this scrap," he had said.

Kelly had glared triumphantly at Alice, who had openly glowered at Graham.

Graham had ignored them both, wondering briefly what had possessed him when he had agreed to lodge with two women as opinionated as Alice and Kelly.

October swept by. Alice hired, and soon fired, another pharo dealer. This morning, she was disgusted by the idea of having the pharo table shut down again, and she stepped out into the kitchen to find Kelly seated at the table reading a book.

"Did you get breakfast?" Alice asked her.

"I made some biscuits and fried some ham," Kelly said. "I made enough for all of us. It's in the stove."

"That was right thoughtful of you," Alice said, getting a tin plate from the cupboard and going over to the stove.

Kelly closed her book when Alice sat down at the table with her food. Alice glanced at her speculatively. Alice was sure now that Kelly and Graham were not and had never been lovers. She wasn't too sure why they hadn't been or what they felt for each other; those were mysteries that she would investigate during the weeks to come. All that mattered right then was that Kelly was a free woman, and as such, Alice could ask her to run the pharo table and not have to worry about Graham getting all in a tizzy over it, even though she had a feeling that he might anyway.

"You make good biscuits," Alice said.

"Thanks."

"I wonder if you would be interested in working for me," Alice said.

Kelly was startled.

"Doing what?"

"Running the pharo table."

Kelly thought about it. Bad weather was setting in soon, and she wouldn't be able to ride. Although money wasn't a problem, she did think she ought to help Alice out if she could, and she did need something to do.

"I don't know how to play pharo," Kelly said at last.

"I can teach you. It's easy enough," Alice said. "I'll split the take sixty-forty with you. I'll even give you a dress to wear so you won't have the expense of buying one."

"All right," Kelly said. "I'll give it a try."

"Good," Alice said, finishing her ham. "We'll try the dress on you after breakfast. If it fits good enough, we can go down to the saloon this afternoon and teach you the game."

Kelly opened her book and read until Alice was done eating. They did the dishes together and, when they were done, went to Alice's room.

Alice's room was as cluttered as Kelly's was empty. Besides the bed and washstand, there was a tall chest of drawers and a huge wardrobe. Kelly stripped down to her underwear while Alice rummaged around in the wardrobe.

"This ought to do," she said, pulling a vivid green dress from the wardrobe. "I bought this when I was about your age. It ought to fit, except maybe we'll have to hem it some, since you're a mite shorter than me."

She helped Kelly get the dress on over her head, then hooked it in the back. Kelly stood uncomfortably. The dress was very low in the bosom, and the color was too bright.

"There," Alice said. "What do you think?"

Kelly surveyed herself in the mirror on the wardrobe door.

"I look common," she said. "Like one of those women from Maybelle's house."

"Watch who you throw down on, missy," Alice said sharply. "That used to be my dress."

Kelly flushed. It had never occurred to her that Alice might have also done such things.

"I'm not throwing down on anyone," she said. "I don't care how anyone makes their living, but I don't like looking like this, and I won't wear this dress."

Alice started to unhook her. If Kelly said she wouldn't wear it, then she wouldn't. Besides, she was halfway right. Although she didn't look common, she did look like a prostitute and, since she wasn't one, that could lead to some unpleasant scenes. Also, Alice had a feeling that Graham would skin her if he found out that she'd put Kelly up to it.

"Well, you can't deal pharo dressed like a cowboy," Alice said, putting the dress back in the wardrobe.

Kelly thought a minute. She personally didn't see why she couldn't deal pharo while dressed like a cowboy, but she had to admit that Alice knew more about these things than she did.

"Fine," she said, an idea coming to her. "I'll go downtown and get the dressiest respectable dress I can find."

"No one's going to beat down the doors to watch a school teacher deal pharo," Alice said.

"I won't look like a school teacher," Kelly said. "And I won't look trashy, but I bet they will beat down the doors. You wait and see."

Alice gazed at her shrewdly. Kelly met her eyes squarely. Alice smiled and nodded.

"All right then," she said. "I'll take my chances with you. Now let's go down to the saloon and teach you to deal."

The game wasn't difficult to learn. Kelly picked it up quickly, but Alice made her practice for several days before letting her play for real. During those days, she and Kelly would spend their afternoons at the saloon. Between her afternoons with Alice and her mornings with the horses, Kelly saw very little of Graham, who slept most of the day because he was out most of the night.

Alice sometimes thought they were avoiding each other. Graham had stated that he was spending his nights at the saloon in order to assist Alice if there happened to be trouble. While Alice appreciated the thought, she and Lars were more than able to handle any trouble that might come along. Having Graham around was probably more dangerous than safe, but he had such a reputation that people came in to drink just so they could whisper about him, and Alice was enough of a business woman to appreciate it.

Because he and Kelly saw so little of each other, it wasn't difficult to keep him from discovering her and Kelly's plan concerning the Pharo table. Alice herself certainly didn't intend to say anything to him about it, and it never occurred to Kelly that her plans were any of his business.

The first he knew of it was the day Kelly brought her dress home. Fancy dresses weren't all that hard to come by in Denver, but Kelly was terribly fussy over it, in Alice's mind, and it took her three days to find one that she liked.

Alice helped her into it, thinking how much neater Kelly's figure was with a corset on, even though Kelly wouldn't let her lace it very tight.

"That's enough Alice," she said, gasping. "I can't breathe."

"You'll get used to it," Alice assured her as she tied the strings.

"I don't know how anyone can get used to not being able to breathe," Kelly said crossly as she stepped into her petticoats. "Not unless they're dead."

"I thought all you eastern girls wore corsets twenty-four hours a day."

"Not me," Kelly replied. "If I wanted to be an eastern girl I would have stayed east."

That was true enough, Alice thought, picking up the dress as Kelly fiddled with her underclothes. It was a pretty shade of deep blue that Alice thought would look very well with her eyes.

When the dress was on and hooked up, Alice began to think that maybe she ought to give Kelly a little more credit for knowing about things. The dress was very becoming to her, and she looked very respectable, but she didn't look even remotely like some old maid school teacher.

"It's a little long," Kelly said, twisting around in the mirror.

"I expect that's so you can wear hoops under it, but there ain't no hoops in Denver." Alice said. "Though we could probably order some from St. Louis."

"No," Kelly said. She was beginning to regret having gotten herself into this.

"You'd look ever so much more stylish," Alice said, trying to cajole her into changing her mind.

"Order all the hoops you like," Kelly replied. "But I won't wear them, so you might as well forget it."

Alice sighed and decided not to press the issue.

"Let's go on into the kitchen," Alice suggested. "You can stand up on a chair so's I can pin the dress up for you."

"I can't sew very well," Kelly said. "Will you hem it for me?"

Alice opened her sewing box and found a box of pins.

"I reckon so," she said. "Whatever was your mother thinking of when she let you get to the age of seventeen without being able to hem a dress?"

"She died when I was a baby," Kelly said, picking up her skirts so she could walk to the kitchen without tripping over them.

Alice opened the door for her, feeling a little bad about having brought up what must be a sore subject for the girl.

Graham was sitting at the table drinking a second cup of coffee when Alice and Kelly stepped into the room. He did not recognize Kelly at first and was wondering why Alice had company, when Kelly greeted him with a cheerful good morning. He recognized her voice immediately and stared at her.

Alice noted his reaction with some amusement, though Kelly seemed oblivious to it, not even seeming to care that he was too tongue tied to return her wish of good morning.

"Go on and stand up on that chair," Alice said to Kelly as she set her pins on the table.

Kelly gathered up her skirts and put one foot up on the chair. Agile though she usually was, Kelly was not used to wearing so much clothing, and she almost lost her balance. Graham rose immediately and, taking her elbow, helped her stand up on the chair.

"Thanks," Kelly said, looking down at him as he took his chair again. "Are you going to say good morning or not?"

"Good morning."

Hiding her smile, Alice knelt before the chair and turned up the hem, fiddling with it until she was satisfied that it was the perfect length. Then she started to pin the dress up.

Alice took her time, and Kelly began to fidget. She hated standing still, and she hated wearing dresses. She wondered how long she would have to deal pharo in order to get enough money for a horse farm.

Graham watched her fidget and smiled inwardly. Whatever Alice had cooked up, Kelly didn't look all that enthused about it. He would get Alice alone when they were done and find out exactly what was afoot. Creating a fuss now would only put Kelly's back up.

When Alice finished, Graham helped Kelly down from the chair.

"Excuse us for a minute," he said to her. "Mrs. Wesley and I have something to discuss."

Kelly watched in surprise as he half-dragged Alice from the

room. She shook her head. He acted so strange sometimes.

Kelly went back into Alice's room and waited for her. She couldn't unhook the back of the dress by herself and wondered idly what good were clothes that you couldn't get into or out of by yourself. It took a long time for Alice to show up. She helped Kelly undress, and Kelly, glad to be back in her jeans, left the house and went happily down to the stable. The weather was fine, and she rode well out of town that afternoon. Alice had said she could start at the saloon as soon as the dress was hemmed.

Inspired by the money she was losing because of the closed pharo table, Alice hemmed the dress that very evening. Kelly tried it on again, and it fit perfectly.

"You can get started tomorrow night," Alice said pleasedly.

"Good, now will you get me back out of this contraption?" Kelly asked irritably.

"Surely," Alice replied, her doubts returning. If Kelly was going to be snappish, it would hurt the trade.

But after a week, her doubts had been put to rest for good. Standing the bar watching the crowd at the pharo table, Alice had to admit that Kelly had been right on all counts. Not only were they beating down the doors, they weren't paying much attention to their playing, which meant they lost more and she made more money. On top of it all, Kelly had turned out to be a sharp dealer. East was looking closer all the time.

There hadn't been any trouble yet, either. Many of the men would talk to Kelly, but not one had made her an indecent proposal. Not even the hardest of hard cases had created a fuss over their losses.

It paid to know what risks to take, Alice crowed to herself. Taking in that cowboy riding female had been the best bet she'd ever made. If Kelly stayed on for a while, Alice would be back east in no time.

It didn't exactly figure though. How Kelly could wring such respectful treatment out of a bunch of dirty miners and smelly buff hunters was beyond her. She looked damn fine in that dress she had bought and with her hair up pretty, but no one had offered her so much as a lecherous look. Maybe it was the polite, distant attitude she affected, and the precise, proper way of speaking that was friendly, but which reminded you she was educated and refined and you weren't. Not stuck up, but genteel, Alice thought.

Whatever it was, she had that raggedy bunch so whoorahed they opened doors for her and were just itching to shoot each other over some imagined slight to her honor. All just to prove what gentlemen they were.

Of course, Graham hadn't been any too pleased about the idea, Alice thought. She remembered how his eyes had nearly popped out of his head when he had seen Kelly wearing the dress for the first time, and he had dragged her from the room by her elbow and told her flatly that if he heard of Kelly doing anything more than dealing pharo, he'd hold Alice personally responsible. The look in his eye as he said it had made Alice fear to think what he might do to settle the account.

So he sat at the bar, not playing poker and not drinking, but just watching the pharo table for signs of trouble. It seemed to Alice that he flinched a little every time she smiled or laughed as she bantered with the players as though she were born to it.

Kelly was aware of him sitting there too. Although she had not heard what he'd said to Alice the other day and Alice had not said a word to her about it, Kelly had a pretty good idea what the trouble was. It was a little annoying that he thought her so dumb, but it warmed her that he was concerned over her welfare. After all, they had made it to Denver, and he had kept his word. He didn't have to feel a responsibility to her anymore.

That evening, Alice didn't close up until nearly dawn. By the time the last stragglers had been shoved out the door, Kelly was thoroughly beat. Alice and Lars cleaned up, and Kelly put her coat on. It was cold, and her dress had a low neckline.

"Let's go," Graham said. He had his coat on.

"Sure. Goodnight Alice, Lars," she called.

"G'night," Alice called back. Lars didn't answer; he was busy in the back room and didn't hear her.

Outside, the sky was still blue-black with the dark that heralds the hour before dawn. Graham took her arm and started for Alice's, walking so quickly that Kelly almost had to run to keep up with him.

"Slow down, will you?" She asked. "My legs aren't as long as yours."

He walked a little slower. She found she could keep up with him better, at any rate.

"You don't have to worry so much," she said. "I'm a little smarter than you give me credit for."

"It's not your smarts I doubt," Graham replied. "It's your understanding of how easily things can slip from one thing to another."

"That's something I've considered," Kelly said. "Alice warned me about it too. There's plenty of other ways for me to get by without turning to such means."

Kelly was glad of the dark, for she was blushing furiously. Graham seemed undisturbed by the conversation, and she was glad; it helped ease her embarrassment.

"Besides,"Kelly said. "I imagine it'll take years before they forget seeing you sitting at that bar staring them down like you do."

Graham didn't answer, and Kelly feared she had sounded ungrateful.

"Not that I don't appreciate it," she said. "I'm glad you're

there."
    They turned onto Alice's street. Kelly looked at Graham to see if he were angry. He didn't seem so. The light was uncertain, but he looked, well, he looked troubled, Kelly thought.
    They went in through the back door. Graham paused to shuck his boots, and Kelly took her coat off, waiting for him to come inside so they could finish talking.
    But when he came in, Graham looked just like his usual self. He tipped his hat to her, said goodnight and went to his room. Kelly sat at the table. There was something formal and distant about his saying goodnight that bothered her.
    She went to bed, thinking that she could figure her unease out better after some sleep, but as it turned out, sleep was hard to find that night, and when it came, it didn't help at all.

Chapter 19

The last days of November passed by and December was halfway over before Alice was able to get anymore clues to the mystery that lived in her house. Kelly did wonderfully at the pharo table, and Graham played poker and drank whiskey. They were friendly to each other, but Alice thought there was some fight between them. It seemed to her that Kelly was also puzzled by it but was too occupied with her new job to pursue the issue.

But that December night, Alice thought she caught a glimpse of what was troubling them. As usual, Kelly was at the pharo table and Graham was playing poker. Alice worked behind the bar with Lars and watched them both during her free moments.

Graham pulled up to the bar after his game broke up. He was minded to go back to Alice's and get some sleep, but it wasn't closing time yet, and he wanted to walk Kelly home. He stood at the far end of the bar near the back wall where he could keep a good eye on everything.

A tall, fat man dressed like a miner came up beside him and ordered a whiskey. Graham noticed with some irritation that he was staring at Kelly.

"I do like blonde-haired women," the miner said to him. "Thet one there looks as ripe as a peach."

Graham concealed his disgust; the man's breath was rank with whiskey and rotten teeth.

"I don't like a man who talks disrespectful of a lady," he said mildly.

The miner laughed.

"Ain't no ladies west of Kansas City," he said. "Though

there's some whores a mite fresher than others."

Graham grabbed him by the back of the shirt and the hair and slammed him face first into the wall. Blood sprayed. The miner yelled. Graham pulled him back from the wall and toward the door; the miner stumbled along screaming and grabbing his broken, bloody nose. Graham threw him out the door and into the street, then turned back into the saloon.

All conversation had ceased, and everyone stared at him as he straightened his collar and went back to his place at the bar. Conversation slowly started up again as it became apparent that the excitement was over.

Alice took the miner's whiskey glass away without comment, although she raised an eyebrow at Graham. He shrugged at her and went back to watching the crowd. It wasn't like he'd started a brawl or done a shooting, so what did she have to complain about?

The bar cleared out a little, and Alice walked over to him. She poured herself a drink and set the bottle on the bar between them. After looking at him a moment, she tossed her drink back. Graham didn't care for the look in her eye.

"So tell me, Mr. McNair," she said. "Just what are you doing dragging that girl all over creation?"

Graham picked up the bottle and poured himself a drink from it.

"I'm not dragging her anywhere," he said. "She's running away."

Alice snorted. "From what?"

Graham didn't answer for so long that Alice almost repeated the question.

"I don't know," he said, taking a sip of whiskey. "We've never discussed it."

Alice raised her eyebrows unbelievingly.

"I never figured you for the chivalrous type. Take her back to wherever you found her," she said. "You know she don't belong out here."

Alice watched Graham closely. There was never any telling how far he could be pushed, although Alice had noticed that Kelly could push him a lot further than anyone else dared.

"She doesn't belong back there either," he replied.

"Maybe not, but at least she won't get kilt."

Graham finished his whiskey and poured himself another. He did not answer her.

"I call it selfish," Alice said, her eyes glinting, "keeping her out here 'cause you can't stand to have her out of your sight."

It was a shot in the dark, and Alice watched to see how it would hit him. A twisted expression flitted swiftly across his face.

"I'm not keeping her anywhere," he said. "I couldn't keep her anywhere if I tried. Neither could you. Neither could anyone else, for that matter."

Graham sipped his whiskey and smiled inwardly at Alice's frustrated face.

"Talking with you is like fighting bees," she said. "You know damn well what I meant."

"I do?" He asked blandly.

Alice threw her hands in the air walked to the other end of the bar. They just didn't get any closer than Graham McNair. How could you argue with a man who never lost his temper?

Busy at the pharo table, Kelly had not seen what had happened, nor did she observe Alice's conversation with Graham. She was always a little surprised at how there was always a sizable crowd of players. Fortunately, they kept a respectful distance; most of them needed a bath. For the life of her, Kelly couldn't understand why men crowded into these smoky, smelly, dirty little saloons when there was the whole great big west just outside the door.

But they did, and they liked to play pharo even though they almost never won. Despite her dislike of the crowd, Kelly enjoyed running the pharo table and helping Alice out, even if she did wish Alice ran a livery stable instead of a saloon.

Dawn was fast approaching by the time Alice shooed the last stragglers out of the place. Kelly closed up the pharo table and sat at the bar. She noticed there was blood on the wall and wondered if it had something to do with the trouble earlier in the evening.

Graham sat beside her. The whiskey bottle that Alice had placed on the bar earlier in the evening was nearly empty. He set his glass down, thinking that he had been drinking entirely too much since their arrival in Denver.

"Win much tonight?" Kelly asked him.

"Enough."

Kelly noticed that his eyes were red and knew he'd been drinking quite a bit. That made it less use than usual to try to talk to him. She yawned and leaned on the bar.

"I'm going to go for a ride later today," she said. "Do you want to go with me?"

Graham shook his head. He never rode for entertainment.

"Are you angry at me over something?" She asked.

"No."

"Yes, you are," Kelly said. "And I wish you'd tell me about it so we can clear the air."

Alice stood at the other end of the bar, half-heartedly wiping glasses and wholeheartedly listening to their conversation.

"You ought to have asked me about this pharo dealing," Graham said.

Kelly considered it. Really, it was none of his business, but she could see where he might be offended by her thinking so.

"I didn't see where it would trouble you," Kelly said. "But I didn't mean to slight you, either."

She sat up and rubbed the back of her neck, which was sore from looking down at the pharo board all evening. She did not notice, but Graham watched her.

Her hands were small and fine and soft-looking, for all that he knew how strong and capable they were. The dress she was wearing showed off her neck and bosom, though it curved up around her shoulders. He wished that it didn't, then remembered the scar on her shoulder, and then, he still wished her shoulders showed. Scar or no scar, there was no doubt in his mind that her shoulders were as pretty as her hands.

Alice saw the path his eyes followed and nodded to herself. The girl did look good, and a man would have to be made of stone not to notice. Still, there was something more fleeting and less obvious than lust in his eyes. It was something that vanished so quickly Alice could not be sure whether she had imagined it or if it had really been there.

There was no more opportunity for observation that night. Graham stood abruptly and got both their coats, and then they were gone home. Alice shook her head, thinking on it. Alice had always been fascinated by people. In her opinion, even the dumbest, dirtiest sodbuster had something interesting about him. She prided herself on being able to ferret out those interesting things, no matter how close a person held them, but Kelly and Graham were a puzzlement to her.

At first glance, anyone would think they were together, but when you looked closer, it seemed they were apart.

Alice had known Graham for many years. She had talked with him, danced with him, drunk with him, and played poker with him, but she had never understood him, whereas Kelly seemed to read him like a book. Kelly knew when he wanted to be left alone and when he didn't. She knew how he thought about things and what was important to him. Of course, the girl tended to be contrary and often chose to act as though she didn't know these things, and it nettled Alice some to see that this girl from back east seemed to have figured him out well enough to have that luxury.

For his part, Graham became more animated around Kelly, although Alice doubted he realized it. Alice had seen the two of them talk all night, and Graham was a man who only talked when there were important things to say. He was also very protective of Kelly, a fact that he took pains to hide. He never tried to charm her (and Alice knew that he could be very charming when he wanted to), and he never complimented her.

Alice thought that, perhaps, he had tried such methods to get her attention and had failed. Since her arrival in Denver, Kelly had received such attention from many other men, but was entirely oblivious to it, as though she didn't see it and would not have known what it meant if she had seen it.

Alice had observed such scenes time and again as Kelly worked the pharo table, and it puzzled her. The girl was as hard to figure as McNair. She treated Graham in the same straightforward and often brusque way that she treated everyone. Still, Alice felt that Kelly was deeply attached to him, but she couldn't put her finger on why she thought so. Unless it was because of the interest she displayed in where he went and what he did and her careful attention to stories about his past adventures.

Alice had noticed that most people were frightened by or uncomfortable around quiet people. She herself was a little unsettled by Graham's quiet intensity, but it never bothered Kelly even remotely. Alice had never seen anyone dare to speak to Graham McNair the way Kelly Knowlton sometimes did. She had mentioned this to Kelly once, but Kelly had just looked puzzled, "Graham and I straightened all that out a long time ago," she had said. "I speak my mind, and if he doesn't like it, he tells me so." The fact that Graham was a renowned shootist seemed to carry no weight with her.

So Alice puzzled over these two, alert for any clues that would solve the mystery, and occasionally, she prodded one or the other of them for information. It was a frustrating procedure. Graham was quieter than a Sioux, and Kelly, for all that she was more open-natured, listened attentively when the conversation turned to Graham but volunteered nothing.

December and January passed much as November had. When the weather was bad, the three of them would gather in Alice's kitchen near the potbellied stove, drink coffee, and talk and eat biscuits and baked beans. After a while, Alice hardly listened to their conversations. They never talked about interesting things like the Indian raids on northern Kansas or the latest town gossip, nor did they ever talk about personal things. When the weather was good, Kelly would exercise the horses during the day and work the pharo table at night. So Alice had almost despaired of ever solving the riddle until one evening, when quite unexpectedly, she stumbled on the biggest clue she'd had yet.

The weather had been clear for nearly two weeks, and there was a good business at the bar that night because some travelers had come in from the east. Kelly kept the pharo table hopping until a big drunk miner lost his balance while playing, and in an effort to steady himself, grabbed the table and put his hand through the cue box.

Angered, Alice closed the table for the night. She would have to send all the way to St. Louis for another box. Kelly sat out at the bar. Alice's misfortune aside, she did not especially regret the accident, now she could have some time out of the smoke and away from the crowds. Graham was occupied with a high stakes poker game, and so Kelly sat alone, talking to Alice now and again.

One of the travelers, a young man of about twenty-four, left Graham's game and sat down near Kelly. Alice was waiting the bar and could hear their conversation. The young man had heard that Kelly was a wrangler and wanted advice about buying some horses from the local stock dealer. Graham had watched the stranger sit near Kelly, and his face had been as bland as ever as he looked back to his cards. But as their conversation stretched out, Alice noticed that Graham was paying less and less attention to the game and more and more to the conversation at the bar.

Alice was called to the other end of the bar to pour a whiskey. She talked with the customer, a very smelly trapper, for a few moments, and looked up as she heard Kelly laugh. Alice's eyes automatically darted over to Graham, who had looked up from his cards with the plainest expression of jealousy she had ever seen written on a human face. It was gone in a flash as he looked back at his cards, but Alice smiled smugly. He either loved Kelly or was so close to it that the difference didn't matter. And if that were the case . . .

Chapter 20

It had been a long day, and Kelly was tired. She'd talked with the young gentleman from Arkansas until dawn, then had taken both horses out for a ride. When she returned from exercising Graham's horse, the young man from Arkansas enlisted her to assist him with selecting four horses to buy from the stock dealer. Selecting the horses had been easy, but negotiating the sale had been hard and had taken several hours. It was now almost six o'clock as she trudged back to Alice's for a bath and a hot meal.

Alice and Graham were seated at the kitchen table eating when Kelly came in.

"Where've you been all day?" Graham asked as she removed her muffler.

"Out." Kelly was put off by his tone; he knew where she'd been.

Alice smiled to herself and kept her eyes on her plate. Kelly finished removing her wraps and poured herself some coffee.

"The wind is picking up," she said. "I wouldn't be surprised if it snowed before morning."

"Tends to happen in winter," Graham said. Kelly was ready to snap at him when Alice spoke.

"Did you enjoy your ride?" Alice asked.

"Yes. Oh by the way, Graham," Kelly said, "Your horse's legs are stocking up; he needs more exercise than the weather will permit. I'm going to have to rub them down every day, do you know where I can find some grease?"

Graham looked at her and said nothing. Kelly felt her face

flame. She set her cup down.

"You want to tell me why you're so testy this morning?" She asked.

"It's evening," Graham said. "Didn't you notice?"

"Whatever," Kelly said, irritated. "Did you lose your shirt last night to those squareheads?"

"No, they know less about cards than they do about horses."

"There's more to life than cards and horses," Alice broke in, watching Kelly closely. "And that handsome young man you were talking to sure seemed to have a case for you."

Kelly flushed and turned away from the table to remove her hat. Alice always picked the worst times to talk of such things. When she was composed again, she turned back around.

"Maybe. But he sure didn't know which end of a horse to feed," she said. "He wanted to pay two hundred dollars for four of Cyrus's nags. I told him there were mules worth more than those horses. We got him down to one twenty-five for the lot."

Kelly took a seat at the table and helped herself to a biscuit. Graham stared at her; Alice bit her lip to keep from laughing.

"I knew that's where you were," Graham muttered, half to himself.

"Well, if you knew," Kelly said, munching her biscuit, "Why did you ask?"

Graham's face went red. Alice coughed and hastily took a sip of coffee.

"I couldn't believe you took such an interest in squareheaded trash," he said nastily.

Goaded, Kelly threw her biscuit at him. It whizzed by his left ear and hit the wall behind him. Crumbs flew. He jumped to his feet, knocking his chair over. For a moment, Alice thought he was going to leap across the table.

"I ought to tan your hide!"

"I'd like to see you try!" Kelly shot back, leaping up.

But before either of them could say anything else, Alice burst into laughter. She gave herself up to it and laughed so hard that tears ran down her face. Graham left the room with as much dignity as he could muster. Kelly heard him stomp out the back door and slam it behind him, and her anger gave way to bewilderment. She never understood what was going on with these people.

Alice was still laughing, so Kelly got herself another biscuit and a few pieces of bacon and began to eat. Her stomach was upset from fighting with Graham, but that would pass, and besides, she was starving. Alice's laughter didn't particularly interest her, especially since she had the idea that it was directed toward Graham, not her.

Alice's laughter tapered off to giggles, and she wiped her eyes. Kelly finished her biscuit and took some more bacon. She wished now that she hadn't thrown her first biscuit at Graham, because there were none left, and she was still hungry.

"Poor Mr. McNair," Alice said now that she was finally over her laughing fit and able to speak.

"Well, he deserved it," Kelly said around a mouthful of bacon. "He's got no cause to speak to me so."

"Don't he?" Alice asked.

"No one does," Kelly said flatly. "I don't know what gets into him sometimes. He acts right addled."

"You get into him, I reckon," Alice said.

"Not unless he provokes me," Kelly replied, misunderstanding her.

"That's not what I meant," Alice said, rising to clear the table.

Kelly didn't answer. She was busy cutting a piece from the cheese on the table.

"Don't you want to know what I meant?" Alice asked her.

"I guess you'll tell me whether I want to know or not," Kelly said. "Go on, I'm listening."

Alice passed over her rudeness.

"He's been irritable ever since your conversation with that man last night," Alice said. "He got downright bearish when he figured out where you were all day."

Kelly frowned and chewed her cheese contemplatively.

"That doesn't make any sense. He must just have a headache or something."

"Honey, I saw him look at the two of you last night with as jealous a face as I've ever seen a man wear."

Kelly was silent. She could not think what that meant to her. It was pleasing, because that meant he did care, but . . .

"The man has a case for you, dear," Alice said, interrupting her thoughts. "He hides it well, but it's there."

Kelly shook her head.

"No, you're imagining things. You think everyone has a case for me. He's never said a word about it."

"Not everyone says what's on their mind," Alice said. "Graham's used to wearing a poker face."

Kelly considered it a moment, then pushed the thought away. If it was true, the last thing she needed was for Alice to know.

"You're wrong," she said, finishing her cheese. "Are there any more biscuits?"

"No, but there's plenty of bread and butter."

"I'll have some after my bath," Kelly said.

Alice watched her leave the room and sighed. It seemed Graham wasn't the only one who kept a good poker face.

"The poor man," she said aloud to the empty kitchen, "He finally falls in love, and it's with a woman who throws biscuits at him."

She started to giggle as she did the dishes.

Chapter 21

Later that night, Kelly sat in the parlor by the fire reading a newspaper. Graham and Alice were both at the saloon. The outside temperature had dropped considerably, and Kelly was wrapped in Alice's big shawl and had pulled her chair as close to the hearth as she could so her hair would dry faster.

She was very tired but knew that she would not be able to sleep for a while. Her mind kept chasing the thought that Alice had put into it. The newspaper provided little distraction; nothing in it seemed to hold her attention for very long.

She had never tried to analyze her feelings before, or anyone else's for that matter. In fact, she couldn't remember ever having been in a situation that demanded it. At home, things had been very simple. Her grandfather loved her, and he showed it by letting her do as she pleased and saying nice things to her. Her father didn't love her, and he showed it by ignoring her or criticizing her when it wasn't possible to ignore her. The stable hands respected her, and they showed it by obeying her promptly and without fussing.

But now, things were complicated. No matter how she might act or what she might say, she privately thought that Graham was the most handsome, smartest, bravest man she'd ever known. For some reason, these feelings made her feel very shy; nothing in her life had taught her how to deal with them. So despite the fact that, under any other circumstances, she would say anything to anybody, Kelly would rather bite her tongue off than indicate by word or action what her feelings for Graham McNair were.

And it hadn't mattered until now, because she was convinced

that Graham didn't care that much for her anyway. He felt obligated, she thought, because she had helped him back in New York and had since taken a bullet for him. It had never occurred to her that he might feel for her the way she felt about him—until the conversation she'd had with Alice that evening.

She thought over his actions toward her, but couldn't see anything that went beyond friendship. She had to admit, though, that he was not the kind of person to allow himself to be obligated unless he wanted to be. He could have left her after finding out she wasn't really going to San Francisco, but he hadn't. He could leave her now; she was safe and able to take care of herself, but so far he had shown no signs of wanting to go anywhere.

Alice was smart about these things, and Kelly knew that she herself was not. She also knew Alice wouldn't lie about such a thing; if she said it, it had to be so—or at least she really believed it to be so—but it just seemed so impossible.

True, she was pretty, but she wore pants a lot of the time and worked with horses and played poker and cussed when she felt like it. She also spoke her mind and didn't mind arguing. Kelly knew, from her many despairing governesses, that ladies were supposed to wear dresses and corsets and bustles. Ladies only rode gentle horses, and when they did, they rode sidesaddle. Ladies spoke softly, blushed when men were profane, and always deferred to the opinions of others. It went without saying that ladies never played poker or were themselves profane.

Kelly also knew that, since she had run away, the traits that her father and governesses had so greatly deplored had only become more prominent because there wasn't any point in being a lady when there were no gentlemen around. It did not occur to her that there were men worth having who had no interest in ladies.

Sleep began to creep up on her. The newspaper slipped from her hands, and her head rested on her shoulder. Her thoughts became more confused and vague, and the last image that sat in her mind before sleep finally claimed her was that of Graham putting his arm around her as they had walked away from Phoenix's lifeless body.

Graham left the saloon a little after two. It was a slow night and he had not been able to concentrate on his card playing anyway. He had spent the last hour drinking at the bar. Every so often, Alice would stop by and needle him over Kelly, which only made him drink more. He'd acted the fool earlier, but it wouldn't have mattered if Alice hadn't been there. Since she had been, she was prepared to rub his nose in it. It seemed to him that he would have to move to a hotel, and his practical mind told him that he should have done so weeks ago.

But he hadn't. Now, as he approached the house, he was surprised to see a lamp glowing in the front room. He frowned to himself; Kelly should have gone to bed a long time ago; she hadn't had any sleep since the morning before last.

He went in through the kitchen and removed his coat, hat, and gloves and shucked his boots off, then he went in to see what she was up to. He found her asleep in Alice's big rocking chair. From the newspaper that lay on the floor, he gathered that she had fallen asleep while reading.

Noiselessly, he approached her. She didn't stir, which meant she must be deeply asleep. Her forehead was puckered in small frown that he found somehow charming. The firelight made her skin glow and got caught in the highlights of her hair. After looking at her for a few moments, he picked up the newspaper, put it on the settee, and turned the kerosene lamp off. Then he squatted beside the chair and, very gently, shook her arm.

Kelly stirred, and her frown deepened. Graham let go of her arm and watched her. She stirred again, then her eyes blinked. She saw Graham, and her frown disappeared. She stretched in the chair, yawning.

"What time is it?" She asked sleepily.

"After two," he replied softly. "You ought to be in bed."

"Mmm. Yeah." Her eyes closed again, and Graham thought she had gone back to sleep.

"Did Alice close up early?" She asked, her eyes still closed.

"No. Listen, Kelly . . ."

She opened her eyes and looked at him; she seemed a little more awake.

"I'm sorry about this afternoon," he said, still whispering.

"It's all right," Kelly said, surprised that he had apologized. "I didn't mean to throw that biscuit at you, either."

"You don't have to apologize for that," Graham said.

"I'm not," she said, snuggling further into the shawl. "You deserved it."

She closed her eyes again, intending to nap some more, but Graham had taken her arm, and with gentle pressure, he pulled her toward him. Kelly's eyes opened in surprise, but she was hypnotized by the look on his face and did not protest.

She slid forward out of the chair, and somehow, she found herself sitting on his lap, and he was holding her in his arms. She looked up at his face and wondered if he was going to kiss her; she was so comfortable and felt so good that she didn't really care whether he did or not. If anyone had ever told her that she could feel so peaceful, she wouldn't have believed it. She looked up at his face and into his eyes, and suddenly, she knew that what Alice had said was true. He did love her, no matter how he acted. She closed her eyes as his head bent down over her, and he began to kiss her.

His lips were soft and warm and tasted like whiskey and coffee—and like himself. It was a strange feeling, but one she knew she liked, and her arms went around his neck. Even the rough wool of his suit jacket felt somehow comfortable, even if only because it was a part of him.

Graham pulled her as close to himself as he could. After a few moments, he pulled away from her a little and leaned back against the settee, pulling her to his chest. He began to stroke her hair, which was loose and flowing down her back; it was even softer than he had ever thought. He wondered briefly how he had gotten himself into such a position, then decided that he didn't care and bent to kiss her some more.

If being kissed had seemed strange to Kelly, she had gotten used to it quickly. Now it only seemed exciting, and she began to kiss him back. Graham held her face in his hands, and Kelly shivered as one of his hands slipped from her cheek down her neck until it rested inside her robe on the curve of her shoulder.

She moved closer to him, fascinated by the feel and the smell of him. She ran her fingers though his hair, then rested one hand on his chest, distantly surprised to feel the pounding of his heart.

His lips left hers, and she felt them brush her neck, kissing her all the way to the base of her throat. She gasped a little as he paused there, then felt him stiffen and stop abruptly as the kitchen door banged open.

His head came up and he looked past Kelly to the parlor door. Now they could hear Alice swearing and banging around in the kitchen. Kelly felt suddenly empty as his hand left her shoulder.

"You'd better get to your room before she comes in here," Graham said. "Sounds like she had some trouble after I left."

Kelly couldn't have cared less about whatever Alice was angry over, and she didn't care if Alice walked in and caught them like this. But it didn't matter. Looking at Graham's watchful face, she could see that the moment had passed and there was no point in pursuing it.

She stood up and padded silently out of the room, down the hall and into her own room. The door leading from the kitchen into the hall was ajar, but not enough for Alice to see her.

Back in the parlor, Graham sat before the fire feeling dazed. He wanted so much from Kelly. He wanted her companionship and her affection and every bit of her willful, mouthy self. He wanted her love, and he knew she would give it to him—that and anything else he wanted. But he did not feel able to ask for it. It would be like betraying her trust, and maybe, he thought in a confused way, it would be a little too much like incest.

He hadn't meant for any of it to happen, but it had. He had wanted to apologize to her and to get her to go to sleep. But she had sat there looking so beautiful and had smart mouthed him so easily that he had just forgotten what he was doing.

Then she had been so warm and had felt so good that he hadn't been able to stop until Alice's sudden return had startled him back to his senses. There was something to be said for making a strategic retreat in good order.

But like any retreat, it carried with it a sense of loss. Hearing Alice slam the door to her room, he stood and slipped noiselessly into his own room. The last thing he needed was for Alice to see him with his hair all over and his collar askew. He'd never hear the end of it.

Chapter 22

Kelly slept until late the next day. The weather was clear and cold, and it had snowed some during the night. She didn't particularly want to go to the saloon, but knew Alice would expect her to. So she dressed lazily and went down to the kitchen, where she found Alice stirring up the fire.

"Good afternoon," Kelly said. "How'd it go last night?"

"Well enough," Alice said, straightening up. "You're up late."

"I was beat."

"Coming to the saloon tonight?"

"Yes."

"Well, it'll be some days before I can get a new cue box for the pharo table. You'll have to stick to poker."

"It doesn't matter," Kelly said. "Has Graham been up yet?"

"He was up and out, then he came back an hour ago and said he was going to bed. I reckon we won't have the pleasure of his company tonight."

Kelly felt relieved. She fixed herself something to eat. Just after dark, she and Alice went down to the saloon.

It was a quiet evening, and Kelly found playing cards somehow relaxing. She didn't win or lose much either way, but it was good entertainment. Alice closed up just before dawn, but instead of walking home with her, Kelly dawdled on a small rise behind the saloon, watching the sun creep up over the horizon. It was bitterly cold, and so, she started to hurry home before the pink streaks in the sky had completely banished the darkness.

She started up the back steps just as the door opened and

Graham stepped out. Startled, she saw that he was carrying his traveling things.

"Good morning," he said, his voice sounding just as it usually did.

"Where are you going?" Kelly blurted out.

"Kansas."

"But it's the middle of January!"

"Set down here for a second," he said, sitting down on the steps.

Reluctantly, Kelly sat beside him. This had to be bad news if he had to say it sitting down.

"Remember how I told you to never push your luck too far?"

"What are you talking about?" Kelly asked, wondering what playing poker had to do with his going to Kansas.

"You can come with me if you want," he went on as if she had not spoken, "but I think it would be best if you didn't."

Kelly thought for a moment. If she went to Kansas, she never would get to ride up into the mountains.

"If you go, will I ever see you again?" She asked, remembering the vastness of the plains they had crossed. It seemed in impossible to find another person in that immense ocean of grass.

"Kansas isn't that far," he said.

No, it wasn't that far, but it wasn't exactly close either. Kelly shifted uncomfortably on the step. Her rear end was freezing. She thought about going to Kansas and what it would mean. Spending her days dealing pharo and playing poker in a lot of dirty saloons held no attraction for her, and now that her surprise at his leaving had worn out, she realized that, somehow, it was a relief to her. She was uncomfortable with the way he made her feel. It had all seemed simple enough the night before last, but in the broad daylight, it made her nervous and uneasy. As much as she would miss him, it seemed like she ought to let him go.

"I guess I should stay here, or else I'll never get into the mountains," she said at last.

"Kansas is pretty flat," Graham said, standing up. He was neither surprised nor disappointed at her decision, for now that it was made, it seemed like he had always known what her answer would be.

Suddenly he grinned at her—the same grin he'd given her the first time she'd seen him. It was impossible not to grin back, and so she did.

"Goodbye," she said. "Steer clear of rivers and Pinkerton men."

"Good advice for us both," he replied. Then he turned and walked away down the street.

Kelly stifled the impulse to run after him. Instead, she

watched him until he disappeared over the hill at the end of the street. Then she went into the house. Alice was sitting at the table. She generally went straight to bed after such a long night, but she couldn't believe that Graham was going to up and leave in the middle of winter. From the look on Kelly's face, however, Alice knew that he had.

Kelly sat down without a word. There was a pit in her stomach, and she felt ill. It seemed impossible, when you considered it, that this time last year she hadn't even known Graham McNair had existed, and yet now, his leaving made her feel so terrible. What had happened?

"Why did he want to leave?" She asked Alice plaintively. Alice always knew the answers to questions like that.

"I guess his wandering foot got to itching," Alice said although she knew it wasn't true. If ever she'd seen a man in full retreat, it was Graham McNair this morning, but she had no idea of how it had come about.

But now Kelly had gotten a better grip on herself, and she thought that she understood a little of it.

"I guess I shouldn't have kissed him," she said aloud before realizing it probably wasn't a good idea to say such a thing in front of Alice.

"What's all this?" Alice asked. "What happened?"

It was too late to unsay it, and Kelly was too troubled to think of some plausible lie, so she found herself telling Alice what had happened the night before last. Alice nodded sympathetically and revealed none of the amazement she felt.

"Well honey, I don't know," Alice said at last. "Some men would just rather be off by themselves, I reckon."

Kelly thought it was more than that, but a new thought occurred to her, one that distracted her from her hurt, at least temporarily. She was on her own now. She could go anywhere she wanted and do anything she wanted. She longed to strike out toward the mountains and see the wild places that until now she had only heard about.

"It's more than that, I guess," Kelly said as she stood and removed her coat and boots. "But it doesn't matter. I'm going west in the spring, to see the mountains." As she spoke her eyes were distant, as if she were already on her way.

Alice shook her head. It was no wonder McNair was so taken with Kelly. The girl was just as crazy as he was.

As Alice was shaking her head over the situation, Graham was riding out of town and into the frozen plains. When Denver was nothing but a speck on the horizon, he reined his horse in and turned for a final look back.

He had no doubts about leaving; he knew it was the right thing to do. Sometimes distance helped. It was hard to ride with someone for nearly a year and not feel a solidarity with them, especially when the ride was as wild as the one he and Kelly had made from New York to Denver. It was understandable that he would feel a certain affection for her and that she would feel some for him.

It was understandable, but it would fade with time and the right amount of distance. The poker games and the wild times would distract him, and he would be himself again. His temper would once more be his own, and there would be no one who could make him act against his own will and better judgment just by looking at him.

There was no need to worry about Kelly; there never really had been such a need. She had the strength and determination to live as she choose, and now that she was free of her past she would have whatever wild times were in store for her. It was all as it should be.

Graham wheeled his horse back around east and continued on his way, thinking that it was January and a new year. 1873 had been wild, he thought, and while the omens had been right about that, they had given him no clue about the manner of that wildness or about the tugging he felt in his heart the farther he rode from Denver.

Chapter 23

Graham passed that next year marshaling in a Kansas cow town—a town so beset by its rowdier element that its citizens actively sought a shootist of deadly reputation to keep the peace. Graham wasn't sure that peace was much worth keeping, but they paid him well to try, and he had been successful at it.

But it wasn't the kind of living that held his interest for long, and when the warmer weather had beckoned again, he had turned in his badge and ridden off without a regret or a backward look. Now Graham squatted by a fire, sipping his coffee. The night was as clear as glass and as fine as anyone could wish for in early spring. The moon was small and new and gave off little light.

He considered where to go next. Leaving off with marshaling had been as much a matter of common sense as it had been a matter of boredom. Wearing a badge was like wearing a target on your chest, and besides, if he ever succeeded in really cleaning the town up, he knew the decent folks would see to it that he was next on the gallows.

The way he saw it, the decent folk let the army clear out the Indians, and they let the miners and the gamblers and the whores go to the wild places and start the towns, then they moved in with their stores and their churches and their laws and tried to regulate everything. In his opinion, everything east of the Ohio river was already a graveyard, and in another fifty years or so, the rest of the country would be too.

That's why he'd quit the army, aside from being tired of military life. The slaughter of the plains Indians had sickened him. Why clear out the Indians for a lot of farms and courthouses? Didn't they have enough of such things back east?

His eyes left the flames, and he looked around the fringes of the firelight. His horse dropped to its knees and rolled onto its back, kicking its legs up in the air. With a snort and a grunt, it hauled itself back to its feet and shook itself. It put him in mind of the day he and Kelly had crossed the Little Powan river. He remembered turning around and seeing her horse's legs waving in the air. It had given him quite a turn.

Graham set his coffee cup down and rubbed his chin thoughtfully. He wondered if Kelly were still in Denver with Alice. He doubted it, but he thought he might as well head that way and see. It would be interesting to hear what she had been up to this past year. During his marshaling, he'd kept his ears open for news of her, but if she had stayed in Colorado, it wasn't likely that any news of her would travel so far east. Most travelers in Kansas came up from the south these days.

The moon was about to set. Graham made sure the fire was well banked, then stretched out on his blankets, but sleep did not come easily. Sometimes, it seemed to him, if you started out thinking about something, your mind would not let you alone about it.

The day Graham headed west for Colorado, Kelly stood in a stock dealer's yard looking at horses. After leaving Denver the previous May, she had made some good money racing Arnie and had sold him for two hundred dollars in mid-July. With that money she had bought a shorter, sturdier horse, outfitted herself, and ridden into the mountains.

She had not come down until the weather turned bad and even then did not leave the mountains entirely. She spent that winter in an abandoned cabin in the foothills and had made some money by hunting and then selling the meat to a mining town below.

Now it was early summer, and her horse had gone lame. As Kelly had never thought too much of him anyway, she had decided to sell him lame, even though it would lower the price that she would get for him, and find a horse with a little more style. She had ridden out of the high country less than two weeks ago. It was something to have the mountains swelling all around you, but it was something else to be in the midst of people. Kelly wasn't yet sure which she preferred.

She turned her attention to a paddock filled with horses of all descriptions. They were milling about, and it was hard to get a good look at them. As she walked closer to the paddock, a short, wiry man with a bristling beard approached her.

"Looking fer a horse miss?"

Kelly nodded.

"Well, we got aplenty of 'em," the man said. "Lemme know if you want to see one up close."

Kelly surveyed the horses. There didn't seem anything special, and she reminded herself that she should have expected such. She cast her eyes about one last time, and they fell on a horse penned up alone.

It was a smallish mare, not over fifteen hands, but strong, with powerfully muscled haunches. Her dirty, matted coat was reddish-brown flecked with gray and marked with large black spots. For all that the mare was well-built and had a proud arch to her neck, Kelly had never seen such an outlandish looking animal.

"What about that mare?" She asked.

"Thet horse is mean, ma'am," answered the man. "Been with the Indians, I reckon."

Kelly looked the mare over more carefully. The animal definitely had a wild look in its eye. When Kelly stepped closer, the mare snorted and laid her ears back. It wasn't hard to see she was ready to bite anyone who came into the paddock.

"Give me a rope," Kelly said.

"You'll get bit," he warned her.

"Give me a rope. How much do you want for her?"

"I'll git the boss," the man said, handing her the rope then scurrying over to the barn.

Kelly fashioned one end of the rope into a hackamore. The wrangler came back with his boss.

"We ain't been able to get a saddle on that mare," the boss said to Kelly. "You better come have a look over here, we got some fine . . ."

"How much do you want for her?" Kelly interrupted.

The boss looked Kelly up and down for a moment.

"One hundred dollars," he said grandly.

"Tell you what," Kelly said. "I'll bet you a hundred dollars against that mare that I can ride her."

The boss laughed.

"That's no bet atall," he said. "You'll just be payin' a hundred dollars for a broke neck."

"Is it a bet then?" She asked.

"Sure enough."

They shook on it. Kelly went over to the paddock and climbed the fence. The other stable hands and a few idlers were gathering to watch, and she could hear them placing bets of their own.

Kelly jumped lightly down from the fence and into the paddock. One of the wranglers called after her, asking if she wanted her saddle, but she hardly heard him. She was concentrating on the mare, and she knew it was no good trying to use a saddle. There was a way to every horse; finding it was a matter of sensitivity, patience, and firmness. In this case, Kelly knew that this horse could be dangerous and that she could not afford to be careless.

She approached the mare slowly but confidently from the off side. The mare saw her and rolled her eyes, sidestepping for a few paces, but Kelly did not hesitate. When she was close enough, she patted the mare's neck with one hand, then took a handful of mane. The mare tossed her head, snorted and stepped away. Kelly stepped with her, then with her other hand, she pulled the hackamore over the mare's nose and up over her ears.

Quick as lightening, the mare snapped her head around and bit at Kelly, who, although she had expected the mare to bite, could not jerk her arm away fast enough. The mare bit her hard on her upper left arm.

Kelly gritted her teeth and did not cry out, although the bite was painful enough to bring tears to her eyes and make her stomach turn over. She could hear the bettors laughing. The mare shied away from her now, but Kelly kept hold of the end of the rope. She followed the mare, keeping the rope slack so the horse wouldn't feel her at the end of it.

When the mare stood still again, Kelly again approached her from the right side; she knew that, as a precaution against horse thieves, Indians frequently trained their horses to only take a rider from that side. She stood by the mare's flank for a second, then, taking a grip on her mane, swung lightly onto her back.

The mare stood stock still for a second; Kelly found her seat quickly. She could feel that every muscle in the mare's body was rigid. The mare bucked twice explosively; Kelly kept her weight low and didn't try to grip with her legs. After a short but wild ride, the mare came back to earth and stood as if in doubt. Kelly patted her neck. She knew the mare was puzzled because she was not used to having so light a rider on her back and because Kelly had not yet tried to bully her.

While she was undecided, Kelly sat still, waiting for her to buck again. When it seemed the mare had accepted the situation, Kelly squeezed her gently with her legs. The mare kicked with her back legs and sidestepped, but Kelly maintained the pressure until she began to walk forward. She walked the mare around the paddock for a few minutes and decided that was enough for one day. Kelly tugged the hackamore until the mare stood, then she slid to the ground, alert in case the mare tried to bite or kick. Kelly removed the hackamore, and the mare did try to bite her again, but this time, Kelly jumped back in time.

She walked warily out of the paddock, thinking that it was entirely possible that the mare would attack her now that she was afoot.

There was some cheering as Kelly climbed the paddock fence. The stable boss rushed forward and shook her hand.

"You just won yourself a horse, young lady," he said. "Don't know why you want such an animal, but she's yours."

"Can I keep her here for a while?" Kelly asked. "She needs some work yet."

"Sure can. As long as you like, free of charge, too. I ain't seen anything like that in twenty years of horse dealing. If you want a job, I could put you on at good wages."

"Thanks. Let me think on it," Kelly replied, unsure of how long she wanted to stay in town.

The small gathering of spectators was dispersing, since all bets had changed hands, and Kelly was suddenly reminded of her throbbing arm. Her shirt was bloody. She felt the bite gingerly and winced. The mare's meanness did bother her, indeed, it could be useful, but the animal had to learn not to bite her and to wear a saddle. Kelly thought she could accomplish both tasks in a month or two.

She decided to take the job. It probably wouldn't pay well, but it would pay enough, and it would give her plenty of opportunity to work with the mare. The work itself couldn't be anything that she hadn't done before, and Kelly had to admit that she had missed horses a lot more than she had missed people over the past months.

Occasionally, she wished Alice were around. Alice was the one thing that had made leaving Denver difficult for Kelly. Although Kelly didn't realize it until the winter she'd spent in the high country, Alice was the only female friend that she had ever had. Alice might have been a little bossy, but her bossiness sprang from genuine concern over Kelly's well being.

That had been a little hard to keep in mind when the time had come for Kelly to go. Alice had watched her prepare to leave, confident that Kelly would change her mind at the last moment and stay.

But that hadn't happened, and on the morning Kelly left, she made a last ditch attempt to talk Kelly into staying. She had told Kelly of all the dangers in going, the advantages in staying, and that getting over a man could be done in easier ways.

"That's got nothing to do with it," Kelly had said, interrupting her. "This is what I want to do, and I'm going to do it, so you might as well get used to the idea."

Alice had fallen silent. Kelly wasn't stupid; she knew what she was getting into. Obviously, she wasn't going to be able to change the girl's mind.

"I'm sorry for speaking so to you," Kelly had gone on. "But all this fuss is trying my patience. I'm very grateful to you for helping me out this winter, but I'm going to strike out on my own now and see what there is to be seen."

Alice had shaken her head.

"It weren't no trouble to me to have you here," she had said. "You paid your own way and then some. But you ain't got to prove anything to anyone, and I'd be pleased if you'd stay on here."

"I appreciate it," Kelly had replied, her voice softening. "But I'm going to go anyway. I do want to ask a favor, though."

"What?"

"Hold on to my savings for me," Kelly had asked. "I've been building up for that horse farm I'm going to have someday, and I hate to run around with so much money on me."

"Don't you trust banks?"

Kelly had shaken her head, remembering how she had hooked up with Graham.

"Well, sure," Alice had replied.

So Kelly had given her the fifteen hundred dollars that she had saved. Alice hid it in her wardrobe, relieved that Kelly seemed to have some kind of plan to her wildness. Maybe that would keep her out of the kinds of trouble that tended to happen when a person wandered around aimless.

They had walked outside together. It had been a cloudy day, and Alice had hugged her tearfully in parting.

"Don't take no more risks than you need to," Alice had said.

"Don't you, either."

Kelly had ridden off feeling a little sad but knowing that she could return to Denver anytime she wanted. Privately, she doubted that Alice would ever make it very far east. Since Alice was rooted to one spot, Kelly felt certain of finding her again, unlike Graham, who wandered about at whim, and who she didn't really think would ever turn up again.

Despite what he had said, she felt that he was gone for good. The world was just too big, and he had gone too far away. For all that, her thoughts had often turned to him—where he had gone and what he might be doing. But despite the realization that she missed him, she never felt lonely. There was something about the clarity and immenseness of the high country that had kept her from feeling much alone, aside from an occasional wish that she had someone to talk about it with.

Now that she had come back down, her work at the livery stable kept her far too busy to miss anyone. There were just two wranglers, herself and a tall, lanky man from Texas named Shubel Ratchford. Most of the stable's business came from selling horses to ranchers and to the army, and they dealt mostly in wild and half-wild horses that wouldn't take a rider without a lot of persuasion. There was rarely less than thirty horses on the place.

Kelly and Shu did all the breaking, and there was a lamed-up old man named Ernie to do the stable work, of which there wasn't much. The place's one barn was reserved for boarders and only had ten stalls.

By the end of August, Kelly had halfway decided to stay on through the winter. Work would slow down some then, and she was making some good money at night by playing cards and by day through betting on who could ride a breaking horse longer. She and Shu never bet against each other on such things; they never had to because there were generally some no-account idlers loitering around and watching them work, eager for a bet. It did not occur to Kelly that she had been the talk of the town since her arrival in June.

There was such a crowd of maybe four or five loungers, as she called them, on a fiercely hot day at the end of August. Since neither Kelly or Shu had the time to work any bets that day, Kelly ignored them entirely as she sat on the fence of the breaking corral and watched Shu's struggles with a little dun pony that was throwing itself around in an attempt to dislodge him.

"Keep his head up!" Kelly shouted.

Shubel either didn't hear her or ignored her advice. The pony got his head down between his front legs and kicked straight up in the air with all four feet off the ground. He twisted hard in mid-air, and Shubel came tumbling down to earth with a thud.

It was an amazing thing to see, how such a small pony could kick so high and dislodge so heavy a rider. Kelly was speechless from having witnessed it. Shubel, who did not seem to be hurt, jumped to his feet, cursing, as the pony continued to buck, eventually coming to rest as far from him as the fence would allow.

"Hey, Shu," Kelly called. "Let me give 'em a try."

"Go right ahead," Shubel replied. "They ain't payin' me fer a broke neck."

Kelly hopped down off the fence. Shubel caught the pony by the reins.

Kelly adjusted the stirrups, then paused to focus for a moment before mounting.

"Get up there quick," Shubel said. "And once yer up, grab hold fast."

The advice was good. The instant her rear end hit the saddle, the pony renewed its contortions. It was a wild ride, but not a scary one. It required attention to the pony's tensing haunches and twisting head. Kelly kept him from lowering his head as much as possible, preventing him from getting all the strength of his powerful hind legs into his bucking.

After a few minutes, he began to tire. His bucking became less powerful and more sporadic. At last, he stopped bucking and started trotting nervously around the paddock, kicking with his back legs occasionally.

Kelly let him trot until, tired from his exertions and nervousness, he began to walk.

"Ride 'em out Kelly," Shu called to her. "Else he'll forget by tomorrow."

Kelly walked the pony over to where Shu sat on the fence. She meant to ask him if he'd take over, but instead, her eyes fixed on a figure standing by the barn door. He was wearing traveling clothes instead of his familiar black suit, but it was Graham.

Kelly flinched and looked away, prodding the pony into a canter. The pony bucked twice in protest, but Kelly rode it out and cantered him around the paddock several times. He would not keep a consistent gait, and Kelly worked him around until he was sweating and too tired to argue further.

"I reckon that'll do it for today," she said to Shubel, who opened the gate for her. "He'll be ready to sell by the end of the week."

Shubel nodded and went off to get another horse. Kelly rode to the barn; Graham stepped up to her as she made the pony stop.

He grinned up at her, and her initial awkwardness slipped away. She grinned back.

"This is a bit far west for you, stranger," she said.

"You can't get too far west, in my opinion," he replied. "Come on down from there before you get your neck broke."

"Oh, he's too tired for such things now," Kelly said. "Though he'll be fussy again in the morning."

"I hear you're working a steady job," Graham said. "Good wages?"

Kelly shook her head.

"Not to speak of, but it keeps me out of trouble. Besides, I need a place to work my new horse. She's too raw to trust."

"She? I thought you didn't like mares."

"I don't, in general, but wait until you see this one," Kelly said, dismounting. "A real Indian pony."

Kelly lead the pony into the barn; Graham followed them. He had watched all of her ride and privately thought she was asking for a broken neck by working at such a job. He did not say so because she would take it as a slight to her wrangling abilities.

He could not help but think that she looked different than she had when he'd first seen her in New York. Then she had been self-confident and aggressive, and she still was, but there was also a dangerous air about her. From long experience, he knew that successful living in the wild places bred such an air, though many lived all their lives and never developed it. It was no surprise to see that Kelly had adopted it so quickly.

She unsaddled the pony and started brushing it down.

"So what have you been up to all this time?" She asked.

"Marshaling over in Kansas," he replied, sitting down on a hay bale.

"Really? How did that come about?"

"Mostly through the town being full of people worse than me."

His tone was jesting. Kelly smiled.

"Oh, you aren't so bad. When'd you start west again?"

"Last month," he said, hoping she wouldn't ask him why. "Where all have you been?"

"I left Denver last May," Kelly said, knocking the brush against the wall to clean it. "I traveled 'till July then went up into the mountains for a while."

She paused, thinking of it. Suddenly, staying in this dirty little town through the winter was seemed less attractive.

"I came down a bit for the winter and packed meat for a mining camp," she went on. "Come spring, I came into this place for a horse and got this job."

"I hope they pay you as well as you work," he commented.

"Hardly," Kelly said. "When'd you ride in?"

"This morning."

"Didn't take you long to find me," she mused.

"I'd be stupid if it took any longer," Graham replied. "You're the only thing anyone in this town talks about except whiskey and gold dust."

Kelly felt the pony's chest to see if he were cool.

"Idlers." She said. "It's no wonder they've got nothing else to talk about. They never do anything."

She lead the pony from the barn. Graham followed her. She turned the pony loose in a large paddock and shut the gate after him.

"How long are you working?" Graham asked her.

"Until six. Where are you staying?"

"Mame's Hotel."

"Me too," Kelly said. "Watch what she charges you. She never serves meat for breakfast."

"Play any cards lately?"

"Now and then," Kelly said. "You won't find it hard to make a living. These miners like to play when they're drunk. But they do get short tempered when they loose."

"Most do," said he. "Have you run into any trouble?"

Kelly shook her head.

"Are you coming back to Mame's for dinner?" He asked.

"Sure."

"I'll see you then," he said. "Maybe we'll go play some cards later."

"All right," Kelly said.

He left the stock yard. Kelly turned back to her work. Shu had roped the next horse and tied him to the stake in the center of the breaking pen. He would need her help to get the saddle on; she ran over and climbed the fence.

Graham walked back toward the center of town. On his way in that morning, he had noticed a bath house not far from where they were staying. He decided to buy a change of clothes and a bath, remembering suddenly how ripe a long ride tended to make a man.

That evening and every evening for the next two weeks, they worked the saloons and card games together. Kelly had been too preoccupied to get around the town much, and now she was surprised to see exactly how much it had grown since summer had begun. She was also surprised to find that it took no time to get used to Graham's company again, despite the solitary life she had lead since having left Denver.

But the late nights and long days began to tire her. Graham suggested that she quit her wrangling job, but Kelly balked at this. He never seemed to understand that she wrangled because she liked to, and she played cards mostly because he liked to.

Halfway through September, he announced that he intended to head back for Denver. Kelly decided to go with him. She wanted to see Alice again and give her the money that she'd saved over the past year and a half. Besides, she was tired of the town and was not yet ready to go back out on her own.

Graham was pleased when she told him she wanted to go along. Though tired of the mining town, he was not tired of her company. He was a little unsettled by how untired of her company he was, but he put it down to having lived almost respectably during the time he had been marshaling. Such things could turn a man's mind.

So Kelly quit her job and said goodbye to Shu, who genuinely regretted her leaving. He had worked with few people who worked as hard and as uncomplainingly as she did. She never shirked and never showed up drunk.

Their first night out, Kelly and Graham camped early. Kelly's mare had to be hobbled because she kept trying to attack Graham's horse. Graham didn't like the mare and thought Kelly was crazy for having her but said nothing about it. Although he knew that Kelly wouldn't agree with him, he personally believed that life was dangerous enough without having to worry about your own horse trying to attack you.

Now they sat around the fire. Kelly was cleaning her rifle, which had seen no use since she'd taken her wrangling job. Graham lay back on his saddle and watched her. His own rifle lay within reach, and as always, he wore his gun belt.

Kelly finished cleaning her rifle and pulled a handful of bullets from her pocket to reload it. She looked up abruptly as the horses seemed suddenly restless, and Graham sat up. Her pony neighed shrilly, and before the sound had even registered in her brain, Kelly saw Graham leap to his feet, revolver drawn, and kick dirt into the fire.

Kelly jammed a bullet into the breech of her rifle and a gunshot sounded. Dirt sprayed beside her. She rolled away from the shot as she saw a shadow move and leap at Graham.

"Behind you!" She shouted. He whirled, and fired once, but the next thing Kelly could see, he was wrestling on the ground with a burly, bearded man. A second figure leapt into the now dimmed firelight, revolver raised and aimed at Kelly. Kelly fired once from the hip, and he flew backward off his feet, the slug having taken him in the throat. A twig snapped behind her, and she whirled, a man on horseback rode into the clearing, straight for her. Kelly used her rifle as a cub, swinging it at his horse's head. The horse reared and shied, spilling his rider to the ground.

As he scrambled to his feet, Kelly swung her rifle again, catching him hard on the chin and knocking him backward. Before she could move in to hit him again, a revolver roared, and she jumped, thinking that she'd been shot.

But instead, the man before her fell forward; his face dissolving into a bloody mask.

Graham had fired from behind her, and she could see a knife handle protruding from the chest of the man he had been struggling with.

They both stood, breathing hard, each looking to see if the other had been hurt. In that silence following the noise and confusion of the fight, Kelly could suddenly hear hoofbeats, and she realized that Graham's horse and the thieves' horses had run off, frightened by the gunshots. Only her Indian pony remained tethered.

She ran over to her horse, hastily unhobbled her, and started her running, leaping onto her back. Though it was dark and the moon was small, she could see the runaways far ahead, and she urged her mare to go faster.

The ground pounded by beneath her, and the breeze whipped her hair as she neared them. She ran her mare alongside them for a moment, then surged ahead and cut them sharply to the right. They pulled up in confusion, and Kelly singled Graham's horse out, leaned over and caught it by the picket rope that dangled from its neck. She galloped back to the camp, dashing up to the firelight and stopping hard.

Graham was dragging the bodies away from the firelight. She slid down from her pony's back and retethered both horses.

"That pony's as good as a watch dog," Graham commented after all three bodies were out of sight.

"What do you think they wanted?" Kelly asked.

"Horse thieves likely," Graham replied. "You take hold well in a fight."

"I'll never clean my rifle at night again," Kelly said, as she sat down and reloaded.

Graham sat back down near the fire, watching her. She had become dangerous all right, but she was still beautiful, especially with her eyes sparking from the excitement of unexpected danger successfully met.

She looked up abruptly and caught him staring. He cut his eyes away. Kelly wrapped up in her blanket and lay down to get some sleep, but it was a good hour or more before he heard her breathing even out into the rythm of sleep.

The rest of their ride into Denver was uneventful. The town had grown some more while they'd been gone, but they still rode straight through to Alice's. It was too early for the saloons to be open, so they went to her house and found her hanging up her laundry on the clothesline behind the house.

She waved happily when they rode up and dismounted. Leaving their horses tied out front, Kelly and Graham walked around back.

"Hidy!" Alice called. "Ain't it good to see the two of you again." This was mostly directed at Kelly, who she had firmly believed would end up dead when she had insisted on leaving Denver alone.

"Hey Alice," Kelly said happily. "How've you been keeping?"

"Well enough," she replied. "Looks like I'll be heading east next spring."

"Wonderful," Kelly said. Graham looked a little amused over it; he had never understood why anyone would want to head east the way Alice did.

"You all need a place to stay?" Alice asked.

"Sure," Kelly replied, but Graham shook his head.

"I'll get a room at the Monarch," he said.

"Well, come on inside and let's get caught up," Alice said, but again Graham declined her offer.

"I'd best head over there and get settled."

"See you later then," Kelly said.

He tipped his hat to both of them and walked back to the horses. Alice watched him curiously, but Kelly seemed unconcerned about his going.

They went into the house, and Alice questioned Kelly about her goings on over the past year. It was Alice's turn to listen with disbelief, although she did not doubt Kelly was telling the truth, it was hard to believe, for example, that anyone would want to spend a winter alone in the mountains.

That night found all three of them at Alice's saloon. To Kelly it seemed a lot like old times, except that Alice had a new pharo dealer, leaving Kelly free to do as she liked. Mostly, however, she and Graham teamed up to cheat at cards.

Kelly did not much care for poker as a way of life, but that fall, it did not bother her much. It was a lot easier than wrangling, and it was good to see Graham again. Since she wasn't tied to the pharo cage and didn't have to wear a dress, she felt more relaxed and confident.

But when October came to a close, Kelly began to feel restless. The mountains loomed so close, beckoning to her. She was half way minded to ride back up into the high country as she had last year, but Denver had a hold on her. Living with Alice was good, and of course, Denver was where Graham was.

Though she saw Graham nearly every day, she almost never saw him alone, which irked her for some nameless reason. She felt he was avoiding her, which touched her pride. It wasn't as though she were chasing around after him or anything.

Graham was avoiding her. He had ridden out to find her purely out of curiosity. He had thought that being away from her would make her seem more like other people. Now he found that watching her ride or play cards or just sit and frown over a book fascinated him just as much as watching her wrestle with that stallion back in New York had.

This discovery unsettled him. At the base of his nature, Graham McNair was essentially a solitary person. To his mind, people were at best harmless and at worst dangerous. He had never craved human company and found most people annoying. Now his mind turned more and more toward Kelly, and it disturbed him.

And so he found himself trapped, wanting to leave but unable to. He avoided being alone with her, but wanted to see her every day, as long as there were other people around so this weakness of his would not be noticed. Surely, he thought, it would pass in time.

But as November approached, he found himself wanting more of her company instead of less. Kelly, who was chaffing at being confined to a rapidly civilizing place like Denver, was oblivious to his internal struggle. She sometimes caught him looking at her with an odd expression on his face, but it meant nothing to her.

The weather turned cold. Kelly generally stayed at Alice's until closing to help with the cleaning up, and early one morning, she found herself sitting at the bar beside Graham. Alice ignored them both and carried a tray of glasses into the back room to be washed.

Kelly was thinking that she ought to go soon, if she planned to go at all. Graham was thinking that her hat looked a bit weather-beaten but was pleased because it was the hat he had bought for her and she was still wearing it.

"I guess I'll head for the mountains," Kelly said aloud. "The weather'll turn bad soon."

Graham had not realized that such a thought was in her mind.

"The weather's already turned bad," he said. "I'll bet the high country's seen a foot of snow already."

Kelly shrugged. She had lived through worse when she was green to the gills, now that she had a bit of experience, it would take more than that to keep her in Denver.

"It's still better than being here," she said. "This town is getting too big for me."

"Let's ride south then," he said. "Ever been to Creed?"

Kelly was surprised by the offer—almost as surprised as he was. It had just sort of popped out.

"No, but I thought you were kind of tired of my company," she said.

144

He did not answer but looked straight ahead at the bottles across the bar.

Kelly had thought a lot about him since they'd first parted nearly two years ago. Something in the solitude of the mountains and in her pride at being independent in wild places had left her comfortable with her feelings for him. Somehow during that time, it had become clear to her that she loved him, and that clarity made her wonder how she could have ever not known it.

Now, looking at him and thinking back on things, she guessed that she had fallen for him before they'd ever reached Denver. She remembered the night he'd rejoined her after his mysterious side trip and how he had seemed to her then as she had looked at him across their campfire. Yes, she thought, that was the moment. And nothing about it seemed scary anymore.

"Let's ride south then," she said, unaware that her voice had taken on a reflection of her thoughts.

But Graham heard it. Startled, he looked at her and saw her face all bright with passion. All the long years of aloneness rushed up around him—a reflex of long habit released by his shock at seeing love for himself in her face.

"You can if you want," he said. "I'm heading for Topeka at first light."

Kelly flushed red. It hadn't been her idea anyway. Why did he suggest it, then slap her in the face with it?

"Why'd you ask then?" She asked,

"I didn't ask," he said. "You misheard me."

Kelly flushed redder, thinking at first that perhaps her feelings had mislead her. Then, when she thought on what he said, she was sure they hadn't. But both options were humiliating; she stood and went into the back room without another word.

Alice saw her upset but did not immediately inquire about it. Kelly helped her for a few moments, then they both heard the front door open and close. That's him leaving, Alice thought.

"I couldn't help overhearing some of that," she said to Kelly, who flushed deeper at the words.

Kelly continued to wipe glasses.

"I expect if you pursued things a little more vigorously," Alice went on, "You might get better results."

Kelly picked up another glass.

"No I wouldn't," she said. "I'd get temporary results, and that's not good enough."

Alice stopped working and sat down. Such a conversation was much more interesting than working.

"You seem to have awful set ideas about it."

"Of course," Kelly answered. "I don't need anyone badly enough to run around after them or settle for less than it being right. If he's going to act so, I'm better off on my own."

Alice stared. This was not the blushing Kelly Knowlton who

had been all upset by his leaving before. There was plenty of hurt pride in her voice, and not a little soreness of heart, but her words were spoken from a firm belief and purpose. They were steadfast, not defiant.

By the time they finished clearing up, it was full dawn. As Kelly and Alice walked home, they saw a rider who looked very much like Graham crest the last ridge out of town. Kelly resolved to ride for Creed the very next day. Graham was headed east, and so, she would go south and see what there was to be seen.

Chapter 24

Kelly couldn't forget Graham entirely, but over the next year, she had little time to dwell on her hurt. She wandered through most of the territory, through the high country and the low, making what money she needed from card games, bets on how long she could sit a wild horse and, in the colder months, by shooting meat and hauling it to more settled areas.

Creed became her favorite stomping ground, and she made several good acquaintances there. When it came again, winter found her holed up in a Creed hotel room, flush with enough money to see her through until spring.

Still, she played an occasional poker game, more for practice than for need. Her favorite saloon was the Gold Nugget, owned and operated by Anderson Whitehead who, she learned by accident, had been in the army with Graham. Like Alice, Anderson liked having Kelly in his place; men always crowded in to see her.

Kelly didn't care for the crowds, but she liked Anderson and his blowsy wife Sara. Days and even weeks would pass between her ventures to the poker tables, but sooner or later, she always went back.

That winter was milder than the one before it. February was drawing to a close and the ground was bare of snow. Kelly rode out of town one crisp morning, took a bath in the afternoon, and went to the Gold Nugget that night. She played a few hands of poker.

Unnoticed by her, a man at the bar was staring at her. It was nothing unusual for Kelly to be stared at, and she would not have cared if she had noticed him. But this man, recently arrived from the Arizona territory, did more than stare. He beckoned to Anderson who, as soon as he finished pouring another patron a drink, walked down the bar to see what he wanted.

"Hey Andy," the man said. "Who's that pants-wearing woman over there?"

The man pointed to Kelly, but Anderson answered without bothering to look.

"Goes by the name of Kelly Knowlton," Anderson said. "What's it to you?"

"Nothing," answered the man, flashing a friendly grin. "Maybe I want to buy her a drink is all."

"You can if you want, Jackson," Anderson replied. "But I bet you a shot of the best in the house that she fourflushes you."

Jackson grinned a little wider.

"I ain't seen a woman yet that could fourflush me," he said. "Send her a drink of your finest and tell her it's from me."

Anderson shrugged. He took a bottle from behind the bar and poured a shot from it, then he walked from behind the bar and over to Kelly.

Kelly, who had been concentrating on her cards, was startled when Anderson tapped her on the shoulder and gave her the drink.

"What's this?" She asked. "I didn't ask for a drink."

Anderson jabbed his thumb at Jackson. Kelly looked and saw him smiling at her. He was tall, two or three inches over six feet, and although he was maybe a few years older than her, there was a boyish impudence in his grin that almost made her smile.

"It's from him," Anderson said. "His name is Jackson Taylor."

Kelly lifted the glass as if to drink from it. Anderson left the table. Jackson was still smiling at her when she suddenly returned his smile and poured the drink out on the floor.

The other players began to laugh. Jackson's smile vanished. Kelly went back to her cards wondering why such a handsome man would act so foolish.

Anderson stepped behind the bar and poured himself a shot from the same bottle he had gotten Kelly's from.

"You'll understand if I add this to your bill," he said to Jackson, who was still staring in disbelief.

Jackson nodded and turned back to the bar. Anderson tossed back his drink and noticed that Jackson's grin was coming back awful quick.

Kelly played two more hands, then took her winnings and left, guiding her eyes carefully so they would not meet Jackson's.

Jackson watched her go from the corner of his eyes. Anderson had come back over to him.

"Where's she from, anyway?" Jackson asked him.

"I ain't too sure, but she wanders around right good. Spends some time further north."

"What's she do besides play cards?"

"I reckon she wrangles. I seen her do some amazing things with horses."

Jackson had never heard of a female wrangler, and he was inclined to think Anderson was exaggerating.

Still, it intrigued him. Until the previous fall, he had been a civilian scout with the army down in the Arizona territory. The Apache wars were his true calling, but the Army had up and fired all the civilian scouts on account of some peace treaty that everyone knew wouldn't last a year. He had drifted north aimlessly, doing whatever a man could when he knew little besides tracking, hunting, and Indian fighting.

Maybe Anderson wasn't exaggerating, he mused. She certainly had cleaned up at her poker game. Maybe he ought to get to know her. Any woman bold enough to wear pants, play cards, and wrangle horses was bound to be good company, and the last months of winter would drag in a place that was often snow bound.

After a short winter squall that dropped a foot or so of snow on the town, Jackson set out to unravel the mystery of Kelly Knowlton. From the talk he picked up here and there, he gathered that no one really knew where she had come from originally, but it was generally agreed that she had arrived from the east three or four years ago. Not that anyone had ever dared to ask her; her speech and bearing gave her away.

It was also generally agreed that she was fearless around horses, and that her opinion was often sought when fights having to do with horses arose. No one claimed to be her friend, although many claimed to know of her. Jackson was surprised at all the crazy stories that were told about her. Some, no doubt were true, and some might be exaggerated, but most were pure imagination on the part of the teller, no matter how he might swear it was the truth.

Once having heard all the talk, Jackson started to watch her. The weather was poorly, so he had no chance to see for himself how good a wrangler she was, but she was good with cards, that he saw time and again in this saloon or that.

This particular evening, she was playing with two no-account looking drifters and a card sharp from Salt Lake City. She and the card sharp were faring the best. The no-accounts were quickly losing their road stake.

Since she didn't really need the money and felt certain that the card sharp was cheating, Kelly decided to bow out of the game. The two dirty-looking men across the table looked as though they would make poor losers, and she was not in the mood for a scrap.

She played the hand out; her two pair beat the taller drifter's pair but not the card sharp's three of a kind. The shorter drifter had folded two antes ago.

"That's it for me, gents," she said, standing. "It's been a pleasure."

The card sharp rose when she did, tipping his hat to her. Kelly started to pick her winnings up, but the taller drifter reached over and grabbed her wrist.

"We ain't done playin' yet. Set back down."

"Let go of me."

"Set back down."

His grip was too strong to break, so Kelly sat down again. He released her wrist, and she shoved her chair back, standing up again. Since she was too far away to grab, the drifter stood up threateningly.

"I said we ain't done yet. Set back down. Me n' Henny are out a hunnert dollars, and we got a right to win it back."

Kelly looked him over. He was over six feet and weighed close on to two hundred pounds. She hated this kind of disturbance, but she also knew that she could not let him bully her.

"I said I'm done playing," she said calmly. "Take your gripe some place else."

She scooped her money from the table and put it in her pocket. Everyone in the place was quiet, waiting to see what would happen. The card sharp moved his chair back from the table, and Henny, the shorter drifter, got to his feet.

"You got 'til three to set back down," he said.

"I'm surprised you can count that high," Kelly said, looking at him contemptuously and turning on her heel.

Out of the corner of her eye, she saw Henny come after her. Swiftly, she sidestepped; he stumbled past her, and she shoved him so that he lost his balance and crashed into another table.

Dazed, Henny tried unsuccessfully to get to his feet.

"Get 'er Cal," he shouted to his buddy.

Kelly took a swift look around the bar. No one was going to help her, but she was not afraid. Both men were half-drunk and clumsy as lame buffalo. She could stay out of their reach for hours if she had to—or until they passed out, which was far more likely. And if they got a little too close, she always had her revolver, though in this case, there was no particular need to use it as neither of the two men were carrying guns.

Cal came at her as clumsily as Henny had, and snatching a bottle from the bar, she broke it over his head. Though stunned, he still took a punch at her, which she was able to duck.

But now Henny was on his feet and looking determined. He drew his knife.

Kelly backed away from him calmly, wanting to give herself more room and a few seconds to think; she could not shoot him without some clearer threat to her life or else she'd end up in jail. She bumped up against someone and jumped in surprise.

Turning, she saw it was the man who had tried to buy her a drink a few nights ago. What was his name?

"Jackson Taylor, at your service, Ma'am," he said politely, tipping his hat as though they were in church.

Kelly looked him up and down. She had no idea why he would want to take a hand in this scrap and didn't need his help, but there was something daring in his grin that appealed to her.

"Think you can get that knife away from him, Mr. Taylor?" She asked flippantly.

"Like candy from a baby," he replied, drawing his own knife and stepping toward Henny.

Kelly only had a few seconds to watch them slash ferociously at each other, for Cal had regained his senses and was making ready to leap at Jackson from behind. Kelly grabbed a chair and broke it over his back. He turned and grabbed at her, but she was too agile for him. Since he couldn't get a hold of her, he tried to hit her, but with the same result. In a few minutes, he was panting from his exertions. He made one more lunge at her, and Kelly pistol whipped him. He sprawled to the floor unconscious.

She looked around to see that Henny was lying on a hastily abandoned poker table, Jackson's knife protruding from his chest. Jackson yanked his knife free and wiped the blade clean on the dead man's shirt. Kelly shook her head. There hadn't been anything going on worth killing a drunk over, but it was on Jackson's conscience, not hers.

Jackson, who was unhurt, smiled over at her, but they had no time for conversation as the sheriff arrived somewhat belatedly and arrested him, Kelly, and the still-unconscious Cal.

When they arrived at the jail, the sheriff took their names and grumbled as he reshuffled the other prisoners so that Kelly would have a cell to herself. Jackson was locked up in the cell across from her.

"I appreciate your assistance, Mr. Taylor," she said to him through the bars. "I'm sorry you're in such trouble over it."

"Call me Jackson," he replied. "There won't be much fuss over it. Don't worry."

Although she was unconcerned for herself, Kelly did not have much faith in his prediction about his own crime being treated lightly, but she said nothing more about it.

They were held overnight and were lead to trial the next morning. As there was no courthouse, the trial was held in the one-room school house at the north end of town. Kelly had not had much experience with courts and trials, but the proceedings struck her as being very informal.

The judge had his feet up on the desk, for one thing, and there were no lawyers, for another. The back of the school house was crowded with spectators, some of whom stepped forward to testify. Their testimony, however, was interrupted by catcalls and hoots from the audience. The judge questioned the witnesses, then told them to stand back. He also questioned Cal, who began cursing at Kelly. The judge ordered the sheriff to silence Cal, and the sheriff pistol whipped him.

"Poor man," Kelly muttered. "His head must be full of cracks by now."

"You there," said the judge, pointing to her. "Miss Knowlton. Is that your name?"

"Yes sir, your honor," Kelly replied.

Her response drew an approving look from the judge, who was not used to people who spoke quietly and addressed him as "sir" and "your honor."

"Tell the court what happened, please."

Kelly recounted the incident as briefly as possible, wanting to get the whole business over with quickly.

"And I must say, your honor," she concluded. "There is no telling what violence those two ruffians might have done me. I am very grateful to Mr. Taylor for assisting me, since the sheriff was nowhere about, and no one else was chivalrous enough to come to my aid."

The judge mulled over her testimony for a moment.

"Were you cheating during that game?"

"No sir, your honor."

The judge leaned back in his chair in his chair for a long while, considering everything that had been said, the calm demeanor of the poker-playing female, and the scurvy appearance of the man who, by all accounts, had attacked her. Then he sat up and looked sternly at her and Jackson.

"I'm going to let you all go free," he announced. "Seems clear to me that them two drifters were itchin' to take their bad temper out on someone. But you, miss, ought not to be playin' cards with such types, and you, sir, ought to be slower to stick someone in the chest. A leg or an arm would have done just as well."

The judge stood up and surveyed the crowd of spectators.

"And none a this would a happened if them others in the saloon had broken things up peaceful. Court adjourned."

He banged the flat of his hand on the desk, and everyone began to spill out of the crowded school room. Kelly waited until the crowd had gone, then she sat down on a desk and scratched her ear, thinking that she ought to leave town as soon as the weather cleared some.

"See, I told you not to fret."

Kelly looked around and saw Jackson standing near the door.

"You were right," she said. "I never saw such a spectacle in all my life."

Jackson laughed and walked over, sitting on the desk beside her.

"This weren't so bad for a courthouse," he said. "Down

south, we hold court in a saloon. Ain't no schools."

"Where south?" Kelly asked, intrigued.

"Arizona territory," he replied. "That's where I hail from."

Kelly had never met anyone from so far south. However, she had heard that it was plenty wild down there—wild and dry.

"So what brings you north?" She asked.

"Oh, I thought I might have a look around," he said. "If I'da known the women up here were so pretty, I reckon I would of come sooner."

He was looking at her with an openly appreciative look as he spoke, and Kelly felt herself flush. She looked away out the window, trying unsuccessfully to remember the last time she had gotten any such compliment.

Jackson noted her reaction with interest.

"You from around here?" He asked.

"Sometimes," Kelly replied. "I hang around Denver some, too."

"Denver?" Jackson said. "Now, there's a place I always wanted to go."

"I wouldn't recommend heading that way until March gets better started," she said. "Winter storms come up awful sudden around here."

"That's a fact."

Now that he was up close to her, Jackson was even more intrigued. She was prettier than he had thought, and since his comment about her looks, she seemed kind of shy about looking at him. This seemed odd to him, after all, she had not turned a hair during that fight and had seemed totally unafraid of being arrested and tried.

"You heading that way anytime soon?" He asked her.

"At the first of April, maybe," she replied.

"Well, maybe if you want some company, we could ride that way together," he said. "Since I ain't never been so far north."

Kelly hesitated. Though she found herself liking him very much, she did not quite trust him that much and felt the invitation was rather sudden.

Jackson noticed that she seemed put off some by what he'd said. He would have to slow down some.

"Of course, that won't be for a month yet," he said. "I might drift off somewhere else afore then."

He paused to see if she would speak. When she did not, he went on.

"But I'd admire to play some cards with you, if you please."

He smiled so charmingly that Kelly heard herself say yes even though she was tired and wanted to go take a nap.

They stood and walked out of the school house, Jackson holding the door for her on their way out.

The day was blustery, but smelling the wind, Kelly knew that spring would turn up soon. There was something in the breeze that made her blood run a little faster and her heart beat a little harder.

Chapter 25

Kelly saw quite a bit of Jackson during March. He turned up nearly every day, sometimes at the stable as she tended to her horse, sometimes in the saloon where she was playing cards, sometimes on the street as she walked from one place to another.

She began to look forward to seeing him, for he always smiled in greeting and talked happily to her. He always seemed cheerful and often paid her compliments, and he told wonderful stories about the Arizona territory and the adventures that he had seen there.

She was surprised to learn that, like Graham, Jackson had been a scout for the army, although Jackson had always been a civilian. When he spoke of the Apache, his voice had the same tone of respect and admiration that Graham's took on when he spoke of the Cheyenne and the Sioux.

But that seemed to be the only similarity between the two men. Jackson was not much at card playing and, despite his efforts to conceal it, always seemed annoyed if she beat him. As they saw more and more of each other, he also began needling her to stay out of saloons and act less like a cowboy.

He never came straight out and said so, for if he had, she would have become angry. Instead, he took little pokes at her that she let pass, but which troubled her mind long afterwards.

Like the day he started deviling her over her clothes, for one. They had been down at the livery stable, Kelly to fuss with her horse and Jackson to see if the mare really was as fierce as Kelly claimed. The mare's fierceness had been quickly proven; she had almost bitten a hole in him when he had rested his arm on top of her stall door, but he had snatched his arm away in time.

"Damn!" He had said. "You ought to break her of that if you're such a hand with horses."

"I don't want her broken of it," Kelly had replied. "I travel alone, and she watches my back for me."

Jackson had not responded, thinking that Kelly was being a little fanciful. She had gone into the mare's stall to brush her, and he noticed that she worked warily but had no problems.

"You going to Whitehead's tonight?" He had asked her.

"Maybe," Kelly had replied.

"You know," he had said, "You oughter buy a dress. Them pants make you look like a boy."

A little offended, Kelly had stopped brushing for a moment.

"I wear what I want, and it's none of your business," she had replied.

"I just say it's a shame," Jackson had said. "Letting all them homely women look better when you're so pretty."

Deeply offended then, Kelly had not answered him. As far as she was concerned, she did look better, no matter what she wore, and it hurt that he did not, apparently, share her view on this matter.

But for all that, Kelly found herself becoming attached to him. If a day passed and she did not see him, she felt saddened and wondered where he had gotten to. As April neared, she decided that she would ask him if he wanted to go with her to Denver.

Jackson, who had noticed that she was warming up to him right well, was not surprised by the question and was happy to go with her. He wanted to see exactly how much she had warmed up to him, and that seemed hard to do in a town where there were so many distractions.

They headed out for Denver in the first week of April. Kelly was glad to be traveling again and glad to have some company. That first day out, Jackson told stories as they rode at a leisurely pace. They stopped early by Kelly's standards, but she did not mind.

She tended to the horses while he hunted up some meat for supper. Kelly thought that it was good to be traveling with someone again and wondered briefly where in the world Graham had gotten to.

"Where'd you find that pony?" Jackson said after they had eaten.

"Up northwest near the high country," she said. "I've had her nearly two years. When I travel alone, I sleep underneath her."

"She ever attacked anyone?"

"Only horse thieves and roustabouts," Kelly replied.

It grew late, and the fire died down. Kelly wrapped up in

her blankets to sleep, and to her surprise, Jackson lay close up beside her. After her surprise faded a bit, she decided that it was nice to have him so close, and so, she didn't chase him off.

But she couldn't quite fall asleep, either. She was awake for an hour after Jackson began to snore. He was a little restless in his sleep, and she found that, after she had turned onto her right side, he curled up close alongside her and put an arm around her.

It was a good feeling to be held so, and one she had never experienced before. She was laying there, enjoying it, when her pony snorted suddenly, and she and Jackson both sat bolt upright.

Jackson grabbed his rifle and scouted around for a bit. Kelly kept her revolver ready until he returned.

"Tweren't nothing," he said, setting his rifle down. "Snake, maybe."

Kelly nodded, and they curled back up together, Jackson putting his arm back around her. Her shirt had come untucked and had ridden up some, and his hand slipped onto the bare skin of her side and down across her stomach.

Her stomach jumped when he touched it, and Kelly's heart beat accelerated so quickly that she almost felt faint. His hand brushed over her stomach and up toward her breasts, and she rolled over toward him, feeling suddenly full of an aching need that she had only guessed at before.

His lips met hers, warm and hungry, and she felt him shift his weight on top of her, and the feeling had its own kind of satisfaction. This, she thought, was an adventure that she had waited too long to embark upon.

Chapter 26

Graham had not left the territory after their misunderstanding, as he termed it. Although he had headed east with the intention of going back to Kansas, he had gotten sidetracked and had ended up in Cheyenne, Wyoming, which was crawling with soldiers.

The army was short on seasoned Indian fighters, and Graham soon found himself doing some scouting. He was more familiar with the area farther south, but that did not hinder him much. Knowing how to get around and having a general idea about the lay of the land put him two aces up on practically every other white man within a hundred mile radius.

The summer after he had met up with Kelly in that mining camp, Graham found himself leading a group of forty troopers down to Denver from an outpost east of Cheyenne. The lieutenant in charge was freshly arrived from the east, as were about half the troopers.

Now they rode in a double column across the plains. It was a boiling hot day, and most of the troopers rode slumped in their saddles, the heat and the boredom combining to make them groggy. Graham had been riding ahead and around them and felt certain they were in for some trouble. He had found the remains of a small Indian camp that was not more than a day old. A war party, probably, and not much threat to forty well-armed cavalry. But if the Indians were still in the neighborhood, they had no doubt sighted them.

Graham reported as much to the lieutenant, who failed to understand the importance of the information.

"If it's a small party, they can hardly attack us, can they?" He asked.

"No, but they can tell the rest of their camp where we are and how many of us there are."

"But you don't know that they did see us?"

"I know it. It would be foolish to assume they didn't."

"Even though we passed last night quietly?"

Graham nodded, becoming annoyed with the lieutenant's demeanor.

"It's my opinion that you ought to shore up those men," Graham said, "Instead of having them strung out. You ought to put them on alert and set out flanking guards, too. Some of them are half asleep in their saddles."

"I'll consider what you've said."

That was plainly a dismissal, and Graham reined in so his horse dropped behind the lieutenant's. He did not salute; as a civilian, he wasn't required to, even though most scouts did so anyway. They valued their jobs; Graham did not.

He rode alongside the detachment's sergeant, a grizzled, one-eyed friend of his named Jeff Bowser, for a moment.

"I smell trouble, Jeff," he said. "How 'bout you?"

"Yep. Since last night. You tell lieutenant pissant?"

Graham nodded. "There's no help for us there."

"Don't ah know it," Jeff leaned over his horse's neck and spat. "I'll roust these bastards awake, anyway."

"I'll ride ahead a ways," Graham said.

The sergeant rode up and down the column, bawling at the soldiers to straighten up and ride like they'd been taught.

Graham had not even ridden far enough to loose the sound of Jeff's yelling when movement on the plains to the north caught his eye. He reined in his horse, and removing his spyglass from his jacket, he scanned the horizon.

It was a group of forty or fifty Sioux, all mounted and dressed for war. Graham put the glass away and rode back to the detachment.

He reined in sharply alongside the lieutenant.

"We got a forty or fifty man war party coming at us from the north," he said calmly, pointing.

The lieutenant's eyes snapped to where he pointed. The Indians were clearly visible, though they were perhaps four miles away. Graham noticed that the lieutenant's face went pasty.

"Order the men to dismount," Graham said. "Get 'em in a circle, guns outward, horses in the middle. One man holding four horses."

The lieutenant seemed transfixed by the approaching danger and did not speak.

"Do it man," Graham said. "Do it now while there's time."

"Time?" The lieutenant's eyes snapped on to his. "We need to run for cover while there's time. We can't hold a defensive position out here in the middle of nowhere. We need cover."

"Cover? There's no cover for forty miles. Not a tree, not a rock, not a butte, not a house. If we run now, they'll run us down and cut us up one by one. Give the order to dismount."

"He's right, sir," said the sergeant. "I been in enough such fixes to know."

But to Lieutenant Tull, it seemed impossible to just stand and fight with no protection from the bullets that would fall on them like hailstones.

"Sergeant Bowser, give the order to head east at a gallop."

The sergeant hesitated, knowing the order meant suicide but trained to obey his commanding officer.

"Sir, I . . ."

"Give the order, sergeant."

Graham could not believe that one stupid fool was going to insist on an order that would kill them all. Well, he did not intend to die because of someone else's foolishness.

He drew his revolver and rode up to the lieutenant, who moved to draw his own gun. But Graham was faster. He brought the butt of his revolver down hard on the man's head. Graham caught him before he spilled to the ground unconscious.

"Order those men to dismount and get them ready," Graham said to Bowser. "Do it fast before the wrath of the Sioux nation sets down upon us."

Sergeant Bowser began barking orders. Graham dismounted and helped him get the troopers ready. Bullets began to whiz around them before they were finished.

But when the circle was complete, the Indians were faced with a solid wall of resistance. Their ponies kicked up dust, making it hard to see, but Graham picked his targets carefully, noticing out of the corner of his eye that the recruit to his left was so scared that he was forgetting to shoot. Instead, the trooper levered unspent shells out of his rifle until a more seasoned trooper smacked the back of his head and yelled some sense back into him.

Bowser worked his way around the inside of the circle, barking orders and encouragement. The man to Graham's right fell, and Graham moved over to help close the space. Another soldier, unnerved by the Indians' war cries and the screams of the wounded and dying, broke and ran. He dropped dead without having gotten more than ten paces.

The attack broke off as abruptly as it had been joined. As the remaining Indians thundered away, Graham stood and wiped the sweat from his face. Surveying the battlefield was a dismal chore. Dead bodies—Indians, troopers, and horses—lay everywhere.

"Get 'em mounted up again, Bowser," Graham said. "Find out how many horses we lost."

Bowser did as he was told, even though the lieutenant was

now conscious and on his feet, full of ire toward Graham.

"That will be enough, sir," he snapped. "You're under arrest."

Graham ignored him and reloaded his revolver. Holstering it, he listened as Bowser reported to Tull.

"Twelve dead, six wounded, eleven horses gone, sir."

"We'll have to leave the dead, sergeant. Get everyone else mounted."

Graham felt a little relieved. His orders were starting to show some sense. Being arrested bothered him not at all. The commander in Denver was a seasoned campaigner and would agree that there had been nothing else to do.

The remaining men were mounted, and so were Graham and Tull, when Bowser rode up.

"We have a problem, sir," he said,

"What, sergeant?"

"Private Walker is bad hurt and can't ride."

"Well, pack him over his horse, sergeant."

"I don't think we can do that, sir."

"Why not?"

"You'd better come see for yourself, sir."

They rode over to where Walker lay, gulping at water from a canteen held by a private named Sherman Buser. Though uninvited, Graham went with them and noticed that Lieutenant Tull went pale again when he saw the man's wound.

Walker had taken a lance in the stomach. Someone had removed the blade, and the man's intestines poked up wetly through the hole. There was something else showing too, something torn and bloody and oozing water. Graham supposed that it must be his stomach.

It was plain to everyone that Private Walker was going to die, and that it could take some time to happen. Belly wounds were the slowest and most painful way to die. Graham knew that when the shock wore off a little more, Walker would start to scream.

"Order the men to dismount, sergeant," said Tull. "We'll wait here until . . . until."

"Lieutenant," Graham said. "Those Indians will be back. We need to clear out."

"Have some compassion, McNair, the man is dying. We can't leave him here alone."

"We can't save him, either. Why risk thirty others for this one who we can't do anything for?"

Sergeant Bowser silently agreed, but he had had enough of mutiny for one day.

"If you contest my authority again, McNair, I'll have you disarmed."

Graham looked down at Walker's eyes; they had become wild with agony. There was no comfort for Walker in having his friends about him; he didn't even know they were there. The only comfort waiting for Walker was in the next world, wherever that might be.

Graham drew his revolver again, and before anyone even realized what he was thinking, he shot Walker dead between the eyes. Private Sherman Buser, still sitting beside the dead man, corked his canteen, feeling relieved and glad—now they could move on—and he might yet keep his hair long enough to loose it naturally.

"Now let's go," Graham said. "Unless maybe you want to sing a few hymns or something."

Graham wheeled his horse away. Sergeant Bowser spat thoughtfully and waited for Lieutenant Tull to recover enough to start giving orders.

"That has to be the most cold-blooded thing I ever saw," Tull said at last.

"Yes sir," said Bowser. "But you're young yet, I reckon."

Chapter 27

As Graham had supposed, the major in charge of things back in Denver took no action against him, despite Lieutenant Tull's indignant report of his actions. Major Sanderson had done worse things himself plenty of times when dire circumstances had forced his hand.

Graham spent that winter in Denver and the surrounding area. There was plenty enough work and plenty enough time for playing cards. It puzzled him that Kelly never showed up in all that time, and he wondered if she had run into trouble somewhere.

When spring came, he was torn between going out to look for her and waiting to see if she would turn up in Denver at last. Alice noticed his uneasiness of mind and suggested that he go for a sport over at Maybelle's. He told her not to be so dirty minded.

Along about the middle of April, he was standing outside the Monarch Hotel, enjoying the weather. He eyed the busy street for possible danger and relaxed as much as was possible in public, soaking up the clean sunshine and wondering if he shouldn't head down to Creed.

Then he spotted Kelly walking up the street, leading her horse. Surprised and relieved, he stepped down off the sidewalk. From the gear her horse carried and her trail-stained appearance, he supposed that she had just ridden into town.

He started over to her. She looked up, saw him, and stopped dead. Running into Graham McNair had been the furthest thing from her mind, and now she was too surprised to greet him, even though he hailed her cheerfully, tipping his hat to her.

Before Kelly could even digest his sudden appearance much less return his greeting, Jackson appeared at her elbow, his face cautiously antagonistic as he looked Graham up and down. The import of his expression was not lost on Graham, who, despite his shock, returned Jackson's look with a coldly speculative glance, then ignored him completely and spoke to Kelly.

"I heard you've been mostly in Creed," he said.

Before Kelly could answer, Jackson broke in.

"That's right," he said. "We have been."

"No one here is talking to you," Graham said.

There was no mistaking the animosity sparking between the two men. Kelly stepped between them.

"Jackson Taylor, this my good friend Graham McNair; Graham McNair, this is my good friend Jackson Taylor."

In response to her introduction, they nodded to each other coldly, but politely. Kelly was satisfied.

"I'm going to put these horses up," she announced. "I will see you both later."

Without another word, she lead the horses down the street, leaving both men standing there awkwardly. Graham felt that he could hardly shoot someone who had been introduced to him so politely as her "good friend," and Jackson was wondering what, exactly, she had meant by the term "good friend." Kelly was a good ways down the street before either man had reached a conclusion, and since Graham showed no inclination toward pursuing their disagreement, Jackson followed her.

Left alone on the street, Graham reflected that it was foolish for him to be so surprised over her having taken up with someone. When he thought about it, the only real surprise was that it had taken so long to happen. He frowned and continued on his way, unsettled by the swift and sudden jealousy that he had felt on realizing that Kelly was traveling with someone else. As he walked, his thoughts turned to the poor first impression that Jackson had made upon him. He had no doubt that Jackson was a hard case and a fearless fighter when the moment arose, but Graham would not want to have to rely on him in a scrape.

Kelly reached the stable a minute ahead of Jackson, who barely waited until she was finished arranging board for their horses before badgering her over Graham.

"Who was that?" He asked angrily. "Just how many good friends you got in this town, anyway?"

Kelly unsaddled her horse, struggling to keep her temper down.

"I told you that was Graham McNair. He is an old friend of mine, and there is no reason for you to raise your voice to me."

"There sure as hell is. I saw how you looked at him. What did you mean you're going to see him later?"

"Just what I said. Denver isn't so big that I can stay here and not see him."

"Maybe we ought to move on then."

"You can if you want," Kelly said, goaded into forgetting her affection for him. "I'm staying here."

Seeing that she had been pushed a bit too far, Jackson decided to back off a little.

"We can stay," he said. "But if I catch you fooling around on me with him or anyone else, I'll beat you black and blue."

Startled, Kelly dropped her saddle. He wasn't threatening her; he meant it. She felt cold, and she spoke through numb lips.

"You ever raise a hand to me, and I'll shoot you before it falls," she said.

They stared at each other. Though surprised at what she had said, Jackson did not take it seriously, but he looked away first and left the barn without another word.

Kelly finished seeing to the horses, wondering if coming back to Denver had been such a good idea. She decided to stay with Alice while she was in town. Jackson could take a room somewhere and visit her if he wanted.

On her way to Alice's, Kelly puzzled over the instantaneous antagonism that had sprung up between Jackson and Graham. They ought to get along well, she thought, since they had both been scouts in the Indian wars. True, Jackson tended to be a bit jealous, and Graham tended to be a little protective, but hell, those weren't any good reasons to pull down on someone, which, for a moment, she had feared they might do.

Alice gave her no satisfactory explanation for their animosity. When Kelly had told her of the incident, Alice laughed and shook her head.

"I ain't never seen anyone as dumb as you when it comes to people, Kelly," she had said. "Except for maybe Graham McNair."

Kelly ignored the insult.

"Well, whatever it is," she said. "They'll have to settle it themselves, and without shooting each other over it. I won't stand for such foolishness."

"You better leave town then," Alice said. "People Graham don't like tend to die young."

It rankled Kelly to think that Alice thought Jackson so inconsequential. But despite her feeling for Jackson, Kelly had to admit that, if it came to a shootout, he would probably loose. Though a skilled outdoorsman and hunter and a superior scout, he was not the marksman Graham was, especially not with a revolver.

But she doubted it would come to a shootout, unless Jackson went out of his way to provoke one. Graham had better sense than to be drawn into such a fight, and considering how awkward their meeting had been, it was not likely that she would see much of him during her stay in Denver.

As the days passed, Kelly was proven correct. Jackson did

not often let her out of his sight for long, which Kelly found irksome, and she knew that Graham would avoid Jackson even if he didn't want to avoid her. It was saddening to think that she and Graham were no longer as good friends as they had been, and she could not understand why her being with Jackson seemed to make such a difference. After all, Graham had made his views on such things pretty clear the winter before last. If anything stood between them, it should have been their "misunderstanding" of the previous winter.

Kelly and Jackson had been in Denver almost two months before Kelly saw Graham alone. After a morning's ride out of town, she returned to the livery stable and found Graham waiting for her. Three days earlier, Jackson had taken a trip up to Cheyenne with some new acquaintances. Kelly had not asked him the purpose of the trip, and though she did not admit it to herself, she was glad that he had gone for while. His constant presence was beginning to annoy her.

Annoyed as she was at Jackson, she still felt uncomfortable around Graham. After all, they had not spoken alone since he'd rebuked her last winter, and the memory of that night still made her cheeks redden. In some ways, it had almost been a relief to not see him all this time.

But now that he was standing there, she couldn't ignore him or not answer when he greeted her. So she returned his wave and his greeting and rode up to him, dismounting.

"Good ride?" He asked her.

"Fair," Kelly said, loosening the girths. "We had a bit of a fight on the way out, but she was good as gold on the way in."

Graham waited for her to finish. It would be better to talk to her when she was finished fooling with her horse.

"Been in Kansas?" Kelly asked him, taking the mare by the reins and starting for the barn.

"No," he said, following her. "I never got out there. I've been up north, mostly."

They entered the barn. Kelly led the mare into her stall and unsaddled her. She put the saddle over the stall door and picked up her brushes. Brushing the mare gave Kelly the opportunity to keep her accustomed to being handled.

Graham stood outside the stall as she worked. He had always liked watching her work with horses. Now it almost distracted him from what he had come to say, but with an effort, he brought his mind back around to it.

"I came to say I'm sorry for how things ended up last time we were in Denver," he said. "I never meant to hurt your feelings."

"Well, you did," Kelly said, focusing on her work so she wouldn't have to look at him. "And you sure took your time apologizing for it."

Graham assumed she meant that he should have apologized

when she'd first gotten to town.

"I wanted to before," he said. "But these days, What's-his-name is always at your elbow."

"His name is Jackson Taylor and you know it," Kelly said, wishing Jackson hadn't gone to Cheyenne if it meant that his presence would have saved her from this conversation. "And he and I are going to be here for a while, so you might as well get used to saying his name."

"If that's so, where is he?" Graham asked.

"Cheyenne, for the moment," Kelly said, not liking the baiting tone in his voice.

"Think he'll be back?" Graham could not keep the sarcastic note from his voice.

"He's supposed to be back today," Kelly said, trying to sound as if she didn't care much one way or another.

Graham snorted. Kelly felt her temper flare, fueled as much by hurt as by anger. She had never thought to see contempt for herself reflected in his eyes. She was so preoccupied with her anger that she forgot to watch the mare, who promptly stepped on her left foot.

"Ow!" Kelly said, digging the mare hard in the ribs with her elbow. The mare stepped off her foot.

"What happened?" Graham asked. "Are you all right?"

"Yes. She stepped on my foot," Kelly snapped. "And you might as well tell me what's on your mind and stop talking the long way around it."

"I've already said it."

"Oh really?" Kelly laughed shortly. "Then why are you picking on Jackson and me and acting mean as a snake?"

"I'm not picking on anyone." He said, anger creeping into his voice. "It's just rilesome that you've been hiding out since you got here, and I had to track you down just to talk to you."

"I've got plenty good reason to hide, as you should know," Kelly said as she finished brushing the mare down. "And it's no reason for you to be angry at me now."

"I'm tired of hearing you talk about that damn Jackson, that's all," Graham snapped. Anger showed on his face now, but Kelly was unimpressed.

"Well, who gives a damn what you think?" She said, tossing her brushes out of the stall. They landed on the floor at Graham's feet. He stared at them a moment, amazed to find himself in the middle of an argument and dismayed that she could still make him loose his temper so easily.

"I reckon you don't, anyway," he said furiously. "I came all the way from Sioux country to get things straight between us, and all you can do is make eyes at some worthless drifter from Arizona."

Kelly opened the stall door and slammed it shut behind her, scaring the mare, who jumped backward. Graham had not raised his voice to her since they crossed the Little Powan River in 1873. She did not intend to let it pass.

"Things were straight between us when you left," she said. "You've said nothing except that you're sorry about it."

Kelly sat down on a hay bale. Her foot hurt terribly, and she wondered if it might be broken. Gingerly, she pulled off her boot and sock. The foot was bruised and swollen. She felt it carefully to see if it was broken anywhere.

"That looks nasty," Graham said, concerned. "Is it broke?"

"I don't think so," Kelly said.

She put her sock and boot back on. Her feelings were all confused. Her affection for Jackson was tied up to how she felt about Graham somehow, and it didn't make sense to her. She couldn't decide what she thought about either man, and just then, neither of them seemed worth the trouble.

Kelly stood abruptly. If Graham hadn't been irking her, she thought, she would have been paying better attention, and the mare wouldn't have been able to step on her. But she ought to accept his apology; it had been more hurtful to think they were no longer friends than it had been to think of the insult that she felt he had offered her.

"For what it's worth," she said. "I accept your apology, and I appreciate you having come all this way to make it. I don't like to think of us as fighting."

"Neither do I."

"Will you be in town much longer?"

"No," he said. "I'm going to take a detachment of soldiers up to Bozeman. We leave tonight."

"Be careful of your hair," Kelly said.

"I intend to be."

Kelly stood up, gingerly putting her injured foot to the ground. Wincing, she took a step.

"You shouldn't walk on that," Graham said suddenly. "Let me carry you."

"No, thank you. I'll be fine," Kelly said. "It's not far to Alice's."

She privately thought it would create a spectacle to be carried through town, one Jackson was certain to hear of.

Graham was looking at her oddly again, and Kelly felt herself flushing under his gaze.

"It's none of my business, Kelly," he said. "But be careful of how far you trust him."

Kelly almost replied that he was right; it wasn't any of his business, but the words were such a good summarization of her own thoughts on the matter that she only smiled.

"I don't trust anyone too far," she said.

Satisfied, Graham nodded, tipped his hat to her, and left, thinking it a pity that he couldn't take her up north with him. If it came to a fight, and it probably would sooner or later, he'd rather have Kelly Knowlton watching his back than a dozen troopers.

Kelly sat on the hay bale and thought for a while longer, then got gingerly to her feet and limped back to Alice's. She was relieved that Graham was leaving town, though she wished he would go some place safer. He would come back sooner or later, if he lived, and Kelly wondered how the terms of their truce would hold up when he did.

After hopping to her room, she opened the door to find that Jackson had returned. He was washing up as she limped into the room, and he greeted her in a grumpy voice. Her foot hurt like the devil, and she wished he'd gone to the damn hotel if he was going to be short-tempered.

As she sat down on the bed and pulled her boots and socks off, Kelly thought that maybe he was still tired from the long ride from Cheyenne to Denver, but she was more concerned with her foot than with whatever was bothering him. From long habit, she glanced over to see that her gunbelt was still hanging from the bedpost.

"What happened to your foot?" He asked.

"My mare stepped on it," Kelly said.

"You ought to sell her," Jackson said. "She's a right bitch."

Kelly ignored him and felt her foot over again.

"Come on down to the saloon with me," Jackson said.

"I'm staying in tonight," Kelly replied. "My foot hurts like sin."

"I got a card game together for us," he said.

"I'm not going," Kelly said, standing up so she could go to the kitchen for a tub and some hot water. It was no good playing cards with Jackson; he just got resentful when she played better than he did, plus he always wanted a sizable cut of her winnings.

"I've got to soak this foot," she told him.

"You'll do as I say," Jackson said angrily.

"To hell with that," Kelly replied. "I'll do as I please."

He back handed her across the mouth, knocking her onto the bed. It wasn't a very hard blow, and Kelly had seen it coming, but she had been too stunned at the thought of him hitting her to block it.

But she wasn't stunned for very much longer. Jackson had turned back toward the mirror, apparently considering the matter settled. Kelly scooted back on the bed and pulled her revolver from its holster. She aimed carefully and fired. The gun roared.

Jackson yelped, jumping from the noise. A bullet hole appeared in the wall an inch to the right of his ear. He whirled around to see that Kelly was still holding the gun on him.

"You will leave this room, or I'll shoot you where you stand, mister," Kelly said quietly.

Jackson considered jumping her for the gun, but knew he wouldn't be fast enough. The look in her eye told him that she would not hesitate to shoot him, and as Graham McNair had been her shooting teacher, it wasn't likely that she would miss.

"Can't we talk this out?" He asked.

"We could have until you hit me. Now you leave this room," Kelly said coldly. Her anger at Graham melded with her anger for Jackson, giving her voice a frightening edge to it. "The next time you raise your hand to me you better think hard about it, 'cause if I can get back up off the floor, you're a dead man."

She meant it. There was no doubt about that. Jackson thought he might just stand there—not leave but not aggravate her further—to show her he couldn't be whoorahed by a woman.

Then she drew the hammer back on her revolver. Damn, he thought, she will shoot me if I don't leave.

He picked up his things and left without another word. When she heard his footsteps trail off down the hall, Kelly got off the bed and bolted the door. If he did come back tomorrow, he would have to knock.

Chapter 28

Out in the street, Jackson walked away from Alice's neither angry nor resentful. It had been his experience that most women would take a slap or two if they were enough in love and if you had them properly buffaloed, but he also knew that some women would not stand for it at all. He had misjudged Kelly, that was all. True, he had known that she was a hard case, but even some of the hardest women would stand rough treatment if they were enough in love, especially if it came during an argument.

No matter. He would spend the night somewhere else. She would miss him in the morning and let him come back. He did not question whether or not he wanted to go back; he knew he was not done with her yet, and since she was so independent, it might take a long time for that to happen.

Kelly also did not question whether or not he would return; she knew that he would and having shot at him troubled her not at all. She boiled up some water and was soaking her foot when Alice came in from doing the shopping.

"Land sakes, Kelly," she exclaimed. "Whatever happened to your foot?"

"My mare stepped on it," Kelly said for what seemed like the ten millionth time.

"Well. Hasn't that Jackson Taylor come back yet?"

"Yes, Alice, he has. He came back, and I threw him out."

Alice smiled broadly.

"That's the first smart thing you've done in three years. That man wasn't worth a pisshole in the snow."

"Alice!" Kelly said, surprised that she would use such

language. Of course, it was no surprise to discover that Alice didn't like Jackson. She'd been all but rude to him since the day Kelly had introduced them.

"It's a true fact," Alice said calmly.

"Maybe and maybe not, but I reckon he'll be back in the morning. We just had a little fight."

"Humph," Alice said, putting the groceries away. "You see Graham today?"

"Yes," Kelly said shortly.

"I saw him ride out a few minutes ago with those soldiers," Alice said. "I hope you said goodbye to him properly."

Kelly flushed but did not answer. The news that he had gone did not trouble her particularly. She knew that Graham would turn up again, sooner or later, and then she would see how the cards fell. Despite what she'd said to Graham, she was quickly getting tired of Jackson's bullying.

But when Jackson pounded on her door the next morning, she opened it without hesitation and let him in.

Jackson rushed into the room, and Kelly saw that yesterday's trouble was far from his mind. He looked excited all over. Just like a little boy, she thought.

"We've been called back," he said happily, taking her by the shoulders. "All us scouts. The Apache war's started up again, and they sent word for us all to come back."

Kelly hardly knew what to say. She could not quite understand why he was so worked up over having to fight a war.

"If we leave first light tomorrow," he was saying, letting go of her and sitting on the bed. "We can be there afore ten days're gone."

Never before had Kelly thought of going so far south, but now, the idea intrigued her. Jackson's tales of the country and the Indians and the wild times that he had spent there had caught her imagination. So exciting did it seem, she too forgot about yesterday's trouble and even forgot to be annoyed because he had assumed, without asking, that she would go with him.

Jackson left to see about getting the horses and provisions ready. Kelly packed her things. If they were to leave at first light tomorrow, she had better speak to Alice about it as soon as she could.

Alice was still eating breakfast when Kelly broached the subject.

"I've got some news," Kelly said, sitting down across from Alice. "Jackson and I are off for the Arizona territory at first light tomorrow."

Alice choked on her eggs and hastily gulped some coffee to clear her throat.

"Sakes!" She said once she caught her breath. "Why in heaven's name would you do such a thing?"

A little annoyed, Kelly thought for a way to explain it.

"There's things to see and do down there that can't been seen or done up here," she said at last.

"Sure are," Alice retorted. "Like getting scalped. I don't care how buffaloed you are by his saucy ways, Kelly, Jackson Taylor ain't worth a scalpin'."

Kelly shook her head impatiently.

"You fuss too much. I'll stay in a settled town."

"There ain't any settled towns down there," Alice replied.

Kelly's face set stubbornly. Alice softened a bit.

"He's just filled your head with moonshine," she said. "Handsome men can do that when they're deadset after you. Don't go, honey. If he really cared, he wouldn't take you into such a place."

Kelly said nothing, and Alice saw that no words would change her mind. She ate silently for a moment, then an idea came to her.

"Whyn't you at least wait until Graham comes back," she said. "So you can tell him where you'll be?"

Kelly flinched as though she had been goosed.

"He might not be back for a year or more, that's why," Kelly said. "We want to leave tomorrow."

Alice felt encouraged that Kelly did not quibble over whether he would come back at all, which meant that she took it for granted that he would.

"He will be back, though," Alice said shrewdly. "And I reckon he'll have feet of clay. I bet it's eating him raw to think of you givin' your lovin' to that no-account Jackson."

Kelly reddened a little and stood up. She took a wad of bills from her pocket and handed them to Alice.

"You'll be heading east soon," she said. "Add this to my savings. I'll turn up for it sooner or later."

Alice accepted the bills. She thumbed through them, doing a little quick figuring. It was close on to three thousand she was holding for the girl. She felt touched; such trust was a warming thing.

"I'll take good care of it," Alice said, pocketing the money and standing up. "And you take good care of yourself. That's no safe country down there."

They hugged. Kelly thanked Alice again and left, excited by the prospect of tomorrow's adventure and wondering where it would lead her.

Chapter 29

They left Denver an hour before dawn and rode toward the high country. Jackson believed, as Kelly did, that it would be safer to travel along south through the mountains since it was summer and the weather was good. There was less danger of horse thieves and other reckless types.

As they rode, Kelly wondered if that wasn't just an excuse they made to themselves. Jackson loved the high country as much as she did, and riding though it for any reason was worth the trouble.

Four days out, they decided to camp over a day. Jackson took both horses and went to shoot some meat. Kelly sat near the fire and trimmed her fingernails with her knife. It was broad daylight, and the fire was nothing but embers. Her rifle was leaned up against a tree behind her, and she wore her gunbelt.

Enjoying the sunshine and the breeze that blew every now and then, Kelly sheathed her knife. Their trip so far had been uneventful, and she wondered at Alice's spookiness about travel. A little way off, she heard a rustling sound, as though someone or something was moving through the bushes. She froze, listening carefully, and heard the same sound again.

Kelly stiffened; something was out there. She picked up her rifle and cocked it. The woods went silent, and she stood tense, ready to act. Then she heard a heavy movement in the trees, and a bear lumbered into the camp. Kelly kept still and waited to see what it would do. She didn't want to provoke it with a sudden motion.

The bear was an awesome sight. Four feet high at the

shoulder, heavy muscles rippled beneath its shaggy, silver-tipped coat as it walked. It sniffed hard, wrinkling its nose and revealing its long yellow teeth.

The bear looked Kelly over and started to growl. Kelly longingly scanned the camp perimeter, hoping that Jackson would suddenly reappear. He didn't, and it could be hours before he returned. She began to edge toward the tree behind her; it had low branches, and she could climb it easily. She remembered hearing somewhere that grizzly bears could not climb trees.

She moved slowly and carefully to keep from alarming the bear into attacking her. The few yards to the tree looked more like miles. The bear swung its head from side to side, and its growling grew louder. Kelly felt her blood rushing through her body and thought that her heart was beating so loudly that the sound of it must be angering the bear.

Then, with a snarl, the bear reared up on its hind legs. Kelly threw the rifle to her shoulder and took aim. She fired once as the bear lunged forward, but the rifle seemed to explode in her hands, and she felt a terrible burning across the right side of her face as her right eye went blind.

Kelly flung the shattered rifle aside and drew her revolver. She paused to aim and saw a confused mass of snarling teeth and matted fur. She could smell warm, fetid breath, then she fired four times and was knocked across the clearing by a single blow of the bear's massive paw. Kelly landed in a heap, too stunned to regain her feet. She brought her revolver up, expecting to feel the bear's teeth rip into her at any moment.

But nothing happened. Her breath seemed to rasp in her ears, and tears streamed from her injured eye. Without thinking, she reloaded her revolver, her fingers deft for all that they were trembling. She snapped the barrel closed and got cautiously to her feet, tense and ready to shoot.

But the bear lay motionless. She could see blood on the ground but, at first, had no idea if it was hers or the bear's. She raised her revolver and fired twice more. Both shots struck him behind the shoulder, but the bear did not move. She hurriedly reloaded, and this time, her fingers fumbled with the cartridges because her fingers were now shaking uncontrollably. Then she approached the bear cautiously.

It was a mess, and Kelly felt her stomach turn. Its entire skull above the nose was gone. Brain tissue was spattered on the ground and all over the bear's neck and shoulders. Kelly guessed that at least two, maybe three bullets had struck the bear in the head, and judging from the blood that was pouring from its neck, it had taken at least one shot in the throat.

Kelly decided it was dead. After all, it didn't have much of a head left. Nevertheless, she crept around it and went straight to the tree. She stood underneath it, ready to climb if she had to, but not wanting to climb just for being afraid of a bear that was probably dead.

She holstered her revolver. Later, she could never remember how long she stood there, but she was beginning to come back to herself when she heard something crashing through the woods toward the clearing. She drew her revolver again.

It was Jackson, leading both horses. He looked out of breath. Kelly stepped forward from under the tree. Jackson took in Kelly's swollen face and the bear carcass with alarm.

"Christ! What happened?"

"Damn rifle blew up in my face," Kelly explained.

Jackson tethered the horses and went to look at the bear. It was dead all right. Even a dog needed more of head than that bear had left. From the looks of the mess, it must have been right on top of her when she had fired. He picked up the remains of Kelly's rifle.

"Looks like we picked up some bad shells," he said after examining it for a moment.

Kelly wasn't listening. She was looking into Jackson's shaving glass, trying to determine how badly her face was hurt. She washed the powder stains off her face with canteen water and her kerchief.

Her cheek and temple were burned, but it was hard to tell how badly. She pried her swollen eye open to see if it had been injured. No metal had gotten into it as far as she could see and feel, although the white of her eye had gone almost completely red.

"Are you hurt bad?" Jackson asked her.

"I don't think so," she said. "But it hurts like hell."

"You're lucky to be alive. Looks like that bear nearly had you for breakfast," he poked a finger into a long gash in the sleeve of Kelly's shirt. Kelly looked at it. Her upper arm was bruised.

"We'd better get this bear skinned and drag the carcass out of camp," Jackson said. "You can't eat griz, though we can probably sell the hide and claws for a good bit."

Kelly sat down on a log and examined her arm. It looked like her shirt had taken the worst of it. She shuddered to think what would have happened if she hadn't had her revolver. She would have been horribly mauled or even dead by the time Jackson had gotten there.

"You must have gotten him in the eyes," Jackson said, poking the shattered remains of the bear's head with the toe of his boot. "A revolver bullet probably wouldn't even dint a bear's forehead."

Kelly hardly heard what he was saying. Though she was still jumpy, the worst of her shakes had vanished, and she was beginning to feel a little silly for still being so scared.

Jackson looked over at her. That was some shooting she had just done, but she didn't seem to think it was any big deal. She looked right steady in the nerves, too. Thinking back on it, he was glad that he had not dared her to shoot him the other day back in Denver.

That night, Kelly lay awake long after Jackson had begun to snore. Looking up at the stars, it came to her that her feelings for Jackson had changed, although she couldn't quite say when the change had occurred. Initially, his obvious and straightforward interest in her had been irresistible. Since then, it had kind of leveled out, and Kelly did not find his company particularly diverting.

She also didn't trust him very much. He was smart, capable and independently minded, but he was not a thinking man, and he was stuck on himself and uneducated to boot.

He didn't love her, though she guessed that he had a certain affection for her. He would back her in a fight and protect her but more to satisfy his pride than for fear she would be hurt, and she knew that if she left him, he would recover from it in no time at all.

Though hurt to realize these things, her practical mind told her it was for the best. After the initial happiness of having her aloneness ended, Kelly realized that she didn't love him either. Kelly guessed he stayed with her because most women either would have made him pay for the nights they spent together or would have prodded him to marry them. Kelly could make money plenty of other ways and had no interest in marrying anyone.

But he respected her, even though he probably would never admit it to himself, and that was all she cared about. She decided that staying with him was the best thing to do for the moment. When they got to Arizona, he would be gone with the army a lot anyway. She would see how things worked out, and if she got homesick, she would ride north without him.

Before she fell asleep, Kelly wondered if such things would be different depending on how you felt about the person you did them with. Alice had told her that men were pretty much the same, and so were the things you did with them. But though she had to admit that she lacked Alice's experience, Kelly thought that Alice was wrong about this one thing. Jackson could never affect her the way Graham did, and surely, that made all the difference—in all things.

The rest of their trip south passed uneventfully. The trees became sparser and the terrain rockier. The air dried out, and the landscape took on shades of purple, red, and orange that struck Kelly as aridly beautiful, and she welcomed the change of scene and the sense of excitement it gave her.

Chapter 30

Graham, meanwhile, quit scouting and spent two months wandering up north. He told himself that he had no destination in mind, but he found himself back in Denver before high summer. He told himself that he had not come back to see Kelly, but he headed straight to Alice's, knowing that, if she was in Denver with Jackson or without him, that's where she was likely to be.

For all he'd not seen much of Kelly the last time he'd been in Denver, Graham knew that her days of being with Jackson Taylor were sharply numbered. Her decison to stay at Alice's gave her away, as did the talk floating around the town—talk of them having arguments that mostly arose from Jackson trying to boss her around. Knowing exactly how little Kelly cared for being told what to do made him confident that Jackson would not be able to hold her interest for long. Sooner or later, she would chase Jackson off, and Graham intended to take the opportunity to mend the things that stood between them.

Alice did not seem surprised to see him as he came up the walk, but he didn't care for the look on her face. Also, she let him into the house without a word and stood silently when he greeted her. Only tremendous worry could keep Alice's mouth closed for so long.

"Aren't you going to say hello?" He asked, casting an eye around and noting that there were packing boxes everywhere. It seemed she was actually going to move east.

Alice swallowed hard and tried to smile; she had seen him come up the walk like a man marching to battle. She could well imagine what was on his mind, especially with the evidence that his face gave. Seeing him look so openly expectant and happy gave her a turn; she was so used to his poker face that she had never fully realized that a poker face was all it was.

"Hidy," she said. Her voice was weak. She hated being the one to tell him what news there was to be told.

"Is Kelly here? Or is she out tearing up the countryside?" Graham asked. Alice's strangeness was affecting him, and his stomach felt quaky. Had something bad happened while he was away?

"No, she ain't," Alice said.

"Which?" He asked, afraid his guess had been based only on hope. "Is she not staying here or is she not out riding?"

Alice squeezed her hands, wishing she could talk fancy like Kelly could when she wanted. Maybe that would make the meaning of the words easier to say.

"What is it?" Graham asked. "Tell me what's wrong."

"Kelly ain't here. She's in Arizona. She and that Jackson Taylor rode down there two months ago."

Graham's face went white. He looked like a man so shocked from being shot that he couldn't yet feel the pain.

"If this is some kind of joke, I'll skin you alive," he said in a voice so cold that Alice knew he meant it literally.

She shook her head helplessly. Grahm turned on his heel and went down the hall. He threw open the door to Kelly's room. Her things were gone. He strode over to the bed and stripped the blankets back. He picked up the pillow and held it to his face, then let it fall from his hands. Even her smell was gone.

He spun around and went back to the kitchen. Alice was standing by the table, looking at him, her face distraught. Graham brushed by her as though she wasn't there.

"Where are you going?" Alice asked, grabbing his arm. Upset though she was, Alice saw murder in his face. If he went out so angry, he was liable to get into killing trouble.

"Let go of me," he said. "Or I'll knock you across the room."

Alice let go and backed away from him, frightened. Graham saw her fear and forced some of his anger to fade. It was replaced by the aching fact that Kelly was gone, and it was his fault. He should never have left. He should have packed her over his horse and run off with her like he'd heard some Mexicans did with their women.

But it was too late now.

"I'm leaving," he said stiffly.

"What? You just got here. Stay over a day or two and rest up," Alice said, disturbed by the look on his face. It was a cold, pained, reckless look that she didn't much care for.

"I believe I'll be going," he said.

"At least let me wrap up some food for you," Alice said.

"I've got provisions enough," he replied. "Take care."

To Alice's surprise, he kissed her on the cheek.

He went out the back door without another word. Alice went out on the porch and waved to him, but he did not seem to see her. She watched after him until he turned around the corner, then she went back inside and sat down, too upset to go back to her packing.

But there was nothing she could do. Kelly was gone, and lord only knew if she would ever be back. Graham, she knew, had taken Kelly's leaving as a sign that she had chosen Jackson over him, but that was ridiculous. He had never given Kelly any choice at all.

After a time, Alice sighed and went back to her packing. No matter what kind of a confused snarl those two had gotten themselves into, she had a train to catch at the end of the week.

Chapter 31

Kelly settled in Tucson, and as she had expected, Jackson was gone much of the time. Kelly didn't miss him particularly and made a life for herself without much fuss. The only thing that irked her was the weather, and the weather seemed to have altered everything about her, her temper, her lifestyle, and her appearance.

These days, she wore cavalry issue pants and boots and a succession of military blouses that had originally been light blue but which were now almost white from the sun and repeated washings. It was just too hot to wear a black hat, so she had traded hers in for a light gray one. She had also cut her hair short. Jackson had pitched quite a fit when he returned from a scouting mission and had seen it, but Kelly didn't care. The sweat and the dust made it impossible for her to keep her hair clean when it was long, besides, short hair was cooler. Jackson could gripe all he wanted, if he wasn't careful, she'd start working in her undershirt like her fellow wranglers, then he'd really have something to yell about.

Not that he wanted her to work either, Kelly thought sourly. He seemed to think she should lay around her hotel room all day and wait for him to favor her with his attention. Kelly didn't think anyone's attention was worth dying of boredom for, especially not in a place as hot as Arizona.

Five months ago, she had stopped playing poker because the stakes had just gotten too high. She'd seen violence before, but nothing like the wildness that went on in this territory. Now, to top off the white men who were killing each other off at an astounding rate, the Apache were making their last stand. The army needed every available man in the field. Kelly had been very relieved when Lt. Rollins, who had heard of her skill with horses, had asked her to help out at the fort.

It was hard work, and the men she worked with were rude and bathed only rarely, but it was a welcome change from the danger-charged atmosphere of Tucson's saloons. Of course, the men had not much liked the idea of working with a woman, and they gave her some rough times, but Kelly went about her business as though it didn't matter. Most of the men, when they saw her do her share of the work and more without complaining and watched her take her lumps silently, gave her a sort of grudging respect.

The only real problem she had was with a little ferret-like man who constantly made lewd comments to her. Kelly generally ignored him so completely he often wondered if she even heard him. One day, however, after he made such a comment, she grabbed him by the shirt front and slammed him against the barn wall so hard he was dizzy for a moment. Just as the dizziness began to pass, she slammed him twice more, and his head hit the barn wall with such a noise that the others had stopped working to see what was going on.

"Keep your damn filthy mouth shut," she had snarled. "Or I'll knock your skinny ass into next week."

She released him, and he fell to the ground cursing, but he had not bothered her again.

The day's work was nearly over. The men were sitting around sharing a canteen of whiskey. They offered it to her, but she shook her head. She never understood how they could drink whiskey in this heat. Her shirt had been soaked through with sweat so many times it was crusty with dust and mud, and she longed for a bath.

Lt. Rollins was walking toward the stable from the bunks. He was in charge of the fort's horses but, as a practical measure, had delegated most of the day to day authority to Kelly. He was busy with other things, and the other wranglers didn't have much sense of how to work out the many things that needed to be done.

"Good evening men," Lt. Rollins said, then he tipped his hat to Kelly. "Good evening Kelly." He felt uncomfortable calling her by her first name, but she had asked him to, and he felt it would be rude to refuse.

"Evening," the men muttered. None of them were regular army, so none of them felt obligated to be particularly polite.

"That wouldn't be whiskey in that canteen, would it?" Rollins asked. The new commander had taken a strict line about drinking.

None of the men answered.

"No, Lieutenant," Kelly said. "It's spring water with fennel in it. It's supposed to help cool you down after a hot day's work."

She was lying, and she knew he knew it. But she also knew that it went against his raising to call a woman a liar even if she was one. It was ungentlemanly. So, as she expected, he let the matter pass.

"Did all those new horses get shod?" He asked, aiming the question to the group even though he knew Kelly would answer.

"Yes sir, every one of them," she replied.

"Good, we need them taken over to Ft. Shelby tomorrow," he said. "Are they fit to ride?"

"Barely. They could use another week's work," Kelly said.

"We need them now. Are they all branded?"

"Yes. We did it the day we got them."

"Thirty-five head, right?"

"Yes, but two have pulled up lame. We can make up the difference from the reserve stable."

"Very well. Have them ready to go at first light tomorrow. There'll be an escort ready for you."

There were some audible groans from the other wranglers. Lt. Rollins silenced them with a stare.

"At first light, men," he said sternly. Then he tipped his hat to Kelly and left.

The men continued to grumble, and while Kelly did not join them, she felt just as disgruntled at the thought of driving thirty-five head of horses across ten miles of parched ground. She hated droving. The dust got so thick you couldn't see, and when it touched your skin, it mixed with your sweat and turned to mud.

There was also considerable danger from the Indians, even if they did have an escort. Thirty-five horses were an easy target; all the Apache had to do was stampede them.

"Mebbe you oughter sit out tomorrow, ma'am," one of the ranglers, a grizzled man named Dave Meyers said to her. "Apt to be some innians about."

"No, they'll need all of us," Kelly said, although she was sorely tempted to make some excuse not to go.

Slowly, the men dispersed. Kelly went back to her room wanting nothing more than a good night's sleep and trying not to be worried over tomorrow.

As they set out, it seemed that her fears had been groundless. She and the four other drovers were plenty able to contain the horses, and they were accompanied by a detachment of twenty cavalry. They kept a fair pace, slowing only as the country became rockier and hillier.

Occupied with her work, Kelly hardly noticed the difference in terrain. She was riding along the right side of the herd. Another rangler was up ahead riding point, one was riding left flank and two were riding the tail. Four soldiers led the way, and the rest rode in formation behind the wranglers who were riding sweep on the herd.

The horses kicked up a lot of dust, and Kelly had pulled her kerchief up over her nose and mouth. Thankfully, there was no wind, which would have made things worse.

They were all armed. Kelly wore her gunbelt and had tied her rifle boot to her saddle. As her mare was no good for droving, she was riding an army horse with painful gaits. After ten minutes of having her tailbone jarred, she wished the whole miserable job were done with.

They were riding through a sloping valley that was crested by low red hills. Kelly wiped the sweat from her forehead with the back of her gloved hand. It came away muddy. When she looked back up, she sat stunned. Indians were pouring over the rise to their left.

Shots were being fired. The horses began to stampede. She and the other wranglers fought to ride them down as the soldiers returned the Indians' fire. The dust thickened instantly, and Kelly could hardly see her own horse's neck. She was not frightened, because as the dust obscured everything, it hid her from being shot at.

They were able to contain the horses and slow them down, but in doing so, they had left their escort far behind. The soldiers had slowed to deal with the attackers. Kelly and the others were at a loss—should they streak for the fort and risk another attack, or wait for the soldiers?

The question was settled for them as a hail of bullets sliced through the air, felling one wrangler and several horses. Another group of Indians swept down from a rise ahead of them. As if at some silent order, they raced with the panicked horses, knowing the fort was their only chance.

Kelly drew her revolver. Indians on swift ponies were running alongside them now. Before she could fix on a target and fire, a bullet struck her horse in the neck, and he tumbled head over heels, spilling her to the ground.

Dazed, but unhurt, Kelly scrambled to her feet. Hooves thudded behind her, and she whirled, unsure if it were friend or foe or stampeding horse. It was an Apache brave, carrying a Winchester and firing wildly.

One shot struck the dirt near her feet. Kelly brought her revolver up and fired twice, knocking him from the saddle. His pony reared at the noise and paused in his running. Kelly dove toward him and caught him by his hackamore. He leapt forward, but Kelly swung neatly onto his back, untroubled by the fact that he wore no saddle.

The herd was now far ahead of her, apparently she'd been spared because the other Indians were focusing on the horses. Kelly spurred the pony on, not wanting to be left too far behind even if her fellow wranglers were in a battle for their lives. She heard gunfire from all sides.

Looking back over her shoulder, she saw the soldiers riding hard behind her. She reached the herd before them. The wranglers were busy fighting for their lives, and the horses were scattering. Amid the swirling dust, Kelly saw Dave wrestling with an Indian. She aimed carefully and fired once, knocking the Indian off of him. Kelly shot the Indian once more, just to make sure, then rode over to see if Dave was all right.

The remaining soldiers swept up behind her, scaring her pony. She had to stop shooting in order to control him. More shots were fired, but Kelly could not see who was winning the fight.

When her horse was calmer, she hurriedly rode forward again, but by then the fighting was over. As the dust settled, Kelly saw bodies lying on the ground Indians, soldiers, and wranglers, but the army seemed to have taken the day. Fifteen of the original twenty were still ahorse, though some of them were wounded. Besides herself and Dave, only one other wrangler was still alive.

The lieutenant in charge was ordering his men to pack the dead up over their horses. Kelly motioned for the two remaining wranglers to help her gather up the remains of the horse herd.

Only twenty horses could be easily found, and no one was in the mood to go looking for the stragglers. They continued on to the fort more hurriedly than before, even though it was much harder to control the now riled-up horse herd with two of the wranglers dead and another nursing a gun shot arm.

At last, the fort loomed ahead. The miles since the fight had seemed endless. They all had twitchy backs, a condition common to those expecting to be shot at every moment—but the last mile was terrible. Kelly had not been truly scared until the possibility of safety rose before her.

Once inside the fort, they drove the remaining horses into a waiting corral, then dismounted. After seeing to their tired horses, they were informed that they would have to spend the night in the fort.

In the morning, the three of them rode back to Tucson with another group of soldiers. The trip passed uneventfully, and as they rode back into town, Dave rode up beside her.

"So how did you like your first Indian fight?" He asked her.

"Not at all," she said with a smile. In truth, the swirling dust and echoing shots had kept her from being scared, because she could not see anything much.

"Well, I sure appreciate what you done for me," Dave said. "And I ain't afraid to say so. You ever need a favor, you just ask me."

"I do appreciate it, Dave. Maybe you can take my turn at stall cleaning sometime."

They both laughed. Stall cleaning was the bane of their existence. Lt. Rollins had been known to go over stall floors with a white glove.

They shook hands and went their separate ways. Kelly left her horse at the stable and walked to her hotel, wearily climbing the stairs to her room, thinking what a relief it was that at least she hadn't been sick with the monthlies on top of everything else. It struck her odd, though, now that she considered it. Usually, she was as regular as clockwork, and she was now over a week late.

She entered her room and pulled off her boots, her mind uneasy with thinking. Alice had told her that not coming sick was a sign that you were going to have a baby, but she had not said whether there was anything else that could cause it. Kelly thought back and remembered that Alice had also told her that feeling ill in the mornings was another sign.

A little relieved, Kelly stripped her clothes off. She was never ill. Next month, no doubt, her period would come back to annoy her. For now, it was a relief not to have it.

She washed herself and climbed into bed, but her sleep was restless that night and for many to come, because her mind was not at ease over things. Her unease grew as the days passed, and still, her period did not start.

Jackson returned. Kelly, who was worried about other things, found his presence more irritating than usual. Her period was now two months late, and she had started feeling ill in the mornings. Jackson stayed a week, and by the end of that week, Kelly was feeling very ill indeed.

The morning he left, Kelly woke up feeling groggy and sick. The bed insisted on spinning around, making it difficult for her not to throw up. The bed stopped abruptly, and after her stomach settled a bit, Kelly managed to sit up. She hadn't slept well, and now, her head ached on top of everything else. She slumped back against the headboard; she was hard pressed to remember ever having felt worse.

Jackson was standing with his back to her, shaving. He saw her struggles in the mirror he was using, and he spoke.

"Don't get up. I'll stop by the fort and tell 'em you're sick. You really look like hell."

"Thanks," Kelly said dryly, "That's just what I needed to hear."

Jackson ignored her sarcasm.

"Just stay in bed. I'll get 'em to send breakfast up to you."

Kelly groaned at the thought of eating.

"Don't you dare. I'll be sick if I eat anything."

"You oughta see a doctor."

Kelly ran her fingers through her damp hair. "I don't think a doctor will help any," she muttered.

Jackson half turned to face her. He looked concerned.

"How do you know?"

Kelly shrugged. It was not an easy thing to say, and she had to work up to it.

"I'm worried about you," he said, turning back to the mirror. "You've been acting right strange lately, and this ain't the first time you've woke up sick."

"I know," Kelly said, smiling a little. He looked funny with his face half covered with shaving soap.

"It ain't anything funny," he said. "Do you have a fever?"

"No."

"There's some kind of fever going through the Apache," he said, scraping the last of the soap from his face. "You got the shakes?"

"No."

Jackson rinsed his face, then dried it carefully. Kelly wrinkled her nose as she watched him preen in the mirror. He was so vain.

"Well, I wonder what it could be then," he said.

"I'm going to have a baby," Kelly said.

Jackson's back jerked as though he'd been stabbed between the shoulders. He dropped the towel.

"What?"

"I'm going to have a baby," she said again.

Kelly could see he was struggling to come to grips with what she'd said. It always amazed her how he had trouble with the obvious.

He didn't say anything for a long time. Kelly watched him with little interest; she doubted he would surprise her, although she kind of hoped that he would.

"What are you going to do?" He asked at last without turning around.

"I'm going back north," Kelly heard herself say.

"I don't want to go north."

"No one's asked you to," she said.

He turned around and looked hard at her. She kept her face expressionless. He looked so like a child that, suddenly, she knew he would never figure into her plans again.

"Why don't you stay here?" He asked. "There are things you can do. I bet someone over at Juanita's will know how to fix it."

Kelly shook her head.

"That's too dangerous."

Jackson looked away from her. He put his shirt on slowly. Kelly watched him disinterestedly. Now that it was said, she was glad, and she couldn't wait to go north.

"Is that it, then?" He asked awkwardly.

"For you it is," Kelly said in a voice that was suddenly full of anger.

Jackson flinched at the sudden change in her demeanor.

"It's not my fault," he protested.

"Well, it's not mine either," Kelly said in a calmer voice. It was too hot outside to argue about things that couldn't be helped.

It hurt her pride to see how quickly he gathered his things to leave. He would not look her in the eye, either. Kelly lay down and stared at the ceiling. She heard the door open, then Jackson spoke.

"I put some money on the dresser for you, Kelly," he said. "When are you leaving?"

"Today," she said, deciding she couldn't spend another day in the Arizona territory. "Tell Lt. Rollins I said goodbye, and I'm sorry for going off so abruptly."

"I will," he said. He hesitated near the door. He seemed to be waiting for her to say something else; Kelly found that very irritating.

"Well, go!" She snapped suddenly, sitting upright. She felt she would burst if she had to look at him for another moment.

Jackson left, slamming the door behind him. Kelly was glad her revolver was out of reach, otherwise she might have shot him through the door.

After a while, she pulled herself out of bed and got dressed. She was two months pregnant; Alice had said that it generally took nine months to have a baby. With this in mind, she laid plans to go back north and then ride east to find Alice. Not only did Alice have her savings, but Kelly knew that, in this situation, being with Alice would comfort her.

She left town by late afternoon without saying goodbye to anyone. The ride north would be long and tiring, but she started it eagerly, realizing for the first time that she had been homesick all along.

Chapter 32

Two weeks later found Kelly in Creed. She didn't see much change in her body yet and decided that she'd better play some cards and see if she could increase her road stake. She stayed for a month. The cards were running well, and she had no difficulties until the morning she woke up to find that her jeans didn't fit. It seemed that her stomach had swollen considerably overnight.

Kelly sat miserably down on the bed, knowing what she should do. She couldn't go in saloons or play poker when she was visibly pregnant. She couldn't ride wild either. Anger rose in her. She snatched up the bed pillow and threw it at the wall. It was a poor choice, for it bounced off the wall silently, and Kelly wanted to hear something crash and break.

But it was no good having a tantrum. She dressed slowly, leaving the top buttons of her jeans undone and her shirt untucked, and by the time she was done, a plan had formed in her mind. If Alice had her long-dreamed of boarding house, Kelly would stay there until the baby was born. Then she would save some more money and buy her horse farm.

While she collected her things, she remembered that Alice had finally retired to Kansas City and wondered how long it would take to get there. Though she had not been east in a while, she had heard that Kansas City was about as safe as a mother's lap these days.

She started out that same day, again without saying goodbye to anyone, even though several of her friends were in town. The last thing she did before leaving was to trade her Indian pony in for a more civilized animal. She would not be traveling in the wild places for a good while.

The ride to Kansas took over two weeks, while she did not hurry it, neither did she savor it. She was too angry to realize that it was to be her last horseback ride for nearly a year.

It was the last week in September when Kelly finally reached Kansas City. Alice's boarding house was not difficult to find. It was in a good location not far from the train depot, on a pleasantly shady dirt street.

The house itself was a huge rambling structure that Kelly guessed had been built before the war. A discreet sign announced that there were "rooms to let" and that "laundry was taken in." Kelly smiled for the first time in two weeks when she saw those signs. It was just like Alice to take in laundry when she didn't need the money just to prove the place wasn't a sporting house.

Dusty and disheveled as she was, Kelly decided to go in through the back door. There was no point in scaring off the respectable trade. She climbed the back steps, hoping this was the last mile of her journey. She was bone tired.

Only the screen door was closed, and Kelly rapped on its frame with her knuckles. There was no answer, so she rapped again, louder this time. Now she heard someone moving around somewhere in the house.

"Don't break the door down!" Yelled a voice that Kelly recognized as Alice's. "I'm comin'!"

The screen door flew open, and Alice stared at her, her mouth open to speak but the words forgotten.

"Hidy, Alice," Kelly said. "Place looks just like you said it would."

"Mercy! Kelly Knowlton! I thought those heathen Apache had gotten you long ago. Come in, child, and let's have a look at you."

Kelly entered the kitchen and sat in the chair Alice ushered her to. Alice had recovered swiftly from her initial surprise and was now looking Kelly over with a careful eye.

"So did you and Mr. Taylor have a parting of the ways?" She asked.

"You could call it that," Kelly said dryly. "I'm going to have a baby."

Alice clucked sorrowfully.

"Did he run off on you?"

"No, I ran him off," Kelly said. "I was mighty tired of his company anyway."

"I hope you at least shot him in the foot or something," Alice said. "So he would regret it a little."

Kelly shook her head. "He's not worth the lead." But secretly, she wished she had thought of it at the time. Now it was too late.

"Well now," Alice said. "You can stay here of course, as

long as you want. I need some help with the banking and the figuring. This ain't quite like running a saloon."

"Thanks," Kelly said.

"Did you ride all the way here from Arizona?"

"I lingered in Colorado for a month."

"That's still a lot of riding to do in your condition. Tell you what," she said, getting to her feet, "I'll have the boy draw you a bath. Take your things up to the first room on the right. Get settled in, take a bath, then we'll have a hot supper. In the morning, we'll go get you some clothes that fit. You'll feel better in no time."

Kelly obeyed Alice's instructions without question; she felt limp now that her journey and the immediate worry of a place to stay were over with, but she didn't really think that anything would ever be all right again.

Chapter 33

As Kelly settled in at Alice's, Graham wandered through the Colorado territory looking for her. After searching Denver, Silver City and a dozen places whose names he could not remember, he rode into Creed. He had not heard that Kelly had left the Arizona territory, but he knew that if she ever left Jackson, she would probably make a beeline north. In his opinion, she was long overdue for getting tired of Jackson.

Creed had always been one of her favorite stomping grounds, and his first stop was the Gold Nugget Saloon, where their mutual friend Anderson Whitehead still kept bar.

"How do," Anderson said as Graham stepped up for a drink. "Whiskey?"

"Sure."

"Ain't seen you in a while, Graham," Anderson said, pouring the whiskey. "How you been keepin'?"

"Fair to middlin'. Yourself?"

"The same. Business is good, but my old lady run off." Anderson shrugged. "I don't need to split the proceeds, but I got to pay for my lovin'. I reckon I break even on the whole transaction."

"Who'd she run off with?"

"Some fancy talking brush salesman from back east," Anderson replied. "A man low enough to sell brushes for a living will do most anything."

"That's a fact," Graham said sympathetically. It was no news to him that brush salesmen were shiftless. He wondered if the one who had run off with Anderson's wife was as fond of cholera jokes as the one that had chased him off that train back east.

"Got any other news worth telling?" He asked.

Anderson scratched his head.

"You know Marshal Alan from Kansas?"

"Would that be Tom Alan?"

"The same. Well, he went lawing down south a little ways. Took a bullet in the back one night. Killed him dead."

"Sorry to hear that," Graham said. "He was a good man."

"Good enough to wear a badge anyway," Sam said. "Hey, you remember Kelly, don't you?"

"Of course," Graham sipped his whiskey to hide his interest.

"Well, she's back up north from Arizona, you know."

"No I didn't know," Graham set his glass down. This was sounding hopeful. "Did you see her?"

"Yep. She was here for about a month in September. Cleaned right up playing cards. Ole Dan Bolton wanted her to hire on at his pharo table, but she up n' left without a word to anyone."

"Didn't say where she was going?"

"Nope. No one even saw her leave. But Whitey Jansen said he saw her in Topeka just a few weeks ago."

Graham frowned. Why would she go to Kansas? She hadn't been so far east since 1873. She might be looking for him, if so, it made sense; he used to spend a lot more time in Kansas than in Colorado.

"I haven't heard of her being in any trouble," he said.

"No one up here has either," Sam said. "We all thought it odd, her going off sudden like that. Some thought she might have trouble following her from Arizona, but no one ever showed up looking for her, and the sheriff ain't got no notice on her."

Graham didn't like the way it sounded. It was just possible that no-account Jackson Taylor had gotten her in the middle of some kind of scrap and had left her in it or gotten himself killed before it was settled.

He had another drink and took a hand in an afternoon poker game. But the play didn't hold his interest, and he left before dark. He went to bed early that night and was up before dawn. He rode back to Kansas, deciding to see if he could find Kelly in Topeka. If she wasn't there, he would go to Kansas City and look Alice up, knowing that if Kelly were in trouble and unable to find him, that's where she would go.

Chapter 34

Kelly moved through the next few months like a caged animal. Her pregnancy was not a particularly difficult one, at least, Alice frequently said that it was not, but Kelly felt that pregnancy was the most cumbersome state she'd ever been in. Used to being active and free to do as she pleased, she found it irksome to be so large and, on top of it, to be confined to the house.

Pregnant women weren't supposed to leave the house if they could help it. Kelly didn't generally pay much mind to such conventions, but she had discovered that people stared worse at a pregnant woman than they did at a woman wearing pants, so she stayed inside. She helped Alice with the housework and did the accounts, but all of these tasks bored her even if they did keep her busy. She missed being outdoors, and she missed riding. She hated feeling so helpless and dreaded giving birth and becoming a mother.

She became snappish and irritable. Alice put it down to the strains of pregnancy and tried to humor her. That only made things worse. Although Kelly never found the words to express it, she felt she was being patronized. She hated being patronized, and the more pregnant she became, the worse it became.

November came, and Kelly had been at Alice's less than two months. One afternoon, she sat at her desk in the little office at the back of the house, going over the shabby ledger Alice kept. It was frustrating work. Though smart and a good business woman, Alice had only a sketchy education and was hopeless at math. The books were always in a snarl. Kelly had never cared much for figuring herself, although she was good at it. Untangling the books always shortened her temper.

She was wearing a dress, too, which also annoyed her. This one was especially irritating because it was very full, and she had to wear several petticoats to help hide her condition. She found it difficult to walk properly when wearing so many clothes.

Footsteps sounded in the hall. Kelly looked up. That wasn't Alice's tread; it was a man's. But there were no boarders at the moment, so who could it be?

There was a knock at the door. Kelly opened her right-hand desk drawer and pulled out her revolver, which she rested in her lap.

"Who is it?" She asked, keeping her voice pleasant in case it was a prospective boarder.

"It's Graham."

Kelly was too amazed to reply, but she didn't have to, for he opened the door and walked in without waiting for an invitation. Kelly stared. It really was him.

"Hello," he said, smiling at her amazed face. "Surprised you, didn't I?"

Kelly nodded.

"I sure had a time hunting you down," he said sitting on a small couch that stood to the right of her desk.

Kelly nodded. "How'd you know to find me here?"

"Just a guess."

Neither of them spoke for a moment. Graham thought there was something bothering her, something more than being surprised to see him. She looked pale. But he did not ask. He would find out in time.

"Well, I'm glad to see you," Kelly said. She wanted to go over and hug him, but if she stood up, he would be able to see that she was pregnant despite the full skirt and annoying petticoats, so she remained seated.

"Did you see Alice yet?" Kelly asked.

"No, I let myself in," Graham said. "The door wasn't locked. I didn't know Kansas City had become so civilized."

"It's not," Kelly said, taking the revolver from her lap and placing it on the desk. Graham laughed. The sound of it seemed to echo oddly in the room. Kelly fiddled with her pencil nervously.

"I heard you dallied in Creed a while after leaving Arizona," Graham said. "I hope you have no troubles with the law or with those who don't care for it."

"No," Kelly said. "Arizona was wild, but I kept my nose clean. I spent the last year wrangling with the army."

"See any Indian trouble?"

"Enough," Kelly replied.

Silence fell upon them again.

"You cut your hair," he said.

"Yes," Kelly said, still playing with the pencil. "Arizona was as hot as Hades."

"I wish you'd put that pencil down," Graham said at last. "You're giving me the fidgets."

The pencil fell from her fingers. Kelly folded her hands in her lap.

"How've you been keeping?" She asked him.

"Fair. I went up to the Dakotas for a spell. You and I ought to take a ride up there sometime."

Kelly turned a shade whiter when he said that. Graham leaned forward, concerned.

"I wish you'd tell me why you're sitting at a desk in Kansas City doing figures and wearing a dress," Graham said.

Kelly did not reply. She looked down at the ledger; she could not conceive of telling him she was pregnant, but it wasn't the kind of thing you could keep a secret either. More than anything, she wished that she had never heard of Jackson Taylor and that she and Graham could ride up north together.

"You won't tell me?" He asked gently.

Kelly took a deep breath, and gripping the edge of the desk, she stood up. Graham looked at her a moment, as though waiting for her to speak, then his eyes fell to her waistline, and his face froze. He looked very much as she had just a few minutes earlier when he had reappeared so unexpectedly.

Kelly sat back down. His surprise was seeping away, only to be replaced with anger. Kelly saw his face cloud over and felt a terrible sadness well up inside her.

"You best go somewhere and get a hold of yourself," she said dully. "I have enough to worry me without you causing a ruckus over something that can't be helped."

Her words reached him, and his anger disappeared. There was no sense in carrying on at her, and Jackson Taylor was too far away to get at.

"Did he leave you?" Graham asked quietly.

"No, I threw him out," Kelly said, wondering why that was foremost in everyone's mind. "He wasn't worth keeping anyway."

Graham did not answer. Kelly had started fiddling with her pencil again, though he guessed she was probably over her embarrassment now that all was known.

Kelly would not meet his eyes, which made him think she was still embarrassed. He tried to think of something to say that would set her at ease.

"Well, I expect Alice is glad to have your company again," he said at last, "and your help with the books. How long do you plan on staying here?"

"Until the baby's born anyway," Kelly replied, still looking down at her ledger. "After that we'll see. I'll want to get that farm of mine sooner or later."

"Sooner, probably, if I know you."

That almost made Kelly smile. She looked up.

"It depends on how the cards fall," she said, shrugging. "But I think I heard Alice come in the kitchen door. I ought to go help put the groceries away."

"I'll do it," Graham said, standing up. "You ought to take it easy."

Kelly snorted. "Don't you start with that; Alice is bad enough. She even takes my arm when I go down the stairs."

"She's just trying to do right by you. After all, you are in a delicate condition."

"I'll never be that delicate."

"And if you ever are, I bet you never admit it. Go on back to the books. I'll help Alice."

He went to the door, but Kelly stopped him with a question just as his hand fell on the knob.

"How long are you going to stay?"

Graham looked over at her, but Kelly's eyes had fallen back to her ledger.

"Until you get tired of my company, I guess."

"That won't happen," Kelly replied, looking up,

"I wouldn't be too sure of that."

He left the room, and Kelly pushed the ledger away. It would be useless to try and unsnarl the accounts now; her mind wouldn't allow her to concentrate, and she'd just foul them up worse.

Alice was in the pantry, putting the groceries away, when Graham entered the kitchen. She stepped out into the kitchen and jumped.

"Goodness! I didn't hear you come in. I must be getting deaf if I can't hear that door squeak."

"I came in from the back room," he replied.

"You've already seen Kelly then."

"Yes."

Alice was relieved—that she didn't have to tell him what news there was to be told.

"I hope you didn't fuss at her any."

"I never fuss at her. I have better sense than that."

Alice snorted in a way that clearly implied that she doubted that he had any sense at all and went back to putting her groceries away.

"You got a room available?" Graham asked her.

"Yes, but we can't have no men in the house when she's in such a state."

"That's foolish," Graham said, annoyed. "Besides, I told her I'd stay. Do you want to be the one to tell her you won't let me?"

"Hell no. You tell her. Tell her it's for her own good. Tell her she won't have no reputation left at all if you stay here at such a time."

"Kelly don't concern herself with such things and neither do I."

"Well, if you cared a rap about her you would. You know how people talk in a civilized place like this. She'll have to live here long after you ride off into the sunset."

Graham said nothing. He could not decide how much truth there was in what Alice was saying, and her comment about his shiftlessness irked him. But she was right about one thing—it would be selfish of him not to do what was in Kelly's best interest. The problem lay in determining what that was.

The kitchen door opened, and Kelly walked in. Graham was distracted from his thoughts by noticing that she was as lightfooted as ever.

"You ought to take that back room on the west side of the house, Graham," she said, taking a sack of coffee from the bags on the table and putting it in the cupboard.

Alice looked pointedly at Graham, who cleared his throat before speaking.

"I was thinking that I would find a hotel nearer the livery stable," he said, his uncertain tone belying his lack of conviction.

"Why?" Kelly asked, frowning.

"It's closer to the saloons," Alice said, trying to cover up Graham's indecision.

Kelly's frown deepened; her eyes looked from Alice to Graham. Alice looked guilty, and Graham looked uncomfortable.

"This is some foolishness the two of you cooked up, isn't it?" She demanded. "Well, I never heard the like. A bank-robbing shootist and a poker-playing female saloon keeper worrying about my reputation."

"Now don't go and get all upset, honey," Alice said placatingly, wishing that Kelly didn't get mad so easily. "We're just trying to do right by you, that's all."

"Then think about what's best for me," Kelly snapped. "Instead of what's best for the neighbors."

"It is best for you," Alice replied. "You might not care now, but you will someday. You may have to live here for a while, and you may never be able to live all this scandal down."

"I don't have to live anywhere I don't want to."

"Honey, please, listen . . ."

"It's bad enough you won't let me out of this damn house," Kelly went on, her anger rising at Alice's placating tone, for she knew that if she had not been pregnant, Alice would have slapped her flat for such rudeness. "Now you want to keep everyone else out to boot."

Alice threw her hands up in the air. Trust Kelly to fly off the handle about something that almost anyone else in the world would take for granted. But Alice knew there would be no talking to her now. Kelly had the bit between her teeth, and she never listened to anyone when in such a state.

"You tell her, Graham," Alice said, making a final attempt to salvage the situation as she sat down tiredly at the table.

At this, Kelly's eyes snapped to Graham, daring him to say anything contrary to her views on the matter. Meeting her glare, Graham smiled wryly. There was nothing of embarrassment about her now, and it pleased him that she seemed to care so much about where he stayed.

"Well," he said mildly, not looking away from Kelly. "Like I said, I'd rather stay here, but I can't if I'm not welcome."

Kelly smiled at him, the anger vanishing from her face as if it had never been there at all. Alice caught the look that passed between them and wondered if there were more to his sudden arrival than just coincidence. After all, she never expected to see Graham McNair east of Abilene again, but there he stood. Alice knew he hadn't traveled all that way just to see her, no matter how fine a boarding house she ran.

"You're welcome here," Alice said, a sly note creeping into her voice "I never meant to say that you weren't. I just didn't know Kelly here had such strong feelings on the matter."

Kelly rolled her eyes. If Alice were going to start up with that nonsense again, Graham had almost better stay at a hotel, but that would allow Kelly too much uncertainty about how he spent his time, so she said nothing.

"If it's settled then," Graham said, "I'll take that room on the west side of the house like you said, Kelly."

"That's fine." Kelly replied. "You'll like the view. You can see clear out of town."

After Graham had gone outside, Kelly sat down at the table and avoided Alice's annoyingly knowing look. She would be subjected to enough looks during Graham's stay, but it would be worth it. Alice noted Kelly's demeanor and crowed silently to herself. It seemed that Jackson Taylor hadn't managed to end this little drama after all. The ensuing weeks ought to be right interesting.

Kelly's spirits rose considerably after Graham's arrival, even though Alice thought they talked less than usual.

It puzzled her, but they seemed to spend a lot of time just sitting in the same room with each other. Graham also fell into the habit of lounging on the settee in her office while Kelly did the books. Sometimes he would forego his evening of card playing and sit in the parlor with them. Alice would work on the mending, and Kelly would read aloud.

But generally they just sat together. Alice never did determine whether or not they were only silent when she was around, although she would have laid odds that they had some conversations when she was not. Alice would have given her eye teeth to be a fly on the wall when they were alone together.

One such evening, they sat in the darkness, Kelly absently patting her stomach. It was good to be around Graham again;

they had not talked much since he'd arrived, but his presence was comforting. It beat Alice's over-active mouth any day.

"It is good to see you again," she said, smiling at him.

Graham jumped a little. Her boldness about saying such things always surprised him a bit, and he never knew what to say back.

Kelly laughed softly. For someone so brave, he could be such a coward.

"You haven't changed a bit," he said. "I missed you too."

It was Kelly's turn to be surprised, and she saw his teeth flash as he grinned at her. She laughed again.

"I'm pretty scared, you know," she said after a moment.

"Scared of what?" He asked, surprised.

"Of having this baby," she said.

Since that first day, they had never mentioned or discussed her condition, but Graham didn't seem embarrassed now that she had brought it up.

"I expect Alice has filled you up with a lot of twaddle," he said. "My mother had six kids, and it never troubled her much."

"Six?" Kelly was shocked. He had never before mentioned his family at all.

"It's different for everyone, I guess," he went on, "but you can be sure Alice has told you the worst she knows of."

"Whatever became of your family?" Kelly asked, temporarily diverted from her fears by her interest in his past.

Graham shrugged. "I'm not too sure. I went back east in '73 and tried to find them, but they were pretty well scattered. My father and two older brothers died in the war. My mother died in '70, and my oldest sister married a storekeeper. That's all I know."

"Is that why you were at the Millersville train station that day?" Kelly asked. She had know for a long time that he had gone east to escape from some trouble, but she had always wondered why he had gone so far east. Once she had gotten to know him, it had seemed an odd thing for him to do.

"Yes," he answered, smiling to think of that day. "I caught a train out of Albany but was driven off it by the most persistent brush salesman I have ever seen."

Kelly laughed. She could just imagine it. When their laughter ended, they were silent again. Kelly thought back to her Grandfather's farm in New York and wondered who the new owners had been and if they had kept it running. For the first time, she was filled with curiosity about what changes time had wrought on her father, her aunt, and her stable hands.

"I wonder what's become of my people in New York," she said finally.

"I'll give you train fare if you want to go see."

Kelly couldn't tell if he was joking or not, but either way, the thought was startling. She could go back if she wanted. There was nothing to be afraid of now. But there also wasn't any point to it.

"No thanks," she said, thinking that would end the conversation. But, to her surprise, Graham pursued it.

"Did you ever regret running away?"

Kelly shook her head.

"Not even with the fix you're in now?"

"I'm not in a fix," she said indignantly.

He grinned. "Most people would think so."

"Most people are fools," Kelly said shortly. She was not worried about making a living or suffering from the scandal or about any of the other things everyone seemed to think should worry her. She was worried about how to raise a baby without giving up everything she enjoyed.

"I'll bet Jackson Taylor thinks you're one. Why ever did you let him off so easy?"

Kelly sat speechless for a moment. Graham had not mentioned Jackson to her since his arrival in Kansas City. Sometimes, she wondered if Graham even remembered there was such a person. Even back in Denver, Graham had ignored her relationship with Jackson as much as possible, and now, he was making a direct reference to it. Something must be rankling him.

"Well, who the hell wants him around?" Kelly demanded. "You sure never liked him, and the only thing he's good for is killing Indians and . . ." her voice trailed off and her face flushed, embarrassed at what she had almost said.

Graham chuckled, and after a moment, Kelly did too. It was not often that he got to see her red-faced over something. He had not meant to provoke her, but the anger he felt toward Jackson was very real, and it puzzled him that Kelly did not seem to share it.

"I never could figure out why you liked him so," Graham said at last. "But I sure know now."

Kelly flushed again. She had never before heard him speak of such things, and she could not get used to it all at once.

"Don't you ever get lonely?" She asked.

"Is that what you call it?" He teased.

"I mean apart from that," Kelly said, impatiently. Her embarrassment gone, she did not want him to become evasive just when things were getting interesting.

"I don't get lonely in general," he said. "Although I sometimes miss certain people."

Kelly wanted to ask if she was one of them, but didn't. She realized then that she still loved him. Time hadn't changed that. Jackson hadn't changed that. It occurred to her that she might always love him, and that he might never love her back. She wondered if she could stand it.

He looked so perfect, sitting there. The way his jacket fit his shoulders, the lines of his face, the way his hair skimmed the neck of his shirt—it all tugged at her heart, and she turned her face from him in embarrassment when she realized that she was wondering what it would be like to make love to him.

Graham had an idea of why she had looked away from him so abruptly. Though he had been jealous at the time, he had not said a word about it when she had gone with Jackson, half hoping that it would turn her away from him, and so he would have a reason to turn away from her. But it hadn't worked out that way.

He stood and said good night. Kelly did not answer, but she looked at him and he could see her heart in her eyes. He backed away and went to his room. He knew he would not be able to sleep, so after he heard Kelly retire, he slipped out of the house and headed to the Buffalo Tongue saloon.

Kelly did not sleep well that night. After tossing and turning until midnight, she finally lit her lamp and tried to read. Her back was achy, and she could not quite get comfortable. She heard Graham come in a little after three and felt relieved that he had not been gone all night, as that would have left too many possibilities for her mind to stand.

She slept a little then, and woke up right around six o'clock. She got dressed slowly and went downstairs to help Alice make breakfast. Tired, Kelly really wanted to stay in bed but did not dare. She had a feeling that today was the day, and she did not want to be alone if she could help it.

The pains began a little after eleven o'clock. They weren't very bad at first, and she ignored them until after two o'clock. She and Alice were washing up the lunch dishes when Alice noticed that Kelly was a little pale.

"Are you feeling all right, Kelly?" Alice asked her. "You didn't eat much lunch."

Kelly set down the plate she had been drying.

"I believe I'm going to have this baby soon," she said, wincing as the worst cramp yet crossed her abdomen.

Alice drew in her breath.

"Are you having pains?"

Kelly nodded. "Since before noon."

"Mercy! Why didn't you say something? Do you want to have that baby while you're wiping the dishes?"

"Don't be ridiculous," Kelly said. "It takes a long time to have a baby."

"Well, get up stairs and into bed. Here, I'll help you."

Alice took her by the elbow and pulled her from the room. Kelly was concentrating on subduing the pain and did not protest.

Upstairs, Alice helped her undress and put her nightgown on. Suddenly, she felt water rushing out of her and down her thighs, as though she had wet herself. Alice saw the startled look on her face.

"Your water break?"

Kelly nodded. Alice got her a dry nightgown. Kelly changed into it and got into bed.

"I'll go get the doctor," Alice said. "How often are you having pains?"

"Every ten minutes or so," Kelly said. "I wish you wouldn't leave me."

She was beginning to feel a little frightened, no matter how sternly she told herself to be calm.

"I'll get Graham to fetch him," Alice said. "You just relax, and I'll be back in a jiffy."

Alice left the room and darted down the hall to Graham's room. She rapped on the door. Graham opened it almost immediately. He had just finished getting dressed.

"What?" He asked her, wondering what was up. Alice looked pretty riled.

"Go get the doctor," Alice ordered, she was not minded to waste time with asking or answering questions.

"Is Kelly . . .?"

"Yes, and we'll need the doctor sometime today, so get a move on."

He brushed past her into the hall and went down the stairs. Alice watched him for a second, thinking on how his face had been even paler than Kelly's, then she went back to Kelly's room.

Chapter 35

Graham sat in the kitchen drinking whiskey from the bottle. Alice and the doctor were closeted in Kelly's room. He wanted very badly to leave the house but couldn't make himself get up and walk out the door. So far there had been no sound from upstairs that he could hear, but what if Kelly started to scream?

As if his thought had summoned the action, Kelly cried out. He stood up, intending to go upstairs but sat back down because he knew Alice wouldn't let him in the room anyway. Kelly cried out again, and he stood back up, walked to the stove and opened the grate. He stirred the fire for a moment, even though it was burning brightly.

Kelly hadn't even yelled like that after having taken a bullet in the shoulder, he thought nervously, hoping that it would be over soon and that she wouldn't have to yell anymore.

Upstairs, Kelly lay in her bed, totally consumed with giving birth. Nothing existed but the need to expel the baby, even the pains had vanished; she had cried out because of the effort it took to push, not because she was hurting.

The doctor bent over and looked to see how much progress she'd made with the last two efforts.

"Almost there, now, I can see the head. One big push now . . ."

Kelly didn't hear him; she didn't need to. She knew without being told that it was time. She bore down with all her might, her body lifting up out of the bed with her effort. She felt something give, something slide, and then something was being taken from her, and she fell back exhausted onto the bed as the thin wail of the baby pierced the air.

She closed her eyes and tried to catch her breath. After a time, she felt Alice place the baby beside her. Alice told her to try and sit up and get it to nurse. Kelly did so, the feel of the baby rooting at her breast giving her a little more energy. She felt more wetness as the afterbirth left her.

Kelly looked down at the baby. As if from a distance, she heard Alice telling her it was girl, and that they were both just fine, but Kelly was fascinated by the red wrinkled face at her breast and did not answer. The baby seemed awfully small to have been such a problem to get out, and Kelly was totally unprepared for how red and puckered it was. Still, when she considered it, these things seemed sensible. Surely getting born was as hard as giving birth, and Kelly probably didn't look any too pert herself by now.

Alice and the doctor were talking and cleaning up the mess, but Kelly hardly noticed them. The baby seemed to fall asleep, and Kelly lay back down. Alice took the baby from her and laid it in the cradle beside her bed. Kelly began to drowse while Alice and the doctor finished their fussing. She felt too tired to ever care about anything again.

Alice opened the door to let the doctor out and ran smack into Graham, who had apparently been ready to disregard her orders about staying out of the way.

"I'll let myself out, Mrs. Wesley," The doctor said, putting his hat on.

"Yes. Thank you," Alice said. She was blocking the door with her body and glaring at Graham. The man seemed determined to ruin what little reputation Kelly had left.

When the doctor disappeared down the stairs, Graham tried to get past Alice, who immediately closed the door in his face.

"Go down stairs and have a drink," she said. "Kelly's fine. She just needs her rest."

"I want to see her," he said.

Alice noticed that he wasn't asking anymore, but she stood firm.

"Let her be. She's tuckered out."

"I want to see her," Graham repeated, and this time, there was grit in his voice. Alice knew she could either get herself out of the way or he would do it for her.

"Make it quick," she said, stepping aside and holding the door open for him.

Despite his insistence, Graham entered the room slowly, hesitating for a moment just inside the door. He could smell blood in the air, and it startled him. Kelly lay still on the bed, so still that his heart skipped a beat. Then he saw her chest rising and falling as she breathed, and he relaxed.

He approached the bed. Kelly was very pale and her face was sunken with fatigue. She was sleeping deeply and did seem to even know he was in the room.

He looked at her for a few moments, trying to feel reassured because she was breathing so strongly and steadily. Then he turned and left the room, brushing past Alice and going down the stairs. Alice, who was tired too, followed him down the stairs and out the front door.

Graham sat down on the front porch steps and ran his fingers through his damp hair. Behind him, Alice's rocking chair creaked as she sat down tiredly.

"Will she be all right?" He asked. His mouth was dry as sawdust. Kelly's appearance had frightened him even more than her cries; he'd never seen anyone look so completely exhausted, and it was unnatural for her to be so still.

"Oh, she'll get over having the baby fine," Alice replied. "She didn't have such a bad time; I've seen lots worse. Now are you going to do right by her?"

Graham jumped in surprise and turned to face her. "What the hell are you talking about?"

Alice stared back at him, her eyes glinting. "You know what I'm talking about. Marry that girl and take her and that baby somewheres no one knows either of you. Give yourself a chance for a decent life."

"Talk sense," Graham said sharply. "Kelly wouldn't marry me." He put his hat back on, suddenly aware that he had been twisting the brim in his hands.

Alice snorted.

"Maybe she wouldn't've three years ago, but I bet she would now. What's the matter? Does the thought of raising another man's baby irk you?"

"Of course not," he felt insulted. "Nothing of the kind."

Graham stood and stepped onto the porch. Alice watched him pace nervously for a moment.

"You're so in love with her you act right addled sometimes," Alice's eyes flashed. "Like right now."

Graham stopped pacing abruptly.

"I ought to find that damn Jackson Taylor and put some lead between his eyes. He is a worthless person."

"Lord above!" Alice exclaimed. "Chasing that man all over Arizona won't accomplish anything. 'Sides, if Kelly wanted him dead, she'd've shot him herself. Whyn't you do something useful? Marry her and take her out of here."

Graham considered it. Alice could see him thinking it over; his eyes were far off, and his face was almost dreamy.

Then his eyes focused sharply on her, and his face reflected nothing but calm.

"Well?" Alice demanded. "What're you going to do?"

"Get a stiff drink and a good night's sleep," he said.

Alice watched him walk down the porch steps.

"I reckon every man's afraid of something, Mr. Graham

McNair," she called after him. "The day'll come when you can't walk away anymore."

Graham walked on as though he had not heard her, but when he got to the saloon, he found it took a whole bottle of straight whiskey to get Alice's words out of his head.

Chapter 36

Kelly recovered quickly. Alice made her stay in bed for three days, and while Kelly felt well enough to get up on the very next day, she did not argue with her over it. Depression had settled deep within her, and she did not care if she never got out of bed again.

But she did. On the morning of the fourth day, she got up and dressed herself. The baby began to cry. Kelly flinched and went to the cradle, wondering what could be wrong since she barely finished feeding it. She wanted to pick the baby up, but was afraid to, so she rocked the cradle a little and patted the baby's back.

The baby continued to cry. Kelly started to worry, wondering what could be wrong. At last, the door opened and Alice walked into the room.

"What in heaven's name is going on?" She asked.

Kelly ducked her head guiltily.

"I don't know," she confessed. "She won't stop crying."

"Pick her up," Alice said.

Kelly hesitated, but didn't want Alice to know how frightened she was, so she picked the baby up; its head lolled about, and Kelly quickly supported it with her arm.

Alice watched her, wondering how anyone so totally unafraid of wild horses could be so completely cowed by a four-day-old infant.

Kelly held the baby close and crooned to her. Little by little, the baby's cries softened, and at last they ended. Kelly felt enormously relieved.

Alice shook her head in disbelief.

"Didn't you have no younger brothers or sisters?" She asked.

"No," Kelly replied. "Why does her head flop like that? Is there something wrong with her?"

"No, all babies're like that. She'll be able to hold her head up in a few months. Come on out on the porch, Kelly, it's a warm day."

Kelly carried the baby out on to the porch and sat in Alice's big rocking chair. Graham was sitting on the porch steps, carving at a piece of wood with his hunting knife. He greeted her cheerfully, and Kelly smiled in return, though she herself felt anything but cheerful.

It was a beautiful day, she thought. There was a cool spring breeze, fresh and alive, that tingled in her nose and made her blood flow faster. It was a day for a wild ride over the hills; such a breeze would make any horse toss its head and strain at the bit.

The breeze stilled, and Kelly felt herself sink again. Alice came out on to the porch, bringing a chair with her. She sat down and cast about for a topic of conversation.

"Well," she said. "Have you named your daughter yet?"

Kelly had. During the time she'd spent in bed, the name had come to her as though she had always known it.

"Laura Anne," she said.

"How'd you land on those two names?" Alice asked her.

"Well, Laura is my real first name," Kelly said. "I was christened Laura Kelly Chapman, but everyone always called me Kelly because Laura was my mother's name, and she died five days after I was born."

"That's a shame. What was the trouble?"

"Blood poisoning," Kelly said.

Alice nodded sympathetically.

"I've seen it happen before," Alice said. "Why I knew a girl in Abilene, and she bled awful when she had her baby. Well, she seemed to recover fine and then, not four days later, down she went with a fever. You could've fried bacon on her forehead. But for all that, I reckon she lingered a week before she . . ."

"Don't you ever get tired of talking?" Graham asked curtly, cutting her off.

Flustered, Alice realized that maybe there were better things to talk about, seeing that it was Kelly's first day out of bed. She cast about for another topic of conversation.

"Well, Laura's a lovely name," she said at last. "How did you decide on Anne for her second name?"

Kelly had not planned on this topic ever coming up, and so had never prepared a good lie. As things were, she was too tired and depressed to be imaginative; therefore, she just told the truth.

"It's a female form of Andrew," she said, looking straight at

Alice.

Graham jumped as though he'd been goosed, and Alice was surprised into silence, Kelly observed with sour amusement. It had always annoyed her that the two of them spent so much time arguing about things that concerned her closely, but they spoke to her of them only rarely. Alice seemed to think she was too simple to understand her own relationship with Graham, and Graham seemed to think that if no one ever spoke of it, then it would cease to exist.

They were both wrong; this Kelly knew for a fact as the days spun out into weeks, and the weeks into months. To her, the only matter of concern was that Graham should stay with them as long as possible. She didn't want to marry him or anyone else for that matter, but she had to admit that she was happier when he was around, and happiness was hard for her to find these days.

She was tired, for one thing, more tired than she had ever been in her life. Wrangling for the army had been nothing compared to taking care of an infant. Besides, it was a different kind of tired. It seemed to pull out from the very core of her body, leaving her numb. And a good night's sleep did little to cure it—not that she ever got a good night's sleep anymore.

She was also depressed. Life had become an endless cycle of feedings and diaper changings and tedious domestic chores. The smallness and helplessness of the baby stirred a fierce protectiveness in her, but one that was tinged with despair and fear—this was a responsibility from which she would never be free. Sometimes the immense finality of it echoed around her like the sound of a door slamming.

She took good care of Laura and did more than her share around the house, but every day she spoke a little less than the day before, and every day, she seemed less interested in her surroundings. Some mornings, her eyes were red, as though she had been crying during the night, and her appetite diminished.

Her temper had always been short, but now it became raw. Alice tip-toed around her, and though Kelly didn't realize it, even Graham chose his words carefully when around her. He was dismayed by the change in her. He had never minded her temper; always before it had been tempered by her humor. Now her sense of fun and laughter seemed to have vanished. But his dismay did not make him want to leave, even though Alice was after him every minute Kelly wasn't around to hear it.

Someone as sharp as Alice should have known how impossible it is to keep secrets in a house, especially a secret as obvious as her opinions about Kelly and Graham. Kelly was fully aware that Alice was after him whenever her back was turned, and overhearing one such exchange, Kelly decided enough was enough and, after Graham had stomped out of the house, went after Alice with determination.

"I wish you'd leave him alone," Kelly said irritably. "You are going to talk him right out of the house."

"I'm only trying to help," Alice replied, unsettled by Kelly's sudden appearance and chagrined that the girl had apparently overheard the entire conversation. "Since you're afraid to say boo to him about it."

"There isn't anything that I'm afraid to say to Graham McNair," Kelly shot back.

Alice had her doubts about that but did not care to get drawn into an argument over it.

"It's my opinion that the two of you ought to get married," Alice said. "I'm damn tired of watching you make cow eyes at each other."

"Married? Married!" Kelly hooted. "Keeping house must've turned your mind. I never heard anything so silly in my life."

"What's so silly about the two of you settling down somewheres peaceful and living decent?"

Kelly made a sour face.

"What makes you think everybody is dying to be decent?" She asked. "Oh yes, I can just picture it. Graham McNair working in a store while I stay at home and burn dinner. Or maybe we could farm. Yes, I'll bet he's a great hand with a plow—almost as good as I'd be at making clothes or knitting socks."

"A little honest work wouldn't hurt either of you," Alice replied, unperturbed by Kelly's sarcasm.

"I've worked hard all my life, Alice Wesley," Kelly said, angered. "I suppose you think running a two-hundred head horse farm at the age of fourteen was easy."

"Run a horse farm then," Alice said. "But stop making excuses. These things can always be worked out, if you want them enough."

Kelly didn't necessarily agree with that. Alice had never understood that sometimes just wanting something badly enough was enough to put fences in your way.

"I'll have my farm one day," she said. "But I don't need any man to help me get it or to run it once I do get it. And I don't need to have any more babies either."

"You're doing right well with Laura these days," Alice said, thinking that maybe Kelly was taking her earlier ineptness a little too hard.

"I don't believe in pushing my luck," said Kelly, who did not think she would ever be as good at mothering as she was at wrangling.

Alice softened a little. Babies were a lot of work, but that wasn't really what they were talking about, was it?

"Well, you aren't going to sit there and tell me you don't love him," she said, the rancor gone from her voice.

"I don't have any interest in such things at the moment,"

Kelly said stiffly.

Alice nodded. Plenty of women felt that way right after having a baby.

"But you don't want him to leave, do you?"

"No," Kelly said, wondering if she could explain it. "It just comforts me to have him around. The other things don't really matter the way you think they do, because we've always been friends. You and he are the only lasting friends I've ever had and I don't want to loose either of you, especially not over something as useless as getting married."

Alice nodded. That made plenty of sense, but Kelly had never had much imagination about such things. She was too young to settle for what she was getting when she had no idea of the possibilities she was missing.

"There was a man I cared for once," Alice said. "Name of Mike Wren. He got away from me 'cause neither of us was bold enough to speak. I regret it to this day. I would hate to see the same thing happen to you."

To Kelly, that sounded foolish. No matter where he went or what he did when he was gone, Kelly knew that Graham would always turn up to see her again. Was there anyone else in his life who could make such a claim? Had there ever been anyone who could make such a claim? She knew him well enough to know that the answers were no and no. He might not ever ask her for anything more than her company, but he treasured it. Wasn't that better than being married and then forgotten?

"Well, if it does, you can say 'I told you so,' and wash your hands of it," Kelly said. "But leave Graham alone. I won't have you troubling us over something that doesn't even make sense."

"If that's what you want, I'll do it," Alice said. "But I've seen him consider my words with a look on his face that would make you think he was a praying man."

True to her word, Alice stopped her campaign that very day. Graham noticed the change with some relief but did not inquire as to the reason. He supposed Kelly had told her stop.

Without needling Graham to distract her, Alice focused her attention on Kelly, who seemed to be getting worse rather than better as time went on, causing Alice to worry over her.

She nagged Kelly to eat more and tried to be extra cheerful. But Kelly just picked at the food and was deaf to her conversation. At last, not knowing what else to do, Alice spoke to Graham about it. He listened to Alice's worrying for a full half an hour before being able to get a word in edgewise.

"I wish you'd talk to her," Alice said. "Get her to see the doctor. He ought to be able to perk her up. I told her to go, and she looked at me like I was speaking Chinese, but I bet you can talk her into it."

"She doesn't need a doctor," Graham said, wishing Alice hadn't brought him into this.

"How do you know?" Alice asked.

Graham didn't answer. Kelly had a baby that she hadn't really wanted, that was the problem. He tried to think what could be done. The obvious solution was for her to give the baby up. But if that was what she wanted, she would have to think of it herself. He was the last person on earth who could suggest it to her.

"Well?" Asked Alice, interrupting his thoughts.

"I'll try and talk to her," Graham said, although he had never believed that talking did much good.

That evening, as he walked past the parlor, he saw Kelly sitting in an armchair. The curtains were drawn, and the room was nearly dark. He entered the room and sat on the sofa, but Kelly did not look up. She did not seem to notice he was there.

Graham watched her for a while. It seemed to him that all her vibrancy had been stilled from deep inside her and that the stillness had changed her face and her manner until she seemed like a stranger. Then he felt angry for some reason, and he reached over and lit the lamp.

Kelly looked at him then, and he could see that she was irritated at him for disturbing her.

"Alice wants you to see a doctor," he said abruptly. "But I never yet met a doctor that could cure a sulk like the one you're in."

"I'm not sulky," Kelly said, offended.

"You are. Why else were you sitting here in the dark moping? Why've you been dragging around the house like a gut-shot buffalo for the past four months?"

Kelly was speechless. His voice was angry, and his words stung. But who was he to sit there and lecture her?

"Shouldn't you be at the saloon?" Kelly asked loftily. "I'm sure they need you at the poker table. There aren't many philosophizing shootists around."

"Why don't you come with me?" He asked, leaning toward her. "It's been a while since you've been out."

"I can't, and you know it," she said angrily.

"Why not?"

"I've got a baby to take care of," she said.

"Seems like Alice would be happy to watch her for a few hours," Graham replied.

For once in her life, Kelly could think of nothing to say. It seemed that there were no words that could hold all the fear and anger and depression that seemed to shadow her wherever she went and no matter what she did. She could not even think of anything to say that would express her resentment of him speaking to her so.

"You're a fine one to talk, you smug son of a bitch," she sputtered. "Sit there and lecture me when you don't have the faintest idea of what you're talking about!"

"If you're that unhappy," said Graham, who was as calm as she was furious, "give the baby to some woman who can't have one of her own. But if you're going to keep her, then get yourself together. You have to get on with your business, and that doesn't mean you have to stay locked in this house and act like someone's maiden aunt."

It was hard to say which of them his words surprised more. Kelly recoiled from him as he spoke and was pressed up against the chair back, as though his words were bullets that she could dodge if she tried. He put his hat firmly on his head and left the room.

Kelly sat there for another hour, then she got up and went to her room. She sat by the cradle and watched her baby sleep. Giving the baby up had been in the back of her mind since the day she realized she was pregnant, but the thought had made her guilty, and she had never admitted having it, not even to herself. Having heard Graham say it was a tremendous relief to her. Now it seemed a practical course of action, one that could be considered and mulled over, instead of a guilty secret. However annoyed she had been with Graham for saying it, she knew he was right. She had to decide what to do.

But hadn't that been why her father had never liked her? Of course, in her father's eyes, he had traded a much loved wife for a baby, and it hadn't seemed like a fair trade. In Kelly's case, she had traded her way of living for a baby, and that didn't seem fair either, but she hated to think that Laura should ever suffer for it. After all, it wasn't Laura's fault.

Kelly knew that, though she had never thought much about it until now, she had suffered from her father's antipathy toward her. Not that he ever beat her, and not that he had ever even raised his voice to her, it was the coldness that seemed to pour out of him whenever she had been around him. All the grandfathers and pet horses in the world couldn't quite make it not matter that her own father had never spoken a kind word to her.

It burned her to think that Laura should ever suffer under such a burden. Kelly hadn't wanted a baby, and Laura hadn't asked to be born, but Kelly had been the one who had wanted to run around with Jackson Taylor. If you wanted to dance, you had to pay the piper, as her grandfather had always said. It was fair enough that she should pay, but not fair at all that Laura should. Of course, Jackson ought to pay too, but there was no point in asking a beggar for money.

The next morning, Kelly was up before Alice. She had been up most of the night thinking, but to Alice, it seemed as though she were a different person. She talked and laughed and cooed at Laura and was more like her old self that she had been since Denver.

Alice was amazed. She could not think what had brought

about such a sudden and drastic change, and she was afraid to ask Kelly about it. She and Kelly sat down to breakfast at the kitchen table. Alice passed Kelly the ham.

"I despise ham," Kelly said cheerfully, taking a large slice of it. "But I'm so hungry I could eat a horse. When did Graham come in last night?"

"He didn't," Alice said. "The egg man said he cleared out last night on account of he had some trouble at the saloon."

Kelly's smile faltered. "Was he hurt?"

"Nope, didn't kill anyone either. I reckon he'll be back before long."

For a moment, it seemed that Kelly's gloom had returned. Then, with an effort, Kelly smiled and put the ham platter back down.

"I think he'll be gone for a while," she said. "Can you watch Laura for an hour or so this afternoon?"

"Be glad to. Where're you going?"

"I'm going to buy a horse," Kelly said.

Alice misunderstood.

"Have you lost your mind? You're not going after him! What about . . ."

But Kelly interrupted her.

"No, I'm not going after him, and I'm not running out on Laura either. I'd just be happier if I could go for a ride now and then."

Kelly chewed her ham and ignored Alice's bewildered look. Kelly hadn't wanted a baby, but she had one now and loved her even though it would be easier if she didn't. She wished she could thank Graham; his words last night had cut through the guilt and resentment and fear and had laid the reality bare. Still, she was not really surprised that he had gone; they had been on a collision course since he had arrived. She did not think that he would be back anytime soon.

And it was two years before she saw him again.

Chapter 37

It was October, a month so bright and sunny that it made the approaching winter seem an impossibility. Kelly was playing peek-a-boo with Laura in the back yard, a game which eventually deteriorated into Laura chasing her in and out of the laundry hanging from the clothesline. Laura was shrieking and laughing, and Kelly was out of breath. She let Laura grab her legs and pretended to fall down.

Laura laughed some more and fell on top of her. When they had finished laughing, Kelly sat up and straightened Laura's dress.

"Ma, see the man," Laura said, and Kelly looked to where she was pointing.

Graham was standing on the back porch grinning broadly at them. Kelly waved at him and finished smoothing Laura's skirts down. She still hated wearing dresses herself and disliked making Laura wear them, but these days, Kelly limited herself to wearing jeans only when she went riding.

She stood up, and Laura grabbed her hand. Graham had come down off the porch to meet them, and for a moment, Kelly was at a loss as to how to greet him.

So she kissed him on the cheek and gave him a quick hug, and before he had a chance to respond to either, Kelly picked Laura up.

"Laura, this your Uncle Graham. Can you say hello?"

"Uncle Graham," Laura said, frowning. Graham laughed.

"She has your eyes, Kelly, and your frown," he said. "Can I hold her?" He asked, holding out his arms.

"No." Laura said firmly, taking a tighter grip on Kelly, who flushed. Graham laughed.

"She has your smart mouth, too," he said.

"And it's no wonder," Alice said, coming out of the kitchen and onto the porch. "You let her run wild. I heard you two yelling like banshees a while ago."

Kelly rolled her eyes. They had been having arguments like this for a year and a half.

"She's two years old, Alice, there's no reason why she shouldn't run and yell if she wants."

"Well, if you're not careful . . ." Alice began, but Graham interrupted her.

"She'll turn out just like her mother," he finished for her.

Alice threw up her hands and went back into the kitchen. Kelly snickered. Laura asked to be put down, and when her feet hit the ground, she went into the house. "I am sorry, though," Kelly said at last. "She doesn't take to strangers very well, and I don't like to force her."

A strange look passed quickly over Graham's face, but Kelly missed it. She was thinking how good it was to see him again.

"It's all right. Alice has to put her two cents in, you know."

"Yes, I know. And it's damn funny, too. For someone who spent ten years running saloons and sporting houses, she sure is an expert at raising children."

Graham smiled.

"I hear you've been cutting quite a rug in this town," he said.

Kelly shrugged. "Not really. I go out for rides sometimes and have been known to play a hand of draw poker now and then. I stay out of trouble though," she said. "Oh, and I have a job at the bank."

Graham laughed out loud.

"You, working in a bank? Who's the bank president? Cole Younger?"

"It's not that funny," Kelly said. She did not like being reminded of the circumstances under which she'd run away from home.

"Well, it's done you good, I reckon," he said, taking a long look at her. She had lost the weight she'd gained while pregnant, and she looked fit and active. The darkness around her had vanished, and she looked as vibrant and alive as ever.

"You look considerably better than the last time I saw you," he said.

"Thank goodness," Kelly said. "That was the worst year of my life, I think."

They went into the house together. Alice was baking cookies. When her back was turned, Kelly snuck a finger full of dough from the mixing bowl. She popped it in her mouth quickly but not quickly enough to escape Alice's notice.

"Stop that," Alice scolded. "It's enough to make a person sick."

Kelly made a face at her and sat at the table. Graham sat across from her.

"So where all have you been?" Kelly asked him. "Not in trouble, I hope."

"No. I went north and did some scouting for the army."

Alice hooted.

"I never thought you'd wear blue pants again."

"Didn't have to," Graham replied easily. "They pay civilians to scout."

"They sure do," Kelly said. "Jackson sure never wore a uniform. Did you really spend two whole years at it?"

Graham had frowned at her reference to Jackson but otherwise ignored it.

"No, I marshaled in Dry Plains, Nebraska, for a spell. They were having some trouble with a rowdy bunch of rustlers and whiskey traders."

"Catch any lead?" Alice asked, taking a tray of the cookies from the oven.

"None to speak of."

"What does that mean?" Kelly asked. "Either you did or you didn't."

"I took a few scatter gun pellets in the leg," he said. "But it didn't even lame me up any."

Alice took a cookie from the tray and gave it to Kelly.

"It's still hot," Alice warned her, turning back to her baking.

Kelly blew on it a little and took a bite.

"These are good, Alice," she said, chewing happily. She broke the remainder in half and offered it to Graham, who declined it.

"Still have a sweet tooth, I see," he said. Part of the reason he had come back was to see if the small things about her had changed at all.

Kelly nodded and finished the cookie.

"I'm a bit low on funds," he said to her. "Care to help me out playing cards tonight?"

"Sure, if Alice'll keep an eye on Laura for me." Alice scraped the last of the cookie dough from her mixing bowl.

"Be glad to," she said. "Just put her to bed before you go."

"Thanks," Kelly said. "May I have another cookie, please?"

Alice shrugged and gave her one. Having her eat them warm was better than having her eat them uncooked. Although Alice liked to devil her over it, Kelly's sweet tooth was the only reason she ever did any baking. Kelly knew it and always accepted the hard time Alice gave her without any umbrage.

The evening passed, and they embarked on their poker playing. Graham realized that playing cards was another reason why he had come back. Kelly was a hell of a card shark when she felt inclined. He had always thought that it was too bad that she was so taken with wrangling. No one ever made any money at wrangling. For him, playing cards with her was one of the most comfortable and least boring things he could think of.

They didn't start playing until after ten o'clock, but the cards ran well, and they played without stopping until a quarter to three. They had come in separately, so Graham left the game first and sat at the bar for twenty minutes or so before leaving.

Kelly excused herself from the game just as he left the saloon. She ordered a whiskey and drank it slowly, then paid the barkeep and left. She was surprised to see Graham waiting for her at the end of the block. There wasn't any reason for him to walk her home in a place as civilized as Kansas City. She had been in a good mood all day, and now, the whiskey made her punchy.

"Pretty good pickings for such a settled up place," Graham said to her as they walked home.

"Yep," Kelly said. "But lord, I miss Colorado in the wintertime. I spent the winter of '74 in the Rockies. I didn't see a single soul from October 'til April. It was like I had the whole world to myself."

"Colorado's settling up quick now," Graham said.

"They'll never settle up those mountains," Kelly said firmly. "You been sticking with towns?"

"Mostly," Graham replied. "There's been a lot of Indian trouble up north lately."

"I never knew you to be afraid of Indians."

"I'm not," Graham said. "Towns just seem friendlier these days."

When they reached Alice's, they stopped on the back porch to shuck their boots. Kelly lost her balance and had to grab the doorpost. She giggled a little, and Graham sniffed audibly.

"Are you drunk?"

"No," Kelly said indignantly. "I lost my balance, is all."

Then she giggled again. Graham raised an eyebrow skeptically, but Kelly ignored him. She was happy.

The house was dark, and they crept in as quietly as possible because Alice always kept a revolver under her pillow in case of housebreakers. Kelly started up the stairs first; Graham was a few steps behind her. When she reached the stop of the staircase, Kelly stopped abruptly and turned. She was eye to eye with him.

She put her hands on his shoulders. Their eyes locked, and after a moment's looking, Kelly leaned forward and kissed him. The nearness and taste and smell of him made her skin prickle in excitement. She was relishing the fact that his moustache tickled in a pleasing way and did not feel his arms go about her waist. She only knew that suddenly she was being held tightly against him, and her arms were around his neck, and he was kissing her back. Her hat fell off as his hands sought her hair. There was nothing restrained about him now, nothing calm and nothing playful. It excited her in some nameless way, and her breath came harder.

They parted for a moment, and Kelly could seem the gleam of his teeth in the darkness. Then he pulled her off the ground; she wrapped her legs around his waist. He carried her up the last two stairs and walked the few steps to his room. Kelly's back was pressed hard against the wall as Graham fumbled with the door handle. He turned his head slightly to see the knob better, and Kelly kissed along his cheek until she reached his ear. He groaned and pushed the door open.

He carried her inside. Kelly kicked the door shut behind them.

The bed skidded across the floor as they fell on it.

The noise made them both stop and listen for a second. The house remained silent. Graham looked down at Kelly, whose face was illuminated by moonlight that streamed in through the window. Her lips were drawn back in what seemed a half-smile, half-snarl, but her eyes . . .

He had meant to slow it down then, to kiss her gently so they could take their time, but he felt that look go all way through him, and the rest of the world ceased to exist. Nothing existed for him except her body and his hunger for it.

As his mouth descended on hers again, Kelly stretched herself out and wrapped herself around him. It seemed to her that she could not get close enough to him, that feeling every inch of his body pressed so tightly on top of hers was not enough. She reached down between them and unbuckled his gun belt. It slid to the ground with a thud, and she unbuttoned his shirt. His chest was smooth and soft and hard with muscles as she slid her hands across it.

Graham sat up, pulling her with him. He let go of her long enough to strip his shirt off, then stood and unbuttoned his trousers. Kelly leaned back and unbuttoned her jeans, and Graham, now that his own pants lay in a heap on the floor, leaned forward and, kissing her, pulled her jeans down over her hips and off, dropping them on the floor.

Kelly scooted back on her elbows as he got back on the bed. He sat Indian style and pulled her into his lap. She began to unbutton her shirt, and his hands folded over hers, helping her with the buttons until her shirt was open and he pushed it back off her shoulders.

There was nothing between them now except the thin cotton of her camisole. Kelly reached up and pulled the remaining pins from her hair, letting it fall down on her shoulders. While she did so, Graham's hands traced the curve of her neck and shoulders and arms, then undid the buttons to her camisole. As he brushed it from her shoulders, the scar from that long ago bullet stood in stark contrast to the white, curving perfection of her shoulders and chest. Kelly watched him, her breath stopped in fascination; he seemed on the edge of some revelation.

It seemed to Graham, as he traced the angry red line with his finger, that he had never understood until now how terrible a thing that shooting had been. Despite all his attempts to protect her, the only scarring wound she'd ever suffered was because of him. He pulled her to him, wanting nothing more than to make it better—all of it—every bullet she'd ever taken for him.

Chapter 38

Just after dawn, Kelly slipped back into her own room and looked in on Laura, who was still sleeping peacefully, then she washed herself and dressed swiftly. She could hear Alice banging around in the kitchen.

Kelly hurried downstairs to help with breakfast. Alice was putting bacon on to fry when Kelly entered the kitchen.

"Good morning, miss," she said tartly.

"Good morning," Kelly replied. "Want me to start the biscuits?"

"No, I'll do it. You turn this bacon."

Kelly went to the stove while Alice mixed biscuit dough. The bacon splattered grease at her, but she liked the way it made the room smell. She was so busy dodging grease splatters that she didn't notice that Alice was watching her with a twinkle in her eye.

"By the by," Alice said casually. "I found your hat on the stairs this morning. It's on the hall stand if you want it."

"Thank you," Kelly said, looking sideways at her. Alice's eyes were sparking. Kelly stifled an urge to sigh. It wasn't any use trying to sneak such a thing by Alice.

"'Course that was a mighty funny place to leave a hat," Alice went on as she rolled the biscuits out. "Seems like if you dropped it, you'd want to pick it up so it don't get stepped on."

The bacon was done. Kelly started forking it out of the fry pan and onto a plate.

"I was occupied with something else at the time," she said, hard put to keep a poker face.

Kelly put the plate on the dining room table. When she reentered the kitchen, Alice was sliding the biscuits into the stove.

"Grits this morning or eggs?" Kelly asked her.

"Eggs, I think. The egg man came yesterday."

They could hear noises from upstairs; the boarders were waking up.

"I'll go get Laura," Kelly said.

"Why'nt you start the eggs? I'll get her."

"Fine. But don't braid her hair too tight, it aches her head."

"At least she don't look like a rag picker's child," Alice retorted.

Kelly greased the griddle with a piece of pork rind. "Two eggs each?" She asked.

"Sure. You n' me can have some pancakes after they go. Is that lazy gambler of yours getting up this morning or did you wear him out last night?"

Kelly turned scarlet and sat down abruptly.

Alice laughed. You'd think someone Kelly's age would have gotten over being so modest, after all Jackson Taylor hadn't exactly been a missionary, and Kelly had a two-year-old baby to prove it.

"Don't speak about it like that," Kelly said in a faint voice once she was able to speak again. She wiped her face in her apron then went back to the stove.

Alice shook her head and went upstairs. Some people were so silly.

By the end of the day, Kelly was also inclined to think she was being silly. Concentrating on her work at the bank had been nearly impossible. Little bits and pieces of the previous night kept flashing through her mind at inappropriate times, making her flush and lose her train of thought. Because Kelly had never cared much for math, she found it especially difficult to do when she had other, much more pleasant things to think about.

At long last, it was five o' clock, and the bank closed up. She walked back to Alice's slowly. She felt much as she had that winter day in Denver when Graham had left for Kansas. She felt as though the night's events had left her naked to his eyes, even though she was dressed and it was broad daylight.

Laura was happy to see her. As soon as Kelly walked into the kitchen, the little girl hugged her legs.

"Whee, ma, whee!" She shouted.

"All right," Kelly said indulgently, picking her up under the arms and tossing her into the air until her head nearly hit the ceiling. Laura shrieked and laughed, and Kelly did it twice more. She set Laura gently back down.

"More Ma, more, more," Laura begged.

"Two more, all right?" Kelly asked. "Ma's back is tired."

Laura nodded. Kelly picked her up and tossed her into the

air twice more. Then she sat down, and Laura scrambled into her lap.

"I swear you'll ruin that child yet," Alice muttered. "My heart fails me every time you do that."

"Sorry," Kelly said in a voice that was not terribly apologetic. "But you better get used to it. When she gets a little bigger, I'm going to get her a pony."

"How much bigger?"

"Maybe for her birthday in the spring," Kelly said. "She's been asking for one."

"That's crazy, buying a three-year-old girl a pony. You shouldn't let her ride in front of you like you do. That's what started it."

"Go for a ride, Ma?" Laura asked.

"Tomorrow, baby," Kelly said. "There's nothing wrong with it. My grandfather started teaching me to ride that way as soon as I learned to walk."

Alice shook her head and sat down at the table with a bowl of beans. "It ain't right. I suppose you'll put her in pants, too."

"Well, you can't teach a three-year-old to ride sidesaddle," Kelly said. "Besides, sidesaddle is the most unnatural thing I ever saw. You can bet a man thought it up."

As she spoke, Kelly heard footsteps coming down the stairs; Graham must finally be awake. She shifted Laura in her lap and tickled Laura's nose with her own braids, making her giggle and squirm.

"Well, look here," Alice said, changing the subject as Graham walked into the kitchen. "It's a miracle. The dead have risen. It ain't like you to sleep through two meals, Mr. McNair."

"That's no reason to blaspheme," Graham returned in good humor. "Sets a bad example for the child there."

Kelly and Laura laughed.

Alice was about to sass him back, but to her complete amazement, he walked straight over to Kelly, kissed her on the top of the head and wished her a good morning. Before he could straighten up, Kelly put her hand behind his neck and pulled him back down. They kissed for so long Alice was afraid one of them would suffocate. She cleared her throat noisily, but neither of them paid any attention.

When they finally came up for air, Graham went to the stove and dished up some leftovers from lunch. Alice shook her head as if to clear it and went back to snapping her beans. No wonder Kelly had turned so red this morning, she thought idly. In Alice's experience there were precious few men worth blushing over, and she'd never imagined that Graham was one of them.

Kelly noticed Alice's reaction with some satisfaction. It was about time the old biddy minded her own business. Although she had been no less surprised than Alice at Graham's greeting and her own reaction to it, it pleased her so that she couldn't be anything but happy.

Graham sat at the table.

"How was the bank this morning?" He asked her.

"Busy. That new teller they hired can't add two and two. I had to go over all his work. It's too bad they won't let me sit in the window, since I end up doing the work anyway."

"Well, bankers tend to run short on common sense," Graham answered. "This chicken pie is good, Alice."

"Thanks," Alice said. Would wonders never cease? Was the man really going to sit there and have a sensible conversation?

"Put me down, Ma," Laura said, and Kelly obliged her. Laura trotted off into the parlor where her toys were; apparently she'd had enough adult conversation. Alice rose and put the bowl of beans back on the counter.

"I'll try that new dress on her now that she's calmed down some," Alice said, wiping her hands on her apron.

"I guess you'd better make her some pants next," Kelly said.

Alice snorted and left the room. Kelly and Graham grinned at each other.

Kelly suddenly felt shy. She stood and went over to the pantry for a few of the cookies that Alice had baked the day before; she felt she could use one.

"Want a cookie?" She asked Graham

"Sure."

Kelly put a few cookies on a plate and set the plate on the table. Before she could sit down again, Graham caught her around the waist and pulled her onto his lap. She put an arm around his shoulders, surprised at how natural it all seemed.

"Will you come with me to play some cards tonight?" He asked.

Kelly was tempted, but she was tired, and she had to be up early the next morning.

"I'm too tired for a late night," she said. "Maybe tomorrow. I don't work Thursdays."

Graham saw her eyes were red and tired. It was certainly true that neither of them had gotten much sleep last night.

"How did you get this powder burn?" He asked, touching a small black mark near her hairline.

"My rifle blew up in my face," Kelly said. "A bad shell stuck in the breech."

He didn't say anything, and they sat there for a moment, but Graham knew Alice would soon be in to bother them some more.

"Well, why don't you stay in my room tonight?" He asked. "I won't be late."

"All right," Kelly said.

Looking at him, Kelly thought he seemed the same as always, but she knew he wasn't. Time had changed them both, though it had not changed their feeling for each other. Kelly thought again of all the time they had spent together, and wondered why such things as had happened in the past two days were suddenly possible, when ten years ago, or five, or two, they had not been.

No answer occurred to her, and she pushed the thought away. Did it really matter?

She stood up, and Graham went back to eating. Laura ran into the room with her new dress on.

"Don't you look sweet," Kelly said, kneeling and giving her a hug. "Did you thank Alice for making such a nice dress for you?"

"Yes. I told her blue was my favorite color, and she made the dress blue."

"Alice is good about such things," Kelly said.

Laura gripped her hand.

"Come on, Ma."

"Where are we going?" Kelly asked, standing up.

"Let's play blocks."

"All right."

Laura dragged her from the room, talking so quickly her words slurred together. Kelly nodded and answered her as though she understood what her daughter was saying, but to Graham, as he watched them go into the parlor, it was so much gibberish.

It was a little unsettling to see how good a mother Kelly had become over the past two years. Laura was a boisterous child, active and full of life, but not disobedient. Graham had not thought that he could ever feel jealous of a child, but it irked him some that Kelly and Laura had their life arranged and that he would have to fit himself in however he could.

Thinking of such things troubled him. He had come to Kansas City solely to see Kelly. As always, he had gotten to missing her, though he had dallied here and there thinking the feeling might pass if he gave it some time. Finally, he had given in and ridden back. Seeing her again made him realize how lonely he had been all that time, and when she had kissed him, he had wondered how he could ever of thought he would forget about her or why he had wanted to.

Now he was prepared to stay for a while, though Kelly clearly had no expectations of him. He wondered if he could convince her to leave Alice's and ride up northwest with him. Kansas City was only an interesting place to be because she was there, and surely she had had more than enough of settled life by now.

He sighed. When he stopped thinking about such things and let his mind consider the spark in her eyes when she was deviling him over something or the pucker in her forehead when she was playing cards or the heat in her face when he touched her, it all seemed very simple. He set his dishes in the washpan and went into the living room. Perhaps he would stay in tonight.

Alice was the only one surprised when Graham walked into

the parlor. Kelly was building a tower out of wooden blocks that Laura knocked over with a delighted laugh. Kelly laughed too and began to build another tower.

But Alice glanced up when he walked in, a shrewd look on her face.

"Off to play some cards?" She asked him.

Graham wavered, wanting to stay but not feeling entirely comfortable about it.

"Yes," he said finally.

Kelly looked up at him, smiling.

"Good luck to you," she said.

"Thanks."

He took his hat from the hall stand and went out the door. Kelly went back to playing blocks with Laura. Alice looked from the now empty doorway to Kelly.

"I'd bet all the money I have that he's back before nine," Alice said.

"That's a bet I won't take," Kelly said without looking up from her game.

Kelly put Laura to bed at eight and stayed in the room until she was asleep. She changed into her nightclothes and went to Graham's room. She usually went to bed after nine o' clock, but tonight she was tired. So instead of reading for a while as she usually did, she turned the lamp down and closed her eyes. She fell asleep almost immediately.

Not much later, she blinked sleepily and came awake to the sound of the door closing softly. Then she remembered where she was and that Graham was supposed to be coming in. He was in the room now, moving noiselessly about as he got ready for bed. Kelly closed her eyes again.

Graham fixed the catch on the door, then removed his gun belt, which he rebuckled and hung from the bed post. This was a precaution that he was so used to taking that he never thought twice about it. He was glad the room was on the second floor so he wouldn't have to worry about bushwhackers coming in through it. Had it been a first-floor room, he would have placed empty bottles or cans on the sash. Anyone opening a window so rigged would make noise enough to wake the dead.

He undressed, tossing his clothes on the armchair, then slid into bed, which, despite the chill in the room, was nice and warm because Kelly was in it.

"Have a good night?" Kelly asked sleepily.

"Fair."

He pulled her close to him so that her head rested on his chest; she put her arms around him.

"Surprised you last night, didn't I?" She asked.

"Pleasantly so," he thought a moment. "I haven't been so surprised since you belted me back in '73."

Kelly chuckled, enjoying the feel of his chest under her

227

hand. She was not surprised at how different these things were with Graham. After all, she loved him. Jackson had never been much but a temporary diversion.

She propped herself up on one elbow so she could see him better. His face was as familiar as always, but in the past twenty-four hours, she had learned that it was capable of reflecting emotions she had never dreamed of, and if she had dreamed of them, not even in the wildest of those dreams had she thought that she could inspire such feeling in anyone.

Like now, when his eyes were hot with a feeling that seemed to sear all the way through her, and she felt he knew everything she was and felt and dreamed about, and there was nowhere for her to hide.

She could feel his hand on the back of her head, drawing her face down to his until his breath brushed her lips an instant before his lips met them, and a shiver of expectation ran down her spine.

Chapter 39

December began. If any boarders came, Alice must have turned them away, for during all that time, no stranger appeared to intrude on the peace in the house. Life slipped into a pleasant routine. Alice saw to the housework; Kelly helped her and continued with her job at the bank. Graham slept through the mornings and did his poker playing in the early aftenoons and evenings. Kelly rarely went with him, but they often played a hand or two in the parlor after Laura went to bed.

One such evening in the middle of the month, Kelly and Graham sat at the table playing cards. Alice sat near the fireplace, knitting something that looked as though it might eventually become a sweater.

"I wish you'd take a hand, Alice," Kelly said. "Two handed poker is no fun. Besides, I'm getting beat pretty bad."

Alice did not look up from her work.

"Play some rummy then," she said. "I want to finish this sweater before Laura outgrows it."

"Well she's not going to grow an extra arm no matter how long you wait," Kelly said. "I never would have guessed that was a sweater."

Alice held it up and looked at it. It did seem a might crooked.

"I declare, it's been so long since I tried to knit I guess I am a bit rusty at it."

"Take a hand then," Graham said. "We can play some stud poker."

"No thanks. I'm even rustier at poker," Alice said. "I believe

I will stick with knitting."

Kelly snorted.

"I call," she said to Graham. They both showed their cards. She had two pair to his ace high. It was about time she'd won a hand. She picked up the cards to shuffle and deal.

"Want to play some gin?" He asked.

"Sure." It never hurt to finish on a winning hand.

She dealt them each seven cards.

There was a creaking on the stairs. Graham was looking over her shoulder, and he smiled.

"I guess we've got company."

Kelly turned around to see what he was talking about. Laura was creeping down the stairs, peeking through the railing.

"Hey there pumpkin," Kelly said. "What are you doing out of bed?"

Laura, picking up on the affectionate note in her mother's voice, ran down the stairs and over to Kelly, who scooped her up and kissed her on the head. "What's the matter?" She asked. "Do you need to go to the outhouse?"

"No. I dreamed bad." Laura settled down on Kelly's lap.

"What about?" Kelly asked her.

"A witch. She wanted to get me."

"And what did you do?"

"I ran."

"Did you get away?"

"Yes, but I was scared."

"I imagine so. Was it an old, ugly witch?"

"Yes. She had claws."

"I would've been scared too," Graham said. "Sounds a little like that school teacher you had staying here two summers ago, Alice."

Alice set her knitting down.

"She paid her rent on time anyway," she said. "And you shouldn't spoil Laura so," she said to Kelly. "Send her back to bed."

Kelly ignored her. She'd had plenty of bad dreams herself as a child. She knew if she let Laura sit up a while she would fall asleep on her lap, and then she could be put to bed with no fear and no fussing. In the morning, she'd have forgotten the dream altogether.

"Since you're up," Kelly said to Laura. "You can help me play cards."

"Two against one isn't fair," Graham protested.

"Oh, it's fair enough. You gamblers always cheat anyway."

Kelly explained to Laura how the game worked. Of course, the child wouldn't remember it all, but it would make her feel grown up. She ignored Alice, who was fuming silently and ripping out a row of stitches, thinking how much she hated to see such a small child in the middle of a card game. Laura fell asleep in her lap less than an hour later, just as Kelly had known she would. She and Graham had had enough cards for the evening, and so he went upstairs with her as she put Laura to bed. Alice put away her crooked knitting and locked the house up.

Kelly tucked Laura into bed and kissed her good night. The little girl did not awaken, but Kelly hesitated to leave her. Laura had been fussy the past few evenings. Waking up in a dark, empty room after a bad nightmare was a terrible thing, in Kelly's opinion.

"I think I ought to stay in here tonight," she said to Graham, who was waiting for her near the door. "Laura hasn't been sleeping well lately. I hate to think that she would wake up scared and not know where to find me."

No sign of hurt crossed his face, much to Kelly's relief. He nodded.

"I can stay in here too, if you like."

That was a surprise to her. Kelly knew he did not sleep well when she was with him. They were both unused to sleeping with another person, but at least Kelly was used to being safe, which Graham never would be.

"We would have to behave ourselves," Kelly said. "But I would understand if you needed a good night's sleep alone for a change."

It was his turn to be surprised. He had not thought that she had noticed his wakefulness. He wondered if she also knew that it was not inspired by worry or habit but by wanting to watch her sleep and to see the dreams that crossed her face in the night.

"I get enough sleep," he said.

"I'd be glad to have the company then," she said. "Can you get the back of this dress for me?"

"With pleasure."

He took his time about it. Kelly remembered how she had once wondered why people made clothes that you needed help to get out of, but all it took to make her understand was feeling his breath on the back of her neck and the chill of the air as her dress fell open beneath his fingers.

Kelly's fears were unfounded, for Laura slept peacefully all night long. The next day was cold and blustery, and after a late breakfast, Kelly sat at her desk going over the month's household accounts. Graham, who was lounging on the settee, watched her frown over the books. The cold weather left him inclined to stay indoors, and he wished Kelly would stop her figuring so they could play cards or talk or something.

He never understood her interest in working so hard. Her skill at poker was enough to make her a good living, so why work in a bank or keep a ledger? He could better understand her interest in horses, though her insistence on doing the hard, mundane work that wranglers were called upon to do mystified him. It was one thing to ride wild horses just because you could; it was another to clean stalls when you didn't have to.

No, he didn't understand her interest in hard work, but he did respect it, especially since it was a choice and not a necessity. She'd told him about working out of that army fort down in Arizona, and he knew that must have been the hardest kind of hard work. Of course, she had been living with Jackson at the time, and probably anything seemed amusing after a day with that worthless son of a bitch.

"Do you ever miss him?" Graham asked abruptly, watching her carefully.

Kelly did not flinch or look up from her books. She erased a number and brushed the dust away. Graham wondered if she had even heard him.

"Who?" She asked disinterestedly.

"Jackson," he clarified.

"Who?" She asked again.

"Jackson Taylor," he said, a little impatiently.

"I don't know anyone by that name," Kelly said looking up briefly and going back to her figuring.

Graham sat back, at a loss for words. Was she joking? Her face was perfectly serious, but how could she have forgotten him entirely?

"Sure you do," Graham said. "Laura's father."

"Oh, him," Kelly said, frowning at her ledger. "No, I never miss him. There's no Indians that need killing around here."

"I thought he was good for something else, too."

Kelly scratched a few figures down and spoke without looking up.

"I was wrong about that," she said. "But even Saul had to have the scales knocked from his eyes by the hand of God."

She began to smile after she had spoken—a knowing and crooked smile—but she did not look up from her work. His question answered, Graham leaned back against the settee, smiling a smile as pleased and knowing as her own had been.

To Kelly, such thoughts and smiles summed that month up very well. In cold weather, surely there was nothing better than curling up with someone who was warm, especially when the boiling point was never far off. It was also a fascination to her that she had know Graham for so long, but had known so little about him when it came to the particulars.

She had always known him to be passionate, for none but a passionate man could get so feeling about the Indians or the intrusions of the respectable folk into the wild places. But she had never realized that she was such a focus of that passion. Likewise, she had always known him to be a humorous man but was unprepared for the small, quiet jokes he made at unexpected moments. He had always been respectful toward her and had never offered her rough treatment, but the gentle affection that turned up in his look and his touch made her insides quake.

Sometimes, their need would drive them so hard that it felt like thunder rolling across the plains or gathering in a mountain valley, making the air tremble and the earth shudder. Other times, a different kind of need kept them awake all night talking about nothing and looking at each other with a kind of pleased bewilderment.

Kelly was a person of feeling, not of thinking. She accepted all these things, and when she thought of them, it was to revel in them, not to analyze them. She had never expected to be so happy and did not question how long it would last. How could she be ungrateful for this miracle that she had never even dreamed was possible? How could she spoil it with regret over things that could not be helped, or taint it with worry that it might vanish at any moment?

For knowing Graham as she did and remembering their past together, Kelly knew that they had come to the very place he that he had been trying so hard to avoid. He had always put different names on that fear and had made varying excuses for it, but she knew in her heart that all those things were no more than masquerades.

Still, those were things that he had to find his own peace about. Kelly could not help him, and recognizing this, she worried hardly about it at all. There wasn't any point to it.

If life inside that blue clapboard house troubled her only a little, then life outside of it troubled her not at all. Kelly rarely went about town. She walked to the livery stable and to the bank, but other than that, she did not go out much. She hated shopping, and generally Alice did it, but every now and then, Kelly ventured into a store when Alice was too busy to go.

That's why she made a quick trip to Henry Woodely's Fine Goods and Hardware Store one warm day at the beginning of February. Alice was busy with the washing, and they were out of coffee and flour. Of course, she couldn't just run in and pick up two things, Alice had filled her ear with a half dozen silly things they didn't really need just so the trip wouldn't be wasted.

The store was a little crowded, and Kelly had to wait to be served, which she hated. Laura was with her, and Kelly amused her by pretending to understand her barely intelligible comments about the book Kelly had read to her the previous evening. When their turn came, Kelly made her choices quickly, hesitating only over what color cloth to buy for a new dress for Laura.

Her shopping finished, Kelly waited for Henry to wrap her things. Several matrons were clustered near the far end of the store, waiting their turn. Kelly glanced at them briefly, concealing her contempt. Then Henry handed her packages to her. Kelly took them, and he gave Laura a piece of candy.

"Thank you," Laura said without prompting. Kelly beamed.

"Thank you, Henry," she said.

"My pleasure, Miss Chapman," he said. "See you soon."

Kelly took Laura's hand as they walked from the store and down the sidewalk. Two women, who Kelly recognized as the pillars of the First Methodist church, were walking toward them. They looked up and saw Kelly at almost the same moment that Kelly recognized them.

As Kelly prepared to smile in greeting, they abruptly drew their skirts aside and crossed to the other side of the street. Kelly walked on, though her legs seemed to have gone numb. From the corner of her eye, she could see that the two women had stopped walking and were whispering to each other. Kelly felt her face flame, knowing that they talking about her.

Damn them anyway, she thought violently, the old biddies. But on the heels of that thought came the realization that one of those old biddie's daughters taught grade school. Laura would be going to grade school in a few years.

Kelly took a firmer grip on Laura's hand. She had never thought that anything she did would attract such attention. After all, she was used to being whispered about. Back in New York, the good citizens of Millersville had talked about her plenty. But that was different, she realized, because back then she had been the only daughter of the district's wealthiest family. She could afford to laugh at their gossip. But that was a good ten or more years ago, she thought distractedly, and things had changed considerably. She was no one in particular here. There was no reason for anyone to even pretend to be polite to her. She didn't care a fig about their opinion of her, but she cared a lot about how it would reflect on Laura.

Her main thought since Laura's birth had been to give up enough of her reckless ways so that she wouldn't meet an early and untimely death. Now she realized that safety wasn't the only thing that she ought to have been considering. Someone—maybe a lot of someones—had been watching her rides and occasional forays into the local saloons with interest. She wondered, with a sudden dart of fear, whether there was talk about her and Graham.

She decided there almost certainly was. There had been no boarders in the house for some time, but it was no secret that Graham was staying at Alice's, and Kelly had gone to several saloons with him. That most definitely would have made sewing circle news.

Once, on one of her occasional visits to New York City, she and her governess, a woman named Eleanor, had gone shopping. They had been in a milliners, looking at dress goods, when a handsome woman in a black dress—a respectable enough dress except that it was a trifle low in the bosom and too tight through the bodice—walked in. Eleanor had looked the woman over with a sharp eye and whispered something to the clerk. The clerk disappeared, then returned with the owner.

"Here now," he had said angrily. "Get out of this shop, we don't want you here."

Kelly had gaped, not understanding his sudden and extreme rudeness. The woman's face had turned red, and her eyes had dropped. She had tried to back away from the owner, who was advancing on her and making shooing motions with his hands as he continued to order her out of the shop. In her haste to escape, the woman bumped against a small table displaying gloves. The table had fallen over, and the woman had stooped to pick them up.

Upset, Kelly had started forward to help her, but Eleanor had grabbed her arm fiercely, holding her back.

"Don't you dare!" She had hissed, dragging Kelly to the other end of the shop.

But Kelly and the woman had locked eyes. On seeing the upset and pity in Kelly's face, the woman had lifted her chin, risen to her feet and swept from the store, spitting in their direction. Kelly thought she understood that defiance now, although it had hurt her at the time.

That day had puzzled her for a long time, and Kelly realized that she had never fully understood what was going on until today, had never understood that the woman must have been a prostitute, and that she had probably been thrown out of dozens of places.

Not that Kelly cared about getting thrown out of dress shops. But what about Laura? Would they let her go to the school? And if they did, would the other children take their parents' views out on her? Although she had not spent much time with other children when she was growing up, Kelly knew that children could be crueler than army mule skinners when they wanted.

Well, all the more reason to save her money and get out of Kansas City as fast as she could. If she couldn't save enough by the time Laura was school aged, then she would just educate her at home. It was likely that she knew more than any ignorant Kansas City school teacher anyway. They could start fresh wherever Kelly decided to start the farm.

But it wasn't going to be easy until then, Kelly knew, and it became a little worse at the month's end, when after a long day at work, the bank president, a prim man in his early fifties, asked to speak to her alone. Once she was seated in his tiny office, Kelly watched him fiddle nervously with his glasses and thought she understood what was about to happen. She stiffened her spine and looked straight at him until he came to the point.

"You needn't come into work tomorrow, Miss Chapman," he said. "We've hired a new teller and no longer require your services."

Forewarned by his demeanor, Kelly was not surprised and did not so much as bat an eyelash.

"I thought I was doing excellent work," she said quietly. "At least, that's what you told me last week."

"Your work is excellent. That is not the issue here."

Kelly felt a thinking calm sweep down over her anger—the same kind of thinking calm that possessed her during any kind of confrontation, dangerous or otherwise. Her anger gave her power, and the calm gave her control over that power. She frowned detachedly, as though considering an abstract problem.

"I'm afraid I don't understand," she said. "Exactly what is the issue?"

He coughed and put his glasses back on.

"You must understand, Miss Chapman, that this is a bank. People trust us with their life's savings. We must inspire confidence. We must be above reproach."

"You've just said my work is excellent," Kelly replied, a glint in her eyes. "In what way, exactly, does excellent work fail to inspire confidence?"

"I was thinking more of your personal conduct," he said. "It pains me to say this, but it has come to my attention that you frequent several of the local saloons and have been seen playing cards with men of questionable reputation."

"I've also played cards with your head teller. Why aren't you questioning his ability to inspire confidence?"

"That is a different issue altogether. Your appearance in such places raises questions about your morality."

"But not about his."

"We aren't discussing him."

There wasn't any point in pursuing the issue, Kelly thought. Aside from the principle involved, she didn't care much anyway. Bank work was boring.

"Very well then," she said. "I'll leave as soon as you give me my week's salary."

He smiled dryly.

"You are hardly in a position to insist, and I think that, considering the damage you may have done to this institution's reputation, it is hardly owed to you."

"A good lawyer may think otherwise, Mr. Jensen, and if I leave here without that money, I intend to hire the best lawyer I can find to get it for me."

"You would risk that scandal?"

"What scandal? I'm not ashamed of anything I've ever done. The only person who will suffer from a scandal is you and your bank. I can assure you that a lawyer will include his fees in the money he sues you for."

Although she didn't realize it, her eyes and face went cold and hard, just as they did when circumstances called for her to look through her revolver sights. Unused to shoot outs, Mr. Jensen blanched and took fifteen dollars from his desk and handed it to her. He did not doubt for a moment that she would do as she had said and feared that a lawsuit would be the least of her revenge.

Kelly took the money and left without a word.

Outside, it was sunny though cold. She walked quickly home, fuming. Pompous judgmental coward, she thought vehemently, how dare he sit there and lecture me? Graham was right. Kansas City had gone to the dogs. Thank goodness that another year should see her away from there.

She stomped up the back steps and slammed into the kitchen. Laura came running into greet her, but sensing her mood, hung back. Kelly picked her up and went looking for Alice.

Alice was sitting in the parlor with her sewing basket, working on the mending.

"Hidy," she said without looking up from her work. "How's your day?"

"Terrible," Kelly said, setting Laura down. "That pasty-faced fool Jensen fired me."

"Fired you? What for?"

"For playing cards."

"There ain't a man in Kansas City he can hire then," Alice replied.

"He will though," Kelly said angrily. "You know how prigs like that think."

Alice looked at her sympathetically. Kelly's news hadn't surprised her; Alice had been expecting it for some time. Alice had seen every form of disreputable behavior in her life, and in her opinion, nothing Kelly did was all that shocking. After all, the girl wasn't mean spirited, and she had never whored, but some people didn't understand those distinctions.

What amazed Alice was that, for someone so smart, Kelly seemed to have no idea of how respectable people thought. Kelly seemed to think she could do as she pleased, and everyone would mind their own business. Alice thought that was terribly naive.

"You didn't like that job much anyway," Alice said.

"That's not the point," Kelly said, sitting down huffily. "I'm so mad I could spit."

"Did you get your wages?"

"Of course."

Alice didn't think that was an "of course" kind of end to the situation but didn't say so. Apparently, it took a harder man than a bank manager to face down Kelly Knowlton when she was on the scrap.

"Is Graham around?" She asked at last.

"He went out about an hour ago. Said he'd be back late."

Kelly watched Laura play for a moment, thinking it was just as well he wasn't around. He had never approved of her working in a bank anyway, though now that she thought of it, he might take umbrage at the insult to her character being fired involved. Maybe if she told it right, he'd go plug that stupid banker for her or at least knock him around a little.

Her temper cooling, Kelly shrugged the idea off. The only way to hurt a bank man was through his money, which she'd done by getting her week's salary. She hadn't begged for it either, so he couldn't feel smug over it. Besides, if she wanted him shot, she ought to do it herself.

By bedtime, she had recovered from the whole episode. She took a bath, and as Graham had not returned, she curled up in bed with a book. If he had told Alice that he was going to be late, she thought, it wouldn't be sensible to expect him before two.

But it wasn't yet ten o'clock when he came in. Kelly was still reading, and although it didn't show on her face, she was very surprised to see him so early. She was also pleased, so pleased that the morning's trouble passed from her mind as she looked up from her book and smiled at him.

"Hidy do," she said,

"Hidy yourself," he said, smiling back. "Living with Alice has ruined your grammar."

"I can speak very well when I am so inclined," Kelly said, amused. He must have won a bundle to be in such a good mood.

She went back to reading in order to give him some privacy to go about taking his clothes off.

He slid into bed, and Kelly sat forward to give him a pillow. He took both pillows, put them behind his back so he could lean comfortably against the headboard, then drew her back so she was laying back against his chest.

Kelly started to put her book aside, but he stopped her.

"What are you reading?"

"A very bad novel."

"Why are you reading it then?"

"I read such things to Alice when she does her mending. She likes them."

Graham could see where Alice's taste in books would differ from Kelly's.

"You do like to read. How long did you go to school?"

"One week," Kelly replied. "My grandfather taught me until I was twelve, then I was sent to Elizabeth Stalling's Academy for Young Ladies. The first day I was there, we had a two-hour lecture on how to use a napkin."

They both laughed. Kelly, who was not given to reminiscing, had not thought of the academy for years.

"What happened?" Graham asked.

"The headmistress asked my grandfather to take me home at the end of the week."

"Why? What did you do?"

"Well, I wasn't used to such a stuffy place, and I wasn't used to sitting still for so long. It got on my nerves. I had a disagreement with the history mistress and was sent to the head mistress's office. I told her that I had never seen such a ridiculous place and that she ought to teach something useful, like higher mathematics. She put me on punishment."

"What was that?"

"Memorizing chapters from the Bible. I refused to do it, and she wired my grandfather."

"I'll bet he had a conniption."

Kelly shook her head. "No, he asked me what had happened, and I told him. He took me home and never spoke of it again, though I bet he had a good laugh over it. After that, I had tutors for French, math, and history. I never went back to school."

"Your grandfather must've been an old rip," Graham said, pleased to know that Kelly had shown spunk at an early age. "Read some aloud."

"Sure."

Kelly didn't know how long he listened or if he fell asleep, but after an hour, he had not said a word. As her eyes were tired and she began to feel drowsy, she closed the book and laid it on her stomach, meaning to rest for a second but, instead, falling asleep almost immediately.

Graham was still awake. He placed the book on the night table and turned the lamp off. Once the room was dark and silent except for the sound of Kelly's breathing, he drifted off to sleep.

They were both awakened three hours later by a wailing cry from Laura's room. Kelly was out of bed and pulling a shirt on before she was even fully awake. She buttoned two buttons and turned to the door. Graham was sitting up in bed, holding his revolver, which he had drawn instinctively upon being startled out of sleep.

"You won't need that," Kelly said as she hurried from the room.

Laura was sitting up in bed wailing. Kelly rushed over to her and picked her up. Laura clutched at her and continued to scream and cry.

Kelly hugged her.

"What's the matter, baby?" She asked, trying to comfort her.

Laura stopped screaming but continued to cry. Kelly walked the floor with her, crooning to her. If it had been a nightmare, it must have been a bad one, she thought. It tore at her heart to hear Laura scream like that.

Graham entered the room.

"What's the matter?" He asked.

"I don't know," Kelly said. "Bad dream maybe."

She shivered, at first she hadn't noticed how cold it was in the room. Kelly took a blanket from the foot of her bed and wrapped Laura in it.

"Hurts, Ma," Laura said. "Ear hurts."

Kelly gently pushed Laura's hand away from her right ear. It was red, but there was no sign of any discharge from it. Kelly felt relieved. There were much worse things than earaches.

Graham had taken Kelly's wrapper from the wardrobe. Now he helped her into it so she wouldn't have to put Laura down.

"Thanks," Kelly said. She thought he looked a little green around the gills. Listening to a child cry in pain tended to do that to people. It was a sound you just never got used to. "Could you stir up the fire in the kitchen and put some water on to boil?" She asked him.

"Sure," he said, heading for the door with considerable haste.

Kelly walked the floor with Laura for a few more minutes, then sat down on the bed. Instantly, Laura began to scream again. Kelly stood back up and walked some more, and Laura quieted down some. When she thought the kitchen might be warm enough, Kelly went downstairs.

The kitchen was still a little cold, and Kelly realized that her feet were still bare. The fire in the stove was blazing though, and the floor would warm up soon. "The water will be ready soon," Graham said. "Want me to go for a doctor?"

"No, she's just got an earache," Kelly said. "I'll get the doctor in the morning if it's not better." Laura's crying had tapered off somewhat, but when Kelly sat down at the table, she began screaming afresh. Kelly immediately stood and paced the kitchen floor until Laura's cries subsided again.

By then, the water had started to boil. She started to make some tea, using one hand to pour the water and the other to hold Laura. But Laura wasn't as little as she used to be, and it was awkward. "Here," Graham said. "I'll take her while you do that."

Kelly privately doubted that Laura would care much for that idea, but her arms were tired so she decided to try it. Laura accepted the change with a minimum of fussing, and Kelly felt a slight twinge of guilt for having underestimated him.

While Graham walked the floor with Laura, Kelly finished making the tea. Then she took Alice's brandy bottle from the cupboard and poured three teaspoons of it into the tea cup. She stirred it well, then mixed in a teaspoon of white sugar. She tasted the resulting mixture, and as it was still bitter, she added some more sugar.

Laura wouldn't let Graham sit down either, so while he stood holding her, Kelly coaxed her into taking the tea a spoonful at a time. Laura didn't care much for it, sugar or not, and a considerable amount ended up on Graham's shirt front. By the time the tea was gone, however, Laura had stopped crying and was half asleep. Kelly put the empty cup on the table and took Laura back from Graham.

Dopey though she was, Laura still fussed when Kelly tried to stop walking or sit down, so she paced the floor for two more hours. Graham offered to take over several times, but Kelly wouldn't let him.

The sky was beginning to lighten when Laura finally began to sleep peacefully against Kelly's bosom. Kelly checked her ears once more. They were still clean. She could hear Alice walking around upstairs. If there had been any borders in the house, Alice would have been awake long ago.

"I'm going to see if I can put her back to bed now," Kelly said. Graham said nothing, but he looked at her so oddly she felt annoyed. "Well, what?" She asked.

"Nothing," he said. "You ought to go to sleep yourself."

"I have to help Alice get breakfast," she replied, the annoyance gone from her voice. He was slouched in a chair, his shirt, which was stained with brandy and tea, was untucked and his braces dangled from his pants. He needed a shave.

Shifting Laura to her other shoulder, she kissed the top of his head.

"I appreciate your help," she said.

Laura was now fast asleep. Kelly carried her upstairs and put her in bed, staying in the room and watching her sleep until she heard Alice's door open and shut. Then she washed and dressed quickly, hurrying back downstairs to help with the morning's work.

Graham was making coffee when she reentered the kitchen, and Alice was fussing with the fire in the stove.

"Good morning, Alice," Kelly said.

"Good morning," Alice said. "Have some trouble last night?"

"Laura had an earache," Kelly explained, going into the pantry for some flour.

"How is she?"

"Asleep," Kelly replied as she measured out the flour for the morning's biscuits.

After breakfast, Kelly went back to bed and did not wake again until late in the afternoon. Graham was nowhere to be found, and Alice told her that he had gone to the saloon. Because Laura was still sick, Kelly spent that night in her own room. She was awake until after midnight, but Graham did not return.

Her need for sleep finally caught up with her, and the next morning, she slept until nearly eight o'clock, when Laura woke her up. Laura was better, so Kelly washed and dressed them both and carried Laura down to breakfast.

Alice was doing the breakfast dishes when they entered the kitchen.

"Good morning to you both," Alice said. "Feeling better?"

"Yes," answered Laura. Kelly nodded.

"Good morning to you too. Sorry I overslept. Is there any breakfast left?"

"I saved you both a plate in the oven," Alice said.

Kelly wrapped her hand in a towel and took the plates from

the oven. Laura sat in her chair, rambling on a little too quickly for Kelly to understand, although she nodded every now and then.

"Did Graham eat yet?" Kelly asked, thinking he might have come in during the early morning.

"He ain't come in yet," Alice said. "I reckon he'll be back for lunch."

Chapter 40

Graham didn't come back for lunch or for dinner either. Kelly considered going to see if he'd ended up in jail over something, but didn't. The thought of running down to the sheriff like a worried hen irked her, especially when it was just as likely that he was holed up in a back room playing poker somewhere.

Two days later, Graham had still not reappeared. Kelly took a ride out of town that afternoon. After tearing over the hills at a gallop for some time, Kelly reined in and let her horse walk for a spell. It was a beautiful day, cold and sunny, and the light had a clarity to it that spoke of spring. Kelly removed her hat and turned her face toward the sunlight, savoring it, letting it drive the worry from her mind.

But even the warmth of the sun did not distract her from her thoughts for long. She was seriously worried about Graham. There had been no news of him having been in a scrape or having been arrested, but if he had planned to leave, why hadn't he taken his things?

Two explanations occurred to Kelly. One, that he had been killed and no one had found his body yet, or two, that he wanted to leave her, but had not wanted to face her over it for fear that she would create a scene.

Kelly was hard put to think which explanation she preferred to be true. Not that she wanted him dead, but it galled her to think anyone considered her so fragile. She had loved him for a long time and had never thought it would come to anything. Now it had come to something, and she had always known in her heart that it would not last long. Both these things had caused her plenty of pain, but neither had ever kept her from doing even one thing she wanted to do. And if she sometimes cried over them, no one knew but her.

It was a mistake, she knew, to expect him to keep still for long in a place as civilized as Kansas City. Hell, it was irksome to her even. The first year or so after Laura had been born had been pure hell for her; she'd nearly gone crazy with boredom. But she had made her choice and stuck to it, and now, she had few regrets. However, without such a motivation, it would be near impossible for Graham to come to such a decision.

And it wasn't just civilization that kept them apart.

"He thinks too much about things," Kelly said to her horse. "He ought to know it's just like being in a scrape. You can't think too much about it, else you'll get the jimmjamms."

That seemed like as close to the truth as she could get. After all, how many times had she looked up abruptly and seen him looking at her, his face all troubled and twisted with longing and wonder and something akin to desperation. It ached her to see it, to see him so troubled over something so unnecessary. It also ached her to realize that he would leave soon, that he had reached his limit and would leave as soon as he realized it.

If he wasn't dead or something, Kelly reminded herself. But the more she thought over how he had looked the night Laura had her earache, the more she knew that he had skipped town. It had been that same look he'd had when he'd left her in Denver.

Kelly struggled with the thought, but she couldn't figure what he saw as the problem. When had she ever asked him for anything? When had she ever indicated by word or by action that she wanted anything more than his company? She could take care of herself without any man's help, hadn't she proven that over the past ten years?

Her horse was rested a little, and Kelly turned him back toward town, not even pausing for a final look westward. She had no time for wishing that day.

Late that evening, Kelly sat at her desk, going over the accounts. She had put Laura to bed several hours earlier, and Alice had said good night about a half hour ago. The house was quiet.

She heard the kitchen door open and close. She pulled her revolver from the top desk drawer and listened. Footsteps came down from the kitchen toward the office door, and Kelly put the revolver down. For her, there was no mistaking Graham's tread, and sure enough, there was a knock at the door.

"Come on in," she said.

The door opened, and Graham walked in. He needed a shave and his collar looked dirty, but otherwise, he seemed his usual self.

"Good evening," he said. "You're up late."

"So are you," Kelly said equably. "Three days late, by my reckoning."

Graham sat down on the settee and pulled his boots off.

"I rode over to Kansas for a spell," he said.

"You could have said goodbye or left word," Kelly replied. "I thought you might be dead somewhere."

She didn't seem angry, and Graham felt relieved. If she were mad about it, she would say so. Kelly wasn't the kind to hold herself in over such a thing.

"I apologize for that," he said. "I just didn't know what I was doing until it was done, is all."

Kelly smiled a little. She was familiar with how such things could happen.

"Well, it happens sometimes," she said. "How was Kansas?"

"Seems like east gets further west all the time," Graham said, and Kelly thought his voice sounded a little sad.

Kelly closed the ledger and put it aside. She was glad he was back and that neither of her thoughts on why he had gone were true. It confirmed her belief that most things couldn't bear too much thinking; the answer was always something that would never have occurred to you anyway.

As Kelly cleared her desk off, Graham watched her, thinking that it would never seem right to see her wearing dresses and sitting at a desk doing figures. She ought to be outside wrestling with horses and riding bareback like a wild Indian. He spoke without thinking, and the calm and the control were gone from his voice.

"Hey, Kelly," he said. "Let's just ride the hell out of here. There's country up northwest like you've never seen before."

Kelly stopped, startled by the vibrant note in his voice and the longing in his eyes. Her heart contracted with emotion, and she felt tears in her eyes. For a second, she could imagine doing such a thing, could see the stars overhead and the wild country all around. She could smell the air and feel the breeze and the tingling in her veins that seemed to be life itself prickling its way through her . . .

And then she was back her sparsely furnished office, knowing that he was offering her something that she could not accept.

"I can't," she said.

"Why not?" He asked, taking her hands and pulling her toward him. "Why not just up and go?"

"Because I love my little girl, that's why," Kelly said, trying to say it as gently as possible. If anyone had told her in May of 1873 that this man could sit here and say such things with his heart plain in his face, she would not have believed it, and now that she saw it, she could not bring herself to hurt him anymore than was necessary.

"We'll take her along," he said so quickly and with such

conviction that Kelly considered it, but despite her longing, she was too realistic not to understand what it would mean.

"I won't drag her through every filthy mining camp and military outpost west of the Mississippi," Kelly said. "I won't take her where the Indians are so riled up even the army is nervous."

Graham continued to look at her, silently asking her to change her mind. Kelly felt a swift and sudden anger at him. Under his gaze, the restlessness and longing and need that she had subdued for so long stirred back into life, and she hated him for it. What right did he have to ask her to make such a choice, to stir her up and make her want and then leave her cold?

She drew her hands away from his.

"You know better," she said angrily. "I can't. I would in an instant if it were just me—and you had plenty of chances when it was just me. But I'm all Laura's got. I didn't want her, may God forgive me for that, but I love her, and I am going to make sure she has choices. I won't put myself above her. It wouldn't be right."

Graham looked deflated. He knew that she spoke of reality, and that he had been speaking of dreams.

"Any life that's what you want ought to be good enough for her," he said. "What choice won't she have?"

"The choice to be decent," Kelly said. "The cards are stacked against her already. I can't bring myself to make it worse for her, and she is not going to have anyone throwing down on her because her mother may or may not have been a whore."

He thought then that she had changed. She was never going to be as wild or as carefree as she had been when he'd first known her. He felt cheated for a moment, cheated and deceived, and it made him angry.

"You might just as well have stayed in New York," he said bitterly. "You've ended up there anyway."

Kelly sat stock still, stunned at what he had said. She could not believe that he would insult her so vilely, even though she had heard him say the words. Anger stormed through her, and she leapt to her feet.

"You arrogant son of a bitch." she hissed. "How dare you sit there and talk to me like that? What the hell do you know about it anyway? You never had a responsibility in your life."

The tears that had risen into her eyes spilled over her lashes, wetting her face. Graham was too taken aback to notice them. He had not meant to insult her; he had been taken with the irony of the situation and had spoken before thinking.

"I wasn't speaking against you," he said. It had never occurred to him that she might face shame or humiliation as part of the price for having chosen a safer life for her daughter.

Kelly sat tiredly down on the sofa. The house seemed so silent she felt she could hear Alice snoring upstairs.

"Sometimes I'm so jealous of you I could scream," she said, looking at him and angrily dashing the tears from her cheeks.

"Jealous of me?"

"Because you can come and go as you please and do as you want, and you will never have to give those things up unless you want to."

Graham went to her and put his arms round her, but she would not relax against him and be comforted. He released her after a moment, feeling crushed beneath the weight of something, something that had been hanging over them for a long time and that had now finally fallen.

"I never thought you would turn respectable," he said sadly.

"I haven't," Kelly replied. "But I want to have that farm I've been planning for, and I want Laura to have good life. Those things are worth a few sacrifices."

"But I'm not."

"Yes you are. You can come and go as you please. I just can't go with you, although I would if I could. I love you."

Those last words just slipped out of her mouth; never before had she told him that she loved him. Now that she had spoken the words, she wished that she could recall them, for the reaction they evoked was completely unlike what she had hoped. Instead of happiness or solemnity or even understanding, anger was on his face. To him, her words sounded too much like an excuse and not enough like something he could settle for, and so, her talk of love was meaningless.

"I guess we've just ended up in different places," he said slowly.

Kelly knew he was talking about leaving. She had always known that he would sooner or later.

"I want you to stay," Kelly said, though she knew it was no use.

Graham went to the window and stared outside. The town had become more and more built up. He couldn't see anything but other buildings. The plains beyond them seemed to have vanished.

"I think I'd better go," he said without looking away from the window.

Kelly stood up. He wasn't taking about coming and going. He was talking about going and never returning. There was no middle ground to him, and Kelly knew she could go no further out of her way to meet him.

"Go then," she said. "Go straight to hell if you want. But in six months or a year or two you'll miss me, and don't you dare think you can dance back here and crawl back into my bed."

She left the room without waiting to see his reaction to her words. Graham stood by the window and thought. All things considered, it would be better if he left before morning. His heart was sore, and he could not imagine ever looking her in the face again.

Chapter 41

At four a.m., the house was dark and silent. Graham went slowly about getting his things together, wanting to slip out before either Kelly or Alice woke up but not wanting to badly enough to hurry. His lack of resolve did him in. Just as he was getting ready to open the door to his room, he heard Alice's door open and close.

He listened as she went downstairs. It was four-thirty, early for her to be awake but not by much. Alice seemed to have a sixth sense for trouble between him and Kelly. He swore silently to himself, then left his room and started down the hall carrying his traveling things. Despite his thought of earlier in the evening, he paused as he passed Kelly's door, and it took a force of will for him to continue down the hall and stairs.

Lamp light flickered from the kitchen. Alice sat at the table, dressed for the day ahead, waiting for her coffee to boil.

"Dressed for traveling, I see," she said. But the baiting tone he expected was absent from her voice.

He nodded. Alice went to the stove.

"I expect you've got time for a cup before you go?" She asked, going to the stove and pouring two cups of coffee out.

Graham set his traps down, but he did not sit at the table even though he accepted the cup Alice offered him. Alice sat back down at the table.

"It don't look like you plan on coming back soon," Alice said. "Did you all have a fight?"

"No, we had a parting of ways," Graham replied.

Alice shook her head sadly.

"Ain't that what you thought when you left her with me in Denver? Ain't that what you thought when she run off to Arizona with Jackson Taylor? Seems to me like you ain't been right yet."

"She told me to go."

"Oh pooh. You riled her up so's you'd have a reason to go," Alice said.

"You talk mighty sure for someone who doesn't even know what was said."

"I know you both is all."

Alice sipped her coffee, gazing at him with wide, speculative eyes.

"Well, it don't matter. You'll ride back out to wherever it is you think you want to be, and after you've played some poker and drunk some whiskey and sat alone under the night sky, you'll realize that none of those things come even halfway close to what that woman can do to you just by smiling at you the way a woman does when she's in love."

Graham set his cup down on the table and picked his things up. Alice always had thought she knew everything, but she was in for some education this time.

"I wouldn't bet the rent on it," he said.

"I would," Alice replied, undaunted by the coldness in his voice because it was the coldness of a man whose heart was sore hurt. "I just wish you'd tell me what is so all fired important about running around the wild country acting reckless. What's the point to it?"

"Ask Kelly," he said, opening the door. "She can say it better than I ever could. And I'll tell you something else, Alice, since you've always taken such an interest in this. I won't be back. Kelly's chosen one way, and I've chosen another, so there's no point to it."

"You've chosen badly then," Alice said. "Even so, I wish you well."

"Thank you," he said. "And I wish you well."

The door banged shut behind him. Alice sat at the table, sipping her coffee and thinking. Kelly was likely to be upset for a while. If they started taking in boarders in again, maybe the extra work would distract her from her hurt.

Although Kelly was not happy with Alice's plan, she did not dispute it. In her present mood, the strain of dealing with strangers made her snappish. Four different boarders came and went during the two weeks after Graham left, but Kelly did not even trouble herself to learn their names.

The degree of her previous happiness was now the measure of her unhappiness. The winter that she and Graham had spent together had aroused a need in her that now became an aching loneliness. She didn't really understand it. After all, they had seen each other off and on for years, and while she always missed him when he was gone, she had never really been lonely. Perhaps, she now thought, it was more a matter of never having realized that she was lonely because she had never had a measure to judge by.

Whatever the reason, she was now unhappier than she had been after Laura was born. Then at least, she had been able to go to him for understanding or a kick in the pants if she needed it. Now their lives were sundered, and for the first time, Kelly realized that Graham McNair was the only person she had ever known who understood every bit of what she was and loved her because of it and not in spite of it.

Those two weeks after he left dragged on endlessly. Everyday, she hoped he would turn up so they could mend things, and everyday, she was disappointed—disappointed and angry at having let herself hope for something so foolish. This time, he was going to be gone a good long while, and he might not come back at all.

So distracted was she with her anguish that she became oblivious to everything else. Sleep was hard to find, for every time she closed her eyes images of regret flashed before them, making her jerk awake. Most nights she spent reading or walking the floors. Only exhaustion could keep her dry, red-rimmed eyes closed long enough to sleep.

March passed and April began. Kelly sat sullenly in the parlor watching Alice darn socks. Laura was upstairs napping, and Alice kept looking at Kelly sideways, which she found annoying.

"What's the matter?" She asked finally. "Did I sprout an extra nose during the night?"

"No," Alice said. "I was just wondering about something."

"Ask away then," Kelly said, thinking that any direct question was better than being stared at, however surreptitiously.

"Ain't you come sick yet this month?" Alice asked her.

Kelly shrugged, wondering why Alice was always so preoccupied with such things.

"No."

"You never did last month either, did you?"

"No," Kelly said slowly, a horrible thought forming in her mind. "But I'm pretty upset, that may be why. I was never sick the month I ran from home, either."

But her words lacked conviction. Alice looked at her questioningly, as though she wondered about Kelly's sanity. The look missed Kelly, who was staring past Alice, her eyes clouded over with a sudden understanding.

"Shit!" She yelled so suddenly and so loudly that Alice jumped in her chair. Kelly sprang to her feet, furious.

"Son of a bitch," she swore, kicking her chair over. It couldn't be. It wasn't fair. But she was sure in her heart that it was true. She was pregnant again, and once again, she was left alone to deal with it.

Anger swept away her previous depression; she stomped from the room and out of house. Once in the back yard, she picked up an old chair that needed re-caning and beat it against the side of the house until it broke apart in her hands. Then she sat down on the back steps feeling as though she had only skimmed off enough of her anger to keep it from boiling over into further violence.

She put her hand to her face and found that her cheeks were wet. Angrily, she dried her face with her skirt. She didn't want a baby; she wanted the baby's father. It wasn't fair that he got to ride off, and she was stuck here with a mess he helped make. It would be one thing if he were willing to help out with things; in such a case she might even be happy to have baby, to see who it looked like and what kind of person it would become. Those things were miracles that she would dearly have liked to share with him. But as things were, it just seemed unfair, and unfairness always infuriated her.

The screen door opened, and Alice poked her head outside.

"Come on in, Kelly," she said. "You'll catch your death out here with no coat on."

Now that Alice mentioned it, it was chilly out. Kelly rubbed her arms for a moment, wanting to stay outside and be alone, but she knew Alice was right. So she stood and climbed the steps wearily.

"I'm surprised at you, Kelly," Alice said. "As crazy as you are about the man, I think you'd be pleased to have this baby. Whatever is the matter with you?"

"I was going to head out on my own next spring and get started on my farm. How am I supposed to do that all by myself with a tot and a newborn? Babies are a lot of work. I don't want to go through all that by myself again."

Kelly plopped down at the kitchen table and sighed. What she wanted didn't matter. She was stuck with the situation, and there was nothing to be done except the best that she could do.

Alice gazed at her sympathetically.

"Well, I can understand that," she said. "But don't fret yourself over it. Graham'll be back."

"No he won't," Kelly said, leaning her elbows on the table. "We threw some very hard words at each other."

Alice patted her shoulder.

"Think what you like," she said. "But I'd bet this house and everything in it that he comes back before that baby's born."

Kelly wished that she could believe Alice's words, but hope seemed to have gone out of her. Long ago, she had realized that getting involved with Jackson had been a mistake. Now it seemed that she should have left well enough alone when it came to Graham. Their love seemed to have burned away so quickly, leaving her without the comfort of his friendship, which she now realized had sustained her for so long.

Annoyed by the thought, Kelly stood up, knowing that she would have to keep busy and keep her mind off of thinking about it.

"Laura's probably up from her nap by now," she said to Alice. "I'll go get her."

She went upstairs tiredly, dreading the months to come.

Chapter 42

April that year was warm and dry. There was no freshness in the breeze, and Kelly often felt that the air irritated her nostrils. Her pregnancy had not, as yet, caused her any trouble. Although her health remained good, her spirits sagged. Her anger smoothed away some of her hurt over Graham's leaving, but it brought her no peace. As May approached and then began, she began to work at feeling better. After all, it was as Alice had said. There was nothing to be done, so she might as well make the best of it.

She spent the first week of May looking for a pony for Laura, who was now begging for one on a regular basis. Despite the little girl's pleadings, Kelly took her time looking. She had to find a small pony, and one with a very gentle disposition. She would not trust her daughter to just any animal.

One afternoon, she returned from having looked at several animals and found Laura playing in the back yard as Alice hung up the laundry. Laura ran to her as soon as she opened the gate.

"Did you find one, Ma?" She asked excitedly, tugging at Kelly's pant leg.

"I think so, pumpkin," Kelly said, scooping her up. "You and I will go see him tomorrow."

"What's he like Ma? What's he like? Is he spotted?"

"No," Kelly said, wondering how Laura had become so taken with the idea of having a spotted pony; it was the one thing she always asked about.

Seeing Laura's disappointment, she tried to placate her.

"He's a pretty black pony with two white legs and a white nose," she said. "I had a pony with stockings when I was your age, and he sure was a good one."

Laura's frown lessened a little. If she could not have a spotted pony, then one like her mother had once had was the next best thing.

"Uncle Graham told me Indians ride spotted ponies," Laura said. "I'm going to be an Indian when I grow up."

Kelly laughed. Alice stopped pinning up her laundry and made a sour face.

"You're a wild Indian now, sugar. Go pick your blocks up. I'll tell you more about him if you'll keep me company while I change."

She set Laura down, and the girl ran over to her playthings. Kelly went over to Alice.

"Don't look so sour, Alice," Kelly said to her. "She'll out grow it."

Alice shook her head and took a clothespin from her mouth.

"No, she won't. You never did."

They both started to laugh but stopped abruptly when Laura suddenly began to cry.

Kelly and Alice both ran over to her. She was sitting in the grass holding her arm.

"What's the matter?" Kelly asked, picking her up.

"Bee stung me," Laura sobbed.

Kelly examined the arm. She could see the small puncture and was relieved that the stinger had fallen out.

"It's OK, pumpkin," Kelly soothed. "It won't hurt long."

"Put some baking soda on it," Alice suggested.

Kelly carried Laura into the house; Alice followed them. Once in the kitchen, Kelly sat down with Laura on her lap while Alice rummaged through the pantry for the baking soda. Laura's sobs had died off some, and Kelly gently picked up her arm to examine it again.

Kelly stared at it, horrified. Laura's entire forearm had swollen and turned red.

"Hurry with that baking soda, Alice," she said, her throat suddenly dry. "It's swelling badly."

Alice emerged from the pantry with the baking soda. Laura began to squirm in Kelly lap.

"What's the matter, baby?" Kelly asked.

"I itch, Ma," Laura said.

Kelly set her down and knelt to look at her. Red splotches were rising on her face and neck. Trying to appear unconcerned, Kelly lifted Laura's dress to look at her legs. They were also covered with red splotches.

"You'd better get the doctor, Alice," Kelly said.

"For a bee sting? Don't be silly," Alice said, not turning from the counter where she was making a paste from baking soda. "She was only stung once."

"Come and look at this."

Alice brought the paste over but stopped in shock when she saw Laura. Kelly hardly noticed Alice's reaction. She felt Laura's face, which was now flushed. She felt hot, as though she had a fever, and her breath had taken on a rasping sound.

"My God," Alice breathed.

"Get the doctor," Kelly hissed. "Now!"

Alice turned and fled out the back door. Laura was crying again, and Kelly carried her upstairs and put her in bed, loosening the buttons on her dress to ease her breathing. She wiped the sweat from Laura's forehead and spoke calmly to her.

"Mum-mum's here, baby," she said. "You just rest easy. Everything's going to be fine, and we'll go see your new pony tomorrow."

Laura's breathing grew harsher, so harsh that it pained Kelly to hear it. Her entire body was covered with red blotches, and her face had begun to swell. She began to cry, and Kelly lifted her from the bed, holding her small feverish body tightly to her and crooning to her as though she had woken from a nightmare.

Laura convulsed in her arms. Kelly held her more tightly, as if she could stop Laura's pain through her own strength. Laura convulsed twice more, and Kelly rocked her, holding her ever tighter. It seemed to work. Laura suddenly went limp in her arms.

Where was the doctor? She wondered desperately, then the thought vanished from her mind as she realized that she could no longer hear Laura's labored breathing.

Relieved, Kelly held Laura away from her.

"Feel a little better now pumpkin?" She asked gently.

But Laura did not respond. Kelly realized with a dull sense of disaster that she was not breathing at all.

Frantic, Kelly felt for her pulse. She could not find it. She listened for her heartbeat, but there was no sound in Laura's chest.

"It can't be!" She cried. "Wake up, pumpkin. It was just a bee sting, that's all. Wake up!"

But Laura didn't wake up, and when Alice and the doctor entered the room ten minutes later, they found Kelly still kneeling there, cradling her daughter in her arms.

The doctor knelt beside them and put his stethoscope to Laura's chest. After listening for a moment, he took it away and placed a compassionate hand on Kelly's arm.

"Miss Chapman," he said. "She's dead."

"I know that," Kelly said in a voice too stunned for tears. "It was just a bee sting. A bee."

"Some people are allergic to bees," the doctor said. "To them, a bee is worse than a rattlesnake. There isn't anything I could have done for her."

Behind them, Alice began to sob, lifting her apron to her face to catch the tears. Kelly gently laid Laura in her little trundle bed and kissed her.

"Doctor, would you send for whichever undertaker you think is best?" She asked.

The doctor nodded and left. Kelly sat by the bed. She could hear Alice sobbing, but the sound was far away from her, as far away as her feelings seemed to be. She remembered, as if from a dream, how she had stood up after having been shot in the shoulder; how she had not felt any pain even though she could see her own blood on the floor. She remembered how she had been able to see and hear everything, but how everything had seemed distant and unreal.

She felt that way now, and that feeling sustained her when the mortician came and took her baby away. She heard herself giving instructions, saw herself doing what had to be done, smelled the grief welling from Alice, but none of it reached her. Not then, not at the funeral, and not during the nightmarish days that followed it.

The suddenness of it had stunned her. In a few minutes, out of a clear blue sky, her baby had been completely taken from her—forever. She could not keep the finality of it in her mind for very long. She found herself listening for the sounds of Laura playing or laughing. During the morning, Kelly's mind would turn to what book to read to Laura in the evening or whether or not she would want to go for a ride in the afternoon. Often, Kelly would find Alice drying her eyes and wonder what could be wrong, then Alice would look at her, and Kelly would remember, and tears would burn behind her own eyes. Grief would seize her afresh, making her knees shake until she had to sit down.

But the tears always refused to fall. They festered there behind her eyes until her head felt swollen, but she could never cry. The anger and guilt boiled inside her, and there was no relief from them, not in tears and not in talking. Kelly did not even believe that time would wash them away, and there was no comfort for her in thoughts of heaven. Laura might be in heaven, but that was the very essence of her mother's hell.

When the boiling became too much, Kelly often though of Graham and wished that he were there. Their fight seemed so unimportant now. If he would just come back for a day—even for an hour. If he were there, she could wail and scream and smash things. She could cry out every bit of her anger, grief, and guilt. If he were there, he would stand there and watch until she was done and then he would take her into his arms and give her comfort. He was the only person who had the strength to stand her misery and the understanding to offer her peace.

But he wasn't there, and there was little reason to think that he might show up any time soon, or ever for that matter. There was no one to help her but Alice, and warm though Alice was, she could not comprehend the storm that raged in Kelly's spirit.

So, stunned and hurting, Kelly stumbled through her days, and alone and despairing, she fought her demons at night.

In her grief, she almost forgot about her pregnancy. When she did remember it, it seemed as distant and as unreal as Laura's death had been. It served to remind her how she had not wanted Laura, and how she had wished that she had never become pregnant. Well, time had taken care of it. She was no longer burdened with Laura, but Laura had not seemed like a burden for years. At some point, Laura had become a flash of light in her life. Kelly could not say when the change had come, but it had. Now it seemed that her earlier resentment had come home to roost.

Kelly lost track of time. She rarely went out, and neither did Alice. The two women comforted each other as well as their different natures would allow. Kelly was not surprised by the intensity of Alice's grief. Alice had loved Laura from the moment that she had been born. Kelly knew that she herself could not make such a claim.

They often sat in the parlor as they had in days past. Alice worked on her sewing, and Kelly read aloud. Though she never said so aloud, Alice often wished that Graham would hurry up and return. Kelly was no worse than she should be, but Alice was worried because she never cried. Alice did not doubt that Kelly had the strength to stand whatever life dealt her, but she did doubt that Kelly had the strength to find her own healing. Without healing, the wound in Kelly's heart would only fester and twist her for life.

True to her nature, Kelly did not wonder about healing. The comfort she craved was beyond her reach, and so she turned in on herself. To her, it seemed only the numbness and the distance would save her from the violence of her emotions.

So great did the numbness become that she did not even react one morning when she woke to find her underpants stained with blood. The sight of blood and what it could mean registered in her brain, but she was incapable of reacting to either fact. Instead, she dressed calmly and went downstairs. Alice was dragging about the kitchen preparing breakfast, and Kelly began to help her.

"You look right peaked this morning, Kelly," Alice said. "You feeling all right?"

"No worse than usual," she said.

A cramp gripped her abdomen, but no sign of the pain showed on her face as she went about making biscuits while Alice fried some sidemeat.

When they had finished making breakfast, Alice carried the platter of meat to the table. She set it down, then turned and went to help Kelly get the biscuits onto a plate. She slipped and nearly fell down.

"Goodness!" She said, catching the counter. "I must have

spilled some water."

Kelly said nothing, and Alice doubted that she had even heard her. Alice took a towel and bent down to wipe up the water. She gasped. The floor was puddled with blood.

Alice looked at Kelly, who was carrying the plate of biscuits to the table. Her skirt was all bloody.

"Kelly, you're bleeding," Alice said.

"Just a little," Kelly replied in a detached voice. "I noticed it when I got dressed."

"Kelly," Alice said. "Look at the floor."

Kelly did. She frowned. That was an awful lot of blood. No wonder Alice sounded so upset. She wondered if she were dying.

"Quite a mess," she said, taking a forkful of side meat from the platter and putting it on Alice's plate. "Is this enough meat for you?"

"Your mind has snapped," Alice said, wonderingly. "Get up to bed. I'll go for the doctor."

Kelly winced. The pain could not be ignored anymore. She did as Alice said.

The doctor came again, and again, there was nothing much he could do. Kelly wondered how anyone could stand to be a doctor. They never did anything much but watch people suffer. She did not react when he told her that she had lost the baby. She was not surprised. What was there to be surprised over? She had not wanted Laura, and now Laura was dead. She had not wanted this baby, and now it was dead.

Downstairs, Alice sat limply at the table, relieved that Kelly would recover from the miscarriage but scared to death when she thought about what impact it would have on her.

"It'd be enough to kill me," she said aloud. "Please God, no more. Bad things always come in threes, but spare us that at least. This house has seen enough grief for a good while."

But she had little faith in that prayer, and as the months passed, she waited for the third thing to fall on them. It was not long in coming, though it came as unexpectedly as the first two had.

258

Chapter 43

The streets of Leadfalls, Wyoming, were thick with spring mud, and the sky was gray with approaching rain. Graham's horse plodded wearily, and Graham looked about the streets without much interest. It seemed tragic to him that over a year of wandering had brought him to no better place than this, a muddy cattle town struggling to shed its winter gloom.

It was tragic, maybe, but fitting. The mud and clouds and dank air suited Graham's mood just fine. Good weather and clean streets would have seemed a further aggravation.

Since having left Kansas City, his travels had taken him through Kansas and Colorado, into Nebraska, and now to Wyoming. Not even in the winter had he stopped in any one place for long, for it seemed that once a place became familiar, boredom crashed down around him, bringing with it thoughts of Kelly.

It irked him. Always before, such thoughts had eased his boredom and lightened his mood, but since they had parted on such bad terms, thinking of her was no comfort. In fact, it made things worse. Time and again, he thought he should ride back to Kansas City and smooth things out so at least he could think of her in peace, but his pride kept him from it. Hadn't she told him not to come back?

From the tales he'd heard others tell, he knew that it took a bit of time to get over a heartbreak—as odd as it was to think of himself as heartbroken. Well, he would give it all the time it took. He had never lacked patience. If it was something that could be done, he would do it.

But here it was, spring again, and things were no better. The hurt had eased but missing her had not. Unbidden, thoughts crept into his mind. Treacherous thoughts of what could be if he would just ride back to Missouri and meet her halfway. On days like this one, halfway didn't seem far at all.

To hell with it, he thought. This town should have some good action, what with all the fat cattlemen in the area. He would settle in for a few weeks and see how the play went. Maybe things would seem more cheerful when the streets dried out.

On his way through town, he rode by the jail. The street was crowded, and he did not notice how one of the two men sitting in chairs on the sidewalk in front of the jail perked up as he rode by.

"Clive," said the man, who was short and wiry. "Go hunt through them notices and see if we got one on Graham McNair."

"Yes sir, Marshal," said the young man beside him, hopping to his feet and going inside the jail.

He returned a few minutes later.

"We ain't got nothing on him, Marshal," said Clive.

"You sure?"

"Yes, sir."

Marshal Jed Gallagher leaned his chair back against the wall, chewing a wad of tobacco and then spitting meditatively.

He'd been marshal for just over a year, and before that, he and his older brother, Jake, had raised some hell down in Kansas. Jake had ridden with Graham in the army. Jed knew Graham was a hard case and a shootist of excellent reputation. Having such a man in town could create trouble, or he thought, it could be a boon—if Graham could be persuaded to use his gun on the right side of the law.

For unlike most Kansas towns of the seventies, rowdy cowboys weren't much of a problem this far north in the 1880s. Here, cattle ranchers fought with the small farmers and sheepherders, and sometimes, the big cattle ranchers fought it out with the little cattle ranchers. If the politics sometimes got confusing, it did not trouble Jed Gallagher, for the largest cattle rancher in Wyoming paid him well, and that money kept the politics of any situation as clear as a May sky.

Getting Graham McNair to assist with keeping the peace in the troubled town should not be difficult to accomplish. Graham had lawed before, and he looked like he'd been on the scout for a while. Plus, two of Jed's deputies, Snakey Potter and Sherman Buser, had ridden with Graham up north in Montana. It would be like a family reunion, Jed thought, spitting and letting his chair set back down. Old folks day in Leadfalls. Jed was twenty-four, ten years younger than his brother, who was about the same age as Graham. Youth, he felt, gave him an edge over both men.

That evening, as Jed made his rounds of the saloons, he kept an eye out for Graham. He finally found him playing cards in the Cattleman's Dream saloon, which Jed took as a good omen.

After greeting several of the patrons, Jed took a seat at the bar and openly watched Graham, who favored him with a brief, cold, questioning look and then went back to his game. Jed took this as an insult but prudently waited for the game to end before taking the issue up.

Jed hailed Graham as he stood up from the table. Seeing the badge on Jed's shirt, Graham obeyed the summons, though he did not hurry about it.

"Good evening marshal," he said, stepping up to the bar.

"No it ain't, not for you."

Graham did not react to the words or to the threatening tone of Jed's voice. He ordered a whiskey.

"I ain't got a notice on you," Jed said. "But if I did, you'd be in jail this minute. We got a peaceful town here, and we don't want no trouble."

"Don't start any then," Graham said, nodding to the bartender, who had just brought his drink.

"I reckon I won't. My brother Jake wouldn't take it kindly as you all wore the blue together."

Graham thought for a second. This bantam-sized big mouth did look familiar.

"Would that be Jake Gallagher?"

"It would."

Graham sipped his whiskey. Jake was a big mouth too, but he was a bona fide hard case and a crack shot. This puppy looked to be neither, though of course, with Jake for a big brother, he was bound to fancy himself both.

"I reckon you know Snakey Potter and Sherman Buser," Jed said.

Graham nodded. Both men had been in the outfit he'd led from Denver to Bozeman. Since then, he had seen them various times in different places. They were the kind of men born to army life. They couldn't button their flies without a direct order, though they feared no danger and never hesitated to kill when there was little chance of being shot at themselves.

Still, there was something to be said for a town with so many familiar names in it. To Graham, a known danger was better than an unknown one.

"Since we ain't got a notice on you, and you rode with m' brother, mebbe you could help out with settling this here town a bit. We need to get shed of the rowdier element."

Graham considered it. He had marshaled before, but working with this Jed Gallagher would be rankling. Also, it sounded funny. The town had seemed quiet enough. Here it was nearly ten o'clock, and the streets were silent; there had been no gun fire or any other sort of disturbance.

"Maybe," Graham said, thinking a flat out refusal would be taken personally, and that would lead to shooting. Graham had no wish to shoot a marshal. Such things generally led to a lynching.

"Well, think on it," Jed replied. "Or come on out with us in the morning, we got a bit of lawin' to do. Cattle rustlers."

"All right," Graham said, deciding that a little marshaling on the side would keep Jed from getting offended for a day or two anyway. "When?"

"Oh, say ten o'clock in front of the jail."

"I'll be there."

"Glad to have you. Can I buy you a drink?"

"No, thanks," Graham said. "I'm done for the night."

He left a dollar for the bartender, tipped his hat to Jed, and left the saloon. Jed looked after him. The conversation had not gone as he had hoped, but then, he should have expected a gambling man like Graham McNair to play his cards close to his chest.

At ten o'clock sharp the next morning, Graham rode up to the jail. Jed, Sherman, and Snakey were waiting for him. The other two deputies, Clive Lee and Dave Meyers, were to be left in charge of the town, though in Graham's opinion, Clive was too wet behind the ears to be left in charge of himself, much less a town. Dave looked capable enough, though, and Graham wondered how he had come to hook up with this dubious crew of lawmen.

They headed out of town and north. All four men carried sidearms and rifles. They rode without talking for several miles, then Jed nudged his horse up alongside Graham's.

"We're headed out to Hobbes place," he said. "I had complaints of them rustling off of Mr. Babcock's place, which lays east of 'em. We're gonna confiscate any rustled steers and take the men folk in, if'n they're about."

The names meant nothing to Graham, though he had gathered from the talk in the saloon that Babcock was the biggest rancher in the territory. Big enough to own a piece of the marshal, Graham thought, beginning to regret having agreed to go on this little foray.

The Hobbes place wasn't much more than a ramshackle house and barn. A few horses milled about in a paddock behind the barn, and chickens scratched in the dirt yard. Clothes hanging from a line behind the house fluttered in the breeze, and two little boys ran out the front door, apparently drawn by the sound of approaching riders. They stared wide-eyed for a moment, then ran back into the house.

At a signal from Jed, Snakey and Sherman circled the place and, finding no one, rode into the barn. Jed and Graham waited in the yard. Graham pulled his rifle from its boot and laid it across his lap. Jed chewed his tobacco and, eyeing the place contemptuously, spat brown juice into the dirt.

A woman appeared on the front porch, drying her hands on her apron. The two boys clung to her skirts. Graham guessed they were about three and five years old.

"What do you want, marshal?" She asked. Graham noticed there was no politeness in her voice

"Where's your husband, Miz Hobbes?"

"Working," the woman answered shortly.

"Rustling, you mean," Jed answered, looking around the place. "I've had a complaint about you all stealing steers again."

"Lies!" The woman said. "And you know it. This is the third time this month you been out here, and you ain't found a thing yet."

"I reckon you all brand 'em too fast for me, that's fer sure," Jed replied.

The sound of frantic squeals came from within the barn, and four pigs and a litter of weaners shot into the yard, chased by Jed and Sherman, who were still mounted.

"See there," Jed said. "Stolen hogs. I knew it."

"We brought those hogs with us from Minnesota," the woman said.

"They weren't here last we came through, were they boys?"

"No, sir," Sherman answered.

"They were too!" Cried Mrs. Hobbes angrily.

"I expect we'll have to confiscate 'em."

"You can't do that!"

"Yes, I can, Ma'am," replied Jed. "I'm the marshal. Snakey, Sherm, go on in the house and see if there's any more stolen goods inside."

The two men dismounted and approached the house. One of the frightened pigs bumped up against Snakey, who promptly pulled his revolver and shot it. It fell down dead.

Graham was disgusted with the entire scene—disgusted and angry. He had not thought that Snakey and Sherm would resort to such base depredations just to make a living. He was also annoyed with himself for having been drawn into such a thing.

His disgust must have shown on his face, for Gallagher sneered at him.

"Never figured you for the gutless type, McNair."

Graham's face went cold so fast that Gallagher's sneer wavered.

"Watch your mouth you two-bit tin-star roustabout," Graham said. "It don't take guts to scare women and little boys, and a badge don't make bullying peaceful folks legal."

"You never cared a damn about sodbusters and squareheads, so what's your gripe?"

"I don't care a damn about fat cattlemen either, or about badge-wearing fools who fancy themselves hard cases just because they like to talk bold and shoot up farm houses."

"You get crossways of me, McNair, and you'll find out about what a hard case is," Gallagher spat. "I can shade anyone as old womanish as you in the blink of an eye."

Graham hefted his rifle with both hands and bashed Gallagher in the face with the butt end of it. Gallagher saw the blow coming but not in time to block it. The rifle connected solidly with his jaw, knocking him from the saddle. He landed on his ass, and his horse danced away. He looked up and found himself staring into the muzzle of Graham's rifle.

"Call your damn dogs off, Gallagher," Graham said.

Gallagher looked up at him, his eyes full of pure, clean hatred. Graham was not impressed. He met Gallagher's look with a cold stare until Gallagher spat to clear the blood from his mouth, and then spoke.

"Snakey, Sherm," he called, still staring up at Graham. "Leave off. We're done here."

Startled, both men looked over and saw their leader with a rifle muzzle in his face. They left off their dirty work, but neither of them thought to pull down on Graham, who, satisfied that he had broken up their little shindig, pulled his rifle off of Gallagher.

"Mount up boys," Graham said to them. "This party is over. Go on back to town and do some honest work."

"You ain't my boss," Snakey said.

Graham made no motion worth mentioning but still fired a single shot that kicked up dirt between Snakey's legs. Snakey jumped in the air and landed with a yelp.

"I said mount up you sorry son of a bitch," Graham ordered. This time both men obeyed him without question.

Meanwhile, Gallagher had picked himself up off the ground. Though enraged at Graham's interference, he kept himself calm. This was not the time to settle matters. Graham was primed for a fight, and even though the three of them might be able to kill him, Graham would no doubt kill or badly wound most of them in return. Gallagher knew that he himself would bear most of Graham's ire if it came to a shoot out. Snakey and Sherm weren't of much account when stacked up next to himself or Graham.

So Gallagher mounted up. Graham let the three of them ride ahead of him a bit, then rode up to the porch, where Mrs. Hobbes stood, unwilling to believe that the scene had ended so easily.

Graham handed her a twenty-dollar gold piece and tipped his hat to her.

"I'm sorry about all of this Ma'am. I should've stopped 'em before they killed that pig."

"You all shouldn't have come out here at all," she said, her eyes flashing.

"That's the truth, Ma'am," he said, thinking that she reminded him of Kelly, except that Kelly wouldn't have needed him to do her fighting for her.

He tipped his hat again and rode after the marshal and his deputies, trailing behind them all the way back to town. Graham had rebooted his rifle but rode with his short gun in his hand. He did not trust any of them, and if it came to a shooting, it would be his word against theirs.

Back in town, he debated whether or not to leave immediately. The question was settled for him by the weather. All that afternoon, it poured down rain, and leaving did not seem so urgent that it had to been done in a deluge.

So Graham holed up in his hotel room with a bottle of whiskey and a mindful of regrets. Night came and went and so did the next day, and still, it rained. He ran out of whiskey and sent for another bottle. The room was damp and cheerless, and even the fleeting warmth of the drink was better than nothing.

At last, the sun broke through the clouds, and the rain stopped. Bleary-eyed, Graham opened the curtains and looked out at the town. It was muddier than ever, but he felt it was time to leave. Maybe he would head east for a spell. Certainly not as far east as Missouri, but maybe over to Kansas, anywhere but here.

He packed his things and went out to the livery stable. The stable was dark in comparison to the outside light, and he paused on the threshold as his bloodshot eyes strained to adjust. He never saw what happened, but he felt a movement behind him, and he spun around, drawing his gun an instant before he felt a crushing blow to his head. He passed into unconsciousness, his unfired gun still in his hand.

"That was a close thing, Jed," Snakey said, stepping out of a nearby stall.

"Not that close," Jed replied, wiping the blood from his revolver butt and reholstering it. "You two get his guns and carry him to the jail. Lock him up tight before he comes around."

Snakey and Sherman did as they were told, and Jed watched them, pleased with himself. The hard part was done. Now all they had to do was wait. He might even get a newspaper story done on him, seeing as he had arrested Graham McNair and had lived to tell the tale. He smiled as his deputies carried Graham's limp body from the stable.

"You weren't so damn hard to shade after all," he said aloud. "I reckon you won't talk so big when you come around."

Chapter 44

It was late afternoon when Graham began to wake up. His head felt terrible, and at first, he thought he was hung over. Then he gingerly felt his forehead, and his fingers came away sticky with blood. There was a large knot on his head, and after some effort, he remembered what had happened. But why had they left him alive?

His eyes opened, and without moving, he looked about himself. He was lying on a cot in what looked to be a jail cell. But what could they possibly have arrested him for?

He lay without moving for another two hours. By then, his head felt well enough, and he sat up. Clive was sitting on a stool in the hall, watching him.

"You all right now?" He asked.

Graham did not answer; he was feeling his head over for cracks. Whoever had hit him had done it hard.

The young man hopped off his stool and left the cell block. A few moments later, Jed appeared. He walked straight up to Graham's cell.

"How was your nap?" He asked snidely.

Graham ignored him. A pip-squeak like Jed was bound to try and needle him. It was best not to play his game.

"Your head bled like a stuck pig," Jed continued. "We was afraid you might peg out on us, which would be a shame. It would deprive these good citizens of their right to try you and hang you."

"For what?" Graham asked, though he did not sound particularly interested in knowing.

"For that sheepherder you shot out on Jenny's ridge. Though I say it's a pity to hang a man that can nail a sheepherder in the head at fifty yards, the folks of this town have had enough of such lawlessness."

"And who says I did it?"

"Well, it were done with a Henry rifle like you carry, and the shooting was too good for it to have been anyone from around here. Plus, old man Hobbes saw you ride over his land on the way out there and on the way back."

Despite the pain in his head, Graham saw that it had all fallen into place. The sheepherder was probably in some cattle rancher's way. The cattle rancher had paid Jed to get rid of him, so Jed used a Henry rifle and spread a lot of talk about Graham being a shootist. No doubt Jed had promised to leave the Hobbes family alone in exchange for the man's testimony—that or had threatened them with something worse than he had yet subjected them to.

"You just rest easy," Jed was saying. "The judge'll be through here on the fifteenth of next month. Trial shouldn't take more than a day or two. After that, this world won't burden you no more."

He laughed and walked out of the cell block. Graham lay back down and tried not to think about anything. There would be time enough for that later, and when that time came, thinking would make his head ache worse than any pistol whipping ever could.

For all of Marshal Jed Gallagher's predictions came to pass. By the time the judge came to town, the people were so set against him that the trial seemed farcical. Though he had never been in any suspense as to what the verdict would be, the proceedings had been mildly diverting. Especially the way that little small-time cattle rancher had quaked when testifying. Graham had amused himself by staring unblinkingly at him the entire time he had been on the stand. By the time he was allowed to step down, he'd looked about ready to vomit on his own shoes.

Graham did not hold the man's lies against him. The man had a family to look out for, and Graham knew that to such a settled type of person, all desperados seemed to be of the same stamp. Certainly the distinctions between a man such as himself and that backshooter Gallagher must seem awful fine.

Graham himself had declined to testify. It would have done no good for him to protest his innocence, since he could hardly be expected to do otherwise, and no one would believe him anyway. Testifying would only give the prosecuting attorney the opportunity to ask him a lot of impertinent questions and slander his past actions.

Well, it was over now, and there was nothing left to do but wait. He'd always known it would come to this sooner or later—this or his luck would run out in a shoot out. But that morning as he watched the sun rise through the bars on his cell window, he felt something like regret, and he wished that Kelly were there. Her presence would be a comfort to him, and he could tell her that he had been wrong to leave, even though it was too late.

He had expected to miss her, after all, he always had before. During the past months, he had worked at not missing her, and he had given getting over her the time that such things took.

A year had passed, and then a year and countless days, but the emptiness had never passed, and it never became any easier to distract himself from it. Now he sat watching the sun rise over the hills, and he remembered what Alice had said to him when he'd last left Kansas City.

Her words had been hard, though she'd spoken them sadly, and he knew he had been too used to ignoring her to hear the truth of she'd said. Of course, he had not been entirely wrong. There were a heap of things to do in this world. There were plenty of card games to be played, plenty of hills to be ridden over, plenty of bars to drink at, and plenty of whores when the need for such things arose.

But sitting in a jail cell, staring down the last days of his life with nothing to distract him from the finality of it, he knew that there was another truth, and it warmed him to think on it.

The truth was that only Kelly had ever looked at him with love and that his need for her went beyond a simple wanting that could be rooted out by force of will. It was true that he could close his eyes and remember every detail of that hour almost ten years ago when he'd first seen her, even though the details of the past year without her blurred and ran together until he could not say if they had happened one year ago or twenty. It was true that he would not regret dying at all, except that it meant he would never see her, never hear her voice, and never touch her again.

The bars on the windows spoiled his view of the endless rolling plains before him, but that morning and for many mornings after, it did not matter. Bars or no bars, he still saw nothing more than a dusty train yard where Kelly argued with a fool shipping agent, wrangled wild horses, then returned his impertinent grin and tip of the hat with a blush that was quickly replaced by a grin as impertinent as his own and an ironical twist of her own hat.

Next to such thoughts, his dreams of the wild places paled. All places, it seemed, were the same, except the place where she happened to be. All roads were the same, except the one that lead back to her. He had always found his feet on that road sooner or later, and maybe the only real mistake he had ever made was to try and leave that road for good.

Why had it been so hard to admit he had been wrong? Was it so impossible to believe he really did love her, even though he'd gladly give a year of his life just to have her lay up against him and read out loud until she fell asleep in his arms?

He had never concerned himself over falling in love, had never thought it would happen to him, but as his remaining days slipped by, each one exactly like the one before it, it made less and less sense to be dishonest with himself. The truth was that he had been in love with Kelly Knowlton from the first moment he'd seen her. Why else had he taken her with him, helped her to find her way, and given her the freedom she needed even when it had about killed him to do it?

It could only be love, and had he not seen the same emotion on her face a million times? He had. What, then, had driven them apart? He could remember their argument, but he could not remember how he had felt, what emotion or fear had prompted him to say such things.

He shook his head and looked away from the window. These days there was little enough for him to do but dream, and sometimes those dreams were more painful than the reality he faced.

During the trial, he had often become distracted by such musings. Such thoughts had occupied his mind the evening after Hobbes' testimony. He had been disturbed by footsteps sounding out in the hall, and Graham had looked up to see Clive at his cell door.

"You got a visitor," he had said.

A runty pasty-faced city-dressed squarehead had appeared at Clive's elbow. The man wore a waxy moustache and carried a note book and a pencil.

"This here is Morgan Howard. He's with some big newspaper out of Wichita."

Clive had opened the cell door and ushered the newspaper man in. Graham noticed there was no asking him if he wanted to talk. Howard had probably paid Jed to let him in; maybe he had even promised him a cut of the money from the story.

Clive had relocked the door and walked down the hall a few steps. He had seated himself on a stool by the cell block door to wait.

Meanwhile, the newspaperman offered Graham his hand.

"I can't tell you how pleased I am to meet you Mr. McNair. I can assure you that no newspaper west of the great Mississippi is providing its readers with a more unprejudiced account of your trial."

Graham looked down at the man's hand then looked back out the window. Undaunted, Morgan withdrew his hand and sat down at the table.

"Now then, Marshal Gallagher assured me that you wanted to communicate the details of your life to an unbiased witness, to let the world know, as it were, the true story of your daring existence."

Graham ignored him and continued to stare out the window.

"Now then, I know you joined the army in 1861. How old were you then?"

After a few moments of silence, Morgan cleared his throat and went on.

"Yes, of course. And you achieved the rank of captain before leaving the colors in . . . what year was it?"

Again, Graham did not reply.

"We'll make it 1870," Morgan said, scribbling on his pad. "Now, by all accounts, you've killed at least thirty men since then, some in shoot outs, some in brawls, some in connection with grudges, is that correct?"

Graham left the window and sat on his bunk, favoring Morgan with a disinterested look.

"No."

"Mr. McNair, if you will only cooperate. I can assure you that the truth is my only interest."

"Is it?"

"I must admit it is something to consider. With that in mind, I wonder if you could tell me something about . . . what was the name . . . ?" He flipped through the notebook for a second, scanning the pages for something. "Hah, here it is. Kelly Knowlton. I heard from Webster Doyle, who knew you from Creed in the 1870s, that you sometimes used to travel with a female cowboy by the name of Kelly Knowlton. Do you know where I could find her?"

Graham's face tightened. He could imagine what this nosey bastard wanted to talk to Kelly about.

"She's dead. She died in 1880," he said coldly.

"Oh?" Morgan sounded disappointed. "Well, is it true she shot a Pinkerton man in 1873?"

"No."

"Is it true she was a deadly hand with a pistol and killed seven men?"

Graham didn't answer. Morgan scribbled some more in his book.

"Now, as to this trial . . ."

"You have 'til a count of five to get your skanky ass out of here," Graham said.

"I hardly think you are in a position to enforce such a threat."

"Would having your head rammed through those iron bars enforce it?" Graham asked.

Morgan paled but remained seated. Graham leisurely cracked his knuckles and began to count.

"One. Two."

Morgan got to his feet.

"Three."

"Violence will not improve your position, Mr. McNair."

"It won't make it any worse, either. Four."

"Deputy! Deputy!"

"Five."

Graham stood. Morgan quaked back against the cell bars as Clive shoved his key into the lock. Sherman held his gun on Graham as Morgan tumbled out of the cell.

A smile twitching his lips, Graham had sat back down and gone back to staring out the window.

"You are an ornery son of a bitch," Sherman had said, shooing Morgan and Clive from the cell block. "Seems like you'd favor the company."

Graham had not answered. Now, thinking back on it, he wondered if anyone ever needed company that badly. He felt sorry for anyone who did. At least his life had not brought him to such depths of desperation.

It was the only comforting thought to take hold of his mind in months.

Chapter 45

Morgan Howard's story appeared in all the Kansas papers and sold well enough to be picked up across the river in Missouri, where it ran in several of the local papers. So it was that Kelly sat down to breakfast one morning, opened the newspaper, and choked on her eggs as her eye fell on Graham's name—and her own.

After coughing to clear her throat, Kelly read the story from start to finish. Aside from being a pack of half-truths, exaggerations, and occasional bald-faced lies, it contained one very important fact—Graham was on trial for his life.

Kelly set the newspaper down. Although she knew none of the specifics, she, like Graham, never doubted that he would be condemned. Whether or not he was actually guilty was, to her, irrelevant—so was their late argument. Maybe they had parted on bad terms, but she could not let him hang, not without trying to prevent it. The danger involved did not deter her. She was not afraid of death. Not even hell could be worse than the life she had lead for the past eighteen months.

She had less than a month, but not even the urgency of time penetrated the coldness that surrounded her as she began to plan. She could take a train to Denver, outfit herself there, and ride the rest of the way. Without even waiting to finish her breakfast, Kelly stood and put on her bonnet and gloves. The bank would be open by the time she could walk over there. The time had come to use all the money that she had been saving for so long.

When she returned from the bank, Alice was waiting for her. Alice had seen the newspaper and knew without being told what

Kelly was planning.

"I suppose it's no use telling you it's a foolish thing to try," she said.

"That's right," Kelly said. "I'm catching the three-fifteen to Denver."

"What good is getting yourself shot going to do anyone?" Alice asked. "Graham wouldn't ask or expect such a thing from you."

Kelly didn't answer. Instead, she went upstairs and began to sort through her things. There was very little that would be of use to her. A few toilet articles, her riding clothes, her gun belt and rifle. She bundled them all together. The guns would need a cleaning, but that could wait until her train ride was over. The only other things she took were a tintype of herself and Laura and a wooden horse that Graham had once carved for Laura.

Kelly looked up from her work to see Alice standing in the doorway watching her.

"You can sell my horse and saddle," she said. "I plan to buy new ones when I reach Denver. Sell anything else I leave that you don't want. I won't be back."

They both knew it, but hearing it said caused them both sadness. Even in the depths of her hardness, Kelly wondered if she had ever had such a good friend as Alice.

"You've been better to me than anyone on earth," Kelly said. "As good as any older sister I could ever wish for. I wish I could do something to repay you."

"I wish things could've worked out better for you," Alice said. "I reckon having you and Laura here were the best times I ever had."

Kelly nodded, her eyes distant.

"Laura did love you," she said. "So do I."

They embraced, and Alice made one last effort to get Kelly to stay.

"I wish you'd think this over some," she said. "You're feeling reckless because you're grieving, but that'll pass."

"I wish I could believe that," Kelly said. "But I'm not feeling reckless. I'm not feeling anything at all."

Chapter 46

As the train steamed west toward Denver, Kelly relaxed in her seat. Aside from her regret at never seeing Alice again, she felt no sadness as Kansas City became farther and farther away. No one could say what the future held for her, and such things did not trouble her mind. She lacked fear, but she also lacked hope. She felt only a grim sense of purpose as her mind roamed over the possibilities of how to perform a jail break, but she knew that no plans could be formulated until she arrived in Leadfalls and saw how things were.

The train stopped over in Dodge City, and in the morning, Kelly started the second leg of her journey. Train travel was soothing to her, and with so much to think about, it was not boring, as she had feared that it might be.

The train put her in Denver the next day—ten days before the hanging was to be. Denver looked much the same as it had when she'd last left it. It was cleaner maybe, and a little larger, but pretty much unchanged. Kelly took a hotel room, changed her clothes, and went about preparing for her trip north.

She bought the two best horses she could find, two saddles, and provisions. Her last purchase was a long canvas duster coat that reached to her ankles. She did not intend to draw any unnecessary attention to herself once she left Denver.

If the escape was successful, she planned to head north and start her long dreamed of horse farm. Graham could go where he liked. She would make sure that he had whatever he needed to make a clean getaway. If she was unsuccessful, she was likely to end up dead or in jail, and he would hang.

She left Denver in the middle of the night, heading east and then circling south and around up north. It was hard to say if such precautions were necessary, but certainly, they could do no harm.

Riding that night seemed an incredible thing, something that she had dreamed of doing during the restless years in Kansas City, though she had never imagined that such a simple wish could cost her so dearly. It was ironic to think how concerned she had been about exposing Laura to danger when Laura had died in her own back yard of nothing worse than a bee sting.

The thought gnawed at her, and she pushed it away. Maybe the path she had chosen after Laura's birth had been a mistake; there was nothing to be done about it now. After all, if she could change her life through hindsight, she never would have gotten tied up with Jackson, and Laura would never have been born in the first place.

Leadfalls appeared on the horizon late in the afternoon of her second day out from Denver. She waited until dark, then rode into town. She located the jail with little difficulty. It was one street over from where they were building the gallows.

The gallows was in a kind of open square to the right of the courthouse. There was a livery stable directly across from it, with a second-story hay loft door that opened over the square. The other buildings facing in were homes or businesses.

Keeping her hat low over her face and trusting her long, baggy coat to hide her figure, Kelly rode through the rest of the town, familiarizing herself with its layout. Then she picked up a copy of the local paper from the sidewalk it had been left on and rode back out of town.

She made camp and slept a little, and in the morning, she washed in the creek, made breakfast, and thought over what she had seen. She had eight days to figure something out.

That night and for several nights after, she rode into town, her hat and long coat working with the darkness to make her seem a very short drifter. She stood in an alley across from the jail and watched the comings and goings. Aside from Marshal Gallagher, there were four deputies. Snakey Potter and Sherman Buser, she knew, had been acquaintances of Graham's up in Sioux country. There was also a young man named Clive Lee who Kelly gathered was the son of a local farmer. The fourth deputy was none other than Dave Meyers, the wrangler whose life Kelly had saved years ago down in Apache country.

Kelly needed an inside man but did not trust Snakey or Sherman. If they had been true friends, they would have broken Graham out long ago. Also, aside from their names and faces, she hardly knew them. Clive was too wide-eyed and wet behind the ears to be of any use to anyone. That left Dave, who was a perfect choice. He owed her a debt; he didn't care much for the law; and from what Kelly overheard of his conversation, he was dying to ride back south.

Five hundred dollars ought to be enough, she thought, but I have to get him tonight. There's only three days left.

Dave left the jail alone a little after nine o'clock. He headed straight for the nearest saloon, but Kelly intercepted him.

"Hey Dave," she said. "Can you spare a moment for an old friend?"

Dave stopped, startled by the voice that spoke to him from the shadowy alley. Kelly stepped forward, tipping her hat back so he could see her face.

"Well, hell!" Dave exclaimed. "Five-Card Kelly Knowlton! Where've you been keepin'?"

"Here and there. How 'bout you?"

"Shit. I left the Arizona a year ago. Worst mistake I ever made. This here north country don't suit me."

"Why don't you ride on back?"

Dave shrugged.

"Don't know," he said gazing at her shrewdly. "I reckon I know why you're here."

"Do you?"

"Sure. That shootist they're gonna hang. A reporter was through here a while back, and he asked a heap o' questions about you. I never knew you ran with such hard cases."

Kelly smiled.

"You know how it is, Dave, I reckon he saved my neck a dozen times while I was still green. I can't let a man like that hang, you understand that."

"Sure do. Least he ain't a damn hypocrite like them damn marshals. Do you know some of 'em used to ride with him? Hell, he even saved that Sherm's life once. I don't know what this world is coming to when a badge comes between a man and his trail buddies."

Dave shook his head sorrowfully. Kelly let him think on it a moment.

"I don't intend to let that happen, Dave," she said. "If you'll help me, I'll give you enough money to go back south and live high. What do you say?"

Dave looked insulted, and Kelly felt a moment of fear. If he went and told the marshal everything, that was the end of her plans.

"I wouldn't take money for such a thing," he said loftily. "You saved my life in that scrape with the Apache. Hell, even if you hadn't, I'd do it just to spite them high-flown hypocrites."

"You are a good man, Dave," Kelly said. "But I'd have to give you a little something. I'd like to think of you having a toot on me."

"Well, that's right generous of you, Kelly," he replied. "I always did say you were a true friend and a good wrangler."

"I'm proud to have your good opinion. Now tell me what

you think of this . . ."

Kelly told him her plan and what she would require him to do. They went over it until she was confident that he understood everything, then she paid him half the money she had promised him with the agreement that he would receive the other half the morning of the escape.

Kelly rode back to her camp well satisfied. Dave was going to make a solid accomplice. She spent the remaining days as she had spent the preceding days, target shooting with her rifle. She only returned to town once more, and it was not to see Dave.

Again, it was just past dusk, and again, she waited in an alley across from the jail. She waited until Marshal Gallagher left for the night.

She approached him carefully from the off side. He stopped abruptly, his hand falling to his revolver butt.

"No need fer that, Marshal," she said, deepening her voice. "I come to ask fer a favor."

He peered at her, but with the uncertain light and her coat and hat, he only thought that she was a very young man, a cowboy, perhaps. Whatever he is, Gallagher thought, he's not packing.

"What favor?" He demanded. "Introduce yourself, boy. Ain't you got any manners?"

Kelly ducked her head as though embarrassed at this reprimand.

"Sorry, sorry," she mumbled. "My name's Lewis Chapman. I hail from Creed, Colorado."

"Well, what do you want, boy?"

"I read in t' paper that you had Graham McNair locked up in yer jail."

"What of it?"

Kelly shuffled her feet and looked down at the ground.

"I'd admire to own his gun rig and rifle, Marshal. He's the best shot I know of, aside from you."

"He ain't dead yet, son," Gallagher replied, thinking it was a shame. Graham's things would probably be sold after the hanging and the money would go to his relatives, if he had any, or to bury him.

"I could pay a hunnert dollars for 'em," Kelly said, seeing the sudden avaricious look in the marshal's eye.

"Shit, boy, after the hanging I could get two hundred."

"Then I'll give you two hunnert now," Kelly said. "That way you won't have to split it with them deputies. Things tend to get lost it jails, I know, after all, you're a busy man."

At that, Gallagher peered harder at her. He thought that a mouthful for such a pup, but his unformed suspicion was pushed away by remembering that Snakey had already laid claim to Graham's rifle. Selling it out from under his deputy would likely cause some hard feelings.

"That's right enough," he said to the boy. "Rifle's gone already. But you can have the gun rig for one hundred."

Kelly nodded, and he started toward the jail.

"Follow me, boy," he said curtly.

Kelly followed him to the jail. He motioned for her to wait outside, and he went in, reappearing in a few moments with the gun belt. Kelly recognized it and both guns immediately.

Gallagher accepted the money and gave her the belt with none too good grace. Kelly thanked him and hurried away after he admonished her to keep it hidden until after the hanging.

Gallagher watched her go, unsettled by the entire incident. There was something wrong with how the boy had walked, but he couldn't quite put his finger on it. Not that it mattered; the boy had vanished, and the thing was done.

Gallagher resettled his hat on his head and headed for the saloon. A hundred dollars would buy a good night's sport.

Chapter 47

The night before the last day, Kelly did not sleep. She rested against her saddle at her horse's feet and stared off at the horizon, watching the stars sparkle and then fade into morning as dawn began to color the sky. It was chilly, and her breath clouded before her. Now and then, her horse would snort, but other than that, no sound spoiled the silence.

The cold air chilled her face and hands, making her skin tingle, but it seemed nothing at all next to the coldness inside of her, the coldness that had crept up over her during the long months after Graham's leaving and Laura's death. It was a coldness that no blanket could cure and no fire could melt. Indeed, she wanted neither warmth nor melting, for the coldness had frozen the firestorm inside of her and had rendered it powerless to harm her further.

Her thoughts roamed briefly over her plans for the morning but rested nowhere for very long. No trace of fear, worry or apprehension hindered those thoughts. Everything that could be planned for had been planned for, and there was no lack of determination on her part. Let the cards fall as they may, she thought, I won't fold, and I won't be bluffing, either.

She had made no fire and had unpacked nothing. When the sun was just barely up, she saddled her horse and rode into town, leading the other horse. It was still early, and few people were out. Keeping her hat low over her face, Kelly rode to a store just to the right of the gallows and tied the extra horse in front of it. Then she rode behind the livery stable and dismounted. The stable hands had finished their morning's work and were leaving to get breakfast. She gathered from their conversation that they intended to go straight to the hanging when they were done eating.

That suited Kelly fine. Leaving her horse standing outside, she entered the stable and, taking her rifle, climbed into the hay loft.

Kelly waited patiently, sighting occasionally down at the gallows. Just before nine, Dave rode up and tied his horse beside the one she had left in front of the store. He opened the right saddle pouch and took the rest of his money. He did not look up to where he knew Kelly was waiting but instead went straight to the jail.

Jed, Sherman, Snakey, and Clive were all gathered in the little office in front of the cell block. Jed was in a high good humor, making crude jokes, and Sherman, Clive and Snakey were grinning up to him like suck-egg dogs. Dave concealed his disgust but privately thanked God for sending Kelly Knowlton to deliver him from such company.

Back in the cell block, Graham stood next to the window. He had watched the sunrise, and now, he could hear Jed and his boys yucking it up out front. The previous evening, he had sat down to write to Kelly, but then, he remembered that he would have to give the letter to one of those no-accounts to be delivered. That, no doubt, would bring a shitstorm down on Kelly's head.

So he had forgone writing to her. She would probably hear of it in the papers, anyway. There was no point in writing for forgiveness. She wouldn't carry a grudge against him right down to the grave, he knew.

A little after eight, they brought him breakfast, which he did not eat, and Clive and Dave kept watch while he shaved. Then he dressed—someone had brushed his suit especially for the occasion—and sat down on his bunk to wait.

The waiting didn't seem very long. His mind seemed to be free of the jail cell and wandered where it would. He had been angry at himself for getting caught like some greenhorn. He had been despairing at the opportunities that he had missed. He had been sad at the things left unsaid. But, this last morning, he was only calm. If dying was the only thing left for him to do, then he would do it as well as he was able. He would not let those other things erode his nerve.

By ten-thirty, a large crowd had gathered in front of the gallows. Looking down on them, Kelly felt a surge of anger at their morbid curiosity. Graham McNair might be a killer, she thought, but at least he didn't view it as sport. Besides, she privately doubted that he had even done this particular killing. It wasn't like him to handle something so badly.

Not that a jury would care about that, she thought. His reputation was such that they would figure even if he didn't do this particular crime, there were plenty of others he was owing for. Jury of his peers my ass, Kelly thought. What do a bunch of farmers and sheepherders know about having someone throw down on them?

"Not a damn thing," she whispered.

No matter, she thought, the more spectators, the greater the confusion she could create, and that would slow down any pursuit.

At a quarter to eleven, Jed, who had been sitting on his desk, stood and stretched leisurely.

"Sherm, Snakey, go on an' get 'em. Tie his hands before letting him out, and you, Dave, keep that shotgun on 'im while they do his hands. Can't have no last minute escapes."

The men went back into the cell block. Graham looked up briefly as they unlocked his cell and came in to tie his hands. They all looked pretty jumpy to him, even though they were all armed to the teeth.

They tied his hands behind his back and led him from the jail. Just over the threshold, he paused a moment, appreciating the fresh air and blue sky. Sherm tried to prod him along, but Jed stopped him.

"Let him take a sniff, Sherm," he said. "We can't hang him 'til eleven, and it's only ten 'til."

"I appreciate that kindness," Graham said to him. "And I'll give you some free advice. It's been eleven o'clock for you for quite sometime. Watch your back."

Jed snorted and spat. He was not impressed with such dramatics. Most condemned men took a moment to try and spook their keepers.

They continued on their way to the gallows, Graham looked about and idly wondered at the size of the crowd gathered to see him hang. Morgan Howard's newspaper story must have been a corker, he thought.

The crowd hushed suddenly as they approached. From her vantage point, Kelly saw Graham, surrounded by deputies, being led to the gallows. For no discernible reason, her hands began to shake violently. With an effort, she steadied herself. This was no time for such foolishness. She'd been in plenty enough scrapes before to be steady as a rock at this last moment. A mistake now would kill them both. Even if there were no mistakes, they were likely to die.

"It doesn't matter," she thought. "Because living with one more death on my conscience would kill me slow; this way, if I fail, I'll die quick."

The scaffold steps creaked as Graham climbed them. Snakey and Sherm were on each side of him; Dave led the way, and Clive and Jed brought up the rear. The hangman and the preacher were already up.

The scaffold was only about ten feet off the ground, but it

gave Graham an excellent view over the crowd, and he could see the open country beyond the ramshackle town. That view held his attention while the preacher preached and the hangman fiddled with the noose.

Kelly was too far away to see Graham's expression, but she knew that, no matter what he might be feeling, his face would be composed. She wished that he knew what she was up to. It would comfort him some.

The preacher lead the crowd in singing a hymn. He went over to Graham, who waved him away sharply. Then Jed read the charge. Kelly could see that at least part of her plan had worked so far—Graham's hands were tied, not handcuffed, and his legs were not shackled. Just then, Sherman knelt to tie his legs together.

Kelly raised her rifle and aimed carefully. Graham was standing over the trap now, and she felt that she could wait no longer. She sighted on that damn Marshal Gallagher and fired.

Chapter 48

Jed Gallagher never knew what hit him. One moment, he was looking over the crowd, and the next, a sharp boom of thunder seemed to sound from the cloudless sky and lightening seemed to snake down and pierce his chest. The impact knocked him backwards, hurtling him from the gallows. He was dead before his body hit the ground.

Two more shots sliced down to the gallows, the first struck Snakey in the head, and he, too, died before realizing what was going on. The second shot drove straight and true for Sherm, but Dave, in his haste to reach Graham, knocked him a little to one side, and the shot took Sherm in the leg. He crumpled to the scaffold floor.

At the first shot, Graham had instinctively flattened himself to the ground. At the second shot, he rolled toward the edge of the scaffold. To him, it made no difference who was shooting or why. The time had come to leave this party.

Dave leaned over and cut his wrists free, and both men jumped down from the scaffold, Dave landing an instant after Graham. Someone was shooting wildly now, and the crowd was screaming and scattering in panic. Motioning for Graham to follow, Dave ran for a store to the right of the gallows.

"Take that horse," he said, indicating the animal that Kelly had left tied there earlier in the morning. "Ride the hell out of here. Ride west. Kelly'll meet up with you when she can."

They both mounted up, pausing a moment to shake hands before tearing out of town in different directions. No one tried to stop them.

The crowd had mostly run off, Kelly saw, pausing to assess the situation below. With the head lawmen dead, Kelly doubted there would be much pursuit, as none of the townsmen would be inclined to risk their lives over an escaped prisoner. And it seemed that her doubts were being proven correct. She could see no one returning fire or even wielding a gun.

Kelly had seen Graham and Dave mount their horses and tear out of town. Dave was heading southwest, a course that would take him back down to Arizona, and Graham was heading due west. Kelly collected her spent cartridges, pocketed them, and climbed down from the loft. Her horse was still tied outside the stable, and she mounted up.

It had been a good ten minutes or more since the first shot had sounded. The streets were nearly empty, most of the townspeople having fled indoors. Clive and the preacher were tending to the fallen, and Kelly saw that the hangman had caught a stray bullet and that Sherman had only been wounded. This troubled her, and she considered finishing him off with her revolver as she rode by but decided there was no point to it. He was a weak-chinned, boneless kind of man and of no real use or danger to anyone without a hard case like Jed to tell him what to do.

Kelly walked her horse past them, looking neither left nor right. She didn't hurry, and no one even noticed her, so occupied were they with the commotion she had created. Once the town was behind her, she picked up Graham's trail and spurred her gelding onto a gallop.

He had a good start on her but not that good, and her horse was faster. She slowly closed the distance between them. As far as she could tell from looking back, there was still no pursuit. Kelly caught up to him about five minutes later. He had pulled up in a small stand of trees to wait for her. She was pleased to see that he looked the same as always. At least jail hadn't hurt him any.

"Hey there, pilgrim," she said. "You sure left a disappointed crowd of folks back there."

"No matter," he replied. "They can get their sport elsewhere. I like my neck the length it is."

Kelly dismounted and untied the bundle of things she'd brought for him.

"You've got a long ride ahead of you," she said, tossing it to him. "You'll need this."

He caught it neatly and tied the bedroll and saddle bags behind his saddle.

"I bought your gunbelt from the sheriff," Kelly said, handing it up to him. "But someone stole your rifle before I got to town."

"Not surprising," Graham said, taking it from her and dismounting. "That was the crookedest bunch of badge-wearing hypocrites I ever saw."

He buckled the gunbelt on and looked at her curiously. As glad as he was to see her, it seemed odd that she would do such a lawless thing as rescue him from the hangman, especially when you considered that she had a baby to look out for.

"I appreciate your taking such a risk on my account," he said. "I hope no news of this follows you to Kansas City."

"I'm not returning to Kansas City," Kelly replied.

It was difficult for her to remember that he did not know about Laura, but his puzzled face reminded her.

"Laura died last summer," she said before he could ask any questions.

Graham was too surprised to ask how or why, and he interpreted the coldness in her voice as anger toward him for not having been there when she must have needed him very badly.

He stepped toward her, meaning to take her in his arms, but she moved away from him.

"I'm sorry," he said, knowing how small the words sounded in comparison to the grief she must feel, but if she wouldn't let him come near her, words were the only comfort he could offer.

Kelly did not answer. She didn't want to talk about it, especially not with him. After all this time, she had finally frozen the storm inside of her, and she had no wish to awaken it.

Kelly went back to her horse. They had precious little time to spend chinning here while a posse formed back in town. She had saved him and outfitted him, and her conscience was free of him. It was time to go make a new life for herself.

"Where are you going to go?" He asked her.

"Canada," Kelly said. "I'm going to get me some land and build the best damn horse farm north of the border, and I am never going to wear another dress until the day I die."

"Was it that bad?" Graham asked, his voice compassionate.

Kelly shook her head. "Words wouldn't halfway cover it."

"Worse than Pinkerton men and wild rivers and horse thieves?" He asked.

"Yes. Worse than grizzly bears and faithless army scouts too." Much to her dismay, she heard her voice shake a little as she spoke.

She hadn't planned on being so affected by seeing him again. During the past months, she had been more lonely than she had ever been in her life. That feeling was gone now, all in an instant. Being with Graham was like riding bareback; it came so naturally she didn't even have to think about it.

She had not thought to do anything more than help him out of his trouble, but now that she had accomplished this, she did not know how to ride away from him. So she stood, unable to believe that all their time together had come to nothing more than this final parting.

Kelly's horse snorted, and she turned around in a flash,

scanning the horizon for trouble. There was still no sign of any riders coming from the town.

"You better get going," she said. "I can't believe they won't follow us at all."

"That doesn't sound like you're coming with me," he said.

"I'm not," Kelly said briefly, not looking away from the horizon.

"Why not?"

"You pick the damndest times to argue, Graham," Kelly said.

"That's no answer."

Maybe she didn't miss him as much as she had thought. How could he possibly want to stand there and pick this thing over not fifteen minutes after almost getting his neck stretched? It seemed to her that he ought to be more concerned with getting his carcass somewhere safer.

He put a hand on her shoulder to turn her around, but she shook it off. Undeterred, Graham spoke his peace anyway. She might laugh or curse or just look at him like he was crazy and ride off without saying anything, but after standing on a gallows and looking through a noose, he found that the only fearsome thing was missed opportunities.

"Kelly, I was wrong to have left. I never realized it until it seemed to late, but I was wrong," he said. "I love you, and I won't leave you again."

"There's no reason why you should," Kelly said bitterly, refusing to acknowledge how her heart sped up at his words. "Laura's not here to be in the way anymore."

"Is that what you think of me?"

Kelly did not answer.

"You have a hard way of looking at things."

"That's right," Kelly snapped. "I've been in some mighty hard places."

Kelly started walking toward her horse. Graham stepped up behind her, caught her by the shoulders, and turned her around. She didn't resist, but neither would she look at him.

"I know you're hurting. But you can't blame it all on me. I'm willing to do what I have to do to make it right again."

"There isn't anything you can do," she said, her voice so low he could hardly hear it. "I just can't anymore, that's all. I'm tired, and I don't have the energy for such things anymore."

Graham tried to take her face in his hands, but she wouldn't let him. The coldness she had felt since her miscarriage was failing her. Cracks were splintering through it, and she was frightened. Why couldn't he just leave her alone? It didn't seem like much to ask for after all this time. And how come he could just touch her the and coldness ended, when it had seen her through a miscarriage, Laura's death, and cold-blooded murder?

"Leave me alone, damn it!" Kelly said, her voice rising as

she twisted away from him.

Graham was pleased to hear her sound angry.

"I've left you alone long enough," he said.

"That's for damn sure," Kelly snapped. Her face was red, but she made no move to mount her horse or to walk away. Graham stood there with that deviling grin on his face. The same grin he'd worn the first time she seen him, the same grin he'd thrown at her when he'd left her in Denver, turned up unexpected in that mining camp, watched her playing peek-a-boo with Laura in Kansas City . . . it was exasperating. The man was incorrigible.

The redness left her face. She could not now remember why she'd been angry.

"Oh hell," she said, looking over at him and trying not to grin back. "If we're both going north, we might as well ride together."

"You mean there won't be room on your farm for a retired gambler?"

"Not for a lazy one like you," Kelly said.

"You ought to take in boarders." Graham said helpfully. "To maintain your respectability. Besides, I could probably earn my keep somehow."

Yes, he was incorrigible. It was part of his charm. She looked up at him from under her eyelashes, and he put his arms around her.

"Maybe you could," she said. "But if you let anyone think I'm respectable for even five minutes, I'll toss you out on your ear."

"That's a deal," he said, and he bent to kiss her.

"Oh damn you anyway," Kelly said breathlessly when they parted, "and I'll tell you this right now. You fourflush me again, and I'll shoot you myself."

Only Kelly could say something like that and make it sound flirtatious, he though pleasedly. He bent to kiss her, but she wiggled away and, before he could catch her, mounted her horse. Enough was enough, in her opinion. Her head was spinning, and she feared she might fall off her horse if they fooled around anymore.

"We'd better scat," she said. "Else we'll both get hung."

Graham shrugged and mounted up. She was right. Under the circumstances, there wasn't really time for such things, even though they were most definitely worth risking a hanging for.

Chapter 49

They rode due west and up into the mountains, both of them knowing it would be easier to shake any pursuit in the high country. Every hour or so, Kelly would halt and look back through her spy glass. At the third such halt, she spotted a far off party of riders making for the mountains. They were no bigger than a speck, but it worried her.

"That's them all right," she said, handing the glass to Graham. "How far off do you think they are?"

"Five hours, maybe," he said, squinting into the glass. "But they'll loose our trail when they get to that rocky gorge we crossed."

"Nonsense," Kelly said. "Our horses scraped those rocks up plenty."

Graham put the glass away.

"It'll be night before they get there, and moonlight won't show up those marks. Besides, I'll bet you ten dollars they don't even get that far," he said. "They don't have the spunk for it. It's not like they were going to hang me for killing the president or something. One nobody sheepherder is only worth just so much trouble."

Kelly couldn't answer that, and despite her misgivings, she didn't take the bet. Instead she got back on her horse and led the way northwest. She wondered if they shouldn't circle around to the southwest to throw off any pursuit, but when she suggested it to him, Graham looked at her as though she had suggested saddling a grizzly bear to ride.

So she didn't argue the point, though she turned a deaf ear

to his suggestion that they stop at sunset. Posse or no posse, she wanted to get up north as quickly as possible.

When they did stop, they argued over whether or not to have a fire and compromised by having a very small fire that Kelly fed carefully with the driest wood she could find.

"I never knew you to be so easily spooked," Graham said after they'd eaten.

"I'd think that one trip up to the gallows would be enough for you," Kelly replied checking her rifle over in preparation for standing watch.

Graham shook his head and unrolled his bedding. If she was determined to be so cautious, that was her own business, but it was late now, and they both needed to get some sleep.

"Stop fooling with that rifle and come to bed," he said.

"I'm standing first watch," Kelly said. "I'll wake you in four hours."

"There's no need for that," he said, disgruntled but knowing there would be no changing her mind.

Kelly ignored his disgruntlement and sat down on a tree stump, her rifle laid across her lap. For this night, it was enough to be awake and alive under the the stars knowing that they were both safe and that life would go on. Kelly felt that she had left a large part of her anger back in Leadfalls, and while peace was still far from her, she could see it somewhere on the horizon.

Graham woke a little after midnight to take his turn at watching. Kelly still sat on her stump, looking off to the east. Graham sat beside her, but she made no move to get up and go to sleep.

"You ought to get some rest," he said. "I'll watch the rest of the night."

Kelly shook her head, unable to remember the last time she'd had a good night's sleep and believing that she no longer needed such rest.

"I'm not tired."

They sat in silence for a while. The moon had set several hours ago, and the fire had died to embers. There was nothing around them but starlight and the dark shadows of the surrounding woods.

"You're still mad at me, aren't you," Graham asked.

"No, I'm not," Kelly replied. "It's just been a hard time is all."

"I know that," he said. "If I had known about Laura, I would have come straight away."

He took her hand. Kelly's eyes left the horizon and fixed on the ground.

"I know you would have," she said. "But that's not all that happened."

Graham waited for her to go on. It had been plain to him that she was carrying some burden along with her, something more than Laura's death, something that was directly connected to him. But the minute spun out, and she just looked silently down at the ground.

"Tell me what else," he said.

She sighed and took the rifle off her lap, leaning it beside her against the stump.

"I was pregnant when you left," she said. "And I lost the baby a month after Laura died."

Graham did not know what to say. He was not upset because the baby had been lost, rather it hurt him to think that Kelly had gone through it all by herself. So much for giving himself airs over Jackson Taylor. Maybe he loved her, but he had done her just as much wrong as a man who hadn't.

"Why didn't you tell me?" He asked. "I wouldn't have left if I'd known."

"I didn't find out until after you'd gone," she said. "Besides, I don't want anyone around me just because they feel obligated."

He put his arm around her, but she did not relax against him, and he knew that she was not done with what she had to say.

"I was so furious when I found out," she said. "I hated you so much for it. I didn't want that baby. And I lost it. I regretted it when it was too late, but that couldn't change anything. It was just like with Laura. I didn't want her, and now she's dead. I regret it, but it's too late."

"You loved her though," he said quietly.

Kelly wondered if that made up for it. Yes, life went on, but it was painful. Sitting there and feeling the night all about her, she no longer really believed that she had caused Laura's death or her own miscarriage, but the guilt had marked her. She moved closer to Graham and pulled his arm tighter around her. He seemed to understand, and he was not repulsed or shocked by that understanding. She was relieved to the point of tears.

Dawn came, and they rode on, Kelly insisting that they maintain their hurried pace and that they take turns watching at night. After a week, they turned eastward in hopes of finding a town. They passed several small settlements before Kelly agreed to stop in one. They had no of way of knowing for sure whether or not they were in Canada, and she saw no point in taking unnecessary risks when they were well equipped and the weather was good.

Then, they came upon good sized town nestled in a valley. Looking down on it from a mountain ridge, Graham thought that it was most likely a mining camp of some type.

"Let's ride down in the morning," he said.

Kelly didn't want to but knew it was unlikely to be dangerous, so she had no rational reason to say no.

"Fine," she said. "We can find out where in the world we are."

They camped a little off the ridge that night. For the first time, Kelly did not suggest keeping a watch, much to Graham's relief, but she wrapped up alone in her blankets and slept under her horse, much to his annoyance.

In the morning, in preparation for their ride into town, Graham decided to shave and remove his moustache. Since Kelly had neglected to buy a razor, he used her nine-inch hunting knife. Kelly couldn't watch.

"You're going to cut your lip off doing that," she said at last.

He looked over at her, pausing to wipe the blade clean. The left side of his moustache was gone but the right side was still intact.

"On second thought," she said. "You'd better risk it. You look right lopsided."

Graham finished up, then wiped his face dry with his blanket.

"Well?"

Kelly cocked her head to one side and made a show of considering it. She had never seen him clean shaven before.

"Your upper lip is three shades whiter than your face," she said at last.

"Noticeable?"

"I think so."

"Well, you're looking for it."

"We aren't worried about people who don't notice such things," she reminded him.

"Maybe, but there isn't anything I can do about it anyway."

"We could ride on a day or two," she suggested.

"You really do have the spooks, don't you?" He was surprised that she was still so jumpy; he had thought that a week or two of calm travel would soothe her nerves. Apparently, he'd been wrong.

"I just don't care to have to ride down to Mexico, that's all," Kelly said brusquely. "If you think it'll be all right, then fine, let's go."

Without waiting for his reply, Kelly mounted her horse. Graham packed up the last of his things and did the same.

They rode down out of the hills and into the valley. Looking around, Kelly thought that she had never seen such pretty country. The bustling little town nestled in the valley spoiled the view for her.

Up close, the town did not seem much better. It reminded her of a dozen other such settlements. In ten minutes, she counted five saloons and two sporting houses. There were a variety of business and two hotels. They took a room at the better hotel, and Kelly went to stable the horses while Graham scouted around to find out where they were.

Kelly had no difficulty in locating a place for the horses, but the stable man spoke mostly French, and it took a little time to make the arrangements. Kelly remembered a good bit of French from her youth, but the intervening years had ruined her pronunciation.

She left the stable carrying both their traps. Graham had taken his rifle with him on his scout, which relieved Kelly, who could not have carried that on top of everything else. She hardly trusted the stableman with their saddles, much less with a rifle.

On the way back to the hotel, she paused to buy a map from the newspaper office. Never having concerned herself much with geography, Kelly thought it might help them get a fix on where to go next.

Kelly walked back to the hotel and climbed the steps to their room wearily. Graham had not returned, and she plopped everything down on the floor. After sorting through her things for her clean clothes, she started to undress. She had asked the woman who owned the hotel to send up a bath.

She was unbuttoning her shirt when Graham walked in.

"We're in Canada, all right," he said. "A good ways in, too, though I can't figure exactly how far. Did you have any trouble with the horses?"

"No."

Kelly sat down on the edge of the bed and pulled her boots off.

"I asked them to send a bath up," she said. "Do you mind going out for a while longer so's I can have some privacy?"

"Not at all," he said. "There's plenty to see here."

He left, and Kelly waited for her bath. The tub wasn't really long enough to get comfortable in, but the water was hot. She scrubbed herself and washed her hair, and by the time the tub had been taken away again, she felt much better.

She put on her clean underwear and shirt. Taking the map from the pocket of her jeans, She sat cross-legged on the bed, drying her hair and studying the map. It was difficult to tell from the map what country would be best for horse raising, but the map did give her a general sense of the huge, wild country that lay before them.

She looked up when the door opened, knowing it was Graham, but leaning over toward her revolver just in case it wasn't.

"Hidy," she said, as he entered the room and bolted the door behind himself. She went back to her map. Graham thought she looked a little more relaxed. He sat on the bed and pulled his boots off.

"Have a good bath?"

"Sure did. You look a shade cleaner yourself, or is it my imagination?"

"There's bath house two streets over. What's this?" He asked, laying up beside her and picking up the map.

"It's a map of Canada," she said, taking it from him and lying it back down. "I think we're right about here." She pointed to a spot roughly one hundred and fifty miles north of the border.

"We did some long riding. I didn't think we'd come so far."

"Neither did I. You hear any talk in the saloons?"

"About Wyoming? No. I don't think anyone up here even knows what Wyoming is."

"That's good, but I think we should go further northwest."

"Whatever. Might as well have a good look around."

He began to rub her thigh. Kelly stiffened, relaxed, and continued to stare at the map, caught between wanting and not wanting.

"Why northwest, especially?" He asked, absently.

"I swore I'd never ride east again."

"This whole country seems to be west," he remarked.

Kelly didn't answer. It had been a long time since anyone had laid a hand on her, and she'd forgotten how it felt. She soon recalled that it could not be easily ignored.

She reached over and pulled his hat off, tossing it onto the foot of the bed. He scooted toward her and pulled her to him.

Their lips met, and Kelly almost recoiled, unprepared for the now unfamiliar feeling of someone wanting her. The force and meaning of it slammed into her like a bullet. It made her feel weak and crumbly inside, and she felt tears in her eyes and on her face.

Graham felt the passion go out of her, and opened his eyes, puzzled by it. Her eyes were screwed shut, and there were tears on her face. Kelly sobbed and tried to push him away, but there was no strength in her effort. Instead of letting her go, Graham held her tighter. She cried quietly for some time, and he held her and stroked her hair until her tears ended and she moved her face away from his chest so she could speak.

"I'm sorry," she said. "It's just been such a long time, and I missed you so much."

Kelly sat up and got off the bed. She went to the wash stand and patted her face with water.

"You want to tell me what that was all about?"

Kelly blew her nose and shook her head.

"Well, you ought to tell me anyway," he said. "It might help."

"It might not."

"I understand most of it already," Graham replied. "It's the specifics you're hiding. Telling someone might be better than staying up all night waiting on a posse that you know won't show up."

"I didn't know it wouldn't," Kelly said. "Neither did you. I've learned not to be so flip about dying."

"Have you? I've stood on a gallows with a rope around my

neck, and that don't make me ignorant of such things."

Kelly sat back down on the bed and said nothing. Dying yourself was a heap different than watching your baby die when there was nothing you could do about it but watch. He knew that, of course, so there was no point in holding it against him.

Graham settled himself comfortably against the headboard and waited. She was aching to tell him about it; he could see that. It was just a hard thing to do. He took it for granted that Alice had not been able to comfort her much. Alice had never understood Kelly's peculiarities very well.

"How did Laura die?" He asked quietly.

"A bee sting," Kelly said, and Graham could hear from her voice that it still stunned her to think about it. "She was stung by a bee, and she got red splotches all over and had a convulsion and died."

Graham had heard of such things happening but had never seen it.

"I just can't believe it," Kelly said, wiping her nose. "It's been a year and more, and I still can't believe it. She was so healthy. She was never sick. A bee sting. I've been stung by bees about forty times in my life. It's not fair."

"No, it sure isn't."

"I had been out looking at a pony to buy for her," Kelly went on, as if he had not spoken. "I found the most adorable black-and-white pony you could ever wish to see." Kelly smiled, thinking of it. "That pony was only about three feet at the shoulder. She was playing in the yard, and Alice was hanging up the washing. She ran over to me like she always did, and I told her all about the pony."

"I'll bet it pleased her," Graham. "She talked about getting a pony all the time."

"It did please her, though she was disappointed when she found out it wasn't spotted. She said you told her that Indians rode spotted ponies and that she wanted to be a wild Indian when she grew up."

"I told her about that Indian pony you had and how fearless you were to ride it. She asked me once if you were an Indian."

"She did?"

Graham nodded. "I told her you weren't, but that you should have been."

"What a thing to say. I'm not sure I like being described so."

"It suits you whether you like it or not."

"Well . . . she was too young to understand anyway, I guess."

She was silent for a moment, considering it.

"So you told her about the pony," Graham prompted.

"Yes, and I told her to go pick up her toys and come in the house. I started talking to Alice about something; I can't even remember what now. Laura started to cry, and we both ran over to her. I was so relieved when I saw it was just a bee sting. I picked her up and carried her into the house. She died not fifteen minutes later."

Her chin began to tremble and jerk as she spoke those last words. She had said them quickly and plainly, lest she start to bawl again before they were said. Once, it had seemed that being able to cry over it would be a blessed relief, but at that moment, it just seemed miserable.

That misery was reflected clearly on her face. Graham caught an echo of it in his own heart, and he pulled her back close to him. This time, Kelly thought that being near him was nothing but comfort, and she could not remember why she had tried to push him away before.

She cried a little bit more but knew that the storm had passed. True, tears would always be waiting for her when she thought of Laura dead and gone from her, but what a small thing those tears seemed next to the happy memories her daughter had given her and the chance for life that each new day brought to her.

"I'll tell you what I think," Graham said. "I think we ought to ride out of here and wander. You're full up with towns, and you need to see the wild places. We'll know when we find the right place for your farm."

That sounded like truth to Kelly, and she slept better than night than she had in well over a year.

Chapter 50

They set out at dawn the next morning and headed straight back into the high country. It reminded Kelly of the trip she and Jackson had made from Denver to Arizona, except that the country stayed green, and they encountered no grizzly bears. Also, Graham was much easier to travel with—too easy, she felt at times. It was hard to keep enough distance between them, and despite all the healing she'd done, she still felt that distance was necessary.

Graham sensed it and tried not to push her, but sometimes things just sparked so well between them that it was hard to restrain himself. On those occasions, her eyes would cloud over, and she would try to start an argument. Graham never let himself be baited into a fight and always insisted that they sleep together, even though she plainly was not interested in resuming their physical relationship. He knew it was only a matter of time and that the closer they were in the meantime, the sooner everything would be back on the right rails.

They spent most of that summer wandering, and in early August, they decided to find a town and see where they were. Kelly was not especially curious to know, though it mattered some to Graham, who was thinking about the coming winter and where they would spend it. They were far enough north to make worrying about winter during August sensible.

That town was smaller than the first one they'd found, but not so small that they didn't have a choice of places to stay. Graham left Kelly soaking happily in a hot bath and went out to find out where they were. Talk was free and easy in the saloons, and it did not take him long to find out what he needed to know.

He stopped at bath house and then at the barber for a shave. Unfortunately, the barber was a Frenchman, and before Graham could stop him, he had slapped Graham's face with some kind of noxious smelling lotion. Short of taking another bath, Graham could think of no way to rid himself of the smell, so he went unhappily back to the hotel, hoping that Kelly would not throw him out, thinking he'd been to a sporting house.

Kelly was just finishing drying her hair went he came in.

"Find out anything worth telling?" She asked him.

"We're about three hundred miles from the border," he said. "Winter sets in during September, and it goes below zero in the bat of an eye."

Kelly combed the last knot from her hair and pulled it back away from her face. Since leaving Kansas City, she'd kept it cut just below her shoulders. It was less trouble to deal with and curled a little since it wasn't so long.

"What's that smell?" She asked.

"I apologize for that," Graham said, sitting on the bed beside her. "That damn French barber splashed me with some concoction before I could stop him."

Kelly tossed her towel on the floor.

"It smells good," she said.

"You must be joking."

She was, but she wasn't. Right then, there wasn't anything he could do, short of suddenly turning into Jackson Taylor, that would annoy her.

She got up and went to the washstand, picking up the book she had left there. Graham watched because her shirt wasn't very long and allowed for a generous view of her legs.

Kelly had to smile when she noticed him looking. Jackson had always gotten red-faced and speechless with embarrassment if he happened to see any part of her uncovered. It was almost insulting, as though she were deformed or something.

But there was nothing insulting about the appreciative look on Graham's face. Kelly set the book on the night table and walked over to him. She stood as close as she could get, putting her arms around his neck, and began to make sniffing sounds.

"Yes, something sure does smell," she said, leaning her face down toward his, breathing down along his ear and kissing the back of his neck.

He fell backward behind the bed, pulling her with him. Her hair fell around them, and he reached up and pushed it back out of the way as their lips met.

They kissed until her lips ached from it, ached from longing and from having been untouched for so long, then Graham sat up abruptly and stood up.

"Where are you going?" She asked sitting up and too

dismayed to be angry.

"Back to the barber," he said. "I want to buy a bottle of that stuff."

Kelly giggled and sat up, leaning forward and catching the back of his pants, pulling him backward until he fell on the bed and began to laugh too. The rest of the afternoon passed without further conversation.

When darkness came, dim moonlight shone in through the window. Kelly wrapped her shirt around herself and got out of bed. After rummaging through her things, she found her last apple.

Taking a bite, she went to the window and looked outside. The half-drawn curtains concealed her from view, but there wasn't much activity in the streets anyway. It had been a hot day, and night had not brought much relief.

A breeze stirred the curtains. Kelly left the window and got back on the bed. They had kicked most of the bedding down to the foot of the bed, except for the sheet, which covered Graham to the waist as he dozed.

Feeling the bed move as Kelly got back on it, he became more wakeful. Kelly sat on her pillow and leaned back against the wall, munching her apple.

"What's that you've got?" He asked, sitting up some and leaning his head against her hip.

"An apple," she said. "We missed dinner."

"So we did. Can you spare me a bite?"

"Sure."

They ate the apple down to the core, which Kelly tossed out the window without getting up. Just then, she didn't care if she never got out of bed again. She put her pillow behind herself and slid down until she was half-lying, half-sitting.

When she was done getting herself comfortable, Graham rested his head on her stomach and went back to dozing as her fingers played through his hair. She felt as though the last of her troubles had fallen away. The peace she had envisioned the first night after the escape was now upon her.

That feeling was tied to this man she loved, and it puzzled her. He could upset her worse than anyone in the world, but he was also the only one who could reach inside her and give her peace. She did not understand it, but she trusted it. There was no need for her to save herself from it anymore. They had come to a place and a time where their feelings for each other were no longer a dangerous thing.

So her thoughts ran until Graham woke up again, and after caressing her stomach for a moment, leaned up on his elbow and brushed her shirt open. Kelly reached up and brought his face down to hers, as he eased on top of her.

There was a kind of satisfaction just in feeling his weight on her pelvis, and she wrapped her legs around one of his and began to kiss him with all the heat and tenderness of a broken heart made whole again.

Chapter 51

Jake Gallagher's first impression of Leadfalls, Wyoming, was much the same as Graham McNair's had been. True, it was now high summer, but the town still seemed dank and gloomy in a way that belied the clear skies and fresh prairie air.

It had been a long trail north from Sweetwater, Texas, where the news of his brother's death had reached him three months after the fact. The details had been sketchy, and so he had ridden to Wyoming with the intention of getting the facts and then deciding who was to pay for killing his little brother. Jed may have had the fatal tendency of overconfidence in his own abilities but, in Jake's mind, that did not absolve the guilty parties of their responsibility.

No one in town could answer his questions about the escape, though he gathered that one of Jed's deputies, Sherman Buser, had survived the shoot out and had lead a posse after Graham. Sherman had taken a bullet in the leg during the escape, and when he had fainted from it in the foothills, the posse had lost heart and turned back.

Now Jed set out looking for Sherman, who had left town as soon as he had been able to ride. Jed found him farther west in a Cheyenne bar room.

Sherman greeted him unenthusiastically, knowing that Jake was a hard one and was probably looking for a way to revenge himself on someone. There was no way of knowing whether Jake would consider Sherman one of those someones. In response to Jake's questions, Sherm recounted the story of how Graham had escaped but neglected to mention how Jed had set Graham up.

"I don't know who done all that firing from the livery stable," he said when the tale was over. "But he sure was a good shot. Got Snakey in the forehead and Jed in the heart. I'd be dead too, except I got knocked outta the way when that goddamned Dave Meyers pushed Graham off the scaffold."

Jake had listened to the story attentively. Only one answer made any sense.

"I know who it was," he said grimly. "It was that goddamn unnatural pants-wearing female Kelly Knowlton."

"You ain't got no way to be sure about that," Sherman replied. "Last I heard she died in '80. Ain't that what Graham told that reporter fella?"

"He lied. I know fer a fact she was livin' in Kansas City just last year."

"That still don't mean it was her that done all this."

"'Course it was. Who else would risk their neck over the likes of Graham McNair?"

"It mighta been one a them hard cases he used t'ride with up in Montana. Anderson Whitehead or one-eye Jeff Bowser or that half-breed Sioux Angry Badger Riley. You can't prove it were her."

"Them's mostly dead now," he said. "Anderson keeps bar down in Creed, n'Jeff got shot down in Texas years ago. Badger Riley ain't been seen since the fight up in Bozeman. It were her. It was all planned out too well for it not have been. 'Sides, look who she picked to help her out. If it were one of them hard cases, they woulda tried to get you or Snakey to help, since you all knowed each other. But she got that shiftless Dave Meyers to help."

"That don't prove nothing."

"Sure it do. Dave used t'ride with the army down in the Arizona territory, and I know for a fact that she knew him down there, and they were in a big Indian fight near Ft. Shelby."

Sherman mulled it over. Aside from hunting down Dave or Graham, there was no way to find out for sure. From the tracking he'd done on the day of the escape, he knew that three riders had left town during the ruckus. A single rider had trailed south, and the other two had ridden due west and into the mountains. If Gallagher's guesses were correct, then Dave had probably ridden south, back down to what was, for him, familiar territory. If he hadn't crossed the border already, he was pretty damn close to it and could probably scoot across it anytime he wanted.

There was no way of telling where Kelly and Graham had gone. He said as much to Gallagher, who laughed.

"They rode north," he said. "I reckon they crossed over into Canada by now. But that don't matter. I'll find 'em."

"You'll find trouble, that's fer sure," Sherman replied. "You'll get a passel n'then some tryin' to bring him back here.

Graham ain't the kinda man to get arrested twice."

"I ain't arrestin' anybody, and I ain't interested in foolin' with Graham McNair," Gallagher said coldly. "I don't care a damn how many sheepherders he killed. But that female cowboy of his shot my brother in cold blood, and I ain't lettin' that pass for a moment."

This was no less than Sherm had expected, but Jake's ice-cold voice made him shiver at hearing the words spoken, and he was filled with foreboding.

"I'm just relieved that it was her," Jake went on. "'Stead a one of them other hard cases that mighta been harder to shade."

"You ain't talkin' sense if'n you think shading Kelly Knowlton'll be an easy thing to accomplish," Sherman said.

"She ain't a killer," Gallagher said. "Least she never was until this happened."

"She ain't a coward either," Sherman said. "She's as hard as they come. Look how she did this escape. That took a heap of nerve."

That was true enough, but it did not deter Jake, who had shaded plenty of hard cases in his time. Kelly might be a good enough shot and bold enough in a dangerous situation, but those things counted for nothing against Jake's cold blooded and carefully calculated malice.

"Well, I'm heading north at first light. You get ready and go with me."

"Me?" Sherman choked on his drink. "I ain't got no grudge against either of 'em."

"You ought to," Jake said coldly. "And even if you don't, I got a grudge against you. You ought to 've plugged that sonuvabitch when you had the chance, then none of this would have happened."

"When did I have the chance?"

"When you all were whoorawing them small-time rustlers, that's when."

Sherman did not argue the point, though he held firm to his belief that the only person who could have been killed that day was himself and maybe Snakey and Jed.

"Leave me outta this, Jake," he said. "It ain't none o' my affair."

"It is now, you yellow dog," Jake said. "You be ready to go in the morning, or I'll kill you just to get myself warmed up to the task ahead."

Sherman swallowed hard and nodded. Meanness ran in the Gallagher family. He had no doubt that Jake would kill him. He also knew that it could take years to track Kelly and Graham down. They might not ever find them. He wondered if he should mention that possibility to Jake, then decided to remain quiet about it. If Jake had thought of it, it obviously did not deter him one bit, and if he hadn't thought of it, it would probably anger him to have it said.

    By the time they rode out of town in the morning, Sherman had reconciled himself to a long trail. It didn't matter anyway. He'd done nothing but drift here and there all his life, and one road was as good as any other.

Chapter 52

In the morning, Graham was up early enough to make Kelly wonder if there was something wrong. She watched sleepily as he shaved and dressed.

"I'm going out to scout around a bit," he said, buttoning his shirt. "Want to come with me?"

Kelly considered it, then shook her head. All the long months of driving sorrow seemed far behind, and now that she could sleep again, she wanted to revel in it.

"No, I think I'll stay here and nap," Kelly said.

"Is there anything else in particular you have in mind to do today?"

"Nothing that can be done without you here," she said, reaching over and taking a book from the night table. She would read and doze the day away like she used to when she was on the tramp in the Colorado territory.

"Well then," Graham said, watching her in the mirror. "Make a few moments in the afternoon so we can get married."

The book slipped from her fingers, hitting the floor with a thump. Kelly sat up swiftly, holding the sheet to her chest.

"What did you say?"

"I said let's get married this afternoon."

"You have lost your mind," Kelly said, retrieving her book.

"Maybe. But let's do it anyway. What do you say?"

"No. I don't want to marry anybody."

"Why not?" He asked, sitting down on the edge of the bed. "I'd be honored to make an honest woman out of you."

Kelly snorted.

"I am an honest woman," she said. "So don't do me any favors."

"Too honest, sometimes," he said. "But you still haven't said why not."

Kelly thought for a moment.

"Well, suppose you start to aggravate me?" Kelly asked.

"I always have aggravated you some," Graham replied. "If it gets too bad, throw a biscuit at me. I am surprised to see you turn so faint hearted. Such things never troubled you before."

They didn't particularly trouble her now, either, except the unexpectedness of the question had flustered her. She had not thought of being married to anyone since she'd escaped from New York. Now that she thought of being married to Graham, it didn't seem like an objectionable thing to do. After all, except for having taken the vows, they had done everything else that married people do.

"Alice once said that men change considerably after they get a legal hold on you," Kelly mused. "They become bullying, and you have to hide your money from them."

"Of course, Alice is an expert on marriage," Graham replied, nettled. "She never even saw a married person until she moved to Kansas City."

"I was just thinking aloud," Kelly said, smiling at his annoyance. "It's hard for me to believe that we're even having this conversation."

Graham was having a little trouble with it himself. But the thought had been steadily growing stronger, and he could not push it away. As strange as it was to think of himself as married, he was determined to use every means possible to make sure that Kelly did not, somehow, get away from him again. Of course, he knew that no vow would hold her to anyone she no longer wanted to be with, but still, he wanted her sacred word that she loved him and would never leave him. It might not hold her fast, but it would hold her long enough so that she couldn't make any quick getaways.

"Tomorrow," she said. "Let's do it tomorrow."

"That means you will?"

"Yes."

"Then I'll be back at three for you," he said, standing up. "I'll scout out a minister or justice of the peace."

"I said tomorrow."

"I don't want to wait."

"It's only a day, and I have to buy a dress."

"No, you don't. In fact, I wish you wouldn't. I never think of you as wearing dresses."

"Oh," Kelly had a sudden remembrance of Jackson hurting her feelings over a similar issue. She shook her head. It was hard to believe that she had ever been that young and stupid.

They were married that afternoon by a justice of the peace

whose English was frequently interrupted by a phrase or two of French. The JP's office was a tent set up on the north side of town, and the witnesses were called in from the street.

Hard packed dirt served as the tent's floor, and Kelly dug at it absently with the toe of her boot while the justice made a short but almost incomprehensible speech about the honorable estate of marriage. She tried to think how all the time and events of the past years had brought them both to this dusty tent somewhere in Canada, swearing to spend the rest of their lives together. She could not arrive at a satisfactory answer.

It was all over in a minute, and they were standing outside in the hazy August sunshine. Walking back to their hotel, Graham pondered what he could do to show her how happy she had made him.

"What do you think about wintering in that abandoned cabin we found on the way here?" Graham asked her suddenly.

"Can we get it weatherproof in time?" Kelly asked, pleased to think that they would not have to winter in town.

"I don't see why not."

"Can you go all winter without a card game?" She asked. "We're liable to get snowed in up there."

"No matter. There'll be plenty to do."

Kelly shook her head, feeling dazed. Apparently, if you stood on a gallows and were lucky enough to get off it unharmed, it changed your view of things entirely, even when your feet were firm on the earth again.

They rode out of town the next morning, stopping on the way to outfit themselves for the winter. The weather was liable to be uncertain, and they could not count on being able to get back to town until spring.

Chapter 53

The cabin was built into the side of a hill; its back wall and floor were made of hard-packed earth; the other walls and roof were made of rough-hewn logs. The chinks between the logs had originally been filled in with mud and sticks, and through several seasons of neglect, much of this had been washed away.

The rest of the cabin was sturdily built and needed little repair, but it took them several days to fill in the chinks—a messy job but not a difficult one. It took another few weeks to build a shelter for the horses and pack mule.

The first snow fell before they were finished, but those few days of wintry weather quickly gave way to nearly three weeks of glorious Indian summer. During that bright autumn, the days slipped by so quickly that Kelly lost track of them. This, however, was more of a comfort than a disturbance. After leaving New York and before going to Kansas City, she had rarely kept track of the days, and now she was glad to be shed of this last vestige of the settled world.

Going to Kansas City had been a mistake, she now realized. She had been scared and had sought refuge there, but she had given up too much of herself in order to do it. Looking back, she could see that this was partly why she had become so angry with Graham during their argument over his leaving. She had let the opinions of the civilized world whoorah her into a compromised existence that had solved none of her problems and had satisfied none of her needs. Every word that he'd spoken that night had been packed with hard, uncomfortable truth—except when it had come to his own feelings.

When the snow finally settled in to stay, they were snugly fixed. Hunting was good, the cabin was warm, and there was plenty to do. During the days, Kelly would take the horses and mule out to graze, letting them paw through the snow and nibble at the trees for their food. She would sit on an exposed rock or lean up against a tree and keep a careful eye on them, her rifle held at the ready.

The walk back to the cabin was always a challenge. The mule was balky, and the horses were frisky from inactivity. Generally, she had far more patience with animals than with people, but leading all three of those animals by herself was a trial. On this day, they were acting up worse than usual, and Kelly thought they seemed more frightened than frisky.

Scanning the ground, Kelly saw some wolf tracks—fresh ones, too. Kelly cast a watchful eye around herself. If there were wolves nearby, they would have to be downwind, or else the horses would be far more upset. Of course, the wolves that had made those tracks might also be miles away by now.

She took a better hold on the leads and quickened her pace. Wolves or no wolves, it was cold out, and she wanted to be in front of the fire, not messing about with flighty horses and a balky mule.

She mentioned the wolf sign to Graham after they'd eaten that evening.

"Where'd you see them?"

"About a half mile north," she said. "They were pretty fresh too, judging from the fit the horses threw."

Graham had grown a beard for the winter months, and now he scratched it thoughtfully, wondering if they both ought to take the horses out from now on. As the winter wore on, the wolves and any other such hunters would get hungrier and more likely to attack the horses—or a person. He had never heard of a wolf actually attacking an armed person, but that didn't mean that it couldn't happen.

"Keep an eye out for more," he said at last. "They may move on, and they may not. I'll go out with you next time."

Kelly nodded. "That would be a help. Those horses are getting frisky."

"Well, you can ride all you like in the spring."

"I know. Are you going to shave that beard off in the spring?"

"Why? Don't you care for it?"

"It's your face, of course," Kelly said. "But no, I don't care for it, although it does tickle nicely at times."

"Maybe I'll leave it on then," he said thoughtfully.

Kelly wrinkled her nose at him and poured herself some more coffee, into which she dropped a piece of molasses candy. There was nothing like hot coffee to warm up with after being out in the cold, but she never could get used to the taste of it.

Outside, the wind was rising. Bad weather was setting in, and Kelly thought it might be a few days before she got the horses outside again. If it was a bad storm, they'd have to go hunting when it was over with.

That was why, when the storm ended and the skies became clear, she and Graham took their rifles and the pack mule and went looking for game. After a long morning of fruitless searching, they came to the edge of a small group of trees and, peering into the clearing beyond, saw a herd of deer pawing through the snow for grass.

They were downwind of the deer, but there was no cover they could use to get closer. Kelly looked inquisitively at Graham, posing a silent question. Graham shrugged, pointed to her, and jerked his thumb toward the deer. Kelly slid her rifle from its boot and, keeping the mule between her and the deer, edged out of the woods and into the clearing, closer to the herd.

When she was close enough, she halted the mule and aimed over its back, choosing a largish animal well within range. She fired once. The rifle roared, and the deer crumpled to the ground. The rest of the deer fled, and in less than a minute, they had disappeared from sight. Kelly hurried over to her kill, and Graham walked out of the trees after her.

The deer was dead, which relieved Kelly enormously. There was nothing worse than a badly wounded animal agonizing in the snow.

"Good shot," Graham said, a little out of breath from hurrying.

"Thanks."

She stuck her rifle stock down in the hard packed snow and drew her skinning knife. Graham was about to do likewise when the mule began to snort and bray, suddenly afraid.

He scanned the snowy hillside, his eyes coming to rest on a clump of trees uphill. A group of shadows disengaged themselves from the trees—wolves. Kelly followed his eyes and saw the wolves a second after he did. She sheathed her knife and picked her rifle back up, glad that she had only fired one shot.

They waited to see what the wolves would do. The mule was terrified and broke away from them, but neither of them chased it. It would get away or it wouldn't; they had other things concerning them at the moment.

Winter lean and drawn by the smell of fresh blood, the wolves loped toward them, moving swiftly. Kelly could not count them at first, but there were ten at least. As the wolves drew near, they fanned out to circle the deer and the two people standing near it.

Without discussing a plan of action, Kelly and Graham found themselves standing back to back as the wolves snarled, wary of coming too close but unable to resist the deer. Neither of them was particularly afraid, and both of them drew confidence from knowing the other was watching their back.

Kelly was fascinated by the wolves; she had never seen any so close before. They could not speak or plan, of course, but they seemed to move and be guided by a single will and of a single accord.

One of the largest wolves drew ever closer to the deer, snarling at them. When it was close enough to be able to leap at them, Graham fired once, killing it. Two more wolves moved in, and they both fired, killing both wolves with three shots. The rest vanished back into the woods.

When the wolves had gone, Kelly and Graham reloaded and hastily gutted the deer and skinned the three dead wolves. Then they bound the deer's front and back legs together. They would have to carry the carcass three miles back to the cabin, and it was already late afternoon.

"Think we've lost the mule for good?" Kelly asked as they started out.

"I'd back a mule that ornery against a pack of wolves any day," Graham replied.

It took them nearly two hours to trudge back to the cabin. The deer was heavy, and the snow was deep in places, which made for hard going. On the way, they saw no more signs of the wolves, and when they finally reached the cabin, the mule was already there, waiting for them. Kelly was annoyed; she had never liked mules, and this one seemed particularly and purposely contrary.

"The first thing I plan to do when we find a town is sell that mule," Kelly remarked later as she pegged the wolf skins out on the cabin floor.

"I've no objection to that," Graham replied. "But do you have to cure those skins in here? They'll stink to high heaven in a day or so."

"I can't very well do it outside," Kelly said, not pausing in her work. "We can leave the door open while the weather's good. Besides, you'll thank me for it next winter when you have a good warm wolfs' fur hat to wear."

"I didn't know you were such a hand at sewing."

"I'm not. I said it would be warm," Kelly reminded him. "I didn't say it would be stylish."

"You don't make it sound worth the smell."

"It might not be," Kelly admitted. "But it will keep me occupied. Were both liable to get antsy when the winter drags on."

"If we get antsy, we'll go down country," Graham replied, a little offended that she anticipated becoming weary of his company.

Kelly, who had noted the offended note to his voice, paused and looked up at him.

"Don't be so gun shy," she said. "You know what I meant.

Being cooped up anywhere can be trying, no matter how cozily you're fixed."

Chapter 54

Had they heard Kelly's words, Jake and Sherman would have agreed with her. They had spent that winter in much less hospitable quarters and became very antsy indeed before it was half over. In the spring, they set out to find Kelly's trail and were ready to make up for a winter of lost time.

The previous fall, they had started out with Sherman showing Jake where he and the posse had given up the hunt. Although the trail was months cold and Gallagher hated the high country, they rode up a ways, guessing at where Kelly and Graham might have gone. Two days later, they found the remains of a small camp site. There was no way to tell if Kelly and Graham had been there, but Gallagher felt certain that they had.

He had squatted by the burned out spot where their fire had been and considered how best to go about finding them. Kelly, he knew, had spent a good deal of time in the mountains and was at home there. Since it was rough country and hard to track someone through, it seemed likely to him that they had ridden north through the mountains.

But their trail was long dead, and Jake himself was no mountain man. It would be quicker to ride across the plains and across the border and then try to pick up their trail. No matter how at home those two were in the high country, they would come down sooner or later and start looking for towns. If Gallagher could find those same towns, tracking them would be easy. Kelly was not easy to forget, since she was so bold about acting unfeminine.

So he and Sherman had ridden back down and crossed the plains, but they had been forced to take a roundabout course to avoid the riled up Sioux, who were tearing up the Dakotas and the Yellowstone. One delay led to another, and they had barely reached the border when the snow began to fly.

They had wintered in a god-forsaken little logging camp, and Jake had had little to do except curse the weather, drink, and hone his plans for vengeance. Jake knew that he and Sherman had been forced to ride much further east than Kelly and Graham had done. He also knew that it could take years to find them, but to his mind, that was so much the better, for the longer it took, the less either of them would be expecting him.

He also had no way of knowing whether or not they were still riding together. Graham, he knew, generally traveled alone, and Jake could not imagine why he would change his habits, especially not for some female wrangler. If they had separated, so much for the better; it would be two against one. If they had not, it would be even odds, and there was a reward notice on Graham. Jake had no particular quarrel with Graham, but killing him would cause Jake to loose no sleep either, especially not when Jake could get a thousand dollars for him, dead or alive.

So they rode west, hugging as close to the border as they dared, traveling slowly. Jake was in no hurry, because hurrying would increase their chances of missing the trail, and time could only work in his favor.

Chapter 55

Kelly and Graham left their cabin before spring penetrated the mountains. Down below, where time had a meaning more precise than seasons, it was probably late March or early April and time to do some traveling and play some poker.

The further down the mountains they went, the friendlier the weather became, and when they reached the plains, it was true spring everywhere. Every morning, Kelly rose early, appreciative of the clear sunrises and fresh air. The spring air always had made her feel more than alive, and she guessed that it had the same effect on almost everything; it was plain to see how the earth came alive and flourished during the spring as it did during no other time of the year.

Neither she nor Graham had any idea of where they were, but they had been traveling northeast since having left the cabin. Of course, it was impossible to keep a straight course in the high country, and they had twisted this way and that during their descent. They might be back in the States, for all they knew.

But they weren't, of that Kelly felt certain. During the next days of traveling, they wandered aimlessly, though they generally headed north and kept the mountains within sight. Kelly supposed that they were looking for a town but that they weren't in any particular hurry to find one.

Hurry or no hurry, a town appeared on the horizon one afternoon, and without discussion, they rode toward it. Kelly in particular was curious to see what kind of a place it was. Maybe towns this far north were less aggravating than the ones further south, she mused to herself. Or maybe, her mood had improved enough to tolerate civilization no matter what shape it took. Either way, she would soon find out.

The town, which they soon learned was named Devereaux, was a small settlement of merchants, trappers, adventurers, and some farmers. Less than a day's ride to the west, it was flanked by the mountains which curved around to the north of the town, where they tumbled down into rocky foothills. Devereaux appeared larger and better settled than the town in which they had gotten married, Kelly thought, and then she was so startled by remembering that they had gotten married that she stopped wondering about the town they were in.

It was just as well to stop wondering and admire the country more, for Kelly had rarely seen a place so prettily situated. She felt she could stay there for some time without becoming anxious to leave. It was good to sleep in a real bed and be able to ride all day and play cards all night.

Though not so impressed with the scenery, Graham was also ready to stay awhile, despite the poor luck that they'd both had playing cards. Going further north seemed useless; they'd just come down from the mountains to the west, and they'd already seen the country to the south. That meant east was the only direction left to explore, and he was in no hurry for that.

Besides, he knew Kelly was thinking of her farm more and more, and he knew that it was the next thing they were going to do. When she was ready to get started with it, she'd say so, and then they would go about finding it. Until then, Devereaux was as good a place to be as any.

Kelly was thinking of her farm. She was enough taken with the country they found themselves in to consider settling there but had never considered starting a farm from scratch. Always before, she had thought of buying a place and taking it over. Now she was faced with the daunting task of having to build barns and a house and fences and anything else she might need.

She had almost decided to ride east, if Graham didn't mind, and look for some place that was for sale. The only thing that held her back was not wanting to ride away from the mountains.

So she kept her thoughts to herself and said nothing about leaving. Since Graham seemed happy enough, aside from his run of bad luck at cards, she had more than enough excuse to stay and keep silent about farm building. Graham, however, brought the topic up himself one evening as they walked back to their hotel after an evening of card playing.

"You still planning on starting up a horse farm?" He asked her.

"Yes," she answered, wondering why he had brought it up, since he wasn't the settling down type.

"I heard talk of a farm for sale five miles north of here," he said. "Some greenhorn from way back east set up in a big way, then his wife ran off 'cause she couldn't stand being so far from civilization. Now he's selling out."

"Where'd you hear all that?"

"Oh, he was talking up a storm at the bar," Graham explained. "You didn't hear because you were still in the game. He said no one's lived in the place all winter, and he sold off all the stock, but the house and barn are still there."

Kelly stopped walking abruptly. She had never suspected that Graham was so adept at eavesdropping.

"Did you happen to hear this man's name?" She asked.

"Shelton Witherspoon. He's the bandy-legged little man with the fancy waistcoat."

Kelly took a few hesitant steps toward the hotel, then stopped again. If this was as it sounded to be, it required immediate investigation.

"I'm going to go talk to him," she said. "I'll be back in an hour or so."

With that, she turned and trotted back to the saloon. Graham watched her go and then went to the hotel. He thought that, perhaps, Kelly had just found her farm.

Chapter 56

A winding dirt road lead up to Shelton's farm, which was closer to ten miles out of town than five, as Kelly found out the next day. The extra distance did not bother Kelly, in fact, it pleased her. Deveraux was all right as far as towns went, but if she bought the place, she would rather have the nearest town be farther than nearer.

"Of course, the barn needs some repair," Shelton said as they rode through the front gate. "But the house is in excellent condition. My wife had all the furniture hauled in from back east."

Kelly examined the barn. The roof was in poor shape, and one wall had a hole torn in it, probably from rot and severe winter winds, but it was a large building with a hay loft, six box stalls, and eight standing stalls.

The fences were also in varying states of decay, Kelly looked them over briefly, then they went up to the house, a rambling structure that looked as though several rooms had been added on to the original building.

"There's a stove in the kitchen, the parlor, and one of the bedrooms," Shelton said as he lead her through the house. "I'll throw them all in, and the furniture too, what there is of it."

There was a kitchen table and chairs, two double beds, two washstands, a wardrobe and two dressers. The house itself was dusty and in need of a cleaning, but it was solidly built as far as she could see and not much worse for a winter of neglect.

After having looked through the house, Kelly stood on the front porch and surveyed the entire spread. The house was atop a small hill and a wide green lawn swept down to the barn. There were two small corrals in front of the barn, and one larger corral behind it. Woods crept up to this corral and up to the fence that circled the house, but to the north, an open field lay and all the country out that way, for as far as she could see, was open but dotted with small stands of trees. Shelton had told her there was a pond in the woods.

Standing there, Kelly was minded of her farm back in New York and knew that she could be very happy here.

"How much are you asking?" She asked Shelton.

"Four thousand," he replied. He had not missed the faintly nostalgic expression on her face as she looked over the place.

The price he named wiped her face clean, however.

"I was thinking two," she said.

"This country's settling up," he replied. "I could get five in another year."

"You don't have another year to wait," Kelly reminded him. "Besides, none of these raggedy settlers have ten cents, much less four thousand dollars."

"But you do, I'll wager," Shelton replied shrewdly. "You have to admit the place is worth it. Why, the furniture alone is easily worth five hundred dollars."

"I don't need the furniture," she said.

"Then I'll go three thousand five hundred."

"Two thousand five," she countered.

"I must think of my expenses," Shelton said. "It will cost me to travel back east and establish myself."

"That's why I'm offering five hundred dollars more than is reasonable," Kelly replied.

They dickered for an hour longer but reached no agreement and rode back into town annoyed with each other.

"I'll have to sleep on it," Kelly said as they parted. "Can we meet tomorrow?"

"Surely. Noon at the Rolling Log Saloon?"

"I'll be there."

They shook hands, and Kelly went back to the hotel. It was getting on toward dinnertime, but her appetite was dulled by her indecision over the farm. Graham was just getting dressed as she entered their room.

"How was it?" He asked.

"It's as close to perfect as I'll find," Kelly said, frowning. "Twenty acres of good grazing land, a house, barn, and some fence work. Of course, it's run down some but nothing that can't be fixed."

Graham knew it couldn't be as good as she said; her creased forehead and pursed lips told him so.

"What's the problem, then?"

"Well, he wants too much for it," Kelly said. "He needs some money and thinks I ought to provide it."

"Is he asking more than you have?"

"No, but I won't have much left over to fix the place up and lay in some stock. Plus, it'll be two years at least before we make any money off the place. We'll need money to live off all that time."

"It won't take much," Graham said thoughtfully. "Hunting's still good, and the cards'll turn favorable sooner or later."

"I still don't know," Kelly said. "I don't like to be so close to nothing. I told him I'd give an answer in the morning."

Graham nodded and finished dressing. Kelly sat on the bed and watched him.

"You do look handsomer without your moustache," she said suddenly. "Though it took me a while to get used to it."

Graham put his hat on and smiled in reply.

"Will you be very late?" Kelly asked.

"Most likely," he said, kissing her. "Bolt the door."

"Of course. Good luck."

He went out, closing the door softly behind him. Kelly got up and bolted it. Frowning, she thought there had been something odd about him. He had not offered her any advice about whether or not she ought to buy the farm, nor had he seemed much interested in discussing it. Perhaps he wanted to wander around a bit more before they came to such a decision, she thought.

She yawned. A good night's sleep would show her what to do, and once she made up her mind, she would ask him to speak freely about his thoughts on the matter. No place was perfect to her if Graham didn't want to be there. She got ready for bed and went to sleep easily, confident that morning would show her the way.

The first streaks of morning light had just fallen in through the window when Kelly was roused from sleep by a knock at the door. Kelly got up and opened the door, then got back in bed. Graham entered the room, looking bright-eyed but wearing his poker face. Kelly snuggled back into bed, hoping that she could fall back asleep.

"Are you going to sleep the day away again?" Graham asked, sitting down on the bed to pull his boots off.

"Yes," then Kelly remembered that she had agreed to meet Shelton at noon. She sat up.

"No, I can't. I've got to go see about the farm."

"Have you decided what to do?"

"I need your opinion on the matter," she said. "And I wish you'd speak plainly. If you want to move around for a while yet, tell me. There'll be other places worth having."

"I wouldn't mind settling here," he replied. "It's the best place we've seen."

"We might go farther and do better," Kelly said.

"Or worse. If the place is to your liking, get it."

"I will then," Kelly said, resting back against the pillows. Graham stood up and took off his gun belt. After hanging it from the bed post, he took off his jacket and shirt, tossing them onto the chair. Kelly was lying with her eyes closed, although he knew that she wasn't asleep.

"Shouldn't you get to it?" He asked.

"There's no hurry," Kelly replied. "I'm supposed to meet him at noon."

"He might sell it from under you."

Kelly's eyes opened suddenly; she had not thought of that.

"He didn't mention having another buyer," she said.

"Would you?" Graham asked.

"No," Kelly said uncomfortably, irked at the thought of losing the place through having been so indecisive about it.

"Hell," Graham said. "He might even loose it in a poker game."

Kelly started to get out of bed, then stopped.

"If I go running to him at six in the morning all worried, he'll just jack the price up five hundred dollars."

Graham began to whistle. Kelly glanced at him sharply. In all the years she known him, she had never heard him whistle, and now that she was completely awake, she noticed that he was having trouble keeping his poker face intact.

"I don't suppose you played some cards with Mr. Shelton Witherspoon last evening?" She asked, watching him alertly.

Graham stood up and picked his jacket up from the chair. After fumbling for the inside breast pocket, he produced a long manila envelope.

"Here," he said, handing it to her.

"What is it?" Kelly asked as she took the envelope.

"Read it."

Kelly opened the envelope and removed the document inside. She unfolded it and began to read. It was the deed to the farm. She scanned it quickly, checking to see if all the legal requirements had been seen to.

Her eye fell on the name of the new owner—Laura Kelly Chapman—her maiden name. The farm was hers and hers alone—the way she had always wanted it.

She could not think what to say, she looked up and saw that Graham was evidently getting great amusement from her speechlessness.

"How did this happen?" She asked.

"A straight flush over two pair," Graham replied. "I pushed him to the wall, and he threw in the deed."

Kelly folded the deed carefully and slid it back into the envelope. She didn't know what to say and did not realize that, to Graham, the look on her face said more than enough.

Chapter 57

To Graham, it seemed that Kelly went about making the farm livable with a kind of furious determination. Only the house was in good repair, and once she had it cleaned and fitted out to her satisfaction, she turned her full attention to the barns and grounds, taking on each task in a systematic way that told him she must have everything all ordered out in her head, even though she never spoke of it.

First, and most surprisingly, she put a vegetable garden behind the house. When he asked her why, she looked at him oddly.

"What did you think we were going to eat through the winter?" She asked.

"I thought we might do some hunting."

"We will, but fried potatos go down good on cold days."

He had to admit that she had a point and that he had forgotten that they were staying for good.

After the garden was started, he had woken up one morning to the sound of hammering from the barn. He had gotten dressed and gone down to see what was going on and had found her patching the ratty east wall.

Though surprised that she knew anything about carpentry, he had not said anything about it, but had pitched in and started to help, feeling a little insulted that she had not asked him to in the first place.

That day, they had examined the barn roof and found it full of holes.

"I'll go get a load of shingles and tar paper tomorrow," he

had said. "Won't take me more than a week to fix it."

Kelly was relieved that he had offered to do it. She did not like heights.

"I appreciate it," she said. "Now that the barn is solid, I plan to start fixing those fences."

The two large paddocks were in fairly good repair, but the smaller one, which she planned to use for breaking, needed a lot of work. Fixing it was likely to take some time, for she would have to make her own fence rails.

In the morning, Graham went into town early for the shingles, and Kelly took the axe and went down to the wood lot. She had never made fence rails before and had only a vague idea of how to go about it, but these things did not daunt her. There was no one else to do it, so if she wanted fences, she would just have to figure it out.

A little before noon, Kelly stumped up to the house. Her shirt was blotched with sweat, and she carried her hat. After stopping at the pump to wash her face and hands, she wearily climbed the steps and plopped down on the porch, where Graham stood, just back from his trip into town.

"I declare," she said. "Making fence rails is the most frustrating thing I've ever attempted."

"Is that what you've been up to all this time?" He asked.

"It is. All those fences have got to be fixed before I can get any stock," Kelly said, drying her face with her shirt tail. "Back home, we always used planed lumber which I bought from a sawmill. If you've got the rails, it's easy, just tie up both ends and pound some nails. But that cussed wedge keeps popping out of the logs. I've spent all morning working like a slave, and I've got two rails to show for it."

"I'm surprised you even have an idea of how to go about it," Graham said. "Since you always used planed lumber at home."

"I've seen it done plenty of times," Kelly said. "Though I never paid any particular attention. It always looked easy enough."

"It is," Graham replied. "It just takes practice."

"How do you know?"

"My father was big on fence rails," Graham replied. "Fence rails and Bible readings—if it weren't for those two things, I might still be up in Vermont, farming."

"Well, I promise not to subject you to any Bible readings if you'll show me how to keep the darn wedge from popping out every two seconds."

"Let me do it. The barn roof can wait."

"No, I want to know how it's done," Kelly said. "Once I get the hang of it, you can take over, and I'll do the barn roof."

"The barn roof can wait. I don't want you climbing around up there. Suppose it caves in?"

"I thought you said it wouldn't."

"There's always a chance."

"This is ridiculous. I suppose when I get the horses, you won't want me to do any breaking either, because I might get thrown."

"Now that's an idea."

Kelly stood abruptly and yanked the door open.

"Where are you going?"

"To get a biscuit," Kelly replied. "You need one thrown at you right about now."

The door banged shut behind her. Graham took off his shirt and rolled up the sleeves of his undershirt. Kelly reappeared a few moments later, brushing crumbs off of her hands.

"You're lucky I had such an appetite. It seemed a shame to waste a good biscuit on you," she said. "Let's get at those logs."

By the time it was too dark to work anymore, Kelly had gotten the hang of rail splitting and felt pleased with her accomplishment.

"That's a good day's work," she said, taking her gloves off. "I can do this alone tomorrow. I'll have those fences fixed in a week."

Graham shook his head. She had gone about learning to split logs the same way she had gone about learning to shoot or wrangling a new horse, with a frown of concentration and an air of determination. Now she was sweaty and dirty from her efforts, but she tugged her gloves off as daintily as a lady at a church supper. It was funny, when he thought about it, but he did not laugh. She would not understand it if he did.

They started back to the house, Graham carrying the axe over his shoulder and Kelly walking beside him, rubbing her sore hands.

"Thank you for the help," Kelly said.

"You're welcome," he said, grinning. It was also funny how formal she was about things. At times, it was almost insulting how she never took it for granted that he was glad to help her, but this evening, it was a fond thought.

In the end, they split fence rails together, then Kelly repaired the fences and Graham patched up the barn roof. It was early July when they finished, and Kelly announced that, as far as she was concerned, the major work was done, and the place was habitable. Graham was relieved; he thought she was looking a little peaked from the work she'd been doing.

Taking advantage of the lull in their work, Graham went into town a few nights a week to play some cards. Although he always asked Kelly to go with him, she always refused. At some point over the years, her distaste for saloons had become outright dislike. Kansas City had been so settled up that the saloons were her only substitute for the wilderness that she preferred. Now that she had all the wilderness a person could ask for, Devereaux's saloons ran a poor second.

She bought three brood mares and a stallion at the end of the month. It was late for breeding them, but she decided to go ahead with it at the end of the summer. That way, the foals would be born in the late spring of the following year.

Breeding was very much on her mind these days, and not just in relation to horses. Her period was late, and as the days passed, she became certain that she was pregnant. More than anything, the thought of it scared her. This was one baby she wouldn't mind having, but her luck had not run well when it came to children, and she thought it might kill her to lose another one.

She said nothing about it to Graham, especially since it was still too early to be sure.

But the thought grew on her mind, and in the last weeks of July, she decided to go into town and see the doctor. He would be able to tell her for sure, and knowing would give her a starting point for everything else.

"I'm going into town," Kelly told Graham after breakfast one morning. "Is there anything you need me to pick up?"

"I'll go with you," he replied.

"No, I want to go alone. Do you need anything?"

"No."

"I'll be back by the afternoon," Kelly said, wondering why he wanted to go with her when he didn't need to go at all.

Later, Graham watched her go, feeling unsettled. It was odd for her to want to go to town at all, much less want to go alone, and he had not cared for her tone of voice when she had refused his company. She had almost sounded guilty about it.

He had never made an issue of it and took great pains to conceal it, but the fact was that he did not like for her to go into town alone. Now, as he watched her ride away, he wondered why he disliked for her to go alone. After all, Devereaux wasn't particularly dangerous, and she was plenty able to take care of herself. After much thought, he still hadn't arrived at a satisfactory answer, so he pushed the whole subject from his mind and vowed never to let Kelly find out about it. She would think he was crazy.

But he could not forget how strangely she had been acting for the past few days. She had seemed less interested in her horses, and he often saw her staring off into space with a puzzled expression on her face. Knowing her as well as he did, Graham knew that something was weighing heavily on her mind, but he had no idea as to what it might be. The farm was shaping up fine, and they had no worries about anything.

It occurred to him that, perhaps, she was annoyed with him or tired of being married, but that didn't make sense either. They had been getting along wonderfully, and Kelly had been extremely affectionate lately. If she were a dishonest sort of person, that might just be a blind for something else, but Kelly wasn't capable of such deceptions and would be furious if she even suspected that he had thought such a thing about her.

Since he didn't know why she had gone into town, he didn't know when to expect her. Therefore, he did a few things that needed doing and then loitered on the porch for a while. Noon approached, and he made some supper for them both, assuming that she would be back soon.

At last, he heard a rider approaching. He went out on the porch and looked down the road. It was Kelly all right. She was riding slower that usual. Most times, she tore down the road and jumped the front gate. Today, her horse walked sedately, and seeing this worried Graham more than anything else.

With the slow pace she was keeping, it seemed to take forever for her to ride that last mile. Graham stood on the porch and waited for her as she opened the gate and rode up to the house.

As she came closer, he was alarmed to see that her face was still and thoughtful, as though she had received some bad news or had been in some sudden and unexpected trouble. She dismounted and tied her horse to the rail.

She stopped at the foot of the porch steps and looked up at him, pushing her hat back off her forehead. Yes, she was worried, Graham thought, her forehead was all crinkled up.

"Bad news from town?" He asked.

Kelly shook her head slowly.

"Unexpected news," she said, "but not necessarily bad news."

"Let's have it then."

"You'd better have a seat first," Kelly said.

"I can take it standing up. Spit it out."

"Trust me on this. You'd better sit."

She smiled a little, a wry smile that eased him a little because she never smiled about things that weren't at least a little bit funny, and something a little bit funny couldn't be too bad. Graham smiled back and sat on the top step. Kelly held the porch rail with one hand and put one foot on the bottom step.

"I went to see the doctor this morning," she said, surprised at how normal her voice sounded.

"I didn't know you'd been ill."

"I'm not," Kelly said. "I'm going to have a baby."

Graham's smile froze on his face, and his eyes went cloudy. Kelly knew that she had looked about the same way when the doctor had told her the news, except maybe he looked a little worse than she had. After all, she had at least had a suspicion.

In that first moment, it was all Graham could do to understand that she was pregnant. After that, it took some time for him to understand that, since he must be the father, what the news meant to him. He had never thought of such a thing happening to him, and he could not say at once how it made him feel.

His eyes focused sharply on Kelly, who stood watching him. Her wry expression had faded, and she looked very solemn. Graham reached up and took her hand, pulling her toward him. She sat on the step next to him, and he put his arm around her.

"What do you think about this?" He asked.

"I don't know," Kelly said slowly. "But, I think I'm afraid to be happy about it, because so much can go wrong."

Her voice faltered a little, and he squeezed her and kissed the top of her head. Kelly appreciated that, and she was thankful that he didn't offer her any trite assurances.

"What about the farm?" He asked. "It's just getting going. Won't this interfere?"

Kelly had not thought much about that.

"I can work that out," she said. "I won't be able to do any heavy work until after the baby's born or for a while after, but I can run things. Besides, there won't be much to do until the foals get to be two years old, and they aren't even bred yet."

Graham nodded.

"When is the baby due?" He asked.

"February," Kelly said.

February was a good ways off, Graham thought. Maybe the time between then and now would give them both some time to get accustomed to the idea.

"Well, let's go have some supper," he said. "After we eat, let's take the day off and go swimming to celebrate."

Kelly smiled—a real smile with no wryness in it. That he wanted to celebrate eased her mind. She had been worried that he might not be happy over having a baby, but apparently, he was happy over it, even if he was cautious of her feelings about the matter. Well, the baby was seven months from being born, and there was plenty of time for his cautiousness to wear away—and hers, too, for that matter.

Chapter 58

But summer just slipped away from them, and fall seemed shorter than it had the year before. October brought snow, and Kelly shut the farm down for the winter. In her sixth month of pregnancy, she found the barn work awkward, and Graham slowly took over doing it. By the end of December, she had stopped working almost entirely, but she often went down to the barn with Graham when he did the chores. Nothing would ever seem quite so cozy to her as a warm barn filled with well-cared for horses.

December also brought several heavy storms, and snow lay deep on the ground. Kelly, who seemed oblivious to both the snow and to her thickening waist line, spent the days reading or playing cards with Graham, who was becoming concerned over the approaching birth.

His concern grew because Kelly never mentioned her condition except to comment occasionally that being pregnant was surely the most awkward state a person could be in. It seemed to him that she wasn't thinking of the birth itself and the fact that, if they got snowed in, there would be no one to help her except himself.

After keeping silent for months, he finally broached the subject with Kelly by suggesting that they move into town for the rest of the winter.

"I don't want to," Kelly replied.

"If there's a storm," Graham said, "I won't be able to get the doctor out here."

Kelly frowned at him. She did not appreciate the implication that she had not been thinking the matter through clearly.

"There might not be a storm," Kelly replied. "And I don't want to leave here and live in some hotel room all winter."

"What's wrong with hotel rooms?" He asked. "You never objected to them before."

"I've had my fill of hotel rooms."

"Well, I never knew you to be a homebody," Graham said, annoyed that she would not listen to reason.

"That's because you never knew me to have a home before," she snapped.

Taken aback, Graham stared at her, then returned to the argument.

"You're not being sensible," he said, maintaining a calm tone despite his annoyance. "Who's going to deliver the baby if I can't get the doctor?"

"I will," Kelly said calmly.

"You'll need some help."

"Nonsense. I've delivered about a hundred foals in my time," Kelly said. "And, it's not like I never had a baby before."

"Foals? What are you talking about? That's not the same thing at all," Graham said incredulously.

"Certainly it is," Kelly said firmly. "Foals just have longer legs."

She sounded so certain that he was almost convinced. Then another thought came to him.

"Well, what about the pain? How are you going to do everything that needs doing if you're in pain?"

Kelly stood up, her annoyance finally getting the better of her. In her opinion, this conversation had gone entirely too far.

"Don't sit there and tell me what it's like to have a baby. You don't have any idea of what it's like. And don't sit there and talk to me like I haven't thought this out, either. I haven't done hardly anything but think about it. I guess I know what I'm talking about."

She stomped out of the room. Undeterred by her anger, Graham followed her.

"You may be thinking about it," he said. "But you're also being bullheaded about it."

"That's my right," Kelly replied. "You once told me you never asked anyone their opinion about a subject on which they were completely ignorant. Well, I follow the same policy."

She went into their room and sat on the bed. Graham followed her, closing the door behind him.

"I'm just concerned for you," he said. "So there's no reason to take that tone to me."

"If you're concerned for me," Kelly said firmly but less angrily. "You'll stop bothering me over this, because I'm not leaving here, and that's all there is to it."

Her chin was stuck out, and her face had reddened.

"Shit," Graham muttered, knowing there was no point in pursuing the argument. The only way he'd get her into town now was to pick her up and carry her. Even that wasn't a sure bet, not even when you considered the fact that she was seven months pregnant.

He sat beside her on the bed. Kelly felt bad over having had to fight with him, but he had insisted. She took his hand and held it.

"It'll all work out, you'll see," she said. "Besides, it might not even be a problem. You know you can't bet on the weather."

"No, but you can bet it will be bad if you want it to be good," he replied. "I just don't want anything to happen to you."

"I know that. But even with a doctor, there's no promises about anything."

That was true enough, but it wasn't exactly comforting. Still, it was her decision, and he had to trust her judgment, which he had never had trouble doing before.

The rest of December was mild. The snow lay frozen on the ground, but no new snow fell. Graham began to think that, perhaps, his worry had been unjustified after all. Kelly noticed that his mood had lightened some but never asked why, guessing it was because of the weather and not wanting to risk another argument. She was in good spirits and health but anxious to be done with being pregnant.

January started out as mild as December. It was cold, but the skies were clear. Kelly continued going down to the barn with Graham when he did the chores even though he no longer let her help him even a little. She liked to get out of the house and into the fresh air, but privately, she was glad that Graham would not let her do any work. Though she said nothing about it, she tired easily these days and doubted that the baby would wait until February or that the weather would hold clear much longer.

Both her doubts were proven accurate. The third week of January brought gray skies and high winds. Midweek, a blizzard set in, the first blizzard they'd had since November. It started early in the morning, and Kelly lay in bed listening to the snowy winds tear around the house and thinking that it would last several days. She patted her distended abdomen, feeling with sudden certainty that her days of being pregnant were sharply numbered.

The blizzard still raged the next day. Again, Kelly lay in bed, listening to Graham's breathing, a pleasant feeling of expectation in her heart as she felt the first cramps pass over her. In a matter of hours, she knew, the baby would be born. For the first time, she let herself wonder if it would be a boy or a girl.

Of course, because of the storm, there would be no one to help her, but that did not scare her. Birth might be a mystery, but it was one in which she had already been initiated. She knew that the pain could be endured, and she knew what needed to be done. There was nothing to fear, unless she chose to fear the awesome power of her own body. There was much that could go wrong, but those things were not in her hands.

She stayed in bed while Graham got up and built up the fire in the kitchen. When the house was good and warm, she got up and put her robe on. After breakfast, Graham suggested a card game, and they sat at the table playing until nearly noon. Kelly had said nothing to him about the approaching birth, knowing that he would want to get the doctor, which was foolishness in such weather.

"That's the fifth hand in a row you've lost, Kelly," he said. "You sure you feel like playing?"

"I have kind of lost interest in the game," Kelly said, shuffling the cards. The pains were becoming steadily harder and more frequent. "Want to play some rummy?"

"Fine." Graham leaned forward, peering at her, then brushed her forehead with the tips of his fingers. They came away wet.

"You're sweating," he said. "Do you have a fever? It's not that warm in here."

"I'm going to have the baby today," she said calmly, starting to deal them each seven cards.

She said it so matter of factly that Graham forgot to be concerned over it.

"Let me know when you want me to go for the doctor," he said.

"You aren't going for any doctor in this weather," Kelly replied.

"I mostly certainly am," Graham said.

"Don't be silly," Kelly said. "Even if you got there, you'd never get back in time. I think it won't be more than a couple of hours now."

"Why didn't you tell me sooner," he demanded, suddenly realizing that the crisis was upon them.

Kelly ignored the question. It was perfectly obvious why she hadn't told him. There was nothing he could accomplish by running around in a blizzard, and she had enough on her mind without having to worry about him freezing to death.

Graham guessed what was in her mind and decided not to argue further. Besides, she was right. She needed him here to help her.

"Let me help you to bed," he said.

"No, not yet," Kelly replied. "I'll let you know when. Just let me sit here for awhile longer."

So they sat and waited. As the time passed, Kelly became increasingly restless. Sweat beaded on her forehead, and she paced the room, panting softly. Walking became too difficult, and she sat down heavily in her chair.

"It's time," she said. And though she said it softly and

calmly, Graham jumped as though she'd fired a rifle.

"Boil up those scissors for me, would you?" She asked. "And I'll need a pan of water. Use that Dutch oven."

He nodded, and Kelly went to the bedroom. Her stride had taken on a spraddling aspect.

When the scissors had boiled, he wrapped them in a clean cloth and went to their room. He rapped softly on the door, and to his surprise, Kelly opened it.

"You ought to be in bed," he said, handing her the scissors.

"I'm on my way," she replied, placing the scissors on the bed table and the pan of water on a chair that she had pulled up to the bedside.

Graham saw that she had covered the bed with her slicker, over which she had placed an old sheet. The washtub stood at the foot of the bed, and she had cut up an old but clean blanket into three smaller blankets, which lay on the head of the bed near a clean nightgown. Everything would be within easy reach once she was in bed.

Concentrating on the pain and the contractions, Kelly briefly debated whether or not she ought to send him out of the room. It would be a comfort to have him there, but the blood and her pain would no doubt upset him, although she knew he would not lose his nerve. In the end, she decided that she needed to do this alone, with no worry or unnecessary presence to distract her from it. If something went wrong, she could always call him.

"You better go on back to the kitchen," she said, getting onto the bed. "I'll yell if I need you."

Graham left the room somewhat reluctantly, but he trusted her when she said that she would call him if the need arose. Kelly wouldn't lie to him about anything, and certainly not about something that important.

When the door closed behind him, Kelly pulled her nightgown up over her hips. Her water broke a few seconds later. She checked to make sure that the scissors and clean towels were close at hand.

The pains had shifted from her vagina to her bottom, which she remembered from Laura's birth as heralding the beginning of the end. She leaned back against the headboard and gripped it during her efforts.

Everything else faded from her senses as she rode the pain and pushed. She groaned from the effort at times, and her back arched with the strength of it, but at last the baby's head appeared between her legs.

Strengthened suddenly, she renewed her efforts, trying to keep her eyes open as the baby slid out of her and on to the bed.

Panting hard, she took the scissors and cut the umbilical cord, noticing with a vague sense of surprise that it was a boy. For some reason, she had expected it to be a girl.

Her fingers shook as she tied the cord off. Steam rose from

the baby, which was squalling heartily. Hot and sweaty from her labor, Kelly had forgotten that the room must be cold. She hastily wrapped the baby in one of the small blankets that she had made and lifted it from the bloody sheet.

The baby continued to cry, but the sound did not frighten her; it relieved her. He had to be healthy in order to make such a noise. She held the baby to her breast and let it grope at her nipple.

A few minutes later, she felt more pains, and the afterbirth slid out of her. The baby had stopped crying, and Kelly slumped back against the headboard, relieved that it was all done with except for cleaning up the mess.

Without getting up, she rolled up the afterbirth in the sheet and put it in the washtub. The slicker, which had been underneath the sheet, was bloody too, so she folded it and put it in on top of the washtub.

The pan of water beside the bed was cold now, but she washed herself as well as she could. She had originally planned to wash the baby in that pan, but she knew the room and the water were too cold. She would have to do it in the kitchen near the fire, and it would have to wait until tomorrow. She did not plan on getting out of bed again that day.

Now that her labor was over, the room felt cold to her, too. The sweat on her skin chilled her, and she wiped her face dry and put on the clean nightshirt, then she climbed back into bed and pulled to covers up over herself and the baby, which she nestled in the crook of her arm.

After laying still a moment, Kelly felt a sudden sweeping sense of exhilaration. The feeling had beckoned to her when the baby had first left her body, but she had pushed it aside, afraid that it would distract her into forgetting to do something important. Now, she stopped resisting it and let herself enjoy it. She slid under the covers and unwrapped the baby, looking it over carefully as it started to wriggle.

His eyes were tightly shut and looked kind of puffy, and his head was covered with fine hair, the color of which she could not determine because he was still all bloody. She was halfway minded to get out of bed and give him a proper bath when Graham knocked at the door and called her name. Feeling a little guilty for having forgotten about him, Kelly hastily wrapped the baby up again and told Graham to come in.

He poked his head in the door as if expecting some unknown adversary to come leaping out of nowhere, and Kelly giggled, still feeling lightheaded and happy. The sound of her giggling seemed to disturb Graham further. Kelly laughed frequently but giggled only rarely.

"There's no boogey man in here," she said. "Come on in and have a look at our baby."

Graham came in and sat gingerly on the edge of the bed.

Kelly looked tired and worn but well. None of the darkness that had haunted her after Laura's birth seemed to be around her now, and he felt relieved.

"Are you all right?" He asked.

Kelly nodded.

"It was much easier this time."

Graham looked at her doubtfully. There was a bloody mess in the washtub, and her hair was stringy with sweat. Much easier looked pretty damn hard to him, but then, Kelly also thought getting thrown from wild horses was entertaining.

Kelly saw him glance at the washtub and then at her. She had neatened things up as much as possible, she thought, but she ought to have combed her hair and pushed the washtub underneath the bed. Well, it was impossible to think of everything.

Feeling a little shy but very proud, she sat up and showed him the baby. Despite his efforts at keeping a poker face, Kelly saw that he was somewhat taken aback by the baby's appearance. She giggled some more, remembering that she'd had much the same reaction when she had first seen Laura.

"Why's she all red?" Graham asked.

"It's a he," Kelly said. "That's blood. I can't wash him in here; it's too cold."

Graham hardly heard her. That day months ago when she had told him that she was pregnant, he had never really understood the meaning of her words. He had not understood that those words had meant that he would, one day, find himself looking a tiny, red, writhing baby that was partly him and partly her and would grow to be a person all its own.

Now he understood, but he could not say what it meant to him, and when he looked at Kelly and saw her smile a knowing smile at him, he knew that there was no need for him to say anything. Maybe, he thought, there weren't any words that could say such things anyway. Maybe such things could only be said in looks and in touching.

"Here," Kelly said, holding the baby out to him. "Hold him."

Graham took the baby. Kelly helped him get his arms adjusted properly. She noticed that he did not hesitate to take the child from her and showed a surprising aptitude for holding it. To her mind, these things contrasted sharply with her own total bewilderment about handling Laura as a newborn.

She watched them for a while, and then her tiredness caught up with her. She lay back against her pillows and Graham placed the baby back in the crook of her arm. She fell asleep almost immediately, glad that this happiness had not eluded her.

Chapter 59

Kelly felt a little dizzy when she saw how quickly the rest of that winter passed. The strain of nursing and caring for a newborn left her tired, but the depression she had feared did not settle into oppress her. There was nothing ahead of them except good things, she felt, and the farm was waiting for her when the weather turned warm.

They never discussed names for the baby. Kelly just started calling him Andrew, and Graham followed suit. Graham was pleased that she called the boy after him and relieved that she had not started calling him Graham. That would have made things too confusing.

Aside from feedings and changings and a bout with the colic, Andrew was, to Kelly, an amazingly easy baby to care for. He was also very quiet. After thinking about it, Kelly decided that she had been foolish to assume that all babies were the same. Laura had been a noisy baby, and Andrew was a quiet baby. No doubt time would reveal other differences as well.

A quiet baby, but not all that quiet, Kelly thought groggily as his cries woke her at three in the morning. She felt too tired to get up and lay still for a moment, trying to wake herself a little more.

"Want me to get him?" Graham asked, sounding as awake as though he had never slept in his life.

"Please," Kelly said, thinking it was good to have a light sleeper in the house, especially one who didn't mind changing diapers.

Graham got out of bed and checked Andrew's diaper.

"He's not wet," Graham said. "He must be hungry."

Nodding, Kelly pulled herself into a sitting position, and Graham brought Andrew to her. Kelly yawned and took the baby, cooing sleepily at him as she unbuttoned her nightshirt.

Graham got back into bed. Kelly leaned tiredly back against his chest as she nursed the baby, who fell asleep immediately after feeding. Kelly buttoned her shirt back up and fell asleep herself, the baby still asleep at her bosom. Graham, however, stayed awake the rest of the night. To him, it had always been a tremendous thing that someone as independently minded and strong-willed as Kelly would lay her head on his shoulder and go to sleep. Now it was more than tremendous to see a baby curled up there too.

Spring brought new life to the farm, and their winter leisure vanished seemingly in a moment. Two foals were born that spring, the garden needed planting, the barn roof needed patching, and the house needed cleaning. Graham was itching to play some real poker, and with this in mind, he offered to ride into town for the supplies they needed. Kelly declined to go with him but took the time to write out a lengthy shopping list.

"I wish there was a way to send Alice a letter," Kelly said as she scribbled the list out.

"She knows what happened in Wyoming, I expect," Graham said. "I'm sure it was in the papers."

"Yes, but it would tickle her to know we got married," Kelly replied. "Check and see if there's some way it could be done."

"She'll just write back to say 'I told you so'."

"Well, she's entitled. I don't grudge it to her."

Kelly stopped writing and read the list over. It seemed like she was forgetting something but could not figure out what. No matter, she could ride in herself in a day or two if it was that important.

"Here you go," she said, handing him the list. Graham read it over.

"I sort of wish Alice were here now," Kelly said. "I do miss her molasses cookies."

Graham pocketed the list.

"I'll be back before morning, but not by much," he said. "All this shopping is going to put me behind in my card playing."

"Sorry."

Kelly did not sound very apologetic. Spring was not an easy time for her to be trapped in the house either, and until he returned, she would have to stay in the house to watch Andrew. Of course, the horses didn't need that much attention and she enjoyed watching Andrew, but it was a rare day for a gallop through the woods.

There was a long line in the general store and a longer one

in the feed store. It was late afternoon before Graham had the wagon loaded, and he was irritated. Everything had taken twice as long as he had expected. The town had grown over the winter and was growing even faster now that good weather had set in.

He was just tying the tarp down over everything when a grizzled old man walked toward him from the hotel. Even from the corner of his eye, Graham could see that the man was too gray and too bent to be dangerous, but nonetheless, his hands hung loose by his guns.

"Mr. McNair?" The old man asked.

"Who wants to know?"

"M' name's Sam Simkin," the old man said placidly. "I heard you got a place and might need some hep w' it."

"Where'd you hear that?"

"T' hotel."

"It's a horse breaking place," Graham said.

The man nodded. "So they say. I been a cook for a cattle outfit down south. I can keep the place fed, all right, and good-fed men work better."

Graham considered it. Neither he nor Kelly cared much for working in a kitchen, and Kelly had been talking about hiring on some wranglers and trading in half-wild horses while the foals grew up. Since Kelly's plans nearly always came to be sooner or later, having a cook might not be a bad idea.

"Why'd you come north?" Graham asked him.

"Passed sixty in the winter," Sam replied. "I reckon they wanted someone feistier."

Graham nodded, satisfied. There were enough feisty people in the house already. An even-tempered cook would be a blessing.

"There's only two of us right now, so you'll have time to work the garden, if that don't irk you," Graham said.

"Sure don't. I'll milk a cow if you got one, too," Sam offered. "And I'm a right good hand with chickens to boot."

They didn't have a cow or chickens, but they probably ought to set about getting some, Graham thought, a little rankled by the thought. It was too much like being squatters to suit him. But if someone else took care of them it wouldn't be so bad . . .

"Room and board and five dollars a month," Graham said. "How's that?"

"Fine. Fine."

"Well, climb up on the wagon. We'll give you a try."

Graham decided to pass on his card game. If, after a few days, Sam worked out, he would come back in and play some cards, and maybe Kelly would come too. Pleased to have landed the job, Sam climbed up onto the wagon. He had been on the tramp for two months and looked forward to settling in somewhere with good people.

Graham finished tying the tarp down and climbed onto the

wagon, picking up the reins.

"I don't suppose you can make molasses cookies," he asked abruptly.

"Sure can," Sam said.

Smiling, Graham slapped the reins on the horse's back. This might be worth missing a night of cards.

Chapter 60

Kelly greeted Sam with some surprise and some doubt. She did not much care to have a stranger in her house. Of course, when she considered the matter, she had grown up with servants in the house, but they had not seemed like strangers. Nell, in particular, had always seemed more like a friend or a family member.

But after the first morning, she felt a little less wary of the situation. It was wonderful to wake up and have breakfast already cooked and waiting, Kelly thought as she dressed Andrew. She sniffed appreciatively as she carried the baby down the hall and into the kitchen, where Sam greeted her cheerfully.

"Good morning, Miz McNair. It's a right pretty day out, ain't it?"

"Good morning. Yes it is," Kelly replied, thinking that she would never get used to being called "Miz McNair," even if she lived to be a hundred.

Kelly sat at the table, and Sam set a plate in front of her—pancakes and bacon—and there wasn't a biscuit in sight. Yes, she thought she could get used to having Sam around.

"I'm aimin' t' hoe the garden today," Sam said as he continued to fry pancakes. "Where's the hoe kept?"

"In the lean-to out back," Kelly said. "There's a hatchet out there too, if you need it. How is your room?"

"Grand. Couldn't ask for better than a feather mattress. Such things mean a lot at this age."

"Well, if you need something, let us know."

"That's right kind of you."

Kelly finished her breakfast in record time, no longer doubting that Sam would work out just fine. Now if she could just find some stable hands, the horse end of the trade ought to pick up. She was minded to trade in adult horses until the horses she was breeding were old enough to sell. But in order to do so, she would need some help with the rough work.

Sam soon became invaluable to her—it was wonderful to be free of the house work, and he made the best cookies she'd ever had. Under his care, the garden flourished mightily, and when they bought a nesting of chickens later that month, he tended them with careful devotion.

Now that she had only Andrew and the horses to look after, she felt as though didn't have enough to do. She was also worried at the way they had been spending money. There was money enough to be made at the poker tables, but to her mind, that was not a sure enough source of income, considering all the responsibilities they now had.

So when summer was good started, Kelly bought a string of half-wild horses and took on two wranglers to help her break them. Both men lived in town and rode back and forth for the day's work. Kelly paid them ten dollars a month and supper.

But though willing workers, neither of the two men were much with horses, and Kelly found that they required constant supervision. Kelly became more and more occupied down at the barns but felt that the time was well spent as horses came and went and she turned a profit in the meantime. There were so many more things that they would need this winter.

As fall began to set in, Graham spent most of his days hunting. Because the town had boomed over the summer, game had become more scarce, and he often went out on two or three day hunting expeditions. Ordinarily, it wouldn't have taken so much time, but Sam was terribly fussy about what sort of game he brought back, and the trips took his mind off the fact that Kelly was so preoccupied with the horses these days.

Chapter 61

By the time the leaves began to turn color, Jake and Sherman had ridden east, almost to the base of the mountains, and had found no trace of Kelly. They stopped to rest in a small, nameless town two days' ride from the border. Jake didn't really feel a need to stop, but Sherm was getting whiny, and Jake figured that a few days of sport and losing at cards would perk him up some.

Preoccupied with his hunt, Jake himself had little time for such things. He had worked as a bounty hunter down in Texas, and aside from marshaling, it was the only work that he had ever been good at doing. The hardest part about tracking people down was figuring out enough about them so that you could second guess them.

With most lawless types, this was an easy task, for he had found most of them to be pretty much on the stupid side. Sometimes, knowing that they were being hunted and gave them a kind of animal wariness, and almost all of them were vicious, but in the end, they always gave themselves away.

Jake had never met Kelly and had never seen her, but from the stories he'd heard about her, he felt he could make some guesses. The best place to look for a wrangler was around horses, and since Kelly liked the high country so well, she might be found there, too. As she was also a good card player, her trail might be picked up by talking with other card players or by overhearing their conversations.

With these things in mind, Jake spent his time in town drifting between the saloons and the livery stable, listening to whatever talk he could. Asking a lot of questions was a clumsy way to go about such work; excessive interest in something was always noticed and remembered and could easily get back to the wrong ears.

It was with this in mind that he idled near the livery stable one day, listening to two scraggly looking wranglers talk. Their conversation was difficult to follow, for they spoke in a puzzling mixture of French and English, and Jake had never understood even one word of French. Still, he gathered that, a few miles north of town, there lived a woman given to wearing pants and carrying guns, who made occasional forays into town to sell furs or meat.

Concealing his interest, Jake listened until the two men drifted off to their work, then he hotfooted it back to the town's only saloon, where he knew Sherman would be. Since it wasn't yet eleven o'clock, Sherman should be over last night's toot and, hopefully, had not yet started out on a fresh one.

Sherm was still sober but unenthusiastic at having to interrupt his sport to go riding out after Kelly. He did not voice any complaints, however. Instead, he kept silent and reminded himself that, if it were Kelly and they finished her off today, he could go back south and finally get shed of Jake.

Jake used all caution as they slowly rode north. After riding for several hours, they spotted a trail of chimney smoke and rode toward it. The smoke led them to a ramshackle cabin surrounded by trees.

Sherman hung back as Jake rode forward, his gun drawn, uncertain as to whether there was anyone in the cabin or not.

Then the door creaked open a crack, and a rifle muzzle poked out.

"That there's fur enough," called a raspy voice.

Jake pulled up; the voice was deep enough to be a man's. Perhaps their quarry lay elsewhere.

"We don't mean no harm," he called back. "We're just lookin' for town. Ain't there one 'round here someplace?"

"Put up them guns then," ordered the voice.

Jake holstered his revolver and motioned for Sherm to do the same.

The door creaked open, and a gaunt, tallish woman wearing overalls stepped out, still holding the rifle ready. Jake cast a glance at Sherman, who shook his head slightly. Sherman had only seen Kelly once or twice, and that nearly ten years ago in Denver, but no one could be more unlike her than the woman who now held a rifle on them. Kelly had been short and lean, though curvy through the hips. This woman was taller than he was and straight as a bean pole. Her black hair was shot through with gray, and Kelly had been yellow haired.

"If it's town you want," she said, "ride south. Ten, fifteen miles, mebbe."

Disgruntled, Jake backed his horse away, unwilling to turn his back on anyone who was holding a rifle on him. When he was out of range, he and Sherm wheeled their horses around and spurred them away.

As he rode, Jake's anger grew, fueled by his disappointment, until he reined in abruptly. Jake fashioned a torch from a fallen branch, his spare shirt, and a generous dousing of whiskey from his flask, then he wheeled his horse about and rode back to that cabin.

Sherm waited for him. He was too far away to see exactly what Jake was up to, but soon, smoke smudged the air over where the cabin stood, and Sherm heard gun shots. He waited, not really caring whether Jake came back or not.

But Jake did ride back, and together, they rode back to town. Sherm never asked what had transpired, and Jake never told him. The blazing fire had improved Jake's mood some, but nonetheless, he decided that Sherm would have to cut his toot short by a day. This town could tell them nothing else. It was time to ride on.

Chapter 62

Winter brought a halt to the horse work, and Kelly let both wranglers go. She could see to the chores herself, and since it was winter, there was no other work to be done. The chores only took three or four hours each day, and that left her plenty of time to do nothing.

But there was never nothing to do. Andrew was crawling, and Kelly often remarked that he crawled faster and better than most people walked. By the middle of November, he would walk, if she held both hands or if he could hold onto the furniture.

"Look here, Graham," Kelly said delightedly one day. A storm was howling outside, and she was walking Andrew around the front room, pleased that he was walking more steadily and that most of the lurching aspect had left his gait.

Graham, who had been lying on the settee, sat up to watch.

"He'll be walking by himself anytime now," Kelly said. "I never saw a baby grow so fast."

Graham refrained from reminding her how limited her experience with babies was.

"I bet Sam a dollar that he would be walking by March," Kelly went on. "Sam says little boys take longer about such things."

"How much longer 'til you teach him to ride?" Graham asked.

"Oh, two years or so," Kelly replied, ignoring the joke. "He's not adventurous."

Kelly steered Andrew toward the sofa.

"Let's go see poppa," she said. "Come on, two more steps,

whoops!"

Andrew lurched forward for the last two steps and almost collided with Graham's knee, but Kelly swung him into the air at the last second.

"There you go," she said, plopping him down on Graham's lap. "That was nearly a boom."

"When will he start to talk?"

"When he's ready I expect," Kelly said. "Laura was noisy from the minute she was born, but both her parents were big talkers. Andrew seems to take after you more, and you sure never speak until you're ready."

"You think he takes after me?"

"Well, he didn't get that auburn hair and those solemn eyes from anyone in my family."

"My hair's brown."

"Now maybe, but I bet it wasn't when you were a baby."

Kelly grinned. It was something to think about—what he had been like as a baby.

Andrew tried to wiggle down off the settee, and Graham helped him.

"He feels wet," Graham said. "Want me to change him?"

"That's OK," Kelly said, standing up. "I'll do it. It's time for his nap anyway."

She scooped the baby up and carried him out of the room, returning about ten minutes later.

"I can't get over how easily he'll take a nap, either," she said. "I never could get Laura to take one with out her having a conniption."

"Well, the conniption was probably what tired her enough to need a nap."

Kelly pushed back the curtains and peered out the window. It was late afternoon but the driving snow blocked out the sun and obliterated everything else. She let the curtain fall back over the window and looked over at Graham, who was still sitting on the sofa, watching her.

She walked over to him and sat on his lap so that she faced him. He leaned forward to hug her, and she put her arms around his neck. Sitting there, with his head resting against her bosom and her cheek resting on his head, Kelly heard the wind rattling the eaves and had a sudden vision of all the long years she had spent alone.

At the time, those years hadn't seem long, and they hadn't seemed lonely, but remembering them now made her hold him tighter and wonder if she had maybe taken him for granted a little over the previous summer and fall.

They let go of each other a little, but Kelly did not get up, and Graham, who was enjoying the feel of her fingers playing through his hair, did not suggest it. Very gently, she kissed his forehead, and when he closed his eyes, she kissed his eyelids, and the end of his nose. Under her kisses, he leaned back against the sofa, and she stopped for a second, touching his face and marveling in her heart at how peaceful his expression had become, then she kissed his lips.

"Sam's likely to come in here any second," he muttered.

Kelly didn't answer, knowing that he couldn't be too concerned about it, since he had started unbuttoning her shirt and knowing that the only conversation they needed to have didn't require words.

Chapter 63

Kelly won her bet with Sam. Andrew started walking just after his first birthday. His seeming cautiousness over letting go of the furniture had worried her some, but when he did let go, she thought he walked like a champ.

"See there," she said triumphantly as he tottered over to her. "We won't be able to keep a hold of him now."

Andrew took two more stumbling steps and gripped her knee. She and Graham were sitting in the kitchen. Sam was down at the barn milking the cow that Kelly had bought the previous fall.

"I don't know about that," Graham said doubtfully. "Looks to me like a breath of wind would knock him flat."

"He'll catch the hang of it in no time," she said proudly. "Now that he's got his nerve up, he can get all the practice he needs."

Graham made no answer, and Kelly watched him surreptitiously. The winter had been a long one, and they had all had a touch of cabin fever; Graham had been slowly becoming more and more silent since the new year. Now spring beckoned, and just the freshness of the air and the greenness that was bursting out everywhere was enough to cure her, and Sam too, it seemed.

Graham, however, did not seem at all cheered by the approach of friendlier weather. He frequently fell into silences that reminded her of when she had first met him. Back then, he had sometimes used silence to protect himself or to punish her, and now, she thought, he was maybe trying to do a little of both.

She had asked him about it once but to no avail.

"Talk to Sam if you want conversation," he had said.

"I don't want conversation," Kelly had replied patiently. "I want to know what's eating at you."

"Nothing," he had said firmly.

But he had not convinced her, and even though it irked her, she thought she understood it some. He was probably bored with such a settled life.

Spring set in with its usual rush of work, and Kelly had little time to worry about Graham's moods. Four new foals were born that spring, and Kelly was relieved when Pete and Andre showed up for work again.

During the first week of June, the last foal was born at four o'clock one morning. Kelly was down at the barns all night to help with the birth, and when it was done with and the long-legged foal was nursing contentedly, the sun was up. She went happily up to the house and woke Andrew, changing his diaper and dressing him.

Sam was frying sidemeat when she carried Andrew into the kitchen and plopped him down at the table.

"Has Mr. Graham been up yet?" She asked Sam.

"Nope. Not yet. Did that horse get born?"

"Yes, it's a little colt with legs ten miles long. Watch the baby for me, will you?"

"Sure."

Kelly went back down the hall to their room. When she opened the door she saw that Graham was still in bed, so she closed it quietly behind herself in order to not disturb him.

She washed her face and hands, then let her hair down and brushed it out. Behind her, on the bed, Graham stirred and sat up.

"Are you just getting in?" He asked.

"I've been in long enough to get the baby up and dressed. That new foal has got a classy look to him."

"That's the last one, is it?"

"Yes, for this year, anyway," Kelly answered, trying to keep the disappointment from her voice.

"Why don't you come in to town with me tonight?" Graham asked, thinking she would jump at the chance to have some fun.

"I'll be too tired," she replied.

"Take a nap after breakfast."

"I can't, there's too much to do."

"Let those useless wranglers of yours do it," Graham said, unable to keep aggravation from creeping into his voice. What was she making excuses for? "Why the hell else are you paying them?"

"I'm paying them to do the things I don't want to do," Kelly said patiently. It wasn't clear to her whether he was needling her for fun or because he was angry over something.

347

"Seems to me," Graham said, his voice becoming flat, "that you enjoy their company a mite too much for just that."

Calm tone of voice or not, that sounded like an accusation—and an insulting one, too.

"What the hell is that supposed to mean?" She demanded.

"Just what I said."

"If you mean to imply . . ." Kelly started, heatedly, but he interrupted her.

"I'm not implying anything. It's a plain fact that you haven't spent a whole night in here with me for almost two weeks."

"I didn't have any idea that I would be missed," Kelly snapped. He was making it sound like she was out tearing up the town or something instead of delivering foals and tending their son. "When I am here, you act like I'm not."

She stomped out of the room, slamming the door behind her. He didn't want to fight; he wanted to aggravate her. She could tell because he had kept his poker face the whole time. When he was really mad, he acted like it. When he was just starting to get mad, he tried to hide it, and if it happened to slip out, he acted like it didn't matter much.

Once back in the kitchen, she sat Andrew on her lap and began feeding him. Graham came in as they were eating and had a cup of coffee but ate nothing himself. Kelly ignored him completely, still wounded by what she considered a malicious attack.

As she cajoled Andrew into taking another forkful of eggs, she happened to look up, and saw that Graham was watching them, his eyes traveling from her to Andrew, with a bewildered but softhearted look on his face. In light of the fight they'd had less than ten minutes ago, seeing him look so surprised her and made her wonder if she could have somehow prevented the fight. She looked away quickly, surprised though she was, lest he catch her looking and close himself up again.

That look haunted her most of the day, and when she thought of it, she lost interest in her work and puzzled over it. By the end of the day, she thought that she had worked things out satisfactorily in her own mind, and she went up to the house tired but ready to try and mend some fences.

Since he plainly did not want to talk about whatever gripe he had, Kelly did not try and force a conversation.

"I'm sorry I can't go into town this evening," she said as she took her bath. "But I would like to go tomorrow, after I'm rested."

Graham was lying on the bed, fiddling with a deck of cards. He heard the conciliatory note in her voice, and it offended him. Andrew could be distracted from a bad mood if she dangled the right toy in front of him, but Andrew was a baby.

"Don't bother yourself."

"It's no bother."

"I know you don't like to leave Andrew here alone."

"I'll put him to bed before we go. He'll never know we're gone," Kelly replied. "I like us fighting less than I like anything else I can think of."

"We're not fighting."

Kelly stood and wrapped herself in a towel.

"We're not getting along, either," she said. "You don't really think I'd mess around with anyone as chinless as those two wranglers, do you?"

Graham set his deck of cards down and got up off the bed. To her dismay, Kelly saw that he was heading for the door. She intercepted him halfway, stopping him by laying a hand on his arm.

"Do you?" She asked softly.

Graham looked down at her. Her shoulders were still wet, and damp straggles of hair hung down around her face. He could see some hurt in her eyes, and some heat, and he could see the scar on her shoulder, reminding him of the first time it had been revealed to him.

"No," he said.

Her hand left his arm and rested on his chest, toying with the buttons in his shirt. They stood so for a moment, then he stepped away from her and left the room.

Frustrated, Kelly stomped her foot and sat down on the bed. She dried herself, then went and looked at her face closely in the mirror, wondering if she had gotten a pimple or something.

Chapter 64

That night, it was her turn to sleep alone. True, Graham rode back from town just after midnight, but he sat in the kitchen and played solitaire until sun up. He maintained his previous silence during the next two weeks, and while Kelly made sure she was up to the house well before dinner and in bed by nine, things got no better; they got worse. Surely there was nothing worse than sleeping in the same bed with someone who acted like you weren't even there and who froze up if you happened to touch him, whether by accident or on purpose.

His silence began to grate on Kelly. She hated being ignored worse than she hated anything else in the whole world. Whether he was purposely blocking her out or whether he was reacting blindly to circumstance, she could not tell, but either way, it was intolerable. Her temper began to strain.

She sat down to eat dinner one evening, alone except for Andrew, who gurgled in his chair, oblivious to Kelly's sour mood. Sam had disappeared to somewhere, and Kelly was nearly done eating when Graham came in and sat down without a word.

"Sam's out done himself tonight," she said to him.

He nodded but did not reply. Kelly fumed silently, but a sudden thought came to her.

"Why don't you ride out for a few days or week or something?" She suggested "Scratch your traveling foot a little. I expect Devereaux is getting tiresome for you."

Graham flinched when she spoke, for he had been thinking of doing just that, but the thought had made him feel a little guilty. It would be interesting to travel for a bit, but there was plenty to be done here as well. Kelly had other help these days, but feeling like he wasn't needed around the place was no comforting thought.

"I'm not that shiftless," he said.

"You're not shiftless at all," Kelly said quietly, pleased that he had answered. "But this farm was my idea, not yours, and I don't hold that against you. This past year has been a lot of hard work; you're entitled to have some fun."

That was about how he had thought of it, but hearing her say it made him uneasy. It was as though she had read his mind, and whenever he realized exactly how close she had gotten to him, it made him antsy.

"Most wives don't take such an attitude," he said shortly. "At least not the ones that still love their husbands."

With an effort, Kelly refrained from uttering the first angry thing that had popped into her head.

"I can't speak for other wives," Kelly said, maintaining her quiet tone of voice. "But I say go if you want. It's better than having you mope around the house. Just stay out of the sporting houses—that's all I ask."

"And how will you know what I do or don't do?" He challenged.

"I'll know," Kelly replied. "Don't think for a moment that I won't."

The sudden sharpness in her tone did not bother him, since he no intention of visiting any sporting houses anyway. Still, he dismissed the idea of leaving. Kelly frequently had crazy ideas. It was best to ignore them.

Kelly realized that the conversation was over when he did not answer. After she finished her meal, she picked Andrew up and went out on the front porch to enjoy the cool June evening.

The next morning at breakfast, Kelly finished eating quickly, determined to spend as little time in Graham's irritating presence as possible.

"You going into town this afternoon?" She asked, rising from the table and going to the stove.

She got no answer. She emptied the tin coffee pot into her cup and looked over at him. He was slouched in his chair, staring at the opposite wall. Sam was standing right there, starting some bread. He ought to at least be polite when servants were in the room, she fumed, setting her cup down and taking a tighter grip on the coffee pot.

"Are you going to town this afternoon?" She asked again, her voice tense with barely concealed anger.

Again, Graham made no reply. Infuriated, Kelly walked over behind him and smacked him on the back of the head with the coffee pot.

"Christ, woman!" Graham yelled, knocking his chair over as he jumped to his feet. Kelly stepped back away from him and put the pot back on the stove.

"Christ yourself," she said calmly. "Answer when you're spoken to."

He grabbed for her, and she dodged behind the table. He came after her, but she kept the table between them. After a few laps around, Graham stopped, and so did Kelly.

"What are you going to do when you catch me?" She asked snidely. "Beat me up?"

"No, I'm going to give you the spanking you should of had ten years ago."

"If you couldn't accomplish it then," she said. "What makes you think you can accomplish it now?"

He lunged for her, and they went around the table again, but he couldn't quite catch her. She was too agile around the corners. They stopped for another moment.

Graham still looked furious, and Kelly saw that she had misjudged his anger some. This, however, did not daunt her in the least.

"I don't know why you're so upset," she said. "The coffee pot's hardly dented at all."

Goaded, he lunged for her so quickly that Kelly was almost caught. At the last second before he laid hold of her arm, Kelly leapt up on to the table and down off the opposite side, banging through the screen door and running lightly down the steps and into the yard.

Cursing, Graham watched her run into the yard, but he did not pursue her. She turned and waved to him, and he cursed some more as she walked calmly to the barn.

He sat back down at the table. Sam, who had retreated into a corner during their fight, resumed his bread making without a comment or a raised eyebrow.

"Shit on it," Graham said, thinking that if she wanted him out of the house that badly, then fine, he would go.

Without further debate, he went back to their room and got a few things together, then he went down to the barn. Kelly was fussing with one of the new foals when he walked in.

"Going traveling?" She asked.

"Yes."

"Take that dun mare if you like. She has easy gaits."

Graham ignored her offer and saddled his bay gelding. Kelly stopped petting the foal and watched, thinking he still looked pretty angry. It was a shame to let him go off mad, but it could not be helped. She considered apologizing for having hit him with the coffee pot, but in order to do so properly, she would have to get close enough to touch him. As his mood had not changed, it was entirely possible that he was still mad enough to try spanking her, and that would give them something real to fight about.

So she hung back until he led his horse from the barn, then

352

she followed him out. He mounted up without a word.

"Enjoy yourself," she said.

"I intend to," he replied in a tone that made Kelly wonder if he'd forgotten what she'd said about staying out of the sporting houses.

Then he was riding away, and Kelly was standing alone in the barnyard, having second thoughts about the wisdom of letting him out on his own. Shrugging, she turned and went back to the barn. Once he fought his anger back down, he would see the truth of the situation, and it would all be worth it if he came back in a better mood.

Peace of mind came from an unexpected source. Sam, who saw and heard everything but never commented on anything, watched her as she fed Andrew that evening. Sam was eating his own dinner. Andrew was fussy that night and feeding him was a chore—and a messy one, too.

"Did Mr. Graham get on his way this morning?" Sam asked her.

"Yes," Kelly said, using a spoon to scrape mashed potatos from Andrew's chin.

"It was right smart of you to send him off."

"What do you mean?" She asked sharply, looking over at him.

"Nothing makes a man appreciate his home life more than having his woman remind him she can do for herself," Sam replied, a little hesitantly in the face of her sharpness.

But Kelly just laughed and went back to feeding Andrew. She had not thought about it in those terms, but if it were true, well, so much for the better. It eased her misgivings over the matter some.

That week passed peacefully enough, but the nights were troublesome. Kelly found that she had trouble sleeping alone, a realization that was discomforting at first, and then amusing, once she got over her discomfort. It was especially amusing when she considered that, for all practical purposes, she had been sleeping alone for a month or more anyway. If, when Graham came back, such matters were not satisfactorily resolved, she would have to take drastic action—maybe a divorce, she thought, bemused by the idea.

She never doubted that he would come back. He always had come back, and they'd had plenty worse fights and far worse troubles. Besides, he had promised that he would never leave her for good, and if he had intended to break that promise, he would have said so. No matter what might be bothering him, she knew that he still had his own sense of honor.

In the end, he wasn't gone half as long as she expected. He came home just at the sunset of a very hot day. He had been gone a week, and Kelly was sitting on the porch when she saw him riding up the road. Pleased to see him, she rose and waved her hat at him in greeting. Of course, how long she remained pleased to see him depended on his mood. As far as she was concerned, if he hadn't cured his sulks, he could ride right back out.

He waved back at her and rode into the barn. Kelly got up and went down to see him. After all, she had mostly provoked the fight they'd had before he'd left. It wouldn't hurt to go a little out of her way to make him feel welcome again.

The barn was all shadowy, except for the sun streaming in through the west-facing windows. Graham was in one of the west stalls, unsaddling his horse.

"Enjoy your scout?" She asked, looking over the stall door.

"Sure. There's some wild towns southeast of here."

"Much different than the ones we saw on the way here?" She asked.

"Fewer farmers and more no-accounts."

Kelly felt relieved that he answered her, and the terseness of his replies did not worry her. After all, poetical descriptions and florid answers had never been much his style, and there was bound to be some awkwardness between them since they'd parted on bad terms.

Kelly let herself into the stall, and Graham put his saddle over the stall door. The sun coming in from the window was filtered with falling dust, making it hazy and somehow hotter.

"I really did miss you," Kelly said abruptly.

Stepping close to him, she put her arms around his neck, and pulled him close. A little surprised at the warmth of her embrace Graham hugged her back. Kelly, who could think of nothing except how good his body felt against hers, rubbed against him until she felt his lips on hers and the sudden shortness of his breath.

His hands slid down her back and onto her behind, pulling her hard up against him, so hard that she could feel his erection. Fully aroused now, she rubbed herself against him, and he responded, propelling them both backwards until Kelly's back was pressed solidly up against the wall.

His hands came up over her breasts, the cotton of her shirt seeming to be no barrier at all as she gasped and yanked his shirt up, running her hands over his stomach. Her jeans felt too tight.

Her hat fell off and drifted slowly down into the straw, but neither of them noticed. With a sense of disappointment, Kelly felt his hands leave her breasts, then she moaned softly as he reached down to the crotch of her jeans, feeling the heat between her legs, then unbuttoning her fly.

Kelly pushed her jeans down off her hips as he undid his own fly, then there was an aching moment of expectation as she felt the tip of his penis brush up against her. She sighed in relief as she felt him slide inside her, warm and solid, and then she realized that she had been without him for far too long.

They strained together, feeling the tension rise unbearably, until, finally it broke. Kelly's back arched and she cried out from the strength of it, and an instant later, Graham slumped against her, his breath hot on her neck.

The moment spun out like the dust hanging in the sunlight, and Kelly wiped the sweat from his forehead. With an effort, Graham stood away from her and buttoned his fly. Kelly pulled her pants back up and tucked her shirt in.

"I guess I missed you too," Graham said wryly. "I apologize for . . ."

His voice trailed off, and with some amusement, Kelly realized that he was embarrassed. She didn't understand how he could be embarrassed about anything they did after all this time, but she felt she ought to put him at ease, if she could.

"Don't apologize," she said, buttoning her fly. "That was the best ride I've had in months."

Chapter 65

Big Jerry had no last name, though occasionally he took the name of some animal particularly worthy of respect. By doing so, he hoped to adopt more than just an alias fitting for a hunter—he hoped to take on some of the animals' own attributes.

Jerry often thought that most people would be better off if they stopped thinking of themselves as being inherently superior to animals. Especially since even a mouse (which surely was as small and insignificant a creature as had ever existed) could pass the winter safely in the most inaccessible mountains—a feat that had killed countless people, foolish and otherwise.

And no doubt the wiry little man speaking to him now, for example, thought of himself as being fashioned in the image of God, but Jerry thought that he looked much more like a wolverine—mean, determined, and totally fearless.

"So we could use a man that knows the ground and can track," the man was saying. "There's some that say you're such a man. Do you want in?"

"You ain't yet said why I should," Jerry replied.

Jake curbed his temper. Hadn't the big dumb half-breed been listening?

"We're looking for a man wanted in the states," he explained as patiently as possible. "There's a heap of reward offered for him."

"How big a heap?"

"Two thousand," Jake said, untroubled by the exaggeration.

"And you say he travels with a pants-wearing female wrangler?"

"I say he might. But she'll be easier to find, and if we can find her, we can find him."

Jerry pulled his coat closer around himself. They were standing in the little swept yard in front of his cabin. It was late fall and approaching dark. The sinking sun robbed the sky of what little warmth the day had provided.

"You ain't findin' anyone before the snow falls," Jerry said. "Come see me in the spring."

"That a yes?" Jake asked. He had resigned himself to having to hole up for the winter, so Jerry's answer was not necessarily disappointing.

"How you plan on cutting the money?"

"Five hundred for you, anyway," Jake replied. "We been on this job four years in the spring, so we feel more is owing to us."

Jerry considered it. Five hundred dollars was a lot of money and, if he stuck to trapping and hunting, five hundred dollars was an almost impossible sum. Of course, he didn't really need so much money; he could live without any money for that matter, but the thought of being in on and helping to end a four-year hunt was stimulating. Wily prey was hard to come by, and he lived for a thrilling chase.

"We can make it to a place I know of before the snow falls," he said at last. "If they ain't been there, I know where to look when the weather turns warm again."

Chapter 66

Winter brought an end to Graham's apparent restlessness. It puzzled Kelly a little, but she never quite made the connection between his restlessness and her preoccupation with the farm. The few times her mind groped toward the connection between the two things, it slipped away from her. It would be conceited to think something like that without better reason, and surely, if it were the case, he would say so. If their positions were reversed, she would speak up the instant she felt even remotely ignored.

But Graham had always possessed more patience than did Kelly. He often thought of the first winter they had spent together after getting married—that was how he wanted things to be. It was irksome to have to compete with a bunch of horses for your own wife's attention.

But Kelly had always been straight with him about wanting the farm, and he had known what he was getting into. So he enjoyed the winter and tried not to dread the approaching spring. Getting resentful again would only make things worse once more.

He had always enjoyed watching her work with horses, and that spring, Graham spent a lot of time sitting on the porch, playing with Andrew and watching her wrangle. This day, Andrew was fooling with the blocks Graham had made for him, and Graham was watching Kelly take a turn at riding a dark bay gelding.

She claimed the gelding was the best horse on the place, aside from the horses that she'd bred herself. That might have been true, but it turned Graham's stomach cold the way that horse flew into the air. Both Pete and Andre had been thrown once already.

Both wranglers held the horse as Kelly got lightly onto his back. At the feel of her weight, the horse went wild, knocking both men to the ground. Kelly had been aboard for less than half a minute and knew the ride would not last much longer.

The horse sprang off the ground, all four legs leaving the ground, and he twisted hard to the off side on the way down. Kelly felt herself thrown from the saddle, and she kicked her feet free of the stirrups.

Kelly flew through the air for what seemed an impossibly long time, then crashed to the ground, landing hard on her side. Graham dropped his whittling and ran to the paddock as Pete caught the still-bucking horse and Andre hopped off the fence to see if Kelly were all right.

As Graham climbed the fence, he could see that she was dazed by the fall, but trying to get to her feet anyway.

"Lie right still," he said, kneeling beside her and checking her over for broken bones. Nothing seemed hurt.

Kelly rested her head in his lap, knowing she ought to get right up and back on the horse but feeling too weak to attempt it. She had been thrown enough times to know that she needed to recover a bit first.

"Do you hurt anywhere?" Graham asked her.

"Nope," Kelly said, although it wasn't exactly true. Her side felt bruised, and her head ached.

Graham didn't believe her.

"Boys put that horse up. There'll be no more breaking today."

Kelly sat up in a flash.

"That's not for you to say."

"You aren't up to it."

"That's not for you to say either," she said, struggling to her feet. Her strength seemed to have flooded back, and she no longer felt the pain in her head and right side.

Reluctantly, Graham helped her up. Kelly stood for a moment on her own, then her eyes rolled back in their sockets and she collapsed.

Graham caught her halfway and eased her to the ground.

"Give me your flask, Pete."

Pete took the bottle from his back pocket and handed it to him. Graham uncorked it and poured a little into Kelly's mouth. She coughed twice, and her eyes fluttered open.

"I guess I must have fainted," she said dazedly. It was hard to believe. She had never fainted in her life. After lying still for a moment, she sat up again.

"Put the horse up boys. Do the evening chores and take the rest of the day off, I'll see you both in the morning."

"Can you stand, Kelly?" Graham asked her as the wranglers

led the horse from the paddock.

"I don't know. Give me a hand."

With his help, Kelly managed to regain her feet but she felt dizzy, and her knees were wobbly. She leaned on his arm, and they started back up to the house. For Kelly, walking took an effort of will. Her head ached, and her vision swam. The ground seemed to rock beneath her feet. A few steps from the porch, she fainted again.

Graham kept her from hitting the ground, picked her up, and carried her up the steps and into the house.

She came around again as he carried her down the hall into their room.

"I think I'd better go to bed for a while," she said.

Graham set her down on the bed. Kelly undressed slowly and needed help getting her boots off. When she was finally in her nightshirt, the door creaked open a little. They both looked over to see Andrew peering in the room.

"Go on into the kitchen, son," Graham said. "I'll be out in a minute."

But Andrew didn't move, and Kelly thought she understood why.

"Come here a second, big eyes," she said, patting the bed beside her.

Andrew ran over and climbed up on the bed. Kelly brushed his hair from his eyes.

"You need a haircut, sprout. I guess I'll have to get the scissors out tonight and see to it. Did you see me fall off that horse?"

Andrew nodded.

"Well, it was a hard fall, and I'm going to go to bed now. But I'm going to be just fine in the morning, so you go play with your Pa."

She kissed him, and he scrambled down from the bed. He began to walk toward the door, and Kelly was taken with how carefully he placed each foot.

"I bet if you asked Sam nicely, he'd give you one of those cookies he made yesterday," she said.

Andrew stopped and turned around.

"Okey dokey, Ma," he said, then he left the room.

Kelly shook her head, though the motion pained her.

"Where did he learn to say that?"

"I don't know. Maybe he heard it in town. Kelly, how do you feel?"

"Not well. My head aches," Kelly got under the covers. "I can sleep it off, though. I've known plenty of wranglers who felt so after a bad fall."

Graham privately thought she was making light of the situation, but he did not say so. If she was bad enough off to faint twice, something must be far wrong. Unless she was better in the morning, he would ride for the doctor.

"Well, get some rest," he said. "Call if you need anything."

"Sure will."

He left the room, closing the door softly behind him. From down the hall came the sound of Sam fixing supper. Though he'd lost his appetite, Graham went to the kitchen and sat down at the table. Sam was occupied with fixing a fire in the stove, and Andrew was playing quietly with his wooden animals. The back door was open, but no sound drifted in from the farmyard.

"Is Miz McNair all right?" Sam asked.

"We'll see," Graham said. "She took a bad fall."

"Nothing broken?"

"No."

Satisfied, Sam went back to his work, and Graham went back to staring out the door. It was eerie how quiet the place had become.

He felt something touch his knee and looked down to see Andrew staring at him.

"Don't you worry, Pa," he said solemnly, patting Graham's knee. "Don't you worry."

Graham laughed and picked the boy up, setting him on his lap.

"No sir, I sure won't."

But he did start to worry when Kelly didn't get up for dinner and showed no interest in the tray that he brought to her. She seemed lethargic and cranky, though she told Andrew a bedtime story. When Graham questioned her about it, she only said that her head still hurt and that she wanted to sleep some more.

In the morning, she got up and dressed herself, but after breakfast, she sat down on the porch with a frown.

"I don't believe I want to work today. Will you please tell Pete and Andre to see to the chores and finish with that bay gelding?"

Graham did as she asked, and when he returned to the house, he found Kelly playing with Andrew on the porch. Kelly was crawling around on all fours making pig noises, chasing Andrew who was shrieking and laughing.

After a moment's watching, Graham went up to the house. As he climbed the steps, Andrew ran to him and begged to be picked up. Graham picked him up.

"No more, Ma," Andrew said breathlessly, and Kelly immediately got to her feet.

"OK, sprout," she said.

"I believe that fall addled your brains," Graham said, though he could not keep from smiling.

"Oh, we play that game a lot," Kelly said. "But mostly when you're out evenings."

Graham sat on the porch steps, and Andrew wiggled away

and ran down into the yard.

"How's your head today?"

"Better," Kelly replied. "But not well. It still hurts some, and my eyes are a tad out of focus."

"I think I should take you to the doctor."

"He'll just tell me to take it easy for a few days. Doctors are only good for taking out bullets and such like things. There's no prescription for a joggled brain."

That was true enough. Graham let it drop, and they sat on the porch and watched Andrew play in the yard. To Kelly, it was amazing how purposeful he was and how he seemed to prefer to play alone much of the time. Laura had always wanted Kelly to play with her.

"You think about Laura a lot, don't you?" Graham asked.

Startled, Kelly looked at him questioningly.

"It shows on your face," he explained.

"Does it?" Kelly asked. She had not thought that her feelings were so plain to see. Then she laughed a little. "Yes, I guess I do think about her a lot. She would have loved it here."

They said no more about it, Graham respecting her need to hold those things close and private.

"I believe I am going to sell off those half-wild scrubs and stick to raising the foals I breed," she said suddenly.

Graham was pleased with this decision and did not comment on it.

"I'll finish with the broncos I've got now and sell them off. When I first went west, I used to get a charge out of bronco riding," she said by way of explanation. "But there's no need for me to do it anymore, and I was younger then."

She sighed and rested her chin in her hands. Graham laughed out loud, either she was joking or the fall had addled her brains. After a moment, Kelly laughed too. Really, she just wanted to spend less time in the barns, so why did she feel compelled to tell such a story?

"How old are you anyway?" Graham asked when they had done laughing. "I never have known."

Kelly paused, reckoning up the years in her head.

"I'll be thirty in November," she answered. "I guess I still have some kick left in me."

"More than just some," he said. "You're still just a pup."

"Don't give yourself airs. You aren't that much older than me."

"Nine years at least," he said. "I don't recall my dates exactly."

"Give yourself airs, then," Kelly replied. "I never heard of a shootist reaching such a settled old age."

"I almost didn't," he said. "And I wouldn't have, if it hadn't been for you."

"Maybe and maybe not. I'll bet if we hadn't had that fight

in Kansas City you never would have gotten into such a fix to begin with."

"That fix or some other, what difference would it make?"

Kelly was quiet for a moment.

"Do you miss all that?" She asked.

"Not particularly," Graham replied. "It's disturbing to find out that I ended up a squatter after all, but I find that I enjoy staying out of trouble."

"We're not squatters, but you're right, peacefulness has its good side, if it's the right kind."

They sat there until supper was ready, both occupied with their own thoughts and both unaware that there are three kinds of trouble—the kind you look for, the kind that happens unlooked for, and the kind that looks for you.

Chapter 67

"They were here all right," Sherman said excitedly. "Three years ago at least, but they were here."

Gallagher was excited too, but no one looking at him would have guessed it. After nearly four years, this was the first concrete news they'd had, but that didn't mean the trail would be over anytime soon.

"Where'd you hear of it?" He asked.

"At the stores, the barbershop, the livery stable, everywhere," Sherman said. "They ain't even bothered to change their names. They stayed a spell, played some cards, then they loaded up a pack mule and headed into the high country."

"And they ain't been back since then?" Gallagher asked.

"Nope," Sherman said. "But here's some more news. They got married before they left here."

Taken aback, Jake spat thoughtfully. This news meant that there would be no getting to Kelly without going through Graham first, and that would not prove easy since he apparently felt sentimental enough over her to have married her.

Still, Jake had surprise on his side—surprise and superior numbers. If Kelly and Graham had given up their reckless ways and settled down to a bit of home life, so much the better, for it had probably made them soft.

"Did you find what time of year they left here?" Jake asked.

"Late summer," Sherman replied. "The store clerk seemed to think they were going to winter up high."

That meant they had gone into the damn mountains again, Gallagher thought disgustedly. Of course, they must have come down at some point; Graham wouldn't go more than a season without a poker game. The trick was finding out where those two had come down when there was no trail to follow.

"Well?" Jake asked Jerry. "Where do you reckon they coulda got to?"

Jerry considered it. Jerry and Sherm had come over from the southeast before he had taken up with them, and since then, the three of them had been moving steadily north. He guessed that they were almost due north from Wyoming, but maybe a little bit to the west, and no one ever rode so straight a course by accident.

"Follow the mountains northwest," he replied finally. "There's some settlements up that way."

Jake stared at him, trying to determine the soundness of the man's judgment. At length, he spat again and nodded.

"You reckon they rode right up north from Wyoming?"

"I do."

"It gets colder the further north you go."

"That's why I don't reckon they went much farther," Jerry replied. "I reckon they settled a bit north and maybe some east, but if they're still alive, there'll be news of 'em."

If they were still alive, Jake thought, annoyed with Jerry for having put that doubt into his mind. It would be a pisser to have ridden for four years only to find Kelly had frozen to death in the mountains or been killed in some bar room ruckus. Even worse, if she'd met her end in the high country, they might never find out about it.

"That's what we'll do then," Jake replied. "Saddle the hell up, and let's get on with it."

Chapter 68

Kelly went back to work three days later, and true to her word, she finished breaking the broncos and started selling them. She bought no more adult horses, and as the previous two years' foals were still too young for much training, she spent more time up from the barns.

The rest of that spring and well into summer, she took a fresh interest in poker games in town. Pleased by this turn of events, Graham forewent his usual trips into the surrounding country until the beginning of July. Even then, he felt reluctant to leave even though he wanted to explore the country a bit farther south. He wanted Kelly to go with him, but did not ask her to, knowing that it really wasn't sensible to leave the place unguarded for so long.

Because he did not want to be gone for more than a week, Graham rode harder than usual, and a four-day ride put him in the midst of a wilderness that he'd never seen before, but his horse pulled up dead lame. Annoyed, he set out walking. Keeping a southeastern course, he hoped to run into a town before long, knowing from their journey north that this course would take him into a more settled region.

A week of walking saw his horse turn sound, and another day of riding put him into a small logging camp. The newness of the few buildings and the cleanness of the tents surrounding them told him the camp was new, maybe not more than a few months old.

There was a saloon of sorts—a large tent featuring a bar made out of a plank of wood propped up by two barrels. In need of a drink and information about where he was, Graham went in.

"What's the name of this here metropolis?" Graham asked the bartender.

"Ain't got a name yet," replied the bartender.

"Is that so? When'd you all put down stakes here?"

"Spring. I ain't sure of the date. Where all are you from?"

"North."

"Don't sound so. You talk like them Yanks what came through here last week."

Graham drank his whiskey and motioned for another. The bartender poured it.

"What Yanks?" He asked.

"Bounty hunters," explained the bartender. "Looking for some hard cases from the States."

"Did they find 'em?"

"Nope."

Graham wanted to question him further but felt it would arouse suspicion. He finished his second drink and took a hand in a card game. Apparently it was not often that travelers came through the camp, and as had been the case with the bartender, Graham's accent stirred talk of the men who had been through the previous month. Without asking a single question, Graham learned that there had been three men traveling together. The leader was named Jake, and he had been accompanied by a man named Sherman and a half-breed named Big Jerry. They had been looking for a pants-wearing female with blonde hair.

It took no particular imagination to fill in the gaps. Graham remembered Jake from his army days. A mean-spirited man, but a smart one, Jake had tenacity and was as experienced a pilgrim as ever traveled the open country. Sherman had probably been bullied into coming along. No doubt they were asking for news of Kelly because she would be more easily remembered by almost anyone who saw her.

Graham left the camp and circled around it until he found the remains of their camp. Picking up their trail, he followed it east for three days, then lost it in a creek bed. Graham dismounted and checked carefully for any clues as to where they might have gone, but the ground kept the secret well.

Squatting by the creek, Graham knew that he had been lucky to follow the trail even this far and that there wasn't any reason to follow it further. There was no reason to think they would deviate from their eastern course, and if they did not, at some point they were bound to strike the path he and Kelly had taken north. It had been years, but people would remember them, especially with the proper encouragement. Once Jake and Sherman started north, they would make good time. Kelly's reputation as a wrangler had spread quickly over the past two years.

Graham stood up. Trying to find them would be a wild

goose chase. It was more important to beat them to their destination. Graham did not put it above either man to vent their desire for revenge on Kelly and Andrew, though he knew that Kelly would not easily permit such a thing.

With that thought in mind, Graham mounted his horse and headed for home. The trip back would take a week or more, even if he wasted no time and rode like the devil, which was exactly what he planned to do.

Chapter 69

Though disappointed, Kelly was not worried when ten days passed without a sign of Graham returning. After all, he had said that he planned to go a little further, and traveling often turned up unexpected delays. It was not until the third week was halfway through that Kelly felt the first gnawings of worry.

He would not be so late unless something had happened. It had to be something pretty bad, too. She could think of few things short of death or terrible injury that would make him take two and a half weeks longer to come home than he had promised. It also occurred to her that he might never come back and that she might never find out why, even if she went looking for him. They were, though she tended to forget it, in the middle of a mighty wilderness.

Work went on as usual, but it became less able to distract her from her unspoken fear. She became restless and unable to sleep. To her, everything seemed stark and disjointed, despite her efforts at seeming cheerful and unworried.

Four weeks to the day after Graham had left, Kelly sat at the kitchen table playing with a fork. It was near midnight, and Sam and Andrew were long since in bed. The fork had been left on the table after supper, and now she was trying to balance it on top of the sugar bowl. This night, she had not even tried to go to sleep. She was still dressed in her work clothes.

The fork teetered and fell onto the table. She picked it up and tried again, and again, until her eyelids began to sag, and she fell asleep, her head resting in her folded arms.

An unknown time later, she came awake with a jerk and a

pounding in her heart. She listened for a moment, then heard a step on the back stairs. Though she had only been awake for a second, sleep was far gone from her when the door opened, and Graham stepped into the room.

He spoke, but Kelly did not understand the words. She felt suddenly and strangely limp, and her eyes dropped to the table cloth.

"I thought you were dead for sure," she muttered, rubbing tiredly at her eyes and finding them wet with unshed tears that willfully began to run and fall and splotch the table cloth.

Graham had expected her to be angry; he had never thought that she would take his absence so hard. He had ridden long and hard, driven by fear over what might have happened while he had been gone. He was full of the need to confront the danger that threatened them, but her tears stopped him dead in his tracks.

Kelly took a deep breath and wiped her eyes with trembling fingers. She wanted to stand up and greet him properly but did not trust her legs to hold her up.

Seeing her distress, Graham went and knelt beside her chair. She hugged him fiercely around the neck.

"Where the hell have you been all this time?" She whispered.

"It couldn't be helped," he said, hugging her back.

Reluctantly, but understanding from his tone that he had something important to say, Kelly let go and dried her eyes again.

"Well, let's have it," she said, sniffling.

"There's bounty hunters after me," he said, standing up. "Jake Gallagher, Sherman Buser and someone I never heard of."

"That's not possible," she said, blowing her nose. "I shot Jake Gallagher dead on that gallows."

"That was Jed, Kelly," Graham explained. "Jake's younger brother. Jake and I rode in the army together. He's won't easily forgive his brother's death."

Kelly shook her head. Her mind still felt numb.

"That doesn't figure. I killed Jed, so why would his brother be after you?"

"From what you told me, no one knows that was you except for me and Dave Myers. Jake probably figures to take it out on me, since I was the cause. And maybe there's a reward involved."

Kelly said nothing. She was tired and worn out with worry and relief. She could not imagine why anyone would spend four years chasing after them for such a cause. Jed Gallagher had been a snake, and who would mourn his passing, much less spend four years trying to avenge him?

"I heard of it about two weeks southwest of here," Graham went on. "I tracked them for a ways and then lost them, so I beelined back here."

He sat down and took his hat off. Looking at his tired face, Kelly could see that she had not been alone in worrying these past days.

"If they've been following us for four years," he said. "They aren't going to give up. It's going to come to a fight sooner or later."

"I thought we'd left all that behind us," Kelly said.

"Almost," Graham said.

Neither of them spoke for a moment. Kelly strove to take in all the possibilities that a fight could involve. Neither of them, she knew, was much afraid of shooting it out with Jake and Sherman, but there were other things besides fear to consider.

"What are we going to do?" Kelly asked. "We can't just sit here and wait for them to show up."

"You're right. We'll end up in jail over it, that or they'll haul me back south. I'm still wanted in the States, and it'd be bad if everyone up here found that out."

Kelly smoothed the table cloth with her hand. They were just getting good settled, and if it got out that Graham was a fugitive, they'd have to move on. She had no intention of spending her life on the run, although there were worse fates.

"What're we going to do?" She asked again.

"It's simple enough," Graham said. "I'll go find him before he gets here, and I'll take care of it."

"I don't like that," Kelly said. "I can't sit here with nothing to do but worry. I'll go with you."

"There's no point in you going," Graham said. "'Sides, we can't leave Andrew here alone."

Kelly picked up the fork and toyed with it. She was inclined to insist on going after them herself, leaving Graham to look after the farm, but she knew that he was better suited to such work. Except for the killing that had been necessary for her to rescue Graham from the hangman, Kelly had never been cold about murder. The other two men she had killed during her reckless years had been both trying to kill her. If she were alone and faced with the situation, well, then she would have done whatever needed doing.

But she wasn't alone, and as much as she disliked Graham's plan of action, she had to admit it was the only one that made sense. She set the fork down.

"I can tell you've thought this out," she said, looking at him with eyes that were sharp and knowing. "And I though I don't care much for that plan, I believe you are thinking of what's best for all of us. When did you want to leave?"

"First light," Graham said.

"I'll fix up some grub for you to take," she said, standing up. "Go see to your horse. You can take that dark bay gelding in the morning. He's broke well now and is the best animal on the place."

Surprised at how easily she had agreed, Graham went back outside. Kelly turned her attention to putting up some provisions, thinking that no plan ever worked out with no trouble or surprises.

Chapter 70

His horse stood ready, tied to the porch rail. Graham was checking his rifle. Kelly watched him from the porch. Her reluctance to come to terms with the situation had vanished, and now she felt no worry over the unknowns, no fear of what might happen, and no resentment at having her life so disrupted. She felt only a fierce, protective kind of love that made her eyes glint.

Graham slid the rifle into his saddle boot and looked up to see Kelly standing there watching him. The expression on her face strengthened his resolve to clean up the mess before Jake Gallagher got within forty miles of the place. He strode up the steps to her, pulling her to him, but she pushed against his chest with her forearms so she could look him in the eye.

"You listen to me, Graham McNair," she said, her voice low and fierce. "I know you. I know how your mind works. If you ride away from here today, you better make damn sure you ride back someday."

"Of course I will," he said uneasily. Her words had named an unformed feeling that had been restless in his mind since the instant he had comprehended the approaching danger.

"Don't you 'of course' me," she said, none of the fierceness leaving her voice. "You'll get out there and start to thinking about how it would be safer for us if you never came back."

He flinched a little at that, and Kelly took his face in her hands.

"I love you," she said, her voice gentle but still determined. "You come back to me, or I'll follow you down, even if it takes me the rest of my days and to the ends of the earth."

She kissed him then, as strongly she had spoken, saying things that words could not express. He kissed her back, pulling her so close and so hard her feet left the porch.

His lips slid off of hers, and she felt his face burrowed in her neck and hair.

"I will come back," he whispered. "Haven't I always?"

He set her gently back down. Kelly's arms slid from around his neck, and she rested her hands on his chest.

"Just so we're straight," she said. "Now go say goodbye to our son."

He kissed her on the forehead and let her go. Kelly watched him go inside, hugging herself and wishing the whole mess were over with.

When Graham came back out of the house, there was a grimness about his face. Kelly walked down the steps with him and watched as he mounted up. Her heart ached to see him riding off alone into such trouble, but she kept it off of her face. Graham was looking at her, and suddenly the grimness left his face and he grinned, tipping his hat to her with a flourish and wheeling his horse around.

Kelly did not wave as he rode away down the lane, but she watched him until he vanished over the horizon, wondering if she would ever see him again.

Chapter 71

After Graham rode away, Kelly went back into the house, feeling cold in the same way she had on her trip from Kansas City to Denver. But there was a difference—this time, if their plans went astray, she had everything to loose.

So thinking, she went to their room and put on her gun belt, which had lain unused since long before Andrew had been born. That morning, she cleaned her revolver thoroughly and loaded it completely, even placing a bullet in the chamber under the hammer, which she normally left empty for safety's sake. If there was trouble, it was likely to be sudden, and she could not count on having enough time to fire twice.

Four days passed, but her tension did not ebb. Caution became a habit, one that she kept close to her at all times. She and Sam took turns watching at night, and she paid only partial attention to the farm itself. Every noise and every shift in the wind required investigation.

Five days after Graham had left, Kelly rode into town for a scout. It made sense to her that if Jake did elude Graham, their trail would be most easily followed to Devereaux, and Devereaux was the only place where Jake could learn the exact location of the farm. She spent two days in town and around it, looking for the approaching danger to crest the horizon.

Just after noon on the third day, Kelly sat on her horse on a tree-covered hillside scanning the approach to town with her spyglass. Three riders rode up over a ridge several miles distant.

They were too far off to see clearly but, Kelly was sure in an instant that these men were on her trail. Without waiting for further proof, she wheeled her horse around and raced for home.

There was nothing else to be done. If she rode out to meet them, that would leave Andrew all alone, and lord only knew what could happen. If she waited at the farm, it would come to her doing a killing in her own back yard and probably getting killed herself. Her best bet was to clear out and hope that Graham would catch up with Gallagher before Gallagher caught up with her.

Two aspects of the situation burned at her. First, it was entirely possible that Graham was dead already, and two, she would have to take Andrew with her. Both thoughts raised the stakes considerably.

"I'll bet it was me he was after all along," Kelly thought as she rode. "If he's been on my trail for four years, he won't give up anytime soon."

On reaching the farm, she jumped her horse over the front gate and rode straight to the house. She dismounted and ran into the house, pausing only to scoop Andrew up in a bear hug and kiss him nosily.

She packed swiftly, long habit guiding her hands without wasting time in unnecessary thought. Andrew followed her about silently, his eyes wide. Only when it came time to go did Kelly hesitate, calling to Sam.

"Sam," she said. "I have to clear out for a while. I'm taking Andrew with me. Keep things going for me. If anyone shows up looking for me, say you don't know where I went or if I'll ever be back. If Mr. McNair returns, tell him I rode west."

There was nothing left to be done. Kelly mounted her horse, and Sam lifted Andrew up to her. As Kelly took the little boy from him, she looked down and had a sudden vision of herself being handed up to her grandfather when she was a little girl. She could remember the feeling of being held under the armpits and lifted so high off the ground it made her dizzy. Then her grandfather had taken her and set her in the saddle in front of him. Sitting there, gripping the saddle horn with both hands and feeling his arm around her, Kelly had never been frightened, no matter how fast they had gone.

Now Andrew sat in front of her, gripping the saddle horn and looking very small. As Kelly had as a child, Laura had always laughed and begged to go faster, but this solemn child waited patiently, unafraid but knowing something was wrong, knowing that something terrible must be happening to have driven his father away and his mother to flight.

Kelly wished he had less understanding, so that he could look on it as an adventure, but he was too observant. He had all of his father's quickness of thought and none of her own wildness to temper it. Even at play, this little boy had a seriousness of purpose, and now when there was no time for play, his seriousness came into its own.

Kelly urged her horse into a trot, and then into a canter, keeping one arm around Andrew so he would not be anymore frightened than was necessary. If he did not get used to riding in a day or two, she would make a sling for him to keep him firmly against her.

They cantered through the open gate and down the road until the farm was out of sight. Then Kelly turned off the road and across country. Her chief hope of safety lay in staying ahead of Gallagher but not in losing him entirely. Such an enemy was better kept within sight to prevent unpleasant surprises.

Chapter 72

At the same time Kelly was riding away from the farm, Gallagher, Sherm and Big Jerry were riding toward it. Once the three of them had reached Devereaux, it had taken them less than a hour to discover the farm's location, and Jake had not permitted them to waste a moment in setting out for it. After a four-year hunt, it seemed the end was in sight.

They did not approach the farm with any particular caution. After all, Kelly had never seen Gallagher and could not possibly know that they were on her trail. Four years of the quiet life had probably dulled her reactions, too. They'd heard talk that Graham had ridden out on some errand and had not yet returned, which meant that she was likely to be alone on the place.

The gate was open; Jake ordered Sherman to stay by it, and he and Big Jerry rode through, slowing their horses to a walk. Two wranglers stood near the barn door.

"Good afternoon, gents," Gallagher said amiably. "I'm looking to buy a string of horses."

"You'd have to talk to Miz McNair 'bout that," said the taller of the two.

"And where might she be?"

"Up t' house."

Gallagher nodded and rode up to the house. Another man stood on the porch.

"Good afternoon," he said. The man was old and bent and wore an apron. "Can you tell me where I might find Miz McNair?"

"Miz McNair ain't here," said the old man.

"Well, I'm aimin' t' buy a string of horses. Can you tell me where I could find her?"

"She's not here."

"When's she coming back?"

The old man shrugged.

"Where did she go?"

The old man shrugged again.

"Is anyone here besides you and them wranglers?"

The man said nothing and went back into the house.

Gallagher sat on his horse a moment, nonplussed. But he had come too far to be stymied by an elderly cook. He dismounted and drew his revolver, then he followed him inside, moving carefully in case it was an ambush.

Sam was in the kitchen, standing at the stove and tending a pot of steaming soup. He did not look up from his work when he heard Gallagher walk in the room. This hard case was apparently not going to take no for an answer.

"Tell me where she went, old man."

Sam did not reply.

"Tell me!"

Gallagher grabbed his shoulder, meaning to pull him away from the stove, but Sam deftly flipped a ladle full of boiling soup at him.

Gallagher yelped and stumbled backward as the liquid scalded his face. His quick reflexes saved his eyes, as he blocked them with his forearm, but the pain in his cheeks and forehead made his eyes water badly, and he was blinded for a moment.

When the burning had stopped enough for him to see clearly, Sam had disappeared. Enraged, Gallagher stormed out the back door and moved cautiously to the front of the house, only to find that the old man and the wranglers had vanished.

He paused to think for a moment. In his guts, he knew that Kelly had been forewarned somehow and that she had run off before he had gotten there. He reasoned that she could not have a very good head start; certainly not more than a few hours. He went cautiously back into the house, looking for any clues as to where she might have gone.

He bypassed the kitchen and walked down the hall. From the looks of it, the first room was probably the cook's. The second was undoubtedly Kelly and Graham's; the dresser drawers were open and clothes hung from them as though someone had packed up in a hurry. Gallagher opened the wardrobe found men's clothes hanging and a couple of suits very much like the ones he knew Graham favored.

Gallagher closed the wardrobe and went on to the next room. From the smallness of the bed and the toys scattered on the floor, it looked to be a child's room. Gallagher frowned. Kelly's daughter had supposedly died in Kansas City. He looked through the dresser, and the mystery was solved. This was a little boy's room.

Gallagher left the house, knowing there were no more clues to be had there but annoyed because he could not make sense of the clues that he had found. Once outside again, he spoke to Jerry.

"They lit out and not too long ago from the look of things."

He told Jerry of the disorder in the master bedroom and of his discovery that there was a child involved. Jerry pondered the information and linked it up with a few things that he'd heard while in town.

To his mind, it was all perfectly plain. Somehow, they had gotten wind of the pursuit. Not wishing to fight it out in their home, they had each ridden off separately. No doubt Kelly was somewhere close by, and Graham had ridden far off, hoping to lead Gallagher away from his wife and son. Wolves often did the same thing when threatened.

He said as much to Jake, who looked at him dubiously.

"I reckon she's the only one out there," he said. "How could they know we was coming? We just caught her while he was out of town."

There was common sense in those words, but Jerry knew that sometimes tracking called for uncommon sense. Still, Jake was leading this party.

"There was some tracks down off the road about a mile from here," he said.

Jake mounted his horse.

"I bet that was one of them. Come on."

He spurred his horse toward the gate, and all three men rode back down the road. Two miles from the farm, they all reined in, and Jerry dismounted, looking for the tracks he'd seen earlier. He found them and, leaving his horse on the road, followed them on foot for a bit. Then he turned and went back to where Jake and Sherman were still mounted, waiting for him.

"One rider, heading due west in a hurry," he said. "He has maybe a two-hour start."

Two hours, Jake thought. That was next to nothing. Of course, they had no way of knowing whether it was Kelly or Graham that they were following, but that didn't matter. It was obvious now that killing the one meant killing the other. Jake didn't believe in leaving unfinished business; it always came back to haunt you.

"Let's go then," he said.

Jerry mounted up, and he led the way down off the road and into the wilderness that surrounded them.

Chapter 73

The further they followed the trail, the more certain Jake became that it was Graham they were following. The country was as rough as any he'd seen. It seemed plain that Kelly must have taken the child with her, and she could not be so desperate as to take a baby up into the high country.

But she was, although he could not have known it. She rode hard and long, pausing only to walk and rest her horse. Darkness fell, and she fed Andrew but had no appetite herself. It became too dangerous to ride, and so she walked, Andrew asleep in her arms.

When she finally stopped, it was nearly midnight. She saw to her horse as best as she could, then sat down and leaned back against a tree, with her boy in her lap. Andrew slept peacefully, and Kelly was comforted by his serene face and his rhythmic breathing. She dozed, trusting her horse to wake her if danger approached.

Big Jerry had lost her trail just as dusk fell. She had ridden up through a stream, and with no light, he could not examine the creek bed for overturned rocks or disturbances in the muck.

"This trail's dead until morning," he told Jake. "We follow it at night, and we'll miss it. Maybe even end up lost."

"Goddamn," Jake swore. "I thought you damn half breeds could track a bird through the air."

"Not without light," replied Big Jerry, who was unperturbed by Jake's anger.

"Ain't there no other sign you can follow?" Jake asked.

"No. But we ain't tracking no man. There's some tracks in

that mud, and I ain't never seen a man with feet that small. There's a baby along with her too, from the looks of it."

That was heartening news, and Jake lost some of his bad temper.

"See there Jake, it don't matter if we can't track her tonight," Sherman said. "She'll have to stop, and she ain't got that big a lead on us anyway."

This eased Jake some more. Burdened with such a small child, Kelly would not be able to ride as hard, and she would have to stop to sleep. Hopefully, he could finish the damn job in a day or two and head back south.

"All right," he said. "Make camp. We'll stay here until it's light."

Satisfied, Sherman started clearing an area for a fire, but Big Jerry did not move.

"I ain't signed up to kill no women and children," he said.

"This ain't a woman we're after," Jake spat. "It's a fiend from hell."

"I reckon you ain't no angel yerself," Jerry said. "But I want it said right now that I ain't about to pull down on no woman, and I won't stand for anyone pulling down on a baby."

"Save your wind," Jake said. "No one's killing Kelly Knowlton but me. If the child worries you, we can leave it with some farmers who need an extra hand."

Jerry nodded and went about tending to his horse. Jake watched him sharply. He had no intentions of inconveniencing himself over some brat. When the time came, Jerry would just have to understand that.

Chapter 74

An hour before dawn, Kelly woke up. Andrew was still sleeping heavily, so she laid him on the blanket as she saddled her horse. She was still tired from the previous day and knew that she would not be able to keep up such a pace for very long.

She woke Andrew and fed him, trying to be cheerful though it hurt her heart to see how tired and scared he looked. They mounted up and started back down the creek bed. She rode slowly, hoping to disturb the bottom as little as possible and fearing that if the horse stumbled, they might be badly hurt or even killed.

Toward noon she rode out of the creek and up a small rise. She dismounted and removed her spyglass from her saddle bags. Taking Andrew with her, she climbed a rocky outcrop and scanned the country below.

She spotted her pursuers coming up the creek bed. They were moving fast, faster than she would dare with Andrew along. They were less than an hour behind her, she guessed.

There was no point in running any further. She would only become more exhausted and more worried. The time had come to turn and fight.

She picked up Andrew and went back to her horse. She lead him into the creek and upstream for about a mile to a fork in the creek. Removing her rifle, bed roll, and saddle bags, Kelly tied the horse's reins to the saddle horn and led him a little way up the right hand fork. Then she fired her revolver just behind him. He tore up the creek in a panic, and Kelly thought he might go several miles before finally stopping.

She shouldered her bed roll and saddle bags and carried Andrew and her rifle up the left side of the fork. She walked through the water for two miles, then left the creek and walked on dry ground. The terrain became rockier, and she had few worries about leaving much sign behind her.

Every now and then, she would use her spyglass to check for pursuit. She saw none but knew that her ruse would not fool them for long.

At last, she came to a high plateau, wooded and rocky. Twenty yards to the right, a tumble of rocks overlooked the trail. Further ahead, the rocks became steeper and more jagged. After scanning the area for a moment, she spotted a kind of basin in the rocks to the right. The basin was fronted and flanked on the uphill side with large boulders.

Deliberately choosing the rockiest and most roundabout path, Kelly crossed over to the cliff and climbed to the basin. It was hard going, and she had to stop several times, but at last she managed it.

The basin provided a natural fortress and a clear view of the path, but it kept her hidden from anyone coming up from the woods below. If Gallagher and company rode up that path, they'd be sitting ducks. She set Andrew down and let the saddle bags and bedroll fall from her aching shoulders. Sooner or later, those three men would ride up that trail and find that she had prepared a nice little welcome for them. She wiped the sweat from her forehead and settled down to wait.

Meanwhile, Jake, Jerry and Sherm followed her course down the stream bed, pausing only briefly when they reached the fork. The right hand side was plenty torn up, and Jake headed down it without hesitation.

Jerry had his doubts about following such a plain course. The woman they were following was no fool, and she was in dire straights. If he had been in her shoes, he would have taken the opportunity to try some kind of dodge.

But Jake's insult of the previous evening still stung at him, so when Jake charged off without asking his opinion on the matter, he kept silent. There was nothing wrong with letting a man make his own mistakes when he was determined to do so.

After a forty-minute ride, they came upon Kelly's horse grazing along the side of the stream. Jake reined in sharply, at first expecting an ambush and then looking around for signs of some kind of accident.

Jerry rode up beside him.

"She ain't here," he said.

Jake turned on him angrily.

"How the hell do you know?"

"I reckon she went up the other side of the fork. It's what I'da done."

"Why the hell didn't you say so afore now?"

Jerry met his eyes squarely but did not answer. Jake nodded as though he had just become certain of something.

"If that's how it is, we'll settle up once this job is done," he said. "Sherm, go catch that horse."

Sherm rode up and caught Kelly's horse, then the three of them turned back downstream. They reached the fork an hour before dusk and followed the trail until dark.

As the sun set, Jake reluctantly gave orders to make camp. It meant one more day until he could finish his self-appointed task, but at this point, it was better to be safe than sorry. It was too easy to lose the trail at night, and now that Kelly was afoot, she would not get very far.

"I reckon tomorrow'll be the day," he said as the three men sat around their fire. "It'll be quick at t' finish."

Big Jerry stared at him. Jake apparently thought that Kelly had believed her ruse at the river would suffice to throw her pursuers off the trail for good. Jake, he thought, was too used to hunting men to understand how this woman was thinking.

Tracking Kelly had put him in mind of a wily mountain lion that he had once hunted. The lion had been clever, twisting its trail and doubling back over its own path, confusing Jerry's dogs, which were brought to a standstill, unable to discern the right line. When at last they had found the right trail, Jerry was confused because the lion had not tried to outdistance them but instead had tried to baffle them.

He had chased the lion another hour before bringing it to bay, the three dogs barking frantically, dancing just out of reach of the cougar's massive paws. But the cougar had not been bewildered by the dogs that attacked from all sides. The cougar had singled out one dog, crushing him to the ground, seemingly oblivious to the other dogs tearing at it, and killing the dog with a single bite that broke the dog's neck. Bloody but undeterred, the cougar had turned on another dog, swiping at it with claws that tore the dog's head into gory shreds.

As Jerry had run up, out of breath, and had taken aim, the cougar dispatched the last dog and crouched to spring at him, its bloody mouth curled into a snarl and hellfire leaping from its yellow eyes. Jerry's first shot had taken the lion in the chest, just before it sprang, knocking it to the ground. To Jerry's amazement, the lion had gotten back to its feet, tottered for a moment and had gathered itself for another leap. A second shot in the head had finally killed it.

Unnerved by the animal's almost supernatural ferocity, Jerry had stood still for a moment, hesitating to approach the animal even though it was dead. As Jerry stood, entranced by the snarl frozen on the cougar's face and shivering from the hatred glaring at him from its dead, yellow eyes, a month-old cougar kitten had tumbled from the bushes.

The memory stood clear before his eyes, and he did not

think that tomorrow would bring a quick finish to anything. Kelly was not running; she had turned at bay, and she was smart enough to have arranged it in her own way and time, not theirs. Jake might not know it, but the play had been taken away from them.

He said as much, but Jake waved his words away impatiently, annoyed by what he viewed as chicken-heartedness. Jake was beginning to regret having brought Jerry along, especially since he seemed to be so spooked by the whole business. Kelly Knowlton was a good shot and a good wrangler and that was all. It would take a heap more than that to get the better of three determined men such as themselves.

Not far away, Kelly dozed against a rock, waiting the night out, restless thoughts driving through her brain. Andrew slept fitfully, his head resting in her lap. During her waking moments, she tried to comfort him with soft words and affectionate hands. There was no moon, and this made the night too dark for tracking; therefore, she knew that she was safe until morning. Her ruse at the river had bought her an extra day. She prayed that it would be enough.

Chapter 75

After riding away from the farm, Graham had ridden to Devereaux and chosen a spiraling course with the town at the center. The extra time such a course took was troublesome, but there was no other way to be sure of striking their trail. Since they would be riding toward the town and he was riding out from it, he should be able to intercept them.

But it was a slow ride, and he had not struck their trail until near dusk on the third day out. Even then, there was no way to be certain it was the right trail. All he could tell from the sign was that there were three men coming up from the south and heading for Devereaux. Nevertheless, he went with his instincts and followed the trail.

The following morning, he had come upon an abandoned camp sight. A scrap of half-burned newspaper caught his eye, and picking it up, he saw it was a clipping of the newspaper story Morgan Howard had written about him back in the States.

His instincts confirmed, he mounted back up and followed the trail hard. Trusting to luck, he rode at night as well, keeping as straight a course for Devereaux as possible. In the morning, he found that his guess had been correct, for their trail was still before him, plain as the words printed on the rag of paper he had found.

Knowing their destination and the quickest way to it gave him an edge, which he now knew he needed. The trail was two days old. If they had not yet reached Devereaux, they soon would. After that, it was only a ten-mile ride to the farm.

Graham made straight for the farm, and his straight course

and hard riding brought him there less than five hours after Jake and his men had left.

Drawn by the sound of an approaching rider, Sam was standing on the porch as Graham raced up to the house, revolver drawn.

On seeing Sam, Graham brought his horse to an abrupt halt, kicking up dust everywhere.

"She went west," Sam said, not waiting to be asked any questions.

Graham sighed, relieved. He should have known better than to think Kelly would let herself get caught like a sitting duck.

"When did the other riders come through?" He asked.

"Four, five hours ago maybe."

Graham nodded, wheeled his horse around and raced back down the lane. Dusk was settling in, but he found their trail and started down it before full dark set in.

He had the advantage of a clearer trail to follow. Three riders cut a noticeable path in the otherwise undisturbed wilderness. But his horse was jaded, and he had to stop long before he had closed the gap enough to feel comfortable about it.

At dawn, he started out again. By the end of the day, he had reached the stream fork, and again, being at the tail end of the chase helped him. It was plain to see that riders had gone up both sides of the fork. Kelly had no doubt pulled a fast one on her pursuers. Without hesitation, he rode up the left fork. Kelly had told Sam to tell him that she had ridden west, and that was all Graham needed to know.

Chapter 76

Kelly greeted the dawn with eyes that were red but alert. A sense of slowly rising tension was upon her, reminding her of the gathering clouds and electric air that heralded the sudden violence of a thunder storm. Danger, imminent and inescapable, was sweeping down upon her, dissipating her tiredness all in an instant and setting her every nerve on fire. She checked her rifle over and sighted down on the trail.

Andrew sat on the blanket, holding the corn pone she had given him for breakfast. He, too, sensed the danger; it had been growing since his father had ridden away so urgently, and his mother had taken to wearing a gun. Kelly saw how his eyes clung to her as she prepared for battle. His normal quietness had taken on a wary aspect that reminded her of a rabbit crouching under a bush as a fox hunts nearby.

She set her rifle down and picked Andrew up, setting him on her lap. She had no idea of how much of the past few days' events he understood, but she was willing to bet that it was more than anyone would ever expect. There was no way she could shield him from the realities of the situation, no matter how much she might want to, and to her mind, knowing the plain truth was always better than being scared of all the things that your mind could dream up.

She rocked him, knowing that time was short now, and that there was little time for such things.

"There's some bad men after me, baby," she said, resting her head on his. "They're going to come up that ridge soon, and there's going to be some shooting. I need you to be brave and do like I say. Can you do that?"

He nodded slightly. Kelly hugged him once more and set him in a sheltered nook in the rocks. It was the best cover around, if only he would stay in it. She would be too occupied with the fight to keep a good eye on him.

The sun was halfway to noon, and still, she and Andrew waited. In the end, Kelly heard their pursuers long before she saw them.

Their horses' hooves clattered against the rocks, and their voices echoed in the valley when they spoke. Kelly sat up, raising her rifle to her shoulder.

The three men walked into her sights. A half-breed Indian led the way, then came a man Kelly had never seen, then Sherm, who led his own horse and hers.

Ignoring the Indian, Kelly sighted on the second man, whose short stature and bony nose proclaimed his close kinship to Jed Gallagher. If she could get Jake, it was likely that the other two would loose their stomach for the fight.

But Jake was walking on the off side of his horse, and Kelly could not get a clear shot at him. Frustrated, she waited tensely. There wouldn't be more than a few moments before they were out of her sights, figured out that they had lost her trail, and started combing the rocks for her. If she did not take this opportunity to lower the odds against her, she might never get another.

Kelly sighted on Sherm and fired. He crumpled to the ground. Kelly quickly sighted back on Jake, but the horses were spooked by the echoing shot; they started rearing and plunging, and again she was unable to get a clear shot at him.

Further down the trail, Graham heard the shot and froze for a second. He could hear the noise of horses going wild, and the sound told him that the shot had not been fired by the men that he was following. From the sound of it, those horses had smelled fresh and sudden blood, blood that had been spilled by a rifle shot.

He swung onto his horse and spurred him up the trail, knowing that the fight had been joined.

Chapter 77

Unlike Graham, Jake Gallagher had not frozen at the rifle shot. His rearing horse had torn free from his hands, and Jake flattened himself to the ground, scrambling for the cover of the trees beside the trail. Four shots punctuated his scramblings, and he felt a clubbing blow in his calf.

Breathing hard and sheltered behind a tree, Jake briefly examined his leg. There was a bloody hole in his boot about five inches up from his ankle. The bullet had exited on the other side. The wound bled freely, but no worse than was to be expected.

Jerry, who had been leading the way, also dove for cover in the trees. He watched the horses run a little way up the hill and then stop dead when confronted with the steep rocky trail just around the bend. Though Jake and Sherm had carried sidearms, Jerry carried only a knife. His rifle was still strapped securely to his panicked horse, just as Jake's and Sherm's were still aboard their horses—not that Sherm needed to worry about such things anymore.

Surveying the scene below her, Kelly reloaded her rifle. Now that the two men had reached cover, the whole game had changed. They could wait her out and come at her at night—if she could wait that long. She looked over at Andrew, who was crouched down with his fingers plugging his ears. She might be able to wait that long, but Andrew could not.

Kelly poked her head cautiously over the rocks. A gunshot whined and struck chips from the rock beside her. She ducked back down.

Below, Jake tried to think. The trees were scanty as far as

cover went, and he had no intention of getting shot like some dumb-ass tenderfoot. Signaling to Jerry to stay put, he inched his way over to Sherm's body.

Kelly fired at him twice but was unable to hit him. He fired once back at her, making her duck while he stripped the gunbelt from Sherm's body. He finished just as Kelly jumped up for another shot.

The bullet struck the ground in front of him, and he hastily scurried backward, spitting to clear the dirt from his mouth.

Once back in the safety of the trees, Jake tossed the gunbelt to Jerry, who accepted it gratefully, thinking that maybe Jake had been right about Kelly Knowlton being a fiend from hell.

"Cover me," Jake hissed to him. "I'm going up around those rocks through these here trees. Keep her busy so she don't see me."

Jerry nodded, removing the revolver from the holster and inching forward so he had a clearer view of the rocks. He fired once. The shot struck not far from where Jake's last shot had scored the rocks. Kelly returned fire, and the glint of the sun on her rifle barrel told him her exact position.

Jerry fired three more times as Jake scrambled through the trees and up on the rocks out of Kelly's sight. As the shots struck the rocks protecting her, Kelly leaned with her back up against them, breathing deeply. Andrew was still crouched down in his shelter, and he made a whimpering noise that stiffened her resolve to finish this before another minute passed.

Less than a hundred yards down the trail, Graham reined his horse in and listened to the gun battle being fought somewhere up ahead. To his ears, it sounded as though three people were having it out. The first shot had been fired by a rifle, and now that rifle was having it out with a double action .45 revolver. Earlier, two shots had been fired from a single action revolver, probably a .44-.40. Kelly carried a .38, so undoubtedly it was she who was firing the rifle. Her first shot must have killed one of the three men following her, and now she was fighting it out with the other two.

Leaving his horse tied to a tree, Graham crept up the road on foot. His horse's iron shoes made too much noise against the rocks, and the situation called for stealth.

Unaware that help was on the way, Kelly popped up over the rocks and fired once at Jerry, who promptly returned fire. She ducked back down and reloaded, knowing that something must be afoot. Only one of the two men still alive was firing at her. She had a clear view of the trail and rocks below her, so if one of them was stalking her, he would have to come up over the rocks uphill from her.

Cautiously, she crawled up hill a short way and peered up over the boulder that formed the uphill side of her shelter. She caught a flash of a man's shirt, then a bullet whizzed by her ear.

She flattened herself down on the ground, breathing hard. The boulder protected her, but it protected Jake as well. She could not fire over or around it without exposing herself.

Kelly scrambled back to her original position. In a matter of moments, she would be pinned down between the two men and that would be it. She grabbed Andrew by the arm and dove out of their vantage point, rolling them both down the rock face and behind a small clump of boulders halfway down the hill.

Jake popped up into her original position a second later, firing wild. He had expected to see her crouched there, ready to fire at him as he came at her. Instead, his bullets struck rock, throwing sparks and stone chips at him. He threw an arm up to protect his eyes.

Behind her questionable cover, Kelly got to her knees and fearfully checked Andrew over. As they had rolled, she had wrapped herself around him, trying to protect his head, and he now looked unhurt—except that he was trembling all over.

But to accomplish their immediate safety, Kelly had been forced to abandon her rifle. Now she drew her revolver with her right hand as she tried to hug Andrew with her left arm. Tears ran silently down his pale face.

A revolver shot sounded and kicked up dust near Kelly's right boot heel, which stuck out on the downhill side of the boulder. That damn Indian was still out there, she thought, but she did not try to shoot back. If she fired at Jerry, she would be a sitting duck for Jake. If she fired at Jake, she would be an easy target for Jerry.

She wiped the sweat from her eyes with her forearm. During her life, she had been many tight places and had faced many dangers, but never before had she faced despair. Now, it was clear to her that she was not going to come out of this fight unscathed, and that she would likely die.

For the first time since she had taken flight, she wondered whether or not they would be satisfied with her death. If she could be sure that it would buy Andrew's life, she would just pop her head up and let one of them get her. If she had been alone, just giving up like that would never have occurred to her, and even now, the idea irked her, though she would do it to save her son's life.

But Andrew's eyes stopped her. She did not trust the world or anyone in it except herself to protect him properly. She could not give up or do anything but continue to fight with every bit of resolve and cunning at her disposal. If it came down to her dying, so be it, but she would not make that an easy thing to accomplish.

Safe in his new position, Jake paused to savor his victory. They had her now. She couldn't fire without one of them getting her, and there was nowhere else for her to run to. It had given him an unpleasant turn when he had sprung into her hiding place and found her gone. She could not have had more than half a minute to escape, but somehow, she had. Now he caught his breath and prepared to finish the job properly.

Downhill, Jerry had seen Kelly dive from her hiding place and roll to safety, but the unexpectedness of it had startled him into inaction. Now he moved forward a little further. She was trapped and surrounded. He would keep her pinned down and let Jake finish his dirty work.

Relieved that the shooting was all but over, Jerry got up off his belly and squatted down to wait, his revolver still drawn and ready. He stiffened suddenly at a rustling sound from behind him and turned and saw nothing but a confusion of motion as Graham leapt at him.

But Jerry's reflexes were good, and he rolled away in time, though he dropped his revolver in the process. He drew his knife, grinning as he saw that Graham also held a drawn knife. No doubt the man had wanted to keep the killing quiet so Gallagher would not realize that he had lost his advantage.

That was clever enough, but no gunman he'd ever seen was worth half a damn with a knife.

But Graham did not wait for Jerry to continue the fight; there was too much at stake. As Jerry raised his knife to throw it, Graham quickly drew his left-hand revolver. He fired an instant before the knife left Jerry's fingers.

A red hole appeared between Jerry's eyes, and he fell backward as his knife sliced through the air, pinning Graham's sleeve to the tree behind him. Graham jerked it out, freeing himself, and tossed the blade aside. Then he switched his revolver to his right hand and picked his rifle up from the ground where he'd left it prior to attacking Jerry. He began to move uphill through the trees, a course that would bring him out behind Gallagher.

Kelly heard the shot Graham had fired and assumed that it was Jerry firing at her again. She put Andrew up close to the rocks, lying him flat and telling him to be still. Then she peeked around the downhill side of her shelter and looked to see where Jerry had gotten to. She had heard him rustling around down there, possibly shifting positions.

But he did not fire at her, and she could see no sign of him. It puzzled her, and she thought for a moment that perhaps he had bugged out or taken a hit earlier and was just now fainting from it. Either way, it meant that she was unguarded from the downhill side, and the odds had just shifted to her favor.

Since no one was covering her from that angle, Kelly could have escaped that way, but the thought did not occur to her. Escape was the last thing on her mind. Victory was unlikely, but this fight had to be finished, no matter how bitter or fruitless that finish might be. Escape was futile and would only delay the inevitable for another day.

So thinking, she removed her hat and poked it up over the rock, making it look as though she was peeping up to take a shot. No one fired at it, which confirmed that the man downhill was either no longer in the game or being very clever.

Gallagher was also puzzled. From his position, he could see a glimpse of Kelly's hat, but couldn't get a clear shot. Why didn't Jerry fire? Then, he remembered Jerry's vow not to pull down on a woman. Now that they had her trapped, the gutless half-breed no doubt felt self-righteous again and was sticking to his earlier promise. Jake fumbled in his pocket for fresh shells so that he could reload his revolver.

For a moment, silence echoed around the hillside. Kelly heard clicking noises from uphill—that's Gallagher reloading, she thought with sudden clarity.

Motioning for Andrew to stay still, Kelly yanked her boots off and, half-standing, half-crouching, moved silently up the hill. As she reached the boulders surrounding Gallagher, she heard a sharp click as he snapped his revolver barrel back into place.

Kelly crouched, her back to the boulders, waiting to see how he would play it. He could not have seen her approach, and she knew that he had not heard her, for he had been far too leisurely in reloading. Now he would either fire over the boulder in front of her or come around it after her.

Less than five feet away, Gallagher was considering those exact options. He was in no mood for a prolonged shoot out. He fired three times over the boulder to clear the way. There was no answering fire, and he charged around the boulder.

He pulled up short when Kelly leapt up in front of him, revolver raised, hammer cocked.

He ran right into the four shots that she fired, but those shots hurled him backward, knocking the gun from his hand even as he fired a single shot that tore through her upper left arm. He came to rest on the stony ground fifteen feet away, his eyes staring up at the sky, and his body feeling strangely numb and cold, except for a searing, burning feeling in his chest as he struggled to breathe.

Then the sky was blocked out by Kelly, who looked down at him for a moment, seeing four torn and bloody holes in his chest, hearing his labored breathing, but feeling no pity. His eyes were confused, and she thought that, in his mind, the battle must have gone much differently, and the surprise he must feel at dying was too much for him.

Well, she could ease his mind for him, she thought, knowing that he would have shown her no such mercy but raising her revolver and shooting him between the eyes. To her, shooting Phoenix on the Kansas plains had been a much harder thing to do.

Gallagher's body jerked once, then slumped into death.

395

Automatically, Kelly reloaded her revolver. As if from a distance, she heard a voice calling her name, and she saw Graham standing on a boulder uphill, holding his rifle aloft so that she would not mistake him for an enemy, hailing her. She waved to him, and he came over the rocks toward her.

When he was close enough, Graham looked her over, thinking that she looked much as he had felt when he had come down from the gallows and had found himself alive.

"You're shot, you know," he said.

"I am?" She asked distractedly, looking over herself and seeing the blood dripping from her left arm.

"You are," he said, setting his rifle down and examining her arm. The bullet had passed cleanly through the muscle of her upper arm. He tore the sleeve from her shirt and bound the wound tightly. She stood patiently as Graham worked, noticing in an amazed kind of way that his hair showed gray at the temples. When had that happened?

Then her eyes snapped back into focus. She brushed the dirt from her jeans when he finished with her arm.

"Andrew must be terrified by now," she said, hurrying over the rocks to where she had left him.

He was still crouched in the nook, his eyes squeezed shut and his fingers plugged in his ears. Kelly patted him gently.

"It's safe now, squirt," she said.

Cautiously, he opened his eyes and took his fingers from his ears. Seeing his mother and feeling the absence of tension, he crawled from his shelter and scrambled over to her, clinging to her. Kelly lifted him and stood up. Graham had followed her, and after a moment, Andrew wanted to go to him.

"I'll go catch my horse," Kelly said handing the little boy to him, then putting her boots back on and trotting off uphill to where the four horses were milling about.

Graham watched her approach the terrified horses, her steadiness and soothing voice calming them until she was able to take her own horse by the reins and lead him back downhill.

"You must have gotten that other one," she said. "I could not figure what had happened to him."

"It was only common sense and justice," Graham replied. "If not for him, they never would have tracked you so fast, and I wouldn't have been so late."

"You weren't late at all. They were after me the whole time anyway. It was my fight," she said, marveling at how bright the sun seemed now that the storm had passed over them. They had overcome the threatened danger, and although she would never know for sure, for only death could bring such absolute certainty, she felt that it was the last danger.

The past and its recklessness was far behind; no vestige of it haunted them. Despite the safety that was now hers, she felt its passing with a some sadness. The smell of a storm in the air had always made her nostrils flare and her blood pound through her veins; it brought her alive, and when it passed, she was stronger, no matter what wreckage lay strewn about her.

Her mind came away from her thoughts, and her eyes caught Graham's. She could tell that he, too, was thinking of storms and avalanches and how it was to get caught up in them. A shadow of a grin crossed his face—reminiscent of his familiar deviling grin, but with a difference of heat. It reminded her that, as long as they had each other, there would always be plenty enough thunder to spare.

About the Author

L. Jean Voss, a native of Columbia, Maryland, resides in Washington, D.C., where she enjoys fencing, the theater, and volunteering at a local homeless shelter. *It Feels Like Thunder* is her first novel—brought to life by a cast of characters she created long ago.

Her reasons for writing are as realistic as her characters: "Writing is entertaining, hard work, an escape, and often frustrating . . . but I write because I have to . . . I have no choice."

L. Jean is a graduate of the College of Journalism at the University of Maryland. Since completing *It Feels Like Thunder*, she has written two other novels that will soon be available.